WHISPERS THROUGH
THE WALL

Also by Bret Kissinger

Forever Fleeting
Gone the Way of the Dodo Bird
The Final Edit
The Winter Tiger & the War Eagle
The Surviving Remnant

WHISPERS

THROUGH

THE

WALL

BRET KISSINGER

ISBN-13: 979-8-9936468-0-0

Book Cover Design by Damonza

Edited by Mark Swift

To the men and women who risked everything to escape East Berlin.
May your courage, sacrifice, and unbroken hope echo through history.

And to my parents and brothers,
who are not just family, but my best friends.

The Christmas Cipher

Christmas had always been Wolfgang Kirschke's favorite time of year. The powdery snow and the scent of fir and warm homemade *Lebkuchen* cookies, time away from school, and the angelic Christmas music were all reasons as to why. But mostly, it was the joy he saw in his parents, where the harsh reality of postwar life could be forgotten about with every glass of *Glühwein* drunk and every carol sung. Every Christmas Eve his parents hosted a party, and each year new faces arrived, everyone in their best spirits. There were few repeat guests, not because they hadn't enjoyed the party, but because they had moved West.

The *Kinderpunsch* chased away the lingering winter chill. Wolfgang and his new friend, Lieselotte Reisinger, sipped the hot drink while they unraveled scarves and peeled off layers of winter clothing. Their cheeks were red and their noses running from the frosty Christmas Eve dusk. Her father, a photographer, had met Wolfgang's father outside Böhm & Söhne Maschinenfabrik, where he was documenting the newly repaired building. What had begun as polite conversation had grown into friendship. But Lieselotte was new to Wolfgang—someone that made him both nervous and curious.

Wolfgang wore his finest corduroy pants and a red hand-knit sweater at his mother's urging. At her own volition, Lieselotte wore a cotton dress with thick wool stockings and a green cardigan. Wolfgang's parents entertained guests in their *Altbau* apartment. The ornate facade had sustained bombing damage during the war. The shady patching prevented the building from regaining its prewar decadence. Just another example of beauty and ruin coexisting in Berlin. His family kept themselves and their guests warm by feeding coal into their stove. Still, the heat was slow to spread through the house.

Two years removed from the end of the Second World War, there was much to celebrate. Wolfgang was ten, and he assumed his new friend was around the same age. Old enough to remember just how awful the end of the war had been. Allied aircraft unleashing death from above. Then the tanks and soldiers of the Red Army storming through the Brandenburg Gate. Though he did not know what the screaming signified, he remembered his father ordering his mother to hide under the bed while he stood guard. The horror had run rampant even if he didn't understand it.

Inside the living room, the adults laughed as Lieselotte's father told a story. Wolfgang cleaned the fog off his glasses with his undershirt, not wanting to miss Mr. Reisinger's pantomiming. The camera around his neck swung wildly as he did. Lieselotte looked on. Her eyes sparkled each time he gestured, her smile widening with every word.

Their apartment was modest, but thanks to Wolfgang's mother, it had a comforting feel. It was home. The Christmas tree, covered in garlands, was the focal point of the living room. The Hoffmans, Wolfgang's older neighbors, sank into the couch as Mrs. Reisinger and Wolfgang's parents sat cross-legged on the floor.

Lieselotte seemed to have inherited an even blend of her parents' features. She had her mother's raven hair color, but her father's wavy texture. Her father's striking blue eye color, but her mother's round, doe-like shape.

As for Wolfgang, it was 99/1 as far as inheritance went. He was his mother's spitting image. Narrow dark eyes, slightly prominent nose, thick dark hair, and a smile that lit up his eyes. The only unfortunate characteristic he had inherited from his father was his awful eyesight. They wore the same style of browline glasses, making them appear more alike than they were.

While Lieselotte's father enamored the adults, Wolfgang led Lieselotte through the living room to the kitchen—the coal stove, square table, sparse cabinets—and then to the private bathroom, a luxury in a city where most apartments shared one. After the tour, they returned to the living room.

The grown-ups laughed and chuckled, enjoying the spicy, warm *Glühwein*. The Hoffmans' two sons had died in the war. So, Wolfgang and Lieselotte were the only children present. Lieselotte's father's story had ended. Now, the grown-ups talked about boring grown-up things like taxing work, crappy weather, and increasing costs.

Wolfgang and Lieselotte finished their *Kinderpunsch*, then headed to Wolfgang's room. They were too young an age for their parents to have concern about such a thing.

"Are you asking for new eyes for Christmas?" Lieselotte asked.

Wolfgang lowered his head out of embarrassment. He was self-conscious about his glasses. He'd never seen how he looked without them. Certainly, he'd taken them off to gaze in a mirror. But the moment he did, the image blurred and doubled. His glasses were a part of him—the same way his mother's features were.

"I already asked other years. Elves don't make eyes," Wolfgang replied, demurely.

"That's okay. You don't look weird in glasses like some people."

Not exactly a great compliment, but Wolfgang looked away, smiling. His stomach knotted as Lieselotte looked around his bedroom. Every single possession Wolfgang held dear up for scrutiny and criticism. She gazed at his books, the clothes hanging in his closest, his well-made bed. She plucked books from the dresser, calling out which ones she had read. To his desk where he assembled wooden building blocks and anchor stone blocks. He prayed she wouldn't notice the teddy bear on his bed—his last gift from Grandpa Mueller. *Am I too old to still have one?* Lieselotte spotted the teddy bear but didn't comment on it. Instead, she focused on the creations on his desk.

"You put all these together?" she asked.

Wolfgang nodded, barely containing his excitement. "I'll tear them down soon."

"Why?"

"So that I can build something better."

After exhausting topics to discuss in his bedroom, they moved into his parents' room. His father held onto trinkets. His mother was always trying to throw old things out. Clothes that no longer fit, broken items like a clock, a locket, and a shattered picture frame. Wolfgang's father rescued them from the trash, vowing they could be salvaged. Wolfgang had explored every nook and cranny of the room. It was old news—his senses diluted from being in here so much. But the way Lieselotte's eyes lit up reminded Wolfgang of the wonder and awe he had once experienced being in here. Wolfgang slid an old green Wehrmacht footlocker from under the bed. Stenciled in white spray paint was his last name, "Kirschke." If she had found other items in the room interesting, this was sure to blow her mind. Wolfgang lifted the double clasps and heaved it open. Inside was a quilt hand-knit by his maternal grandmother. Too precious to even use. His father's gray military uniform. Underneath them all lay a defunct black box. Wolfgang struggled to lift it out of the case; it was like trying to heave an anchor out of deep water.

Wolfgang opened it. Compact with a keyboard, rotating rotors, and a plugboard. A lamp board displayed letters.

"What is it?" Lieselotte asked.

Wolfgang bit his lip, then shook his head. "I don't know."

His father had been mute about the device and the uniform. He never got mad with Wolfgang, understanding it was only natural for a child to be inquisitive. His father fed that fire—but this chest was different. His father would change the subject, sometimes pointing out another object or asking other questions. It was a source of untapped wonders, unlimited possibilities. An obstacle preventing him from truly knowing his father. Wolfgang often lay in bed, wondering what the black box was, crafting stories in his mind.

"It looks like a typewriter. My father uses one," Lieselotte said.

Just then, approaching footsteps made the children jerk their heads toward the door.

"Wolfgang? Oh, there you two are," his father, Rolf, said.

His eyes took in the typewriter-type object on the floor. He stared at the device, then at the children. Whether he had drank a bit too much *Glühwein* or was overcome with Christmas spirit, he didn't tell Wolfgang to put it away. Instead, he sat on the floor with them. "Would you like to know what that is?" he asked.

Is this really going to happen? Wolfgang's heart pounded. Maybe—just maybe—he'd finally get an answer to this mysterious black box. He'd heard of Christmas miracles. He just never thought he'd be part of one.

Both children nodded. Lieselotte's curiosity was at a normal level; Wolfgang's was off the charts. He licked his lips in anticipation.

"This is an Enigma machine," Rolf said. "In the war, I used this machine to encode and decode secret messages. It was Germany's secret weapon … until the Allies cracked it."

In the long lexicon of language, there's nothing that will light up a child's eyes like "secret message."

"How does it work?" Lieselotte asked, beating Wolfgang to the question. Which was fine with Wolfgang. Maybe if she asked the questions, his father would keep answering in his attempt to be hospitable.

Rolf hesitated—deciding how much to tell. "Each day, we had a codebook. That codebook told us how to set the rotors, reflector, and plugboard." Rolf pointed to each item as he called them out.

He rose to his feet and searched for a pen and paper. He scribbled a message onto the paper. The letters he'd written didn't form any word that Wolfgang knew. A quick glance at Lieselotte confirmed she couldn't make a word out of the jumbled mess of letters, either.

VKPQB DZJTF GNXU

"Let's decode my secret message," Rolf said. He plugged the plugboard into the outlet. Then adjusted the rotors and rotor positions. "Now, type the letters you see on this sheet of paper on the keyboard."

Wolfgang took the note and held it out for Lieselotte.

"You type," she said, taking the scrap piece of paper.

"Here," Rolf said, handing the pencil to Lieselotte. "You'll need this to write the decoded message."

Lieselotte read off the first letter: V. Wolfgang searched the keyboard for the letter. Once he found it, he pressed the key. The key for M lit up; Wolfgang and Lieselotte gasped. The lights only added to the intrigue and mystery of it all. Lieselotte wrote the letter. They repeated the process, letter by letter, until each one had been decoded.

Merry Christmas.

"Do you need a machine to do that?" Wolfgang asked.

"No!" Rolf answered with enthusiasm, his eyes lighting up. "All you need is to establish rules."

He asked for the pencil and paper back. Lieselotte handed them to him.

"Pick a number between one and nine," Rolf instructed the young girl.

"Three."

Rolf wrote a few sentences.

"Now, if we look at the third letter of each word, we can decipher. Try," he said, offering the pencil and paper to Wolfgang.

Wolfgang took the pencil and circled the third letter of each word. Lieselotte leaned over his shoulder to decode with him.

"Silentnight. Silent Night?" he asked.

"Yes, you must glean where the spacing between words lie," Rolf said. "Wolfgang, whisper a coded message in my ear."

Wolfgang leaned toward his father, covering his mouth with his hand so Lieselotte wouldn't be able to read his lips. "Starlight shines so bright."

Without hesitation or thought, his father wrote words that would reveal that phrase every third letter at a time. Then he handed the piece of paper to Lieselotte to decipher. She bit her lip, deep in concentration, as she circled the required letters.

Once she completed circling all the appropriate letters, she combined them into one jumbled collection of letters. Then added a slash to break apart the words she found.

"Starlight shines so bright."

"Is that the answer, Wolfgang?" Rolf asked.

Wolfgang nodded, dumbfounded. Lieselotte looked as though she'd just discovered magic. Of all the marvels of Christmastime—*Weihnachtsmann* (Christmas Man), the birth of Jesus—this secret coded message had the same sense of awe-inspiring wonder. Truly mythical and confounding.

Wolfgang and Lieselotte had the ability to communicate with each other in a way no one else could comprehend. That was riveting. Empowering. It was their own language!

They listened for an hour as Rolf went into further detail in teaching them about the Caesar shift, Atbash, Polybius square, Vigenère, and book ciphers. Each cipher turned obscure, general text into a secret. Ciphers that were clearly secret messages as they were just a series of letters, to the deeply hidden messages buried in actual words. At times, Rolf forgot he was talking to two children. It's only natural when we're passionate about something that we forget not everyone shares our knowledge base. Wolfgang had never heard his father this excited. Never seen him this passionate. But Wolfgang's mother's presence in the doorframe cut it short.

"Sweetheart, we have guests. You've disappeared for close to an hour," Freya said.

"He's teaching us," Wolfgang said.

Freya's eyes found the Enigma machine and Rolf's military uniform. Her smile faltered. The look that formed wasn't one of dislike or disapproval, but fear. She had never tried to throw it out, but her eyes betrayed what she felt: they were all dangerous artifacts of a bygone era.

"Let's put that stuff away and come down and join the others," Freya said.

She didn't leave until Rolf had put the Enigma machine away, closed the footlocker, and slid it under the bed where it belonged. She tousled Wolfgang's hair as he passed through the doorframe.

They spent the rest of the night singing carols—boisterous, and, in some cases, drunk voices. Wolfgang and Lieselotte sang along with them, but crafting ciphers filled their minds. *What hidden messages were in those innocuous song lyrics?*

The elation of learning how to create a cipher vanished quickly. Lieselotte lived in Leverkusen in West Germany. Wolfgang was in East Berlin inside East Germany.

"You can write each other," Wolfgang's mother said after their guests had left.

And with that, the elation returned. *Why hadn't I thought of that?* Wolfgang wrote his first letter before the Reisingers' train had made it to Leverkusen. His first reply came shortly into the new year. And so began a friendship consisting entirely of writing letters.

Ink, Ash, and Silence

Holidays came and went, the seasons, too, but the letters came with dependable consistency. Unfortunately, her father's work as a journalist and photographer hadn't brought him back to East Berlin. Many of Lieselotte's letters included photographs. Her father had shown her how photography worked. At first, she couldn't understand why his photos were so much better. He explained composition, lighting, focus—using their photographs to make abstract concepts clear. She did her best to teach Wolfgang, adding notes to the photographs.

The letter on Wolfgang's desk stated Lieselotte had sent it on 2 May 1952. It was now 13 May—far longer than the three days he'd come to expect. The letter had been opened—not by his mother, but by the Stasi, East Germany's feared secret police. A name they dare not utter. Wolfgang unfolded the letter.

Wolfgang,

Things have been going exceptionally well here in Leverkusen. My parents and their friends often talk about the Economic Miracle. I'm not sure what that means, but they sure are happy about it. I am eager for summer. I like school but need a nice long holiday. My parents bought a new car! A Mercedes-Benz 170. My parents argued about whether it was necessary. My father won out, and even though my mother had not wanted it, she cannot hide her smile when she is in it.

He never wins an argument, so we think she wanted it just as badly. Seeing my mother's smile on our drives, it's obvious we are right!

There's a new grocery store in town. I tag along with my mother. It's usually boring.

Bread, milk, eggs, meats, fruits. But this new store has Milka chocolate! My, is it ever spectacular! Do you have Milka by you? Do your parents let you eat it?

I do miss my old home in East Germany, but our new house is quite nice. No one had ever slept in my bedroom before, which I find comforting. Also, we may get a television! A lot of children at my school watch variety shows where they put on sketches and play music. Do you have a television? It'd be fun to talk about these shows!

P.S: This admiration frightens fashion sessions. Maybe fooling frustration.

Wolfgang grabbed a pencil from his desk and decoded the last sentence, careful not to topple his building blocks.

I miss you!

Lieselotte's letter arrived in three days. The envelope's seal had been opened and resealed. She asked her parents if they had done so. Her father crouched down beside her, gazing into her eyes.

"The East government read that letter," he said. It was the first time she heard about the Stasi—registered the way her mother shivered. Once in her room, she read.

Lieselotte,

I drooled thinking about the chocolate. Sadly, it's really hard to come by here. That's exciting your parents got a car and so quickly! My parents submitted to purchase a car. I think it's a Barkas B 1000. But we're not supposed to get it for quite a while—at least five years. How did your parents get theirs so fast?

The foods you eat are so incredible! We have ration cards—we try to get oranges, but the store's supply sells out fast. We eat lots of oatmeal and soups.

What do they do on these television shows? I don't know anyone who has a television. Are you still reading?

With school ending soon, I always wonder which of my classmates won't be at school next year. So many families have moved to the West. More and more follow suit.

P.S: Thick elm aligned. Tossed & tossed thyme. Goods found. Determination took fools!

18 June 1953

Wolfgang,

The light of my life has gone out. My father was killed in East Berlin. I will write more when it doesn't hurt so much. But I don't think that day will ever come.

Lieselotte

30 June 1953

Lieselotte,

I am so saddened to hear this. I thought long and often about what to say. I guess I have nothing better than "I'm sorry." I am here when you wish to talk—about this or anything.

He wasn't sure a cipher was appropriate, but that was how he always ended his letters. And maybe it would provide a needed distraction. So, he wrote a cipher that, when decoded, said:

Your father loved you.

Tears had smeared the ink, warping the text. Her grief seeped into the page. It was an odd thing to hold. Such a harmless piece of paper, but the person holding it had been in so much pain. Letters carry bits of our souls. This one held a fractured piece of Lieselotte's. It was a timestamp.

Wolfgang recalled the events of 17 June. His face pressed against the window—until his mother yanked him away. Over 50,000 citizens flooded the streets in protest of the German Democratic Republic's regime and the increased work quotas. All along places like Alexanderplatz and Stalinallee, they cried out in one voice, "We want free elections!" "Down with the government!" The thundering sound raised goosebumps on Wolfgang's body. There was so much anger in those words chanted out by the powerful voices of thousands. A cry that reached his very bones. The only thing more powerful had been the Soviet tanks and armed police blocking the protestors' path. The grinding of the tanks' tracks, the clacking boots of soldiers stomping toward the protestors.

Wolfgang sensed what was coming. Some of the 50,000 knew, too.

Time stopped. As if it knew it would break itself into a before this moment and an after this moment.

Whether a protestor had thrown a stone, or an armed guard had opened fire first, Wolfgang didn't know. But the snap of gunfire and screams saturated the streets. It was then his mother tore him away from the window. When the smoke cleared and the screams and cries fell silent, some fifty-five people, including Mr. Reisinger, lay dead. Some were executed later for their participation. Mr. Reisinger was found with his Leica 35mm film camera in his hands. He had been a true journalist to his last moment. Someone had stripped away the film, no doubt by orders of the East German government to prevent it from being seen.

Sadly, Wolfgang was in a position of knowing more about Mr. Reisinger's death than Lieselotte and her mother. Details he'd never tell her about. Like how he'd heard his body stayed in the street for hours.

Why didn't my father take part in the protest? From the window view, it seemed like everyone had. After all, the ten percent increase in quota essentially had equated to a ten percent reduction in pay. Instead, Rolf sat in his handmade chair, rocking in silence.

"Because I know you cannot change what is," he said.

Even at fifteen, Wolfgang understood the subtext. His father had been in the Nazi Party, not a vehement supporter, but having joined out of fear. He'd seen and heard about what happened to those who opposed Hitler and the Third Reich.

Maybe his father was right. What hope did those screaming people have? Why would they think yelling would solve anything? They wielded picket signs and loud voices. The other side rode tanks and fired machine guns.

After that fateful June day, knowing the violent lengths the Soviet-backed East German government was willing to go to crush rebellion, the protests never reached that level again in East Berlin. East Berliners, at least outwardly, took Rolf's position and accepted that you cannot change what is. Instead of trying to change East Germany, many continued to leave for West Germany—moving to where those desired changes were already a reality.

Lieselotte didn't write the rest of June, or the rest of summer, or throughout autumn and much of winter. Her lone letter arrived on 22 December. It simply stated:

Merry Christmas, Wolfgang.

Was it possible to see sadness in a single sentence? Hidden inside such an innocuous and ubiquitous greeting? Wolfgang could. There were no tear marks on this letter. But it seemed so desolate. Like Lieselotte had cried all the tears she could and couldn't remember who she was before. The letter lacked the stenciling of her soul all the others had possessed.

Wolfgang's mother told him to be patient. Sage advice that in his youth he couldn't understand. Time and space, to him, made it appear he didn't care. And he couldn't let her think that. He sent letters every week. Some were horribly mundane. About school and dinner meals. When he had something especially exciting to share, those too went unanswered. Wolfgang's letters slowed, then stopped.

But a year after her father's death, a letter finally came. The tri-folded letter glimpsed the black writings through the folds and showed that this letter was different. She'd filled not just one page, but multiple pages. This wasn't a letter; it was a missive. Wolfgang brought the letter into his room. As he reached to tear it open, he paused. Unsure if he wanted to. He'd grown accustomed to life without her. *What if she disappears on me again?*

He set the letter on his desk and decided he'd read it before bed. But it got buried under clean laundry. Days passed. A week. Nearly a month before his eyes found the letter. It was a rainy July day. With nothing to do but be stuck inside, Wolfgang unfolded the letter.

The moment he saw his name written in her hand sent a flurry of guilt. He'd missed this. He went back to his eleven-year-old self, excited about racing through the letter to get to the cipher hidden at the end. It'd been a while since he'd last decoded one. *Third letter of each word, right?*

Dear Wolfgang,

I apologize for being so distant this past year. It has, without a doubt, been the most difficult year of my life. Mother tries to be strong for me, but I can still hear her crying most nights. Our hallway is lined with photographs that just stop … there will never be new ones.

I can't lie and say that life, apart from the loss of my father, hasn't improved. Buildings have been rebuilt, and new ones seem to sprout up every few weeks. The older people call it a miracle—talking about how the city had looked at the end of the war compared to now. My father would have loved to photograph it all.

I've done well in school and discovered I have my father's flair for language. I feel inspired to write what I see. I feel closer to him every time I write. His Leica camera is in my room on my nightstand, but I haven't found the strength to use it. I think he would be proud if I did, but it was our thing. To use it alone … Maybe soon I'll find the courage to use it.

My friends Christa and Brigitte have helped me tremendously. Sometimes, I can't be in my house with all the reminders of him—the sights, sounds, and smells—and to be able to go over to theirs is a welcoming balm.

Summer is always exciting. There are so many clubs and dance halls for us to spend our days. Though I do hope to spend time at the beach—perhaps Strandbad Wannsee or Strandbad Müggelsee.

What about you? How was your year? How are your parents? I want to hear all about it!

The end of her letter contained a brief paragraph, a larger than normal space between the previous one. A cipher. Wolfgang grabbed his pencil and decoded it. He circled the third letter of each word, translating the cipher.

I am sorry for being distant. Thank you for all the letters.

Any reservation he'd had about writing back vanished. He feverishly brought his pencil to a blank sheet of paper. Unloading all his thoughts, surely missing a few words in his sentences. Trying to remember everything that had happened the past year. First commenting on what she had written and then answering her questions. Then asking questions of his own. He asked about her friends, telling her about Gregor and Sigmar, who had been close friends who wouldn't be coming back to school next year. Their families were heading west. Whereas Lieselotte had learned about the Economic Miracle, Wolfgang was hearing about the Brain Drain—the mass exodus of skilled professionals, intellectuals, and educated people from East into West. By 1954, an estimated 1.6 million East Germans had fled to the West. Wolfgang wasn't concerned about the 1.6 million as a whole, only the handful of friends he continued to lose year after year. He told her about Dietrich, deciding to be vague about him. He was a friend. But it seemed they were Venn diagrams whose circles intersected with mutual friends. Now that those mutual friends had moved west, Dietrich and Wolfgang found they were the last two left. At the end of his letter, he planned out his cipher and what he wanted to say.

It's wonderful to hear from you again.

The letters poured in over the next four years—at least two a month. Detailing their final years of schooling. Lieselotte had excelled in writing and history; Wolfgang had strong skills in mathematics. His love had been football, and he'd excelled on the pitch. He'd grown tall and broad-shouldered. But it was his legs that had led to his success on the pitch. Powerful as a mule, he could run up and down the field. He'd been accepted into the Technische Hochschule in Berlin—the prestigious university known for its engineering programs.

Lieselotte would be attending Freie Universität Berlin to study journalism. She'd sent several photographs throughout the years, finally having used her father's camera, realizing it was not a cursed artifact but a treasured memento. Every time she clicked a photo, she felt him. Imagined his smile when she considered framing and lighting. She'd grown from the ten-year-old Wolfgang had met on Christmas Eve all those years ago.

Was it odd that their closest friend throughout their formative years had been someone they'd only seen once? In some ways, it felt like they were figments of each other's imagination. There wasn't anything they didn't tell each other about. Their dreams, fears, disappointments, crushes, and heartaches. An entirely unfiltered friendship.

But little did they know, their friendship was about to leap off the page.

Across a Divided City

Lieselotte needed this winter break from school. The Freie Universität Berlin library was one of the best in Germany, but she'd spent so many hours inside. Her image of Berlin was a postcard view out the window. She toiled over German studies, political science, and sociology, dreaming of being able to spend an afternoon with her camera capturing the life around her unfolding and the growing visible divide between the West and East—from its buildings, to its automobiles, to the fashion.

She owed her mother a lengthy visit. Leaving home to move to Berlin had been hard for her mother. Even if she only ever stated how proud she was of Lieselotte, her departure had left her mother alone. Lieselotte loved her home city, but she wanted to be a journalist, and that meant she needed to go where the news was. Her plan was to travel home on the 22nd. But tonight, her plan was to close her books, clear her mind from her studies, and enjoy the night.

Engineering had seemed like the perfect job for Wolfgang, but the state forbade him from achieving that goal. A state-controlled rigid educational system had shaped Technische Hochschule. He'd grown frustrated with how much Marxist-Leninist principles had factored into everything. *Innovation prohibited. Conformity required.* His father was a conformer. Did what was expected. He'd done it in his military career, and he did so with the Berlin Uprising of '53. Wolfgang questioned his father's passivity more than he had that Enigma machine. He heard the disappointment in his father's voice when he told him he'd been expelled. *Why couldn't he just keep his mouth shut? Toe the line?* But Wolfgang was a question asker. It was how he learned. His unwillingness and inability to conform in a system that prioritized state service and ideals over individual innovation had ended his chances of being an engineer. It's not like it was something he'd dreamed about doing his whole life. It was more of a realization. He had a knack for mathematics. Saw solutions, while others only saw problems. Enjoyed building— creating more and more elaborate structures with his blocks. He hadn't known engineering suited those skills perfectly.

While he pondered his next move, he'd taken a job at a factory. That next move, right now, was heading over to West Berlin to drink his fill of beer and enjoy some prohibited Western culture. Would this help him find clarity in his next step? No, but he needed tonight. And it was nice to raise a metaphorical double bird to the government that had deemed him unfit to pursue his chosen career.

Dietrich wasn't up for a trip into the Western section of the city, arguing they had beer in the East. Dietrich was shy and didn't like to take chances. Wolfgang couldn't fault him for that, as in a lot of ways, Dietrich's personality matched his father's. He had no desire to cause problems, which at times felt a lot like having no desire to live. Eckhart was more easily persuaded. He was a man led by basic principles: women and a good time. Eckhart was by his own admission an average-looking man with average brown hair and average brown eyes. But his personality drew people to him. He had confidence in droves. Dietrich was better-looking with envious, wavy, thick dark hair and handsome features. But for a reason Wolfgang couldn't pinpoint, he lacked self-assurance. The result was a case study on how confidence affects attractiveness.

On the flip side, Wolfgang fell somewhere in the middle of Eckhart and Dietrich. With Eckhart and Dietrich being opposites, the deciding vote on what their Friday and Saturday nights would entail often ended up being Wolfgang's decision. Some nights he sided with Dietrich—wanting to go out for a beer or two or not go out at all. Other nights, he sided with Eckhart—looking for a great time that would lead to a legendary memory. It wasn't often he matched Eckhart's zest. But today was one of those times. He needed a break from his status quo. From that pair of shackles that grew tighter and tighter. It was an itch he wasn't allowed to scratch.

Wolfgang and his two friends waited in line at Friedrichstraße Station to cross into West Berlin. Passports held out, waiting for the Volkspolizei—VoPos—to wave them forward. The guards paced, field caps on their heads, PPSh-41s cradled to their chests.

The wind was blistering, making it feel colder than the mid-twenty degrees Fahrenheit it was. It was that time of year where your coat was your wardrobe. The three friends' dark trench coats hid their turtlenecks and button-down shirts. They wore scarves for practicality, not fashion.

A guard waved Wolfgang forward. He handed his dark blue GDR-issued passport, embossed with the gold hammer-and-compass enclosed in a wreath of wheat emblem, to the scowling guard. The guard reviewed the personal details and scrutinized the black-and-white photo.

"What is the reason for your visit to West Berlin?"

Delivered as if there were no wrong answers, but Wolfgang knew a wrong answer would result in the guards sending him away.

"My grandmother is ill. I was told to visit her before it's too late," Wolfgang said.

Lying about a family member's health wasn't an easy thing to do. He didn't like it. It seemed like putting some jinx out in the world. But the border police needed valid reasons. They were extremely strict. Saying you wanted to go into the Western sector of the city to experience the culture wouldn't be accepted. Even saying he wanted to visit his ailing grandmother may not grant him admittance.

The guard glanced from the passport to Wolfgang. While everything about him looked lazy, his eyes were predatorial. Studying the image of Wolfgang to the real-life person. Then, staring so hard at Wolfgang that he thought the lenses of his glasses would crack.

He pressed the passport against Wolfgang's chest, exhaling a cloud of breath. There was no confirmation that he granted Wolfgang access to the West. But when Wolfgang didn't move, the guard jerked his head for him to cross.

They all claimed the same ailing grandmother, well-rehearsed down to her illness and the song she used to sing to them. While Wolfgang waited for Eckhart and Dietrich to cross, the first thing he noticed in West Berlin was how much cleaner the air was. Even just inside the city's border. East Berlin, and East Germany, relied on lignite, a brown, highly polluting coal. The lack of pollution controls and vehicle emissions from two-stroke engines like the Trabant added to it. The smog and haze were constant. Even with the cloudy sky, the difference between smog levels was striking.

When Eckhart and Dietrich crossed over, Wolfgang was still gazing at the sky.

"Are we sure we want to do this?" Dietrich asked. "Seems like an unnecessary risk. We have beer in the East. Women, too."

Eckhart rolled his eyes. "Open your eyes, Dietrich. Look around!"

It wasn't by pure happenstance how stark the difference between Friedrichstraße in West Berlin was to East Berlin. Where the East Berlin streets had been bleak, here in the West it was a hum of activity.

Dumbfounded, Wolfgang and his two friends walked toward the famed Kurfürstendamm (Ku'damm) that showcased everything the West had to offer, and the East could not. The six-floor department store KaDeWe (Kaufhaus des Westens), Europe's largest, housed high-end clothing and a world-famous food hall. Bookshops and record stores each contained hundreds, if not thousands, of items prohibited in the East. Billboards and neon lights advertised a mix of American and German products, from Coca-Cola to Volkswagen. Cinemas played the hits from Hollywood showcasing legends like Cary Grant and Elizabeth Taylor. If the visuals weren't spellbinding enough, the smells made them nearly drool. Thick air wafted the mingling aromas of sizzling beef and crisp, salty fries; buttery garlic from escargots drifting alongside the deep, oaky perfume of aged Bordeaux; and the hearty scents of golden *schnitzel*, smoky sausages, tangy *sauerkraut*, and frothy *pilsners*.

The area buzzed with passing cars, the sound of clacking footsteps, lively chatter and laughter, jazz and rock 'n' roll drifting out of clubs, and the distant ringing of tram bells. An electric energy that was contagious.

Gazing at the men, women, and children, Wolfgang glanced at his own clothes. They were all Berliners, but he stood out. The men of West Berlin wore sharp suits, slim ties, and polished shoes, while he looked plain by comparison. The women, too, dressed differently than their East Berlin counterparts. Tailored coats, elegant dresses, pencil skirts, gloves, and hats—so unlike the boxy, functional clothes of the East. Even the fabrics stressed the differences—polyester in the East; wool, silk, and cotton in the West.

Sidewalks, filled shoulder to shoulder with people, lined the two-mile-long boulevard. Every store was a reminder of what Wolfgang didn't have and never could have. While officially, the exchange between the East's *Ostmark* and the West's *Deutschmark* was 1:1, that number was symbolic at best. The reality was closer to 1:10, meaning all those tantalizing smells filling his nostrils and making his stomach growl would likely be outside Wolfgang's financial means.

The three men pointed at the different stores, shops, and restaurants, trying to agree on where to go and what to do. They settled on going to the cinema and watching an American movie. They strolled inside, waiting in line. Golden bulbs dazzled across the cinema. The marquee name of "The Majestic Theater" showcased in black letters: Sinatra. Martin. Directed by Milestone with the film's title *Ocean's 11* shown. The crowd was eager to see the Rat Pack on the silver screen.

They paid the ticketer and then followed the crowd to the concessions for Cokes and popcorn. The theater was full, forcing Wolfgang and the others to sit closer to the screen than he would have preferred. He'd been to the cinema before. The East had them but pushed state-approved scripts and messaging. Either informational or propaganda. Never something as exciting as American movies. And those theaters lacked the elegance and opulence this theater had.

As the lights dimmed and the opening credits rolled, and suave Sinatra and magnetic Martin bantered, a camera flashed from the back row. Almost impossible to notice with the flickering screen.

Lieselotte stashed her father's camera into her purse and hurried to her seat.

"The movie's started," her friend Anneliese whispered to her.

Lieselotte apologized with a grimace. *How am I to resist capturing the packed theater?* The way the screen backlit the audience, it was a wonderful opportunity for a photo she couldn't pass up. As she glanced over at Anneliese, the temptation to take a photograph consumed her. She looked so radiant—cinematic. Anneliese had vibrant blonde hair and striking blue eyes. It wasn't a stretch to see her on screen, like fabled blonde German actress Emma Sanders. Her friendship with Anneliese made little sense. They had met their first year in college and had different hobbies, likes, and upbringings. There was little they had in common except for three things: loyalty to each other, a similar outlook on life, and a desire for the other to succeed. If you have those three things, everything else is inconsequential.

Anneliese also had an extra sense to know when Lieselotte's mind was elsewhere. Like now. She put her hand on Lieselotte's leg just as she started to shake.

"Try to let your mind clear," Anneliese said with a reassuring smile.

Though they'd met at university, it felt like they had known each other longer. Anneliese knew about Lieselotte's father's tragic passing. She understood that while what transpired in East Germany was sad for most Westerners, for Lieselotte, it wasn't something she could shake. That she couldn't read the newspaper and move on. That she wanted to make active change. Understood that passive downtime was downright uncomfortable for Lieselotte.

To Lieselotte's surprise, the charm and charisma of the Rat Pack had granted her reprieve, and by the time the credits rolled, and the cinema's lights flared back on, she felt a clear mind for the first time in a long while.

She wanted that rare bliss to last. To not think about the loss of her father, her mother's loneliness, the holidays, and her ever-growing coursework. As she followed the queue out of the theater, her gaze drifted to the line across from her and the men and women stumbling toward the exits. Her eyes glimpsed a tall, broad-shouldered man with glasses. She looked away, then snapped her gaze back, as if someone had rewound a tape. Searching and searching. *Where did he go? Did I lose him?*

Burgers, Brass, and the Berlin Night

E nough of the crowd parted for her to see him again. She couldn't help but stare. They'd sent pictures of each other, but those black-and-white photos didn't do justice. He was tall—well over six feet. He had an awkward gait, as if he didn't want to be as noticeable as he was. But tall and handsome meant he was noticeable, no matter how much he didn't want to be. And he still wore those black browline glasses. Even though they hadn't seen each other since childhood, she knew more about him than anyone in the theater. And he knew more about her.

Wolfgang sighed at how slowly the line moved to exit the theater. Dietrich and Eckhart were in deep conversation about the movie, debating about who had stolen the show and what had been the best scene. The weight of a stare tickled his neck. His body told him so. His eyes went to the left to the woman with dark, voluminous, wavy hair and clear blue eyes. Her facial features were soft yet defined. She was dressed in black cigarette trousers with a navy cashmere sweater and an unbuttoned gray peacoat. Wolfgang marveled at her elegance. As if for the first time, he recognized her as the woman she'd become.

They stared at each other for several moments, both realizing not only was the other who they thought they were, but that they were actually here. Once they came to that mutual conclusion, they smiled. Wolfgang pointed toward the lobby, his way of saying for her to wait for him there. The universe seemed to know the rush he was in, because people walked even slower than they had before. Chatting, forgetting to advance. Impervious to the heat of the cramped theater and the fact they clogged foot traffic.

"What's the matter?" Eckhart asked.

"The girl who was across the aisle, I know her," Wolfgang said.

Even though he had used past tense, both Eckhart and Dietrich snapped their gazes in that direction.

"She's a family friend," Wolfgang added.

"Is this family friend good-looking?" Eckhart asked, straining his neck to see.

Wolfgang had never considered her looks before. She'd always been Lieselotte. But protection surged through him. Yes, now that he had considered her looks, she was good-looking. Incredibly so.

"She's Wolfgang's friend," Dietrich reminded Eckhart.

Eckhart sighed, annoyed. "Fine. Is this family friend traveling with good-looking friends?"

Wolfgang shrugged. Truthfully, he didn't remember a thing about who Lieselotte was with. His eyes had focused on her alone. Once in the lobby, the crowd thinned, splitting into those heading for the exits, the restroom, or lingering behind to decide what to do next. In the middle of the red-carpeted lobby, Lieselotte waited for Wolfgang.

He adjusted his glasses, a nervous habit. They smiled, unsure whether to shake hands or hug—landing on an awkward combination. Eckhart let out a gasp of sorrow at the cringey act.

Lieselotte introduced Wolfgang to Anneliese, Elsa, and Hilde. Eckhart rushed forward, extending his hand to Anneliese. He introduced himself—his eyes focused solely on her.

"And this is my overly eager friend, Eckhart, and that's Dietrich," Wolfgang said.

Dietrich waved, his face blushing. As the two groups of friends made normal small talk, Wolfgang and Lieselotte stared at each other in silence and then broke into a nervous fit of giggles.

"It's great to see you," Lieselotte said.

"Yes, it's wonderful. You look so different from the last time I saw you," Wolfgang said.

"I know. You, too. You don't appear to stop growing. I got your pictures, but they don't …" She tried to find the right word.

"Compare to the real thing?" he finished for her.

"Yes, exactly." She paused. "God, I can't believe I'm actually seeing you."

"I know."

They shared a nervous discomfort. They had poured their souls into their letters. Unfiltered and unabashed. But now they stood face-to-face with that person. Vulnerable. Seeing angles of each other they never had. Hearing each other speak.

"So, what plan do you ladies have for the evening?" Eckhart asked.

Though Eckhart could send a tidal wave of embarrassment that turned every speck of skin on Wolfgang red, he couldn't deny that Eckhart had a grasp on life. He didn't waste time. Where it would have taken Wolfgang minutes, or he may never have asked, Eckhart just came out and said what he wanted to. No rehearsing, no coming up with alternate conversations and possible responses. He said what was on his mind. That was fine here in West Berlin, but that lack of tact could be a problem in the East.

Wolfgang apologized to Lieselotte and her friends with a smile, but his eyes waited for an answer. *What are they doing tonight?*

"Drinks and dancing," Anneliese replied.

"Well, I'll be damned," Eckhart quipped. "That's our plan, too."

Eckhart's confidence gave him such a leg up. People are drawn to confidence. And judging by the smirk on Anneliese's mouth, she was drawn to him already.

The two of them led the way out of the theater. Dietrich, Elsa, and Hilde lumbering behind them, with Wolfgang and Lieselotte a short distance away but far enough they could carry a conversation.

"What brings you into the Western sector?" she asked.

"I needed some time away," Wolfgang answered.

She nodded, not liking the brief reply. They'd had no secrets in their letters, but they were realizing how different it is in person. To get instant feedback to comments and questions. For them, it was a brand-new way of communicating.

"I, ugh, I got kicked out of Technische," Wolfgang said.

"What? You said your grades were great?"

"I said they were good," Wolfgang corrected with a bit of self-deprecation. "I asked too many questions. Or should I say I questioned too much."

Lieselotte shook her head. "I'm sorry. That's stupid. You should be rewarded for asking questions. For questioning things. It's how innovation happens."

Wolfgang nodded. "If you don't question things, how can they expect things to change?"

"I believe you just answered your own question, Wolfgang. They don't want it to."

A moment's pause took hold as they navigated down the Ku'damm. She asked what he was doing now that he wasn't in school. Wolfgang told her about work at the factory, telling her how he helped make industrial equipment. Keeping it vague and brief. Most people lie about their jobs to people. They want to make it sound like they work at the greatest place, have the greatest pay. Sometimes it's true. Usually, it's not. It's a lie we project on others as protection. We won't admit to others that we're trapped in a job we can't stand. Wolfgang didn't want to lie to Lieselotte. He always told her the truth—and he refused to sell the communist lie. So, he told her the undiluted reality. How monotonous and soul-destroying the job was. Eight-to-ten-hour workdays, six days a week. How the factories were incredibly noisy and poorly lit, the dust that caked everything filling his lungs and leaving him with a hoarse cough every day. That wages were equal between men and women, but those wages were pitiful. Sure, there was state-sponsored health care and education. But it still didn't balance the scales.

"But enough about me. Tell me about Freie," he said.

They'd just arrived at a beer hall. People filled the beer garden, polishing off *steins* of beer and glasses of wine. Shouting to be heard over the countless conversations and live music. While the others went to get drinks, Lieselotte and Wolfgang hunted for an open table and had to settle for claiming the end of a long rectangular oak one.

"Freie is incredible," Lieselotte answered, once they were settled. "I'm writing for the university's newspaper."

Wolfgang beamed. "That's wonderful! You didn't tell me!"

"That's because you haven't gotten that letter yet. It's still in transit." She laughed.

Wolfgang's spirits soared when she laughed. "I prefer to get the news this way."

Lieselotte met his eyes. "So do I."

She told him about the paper's motto: *Truth, justice, and freedom.* How the values resonated so deeply with her—and were all foreign concepts to him. The campus was vibrant with not only German students, but students from America, France, and the United Kingdom.

"I went to Paris a few weeks ago to write an article. Oh, Wolfgang, the city is incredible! We ate at this café called the Givre Strudel. It had the best apple strudel I've ever had!"

Wolfgang smiled through her stories, envious in the best of ways for all she had experienced. She had lived a full life, seen other parts of the world, eaten foods he'd never heard of. Listened to music and seen movies that would take months to circulate in the East Berlin underground.

Wolfgang sighed, tension leaving his body. "It feels good to let out my frustration. Back home ..."

"You can't," Lieselotte finished for him.

She'd packed so much into that sentence. Anger, sorrow, understanding. Wolfgang didn't reply. He didn't need to. It was one thing to be frustrated and discontented. It was another thing all together, to deny its existence. To keep it bottled up. That frustration wouldn't stay dormant. It would end one of two ways: an explosion or an implosion.

Dietrich set two *steins* in front of Wolfgang and Lieselotte. Anneliese and Eckhart followed close behind. Wolfgang and Lieselotte went silent as the others gathered around, deciding they wanted to keep their conversation private. Wolfgang had never told anyone about his pen pal relationship with Lieselotte. He never disclosed with his parents what Lieselotte said in her letters. And it was easy to deduce that Lieselotte had told no one about him. That secret was precious, and now that they were seeing each other in the flesh, that secret was captivating. Sexy. Intimately erotic.

The conversation was slow through the first *stein* of beer. The small talk of what each other did for a living. Eckhart and Dietrich answering that they worked at the same textile plant as Wolfgang; Anneliese, Hilde, and Elsa stating they were also students at Freie. Then the follow-ups. *Do you like it? What are you studying?* It wasn't until halfway through those massive *steins* that the alcohol removed the social guards and the chitchat truly became a conversation. Even Dietrich looked at the women with a sense of wonder at the lives they lived—all they had done and seen. His wonder dulled compared to Eckhart and Wolfgang, but it was there. *How could people separated by mere feet live such drastically different lives?*

"You've never seen a Marilyn Monroe movie?" Anneliese asked.

Eckhart shook his head, dejected. "But man, I want to."

"She's so gorgeous."

Eckhart leaned toward her. "You look like her."

Anneliese laughed. "Oh, is that so?"

"Oh, that is so."

Eckhart charmed them with humorous stories of when they'd gotten drunk at their favorite *Kneipe* (pub), the Copper Cellar. Stumbling home, puking in alleyways.

Once the local lederhosen-wearing band inside the beer hall started playing the accordion, tuba, and trumpet, the group clapped and sang along with them. Beer splashed out of *steins*, soddening their shirts and shoes but not shrinking their smiles.

After drinking a third massive *stein*, the world relaxed. The air soothed. Worries disappeared. Strangers became friends.

"I think we're good and drunk now!" Eckhart screamed over the music. "How about that dancing?"

Anneliese returned his smile, reaching out and grabbing a handful of the front of his shirt and leading him out of the beer hall. Eckhart struggled to finish his *stein* as she pulled him away. Dietrich laughed, grabbing the *stein* for his friend and setting it on the table.

"Where are you going?" Hilde called out.

"Dancing!" Anneliese cried back.

Hilde and Elsa elected to call it a night. Wolfgang waited for Lieselotte to decide, hoping she wanted the night to continue.

"Care if I join you?" she asked him.

Wolfgang grinned. "Not at all."

The two of them, along with Dietrich, hurried after Eckhart and Anneliese. The sun had long set, but foot traffic only increased in the Ku'damm. While people exited shops closing for the day with shopping bags in hand, the clubs and bars were just awakening. There was frenetic energy among the people. Everyone looked for a great time, and they didn't have to look hard to find it. It was available everywhere.

Anneliese led them to a club called the Tantalizing Tingle. The wooden floor was scuffed and the hot air thick with cigarette smoke. People packed the dance floor. A U-shaped bar perimetered the dance floor, manned by half a dozen bartenders. American hits blared so loudly it tingled their skin.

The five made it to the dance floor in time for an ultimate dance hit. They obeyed the singer's request and twisted. The lighting was dim enough to erase shyness, but bright enough to move freely. Mixed with alcohol, it resulted in a complete surrender of caring what others thought—the most freeing experience in the world.

Wolfgang's glasses steamed up, forcing him to clean them with his shirt. His dark eyes narrowed as he squinted to see. Lieselotte leaned into him and whispered into his ear. "Looks like you never got those eyes for Christmas."

Her eyes gleamed when she smiled, catching every strand of light. Sweat glistening on her forehead, hair jetting out of the blue ribbon she had kept it in, a blunt realization hit him. One that seemed to always have been there, but somehow, he hadn't noticed. Lieselotte was no longer a childhood friend. A pen pal. She meant more. And no longer were his feelings toward her platonic. He was smitten. His cheeks blushed, heart fluttered, and he grinned so hard his cheeks cramped.

The music played hit after hit, no song offering a break. Dancers stumbled off the dance floor for a drink refill, bathroom break, or breather, only to rush back when the next song was another hit that couldn't be missed.

After ten songs, the group needed a break. They stumbled to the bar for more drinks.

Dietrich waved his hand. "I'm done. One more and I won't make it home."

"That's the idea!" Eckhart said, clapping his friend on the back. Wolfgang grabbed a napkin from the bar and asked a bartender for a pen.

Wolfgang struggled to write the cipher, his brain straining from such a complex task. Once he finished, he slid it over, in clear view of everyone.

"That's an incredibly odd sentence," Anneliese said.

Yes, it is. Odd for everyone but for who it was intended. Lieselotte took the note, deciphering every third letter as she'd done hundreds of times since Wolfgang's father had first showed them that Christmas Eve.

Want to get out of here?

Lieselotte set the napkin down and smiled at Wolfgang. "Sure." She turned to Anneliese. "We'll be back in a bit. Will you be okay?"

"I'll be fine. You have details you need to provide later," Anneliese said.

"Ha. Fair enough."

Stepping outside was like being hit with a smelling salt, making them fully aware of how drunk they were. All the sights, smells, and sounds. Breathing in the refreshing winter air. Feeling the sweat on their bodies freeze.

"So much for a productive Saturday," she said. "I don't think I'll leave my bed."

"I must confess something." He motioned conspiratorially for her to come closer. She did. "I must confess that I am succumbing to intoxication myself."

Lieselotte chuckled. "Oh, really?"

His glistening eyes and droopy smile were dead giveaways.

"Do you know what helps with that?" he asked.

"Sleep? Water?" she replied.

Wolfgang shook his head, then shrugged. Yes, those were both powerful tools, but not what he had in mind. "Food." His front teeth scraped along his bottom lip when he said it.

Lieselotte smiled at how adorable he was. Recognizing the little boy she'd known in the tall, broad-shouldered man and realizing she liked the parts she didn't recognize.

"Have you ever had a hamburger and French fries?" she asked.

Wolfgang shook his head. The East had prioritized practicality and collective needs over consumer culture. Fast food was a symbol of capitalist consumerism. Most restaurants in East Berlin were state-run, offering traditional German fare like sausages, potatoes, and bread. A burger and fries were as American as it gets.

"You are in for the night of your life," she said.

She looped her arm through his and quickened her pace, dragging him along. She led him to an American restaurant called Rosie's Diner. Young people, appearing to be in the same inebriated state as Lieselotte and Wolfgang, packed the hip diner.

They took a seat at the counter on the chrome swivel stools. A server wearing a soda jerk hat laid two menus in front of them. For Wolfgang, it was overwhelming. His face flushed with embarrassment. *A front and back? Where do you even start?*

She watched him, sensing his awe—how foreign this was for him.

"This menu is …" he stopped, at a loss for words.

Lieselotte had become accustomed to choice. In many ways, this menu was symbolic of how different their lives were. The different worlds they came from. One of choice; the other of command. Capitalism versus communism.

"Allow me to order?" she asked.

"Be my guest," Wolfgang said.

When the server returned, Lieselotte placed their order. They filled the time waiting for their food, talking about that Christmas Eve all those years ago. That night had sparked curiosity. Both knew that without ciphers, they likely wouldn't have kept writing—certainly not for this long. Time moves on. You meet new people. You want to share things with people in real life, not on the page. But the cipher had bonded them. Something they could only do with each other. When they were young, it was cracking the cipher they most looked forward to. But now it was the simple presence of the letter that brought the most excitement. To keep in touch with someone they'd never given a name or title to but who had unquestionably been their best friend.

"I'm in America," Wolfgang commented, looking around at the images on the wall.

"Do you recognize them?" she asked, motioning to them. Lucille Ball and Desi Arnaz, James Dean, Marilyn Monroe, and Elvis Presley.

Wolfgang shook his head.

The server delivered the burgers in a red basket lined with parchment paper. The buns glistened, dripping butter. Lieselotte couldn't remember her first burger, but she could relive it by watching Wolfgang take his first bite. He didn't have to say it—his face said it all. The way his eyes lit up when the flavor tantalized his taste buds as he alternated between chomps of burger and fries and sips of Coke.

And after the only thing left on that parchment paper was grease, something Wolfgang contemplated licking clean, the server set two strawberry malts in front of them.

While the burger satisfied his savory itch, the malt obliterated his sweet tooth. Lieselotte smiled the whole while, remembering the same look of wonder he'd had in his eyes that Christmas Eve.

When the check came, she grabbed it and removed the required *Deutschmarks*. Wolfgang would have wanted to pay, but she knew his *Ostmarks* hadn't given him a huge return of *Deutschmarks*.

The rich, fatty food had helped soak up a stomach's worth of alcohol, but now, the prospect of walking anywhere seemed unachievable. They felt the allure of sleep, and if they didn't move soon, they'd be face down on the counter until the staff booted them out.

Lieselotte nudged him. "Come on."

"Ugh. Must we move?" he replied.

"Move we must."

They sauntered back outside, shivering from the cold. Maybe the waning armor of alcohol had something to do with it. The threat of snowfall was growing. Lieselotte popped a piece of gum into her mouth and offered him one. They walked in silence, only zipping cars and the chatter of club-goers breaking the quiet.

Their directionless walk led them to the Gendarmenmarkt, a square framed by the "French Cathedral," the "German Cathedral," and the grand Konzerthaus. Golden light bathed the gorgeous buildings, contrasting beautifully with the crisp night sky.

"Do you still practice?" Wolfgang asked.

Lieselotte was Catholic, though it's natural for young people to go through spiritual lulls.

"I do," Lieselotte replied. "I had to reexamine my faith. Question things I've always accepted because I was told to."

"You must have liked the answers you found."

"I did."

While the East wasn't anti-Catholic per se, they were anti-religion. Much like the Nazis before them, they didn't like any organization that could control the masses and instill ideas. Government could make your mortal life hell; religion could threaten you with an eternity of it. But Wolfgang couldn't blame his lack of faith on the state. His parents hadn't been churchgoers, and he hadn't really considered religion. Never thought of questions or sought answers.

"My mom turned to God after my father died," Lieselotte said, the pain still intact.

"And you? I don't know much about that time," Wolfgang said.

It was the year she barely wrote.

"I got angry. Then sad. I just wanted to shut myself away from the world. I had cried so much I couldn't cry anymore."

Without warning, Wolfgang wrapped her in a hug. "I never got to give you this after it happened," he said.

"Can I tell you something?" she asked, looking up at him. Wolfgang nodded his permission, but the seriousness on her face unnerved him. "I wasn't sure if I'd ever start writing to you again."

Wolfgang's brow furrowed. "Was it something I did?"

"No, not at all. It's just ... you were a reminder of life before my father was killed. Maybe I thought if I lost you, losing my father would hurt less." She sighed. "Oh, that doesn't make any sense."

"No, it does. All your grief was focused on your father. If you lost other people and things, then your father's loss wouldn't hurt so much. That pain would have to be spread around instead of being all-consuming."

Lieselotte stared at him, dumbfounded. That was exactly it. Succinctly put in a way she had never been able to express.

"I'm really happy I didn't stop," she said.

"So am I."

Wolfgang stared at her. She stared at him. Each comfortable enough to let the other study the lines and curves of their face. Their eyes. Their lips. Seeing each other for the first time. Things were different now. They had each felt like a figment of the other's imagination. It was only natural to have built up a fictionalized version of the person you thought you knew. Most times, that idolization had only one result: a complete letdown. But seeing the other now, it had been the opposite. It had been a confirmation. But it was also a change. Platonic friends no longer applied. It didn't apply for Wolfgang looking at Lieselotte biting her lip, imagining kissing her. And it didn't apply to Lieselotte looking at his warm eyes hidden behind those lenses, or the desire to run her fingers along the cord-like muscles in his shoulders and arms.

Without a word, he stepped toward her. She met him halfway. It was impossible to know who closed that final infinitesimal distance. He cupped her face while she laid her hands on his chest. Tasting spearmint, fries, and the sweetness of the malt. Surrendering to a kiss neither had known they wanted but now couldn't imagine going without.

Quotas and Quiet Wars

Wolfgang longed to get back in her orbit. To listen to what she had to say, to witness her smile, the way her eyes lit up when she talked about her passions. He'd had crushes and attractions, but he'd never opened up with anyone the way he had with Lieselotte. That was not a criticism of the women of East Berlin. It was a testament to the fear of letting someone know you. The true you. Your thoughts. Your dreams. Your fears. Your likes. And most dangerously, your dislikes. Never knowing when something that came up in casual conversation would be disclosed to the fearsome Stasi: known for its vast surveillance network, an unlimited number of informants, and brutal tactics to maintain control and suppress dissent. In recent history, Germany had suffered many organizations that instilled terror. Nazis. Gestapo. The *Schutzstaffel*. The Stasi had taken their place in history and infamy.

Wolfgang had always told Lieselotte everything, but as public discord grew, he couldn't be as transparent. There was always the chance the Stasi could read his letters. Now more than ever, he didn't want to hold back. *But how can I safely continue pouring my soul into my letters?* As he glanced at her letter detailing her writing for the student newspaper, the answer came. The cipher that ended all their letters. Now, it wouldn't just be a fun game to end the letter. It would be vital text.

In the West, Lieselotte had the same thoughts and feelings Wolfgang had. Wolfgang had always held an allure. But seeing him in person for the first time in ten years—how much he'd changed, from his broad shoulders to his height, but never losing that child-like smile—had made that allure magnetic. And now, the letters wouldn't cut it. She couldn't go back to just that. Those letters could continue and had served their purpose, but after having a conversation in person, seeing his reactions, how could she go back?

And the kiss ...

She knew how hard it was for Wolfgang to make it into the Western sector, as the East made it harder and harder for people to leave. The manner of passports was complicated. A West German passport allowed visa-free travel to several Western countries. Its holder could travel freely from West Germany to West Berlin. West Berlin residents were issued a special identity card with a notation indicating they were from West Berlin, which was not officially part of West Germany. Despite sectors still being open, Lieselotte sensed the increasing danger—the East German government created an atmosphere of hostility toward all Westerners entering the East. Why would they limit people from entering when they suffered such drastic population losses? To control propaganda, restrict Western influence, prioritize those loyal to communism, and due to an overwhelming fear of espionage. This political hostility and the scrutiny of the Stasi and VoPos monitoring East Berliners looking to get into the West made it difficult for Wolfgang and Lieselotte to routinely see each other.

Lieselotte hadn't been into East Berlin since her family had moved, and had no desire to return to the oppressive East. But many West Berliners flocked into the East to drink at their pubs and eat their foods. Their *Deutschmarks* allowed them to purchase significantly more in the East than in the West.

Lieselotte convinced Anneliese to join her on the venture to the East. It didn't take much persuasion. She and Eckhart had hit it off. Their whole relationship was based on challenging each other, a friendly jest. One more dance. One more drink. From what Anneliese had said, they weren't exclusive—she wasn't turning down dates, and neither was Eckhart. But they both agreed that they enjoyed spending time together and when they were together, they were together.

Winter kept them inside either Wolfgang or Eckhart's small apartment, but when the last stubborn storms passed in late February, spring presented an array of activities.

Throughout the summer, Wolfgang and Lieselotte met most weekends, trading letters in person as keepsakes for their goodbyes. They swam in quiet Märkisches Viertel lakes, lounged in the sun, and rowed together, his strong shoulders powering them forward. When Wolfgang visited the West, they explored beer gardens, the Berlin Zoo, and played football at Tempelhofer Feld. They biked through the city by night—sometimes with friends, sometimes just the two of them—and wandered the Ku'damm, taking in live music, films, and late-night milkshakes. As the summer faded, Wolfgang and Lieselotte's relationship deepened. While Eckhart and Anneliese were happy to keep things casual, Wolfgang and Lieselotte had gone all in. Their relationship had started differently than most. Often, you date and get to know someone. They got to know each other and then dated. But even though Wolfgang was thrilled, only Dietrich and Eckhart knew he was dating a West Berliner. It was safer that way.

As December crept along, the Ku'damm was festooned for Christmas. Wolfgang and Lieselotte, hand in hand, strolled the *Weihnachtsmarkt*, where golden lights were draped along storefronts and wreaths hung from streetlamps. A Christmas tree, branches laden with lights and ornaments, dominated the square. The rich scents of hot chestnuts and steaming *Glühwein* filled the air from street vendors as Christmas music drifted from the shops.

They made plans for the 23rd for Wolfgang to stay with Lieselotte in West Berlin for Christmas. Her mother would take the train to meet them.

Wolfgang had his bag packed, eager to go, when someone knocked on his door. He sighed and opened it. Eckhart and Dietrich came inside. With all three men inside, the living room seemed to have shrunk.

"We're going to the Copper Cellar for a few," Dietrich said, before his eyes fell on the packed bag.

"Where are you going?" Eckhart asked.

Wolfgang buttoned his trench coat. "By Lieselotte for Christmas."

"Wolfgang, you need to be careful," Dietrich urged.

"About what?" Wolfgang asked.

Dietrich gave a look that said, *come on*. "Don't think *they* haven't noticed who you're spending time with."

"It is none of their damn business."

Eckhart lifted his hands in mock surrender. "Relax, we're not going to arrest you. Dietrich's just saying to be careful."

"You don't think I should go?" Wolfgang asked, annoyed with Eckhart's newfound line-toeing, yet appreciative of Dietrich's concern.

"That's not what either of us is saying. But Dietrich's right, they're going to know. It's just a lot of … hassle."

"You spend time with Anneliese," Wolfgang countered.

"I do. And I love it. But we both know …" He exhaled, ending the brewing tension. "I just think you need to be careful falling for her. It could lead to heartbreak."

Wolfgang put his hand on Eckhart's shoulder. "You don't have to worry about me falling for her." He bent down to pick up his bag. "Because it already happened." He clapped Eckhart on the back and headed for the door.

"It's not just that she's a West Berliner. Her father was a vocal opponent to the state. His photos were all over Western newspapers. *They* know that," Dietrich added. Wolfgang stood by the door, undeterred. Dietrich sighed. "Just try to keep it as quiet as you can, okay?"

He had Wolfgang's best interests at heart. Eckhart, too. *But don't they see how wrong that is? To be afraid to tell people about who I love? To keep it secret?*

"Merry Christmas. We'll have those drinks when I get back," Wolfgang said.

Dietrich and Eckhart left the small apartment first, Dietrich casting a concerned look, hoping they'd have the chance to have those drinks. Wolfgang followed them down the steps before they went their separate ways. Eckhart and Dietrich toward the Copper Cellar; Wolfgang toward Friedrichstraße checkpoint. Wolfgang joined the queue near the border control booths.

Considering the date, there were even more people in line than normal, waiting to visit family for the holidays. Wolfgang held his passport in one hand, his bag in the other. The VoPo on duty was young—only twenty. The line crawled forward. Wolfgang gazed ahead, but his thoughts were on the three days he would have with Lieselotte. *What better Christmas gift could there be?*

"Next," the young VoPo stated.

Wolfgang stepped up and extended his passport.

"I will take this one," a crisp, authoritative voice declared.

A man, a few inches taller than Wolfgang, snatched his passport. He wore a field gray double-breasted uniform. His visored cap featured the East German national emblem. His pale blue eyes and ash blond hair complemented a striking face.

"*Herr* Kirschke," he said, before his eyes had even seen the name on the passport. "My name is *Hauptmann* Ludwig Schwarzfuchs," he introduced. "How are you on this majestic winter's eve?"

"I'm well. Thank you."

Schwarzfuchs handed the passport back to Wolfgang without even opening it.

"Something wrong?" Wolfgang asked.

Schwarzfuchs smiled. "I know that's your passport. It's seen considerable use in the last few months."

Wolfgang stayed silent, deciding not to ask any more questions.

"Why do you wish to visit West Berlin?" Schwarzfuchs asked.

"My grandma is—"

"Surely, this sickly grandmother from last December has died?" His eyes penetrated Wolfgang, a facade of charm gleaming on the surface. "Is this Grandmother Kirschke or Grandmother Mueller?"

The fact that he knew his maternal grandmother's last name unnerved Wolfgang. If he knew her name, did he also know she had already passed? Most likely. But he also probably knew that his Grandma Kirschke didn't live in West Berlin.

"Margaret Mueller is buried outside Dresden. Elke Kirschke lives in Schönfeld. So, *Herr* Kirschke. How about the truth?" Schwarzfuchs said.

Goosebumps prickled along Wolfgang's arms. Schwarzfuchs didn't look like a monster. Didn't have soulless eyes or a crazed stare. He was striking and wielder of a fantastic smile; spoke calmly and crisply, each word cerebral.

"The truth requires no pause," Schwarzfuchs said. "Perhaps I can assist. You wish to travel to West Berlin to visit *Fraulein* Lieselotte Reisinger."

Schwarzfuchs gazed down upon Wolfgang. No matter how uncomfortable Wolfgang was, how much fear coursed through him, he didn't look away. He wouldn't.

"Lieselotte Reisinger, the daughter of extremist Johan Reisinger, who instigated violence on 17 June 1953," Schwarzfuchs continued. He paused, waiting to see if Wolfgang would object. Speak at all. When he didn't, Schwarzfuchs continued. "Do you deny this?"

"No," Wolfgang replied, snapping the single syllable from his lips.

The intimidating demeanor Schwarzfuchs had displayed shifted into something more like an understanding that was somehow more unnerving. "I was your age once. I understand the rush of attraction. The abandonment of reason. But we cannot let women plant lies in our heads."

"She hasn't planted anything," Wolfgang said.

"I hope that's true."

There was nothing to plant. He'd sown those seeds himself.

"*Fraulein* Reisinger's article for the Freie newspaper this month has received *attention*," Schwarzfuchs said.

Wolfgang knew the article. She hadn't condemned communism or supported capitalism; the theme of her article was that every person has the right to choose. However, the facts presented were critical of the communist regime.

Throughout history, culture, customs, and climate change, but the cry for freedom has always remained, she'd written.

"I know you wish to be an engineer," the Stasi officer continued. "You have problems knowing what's best for you. That is a sign of immaturity. Perhaps with a bit of self-growth, accommodations can be made to get you back into university."

Wolfgang didn't take the bait. *What does Schwarzfuchs want in exchange? For me to become an informant?*

"I apologize for being brisk, but I am running late. May I cross?" Wolfgang asked.

Schwarzfuchs stared at Wolfgang. Unblinking. Using his eyes to intimidate, like the barrel of two guns pointed directly at him. "You may not. We have met our quota today. Perhaps you will have better fortune in the days to come."

Rage swirled in Wolfgang's veins. His ears flushed with heat. Wolfgang wasn't quick to anger. But at that moment, he wanted to ball his fist and clobber Schwarzfuchs. Thankfully, he had one rational thought to reel in his temper. Even voicing his frustration would be enough to get him thrown in jail. The only rational play was to walk away.

So, Wolfgang did. Biting his lip so hard he could taste blood. Then he bit down harder. Not releasing, because if he did, he'd say one final, snippy thing. He didn't need to spend Christmas incarcerated. He'd have to spend it without Lieselotte, and that was bad enough.

The Greatest of Adversities

Lieselotte waited at the Amtrak station. Wolfgang had been due an hour ago. Three buses had come and gone. Lieselotte's mother stood beside her. Grief had carved the crow's-feet framing her eyes and the deep lines tracing her mouth.

"He would've come if it was his choice," her mother said, wrapping her arm around her.

"I know," Lieselotte said.

Since October, every letter—written in cipher—had centered around spending Christmas together. Her mother was eager to see him. Lieselotte had shared photos and stories, but that couldn't replace the real thing.

"Sweetheart," her mother said, her voice serious, "I'm afraid this conversation may be too late. But as your mother, I feel I must have it."

She took her daughter's hands in hers, struggling to accept they were the hands of a woman, not a little girl.

"Being with Wolfgang … it might only lead to pain. That's the risk with any love. But things between the East and West will only get worse. The East won't tolerate a relationship with a Westerner. Especially not with you given your father's past."

"They won't know."

Her mother smiled at her naivety. "They know."

"You're saying I should end it?"

"As your mother, whose responsibility is to protect you, yes. But as a woman, as your friend—as someone who believes we do not choose whom we love—I say fight. The greatest of loves can only be measured against the greatest of adversities."

Lieselotte let those heavy words weigh on her, considering them. Christmas had once been joyous, rich with tradition when her father was alive. This was the first year since his death that had any sense of joy. Her mother, a devout Catholic, reminded Lieselotte to be grateful and to remember the true meaning of Christmas: the birth of Jesus Christ. It was human to question the path you were on, but it was faith that reminded you your plans didn't always mesh with His plans. Knowing and accepting what He had laid out for you was something Lieselotte struggled to understand. Being with Wolfgang wouldn't be easy. The obstacles were unending, each more difficult.

A memory of her mother flashed before her and the look of love she had watching Lieselotte's father tell a story, sneak a kiss while she was at the stove, and draw a heart with shaving cream on the bathroom mirror. Would she have chosen differently, knowing it would end with the love of her life murdered in the streets of East Berlin? Would she have spared herself that pain? Lieselotte had seen how much joy her father had brought her mother. How many smiles he'd caused. So many more of those than tears.

Her mother often called her father stubborn—once something was in his mind, no argument could sway him. Lieselotte had inherited that. That stubbornness filled her as she lay in bed that cold Christmas Eve.

She wanted to be a journalist—to expose the oppression in East Berlin, East Germany, and across the Communist Bloc. To continue the cry for rights the Berliners in '53 had demanded. To write vivid prose and capture photographs so visceral, so powerful, the world couldn't ignore them, just like her father had. If she gave up on Wolfgang, they won. And she refused to let them win. She would prove to them, to Wolfgang, that with enough resolve, nothing was impossible. She would fight.

A Lion in the Rain

Wolfgang had tried to cross into West Berlin every weekend since his failed Christmas request. He'd only succeeded three times. The Stasi were watching him. Schwarzfuchs loomed—sometimes rejecting Wolfgang himself, other times sending a VoPo to say, "*Hauptmann* Schwarzfuchs said the quota has been met."

Wolfgang knew he was being monitored. He kept his head down—worked hard, took every extra shift without complaint. The letters from Lieselotte had sustained him, but they couldn't mimic her voice, her scent, her touch, or her kiss.

The late July rain pelting through the muggy air wouldn't let up, but Wolfgang wouldn't let it stop him from trying to cross. Such a poor weather day meant fewer people tried to commute between the divided city. Most people were nestled inside. The guards held umbrellas. The sternest of them let the water ripple off their hats. Among them was Schwarzfuchs, standing in front of the checkpoint, looking as if he had been waiting for Wolfgang. *Did someone tip him off?*

"*Herr* Kirschke. What brings you out on such a horrid day?" Schwarzfuchs asked.

"It's a beautiful day." Damned if he agreed with him on anything—even the weather.

Wolfgang extended his passport. Schwarzfuchs took it, examining it with a level of detail he never had before. No doubt to make Wolfgang stand out in the rain a little longer.

"Your birthday approaches," Schwarzfuchs commented. "We are both Leos. Lions. Tell me, *Herr* Kirschke, do you consider yourself a lion? A lion must know its place in the pride."

He handed Wolfgang his passport back. Wolfgang slipped it into his pocket to protect it from the rain.

"You have done well at your place of employment, *Herr* Kirschke. The state believes in rewarding hard work. I will approve your journey into the West."

Is this a trick? It had to be. Wolfgang didn't advance. He'd been conditioned to hear rejection.

"Unless, of course, you've changed your mind?" Schwarzfuchs asked.

Wolfgang shook his head, and with long strides crossed the border, expecting Schwarzfuchs to call out after him and tell him to stop. That there had been a mistake. To hear him chuckle. But Schwarzfuchs did none of those things.

"Enjoy your visit, *Herr* Kirschke!" Schwarzfuchs called out.

A cold tingle spread along Wolfgang's body. *Why did they allow me entrance?* Especially since it was Schwarzfuchs who had. He should feel overjoyed about his access into West Berlin. Instead, he felt unnerved. *Why now? After months of constant rejection?* With the Stasi, kindness was never without an ulterior motive.

But he had to shake that feeling. The weather had already thrown a wrinkle into their plans. He couldn't bring his own dark cloud.

Lieselotte lived on campus, sharing her dormitory with a roommate who hardly left, unaffected by the claustrophobia that would drive most people mad after an hour. A shared dorm room was hardly conducive to private, intimate moments. They played cards, trying to sneak moments of intimacy, whether with a foot rubbing across a leg or fingers tracing along hands.

He was sopping wet by the time he knocked on her dorm room door. But the smile she greeted him with was well worth the sodden trot. She handed him a towel. He dried his hair and cleaned his glasses. He greeted Sandra, Lieselotte's roommate. She offered a polite wave but went back to her reading. Apart from the first time they'd met, she never spoke.

"I'm ready to go," Lieselotte said.

Wolfgang turned his head to the side in confusion. "Go where?"

"You said you had something planned the next time we met."

"I did, but it's pouring out. Or did you think I got dressed in the shower?"

"Am I to believe that we're going to let a little rain stop us?"

Wolfgang smirked. "No. We shan't let a little thing like that stop us."

Though the rain had eased, it still fell hard enough to warrant an umbrella. Lieselotte grabbed one and opened it as they stepped outside. As expected, they had the Western Berlin streets mostly to themselves. Certainly, they were the only ones out for a stroll. Lieselotte led them to the bus station where they took a bus to Schlachtensee, roughly two miles from the university. The lake was empty. No surprise, given the rain.

"Don't just stand there! You wanted to swim!" Lieselotte said.

"You still want to swim?" Wolfgang asked.

"I want to swim with you. I don't care what the weather is like. Do you?" Lieselotte asked.

"Not one damn bit."

She closed the umbrella and stripped down to her underwear, her hair clinging to her shoulders, drenched and dark. Wolfgang looked on, his breathing hitched. The air in his lungs sucked away.

He admired her curves as she strolled into the water. The way the rivulets of water ran down her chest and disappeared into the expanse of her cleavage. His heartbeat thundered. His cheeks flushed. Excitement bubbled in his stomach. He stripped down to his boxer shorts and gasped once the water touched his feet. It only got worse the deeper he went.

Lieselotte took a deep breath and submerged, then rose from the water with a look of shock. Her nipples hardened from the cold, and it was all Wolfgang could do not to stare. Goosebumps mottled her ivory skin; her lips trembled. Heat flashed through Wolfgang, a physical hunger he fought to suppress.

Over the last few months, they'd become more intimate. Touching. Caressing. Kissing. But no further. She had the conviction to wait until marriage. Wolfgang always respected her wish, but *damn*, in moments like this, his restraint frayed.

The change from dusk to nighttime seemed to have come without warning. The sky bled into a dusky blue. Thunder cracked. Lightning flashed.

"We should get out of the water!" Wolfgang shouted.

He took Lieselotte's hand, and they ran for the shore, screaming with excitement as the sky flashed like a strobe light. The storm rattled through the Grunewald Forest, every crack of thunder blurring the line between exhilaration and fear—that place where you feel most alive.

They grabbed their clothes and sprinted into the trees, but in their hurry, they ran to opposite ends. Thirty meters of open grass, sand, and mud separated them.

Both screamed for the other to run over. Laughing. Even though they were already drenched, neither wanted to go back out into the downpour. The relentless pitter-patter of rain, howling wind, and crashing thunder meant it was impossible for Wolfgang and Lieselotte to hear each other.

In the chaos, both ran out. The ground was a slick, muddy mess. Wolfgang slipped, protecting his face with his hands. Mud splattered all over him. Lieselotte didn't last much longer before she slipped on her butt. Their clothes were caked in mud. Lieselotte sat, her body slouched forward, head dipped in embarrassment but grinning. Wolfgang got to his knees; head arched in disbelief.

They cackled into the sky, then locked eyes, the laughter fading. A mutual acknowledgment passed between them that there was nowhere else they'd rather be.

"I'm going to defect," Wolfgang said.

Lieselotte smiled before joy was replaced with want. Lust swelled. Raw and urgent. Primal. Sowed in their souls. They crawled toward each other, leaving handprints in the mud, then rose to their knees when they got to each other. Wolfgang cupped her face. She grabbed a handful of his hair, conditioning it with her muddy fingers. Lips locked together, teeth tracing the lines of their lips.

The mud made it wilder. Sexier. More intoxicating. She sat on his lap, wrapping her legs around his waist. Hands exploring, leaving traces of mud where they'd been, and the taste of the sapid rainwater on each other's lips.

Barbed Wire Sunday

By the time Wolfgang left her dorm room the following morning, all doubts vanished—he was unequivocally, undeniably, and undisputably in love with Lieselotte.

The relentless heat of August assailed both East and West Berlin. The factories were stifling, and Wolfgang sweated through his shift, chafing until his skin burned. Müggelsee, Berlin's largest lake, offered the only relief. For Wolfgang, even an air-conditioned room wouldn't have helped him sleep. He had too much on his mind.

As he lay atop his bed in boxer shorts, sweating into the mattress, he pondered the consequence of his decision. He was going to defect into West Berlin at the end of August. The decision didn't cause his sleeplessness but its consequences. The goodbyes he would be forced to face. His parents. His friends. He couldn't tell them anything. He would hurt everyone close to him. Even though he trusted his parents and his friends, it would be better for them if they had no knowledge of his defection. Otherwise, they risked being labeled accomplices. The Stasi were human lie detectors. They'd be able to tell if they'd had previous knowledge or if they were just as blindsided.

But as Wolfgang lay in bed, dreaming of escape, history was being made. In the early Sunday morning of 13 August 1961, the East German Republic had taken dramatic steps to seal its border.

Wolfgang awoke earlier than normal for a Sunday, deciding a stroll around the city would help his overloaded mind. Immediately after stepping outside, he knew something was different this Sunday morning. Droves of people were heading toward the West, murmuring about what was happening. Wolfgang followed them as far as the barriers near the iconic columns and quadriga of the Brandenburg Gate, looming beyond the barbed wire—a symbol of

Berlin's unity now dividing its people. Streets were blocked off. Barbed wire fences hastily erected. Armed soldiers took up positions along the wall, their gazes not directed to the West, as if the American-backed West was making a move into East Berlin but facing its own citizens. History would come to know this day as Barbed Wire Sunday. For those involved in the barrier's implementation, it was known as Operation Rose. The East's solution to stopping the Brain Drain. Overnight, the border had been cut off.

People shouted questions at the guards, arms flailing toward the West, pleading for passage. Stating they had family, friends, and employment in the West and needed to get through. East Berlin denied each of them en masse.

Schwarzfuchs was among the senior level on the scene. He stood with his hands behind his back, surveying the crowd. When the masses didn't calm, he raised his hands to silence them.

"Ladies and gentlemen!" he repeated himself until it quieted enough for him to be heard. Even so, the sound of heavy machinery, hammering, and the clinking of tools by the people erecting the barrier made it hard to hear. "The West has continued to send spies into the East to undermine our great society! Under the supreme wisdom of Minister Mielke and Secretary Ulbricht, we are creating an anti-fascist barricade for your protection! We must keep these treacherous and treasonous filth from polluting our streets and poisoning our youth!"

Many people accepted that as truth. Wolfgang found one major flaw in that logic. *If the threat is from outside, why are the guards, with their guns at the ready, scanning the East instead of the West?*

Schwarzfuchs had known this barrier was coming. *Did he allow me into the West as a parting gift—or a final taunt?* Seeing the smug satisfaction on Schwarzfuchs's face, it was obvious it was the latter. He wanted the loss to be fresh, so it stung all the more.

For the first time in history, a wall had been constructed not to keep people out, but to keep its own people in. The Iron Curtain entrapped Wolfgang behind it with no way out.

That swim in the rain and the epic embrace he and Lieselotte had shared on the muddy shore seemed so long ago. A relic from another life beyond the other side of the wall. Seeing her had been difficult before. Now, it would be impossible. They'd never allow him into the West again; each scrape of cinder block sliding into place reiterated that point. His strength left him, replaced by lightheadedness. His breathing raced, catching in his throat. This was a nightmare, one he desperately wanted to wake up from. But there was no waking from this nightmare. A new dawn had risen in Berlin.

In the West, news of the wall caused outrage. Lieselotte and Anneliese joined the protestors, gathering across Pariser Platz. The Brandenburg Gate rose just beyond, sealed behind the East's barriers, marking the line between freedom and oppression. They pondered the creation of this monstrosity. Demanding the Western government do something. *How could this happen? Be allowed to happen?* Those not protesting begged for answers on loved ones on the other side of this newly created divide.

August ticked by with no intervention from the West. Then September. It wasn't until 22 October that action took place. American diplomat Allan Lightner attempted to cross into East Berlin without showing identification. US policy stated only Soviet officials, not East German authorities, could check American personnel. US military police escorted Lightner through. The East German government saw it as a challenge to their authority. In response, on 27 October, under the urging of American General Lucius Clay, M48 tanks grinded to a halt at the checkpoint—a mere eighty yards from the border. The Soviets, in response, sent T-54 tanks.

Lieselotte stood by and watched Checkpoint Charlie. For the first time in the Cold War, American and Soviet tanks, separated by a mere hundred meters, faced each other. World War III was only a bullet away. Many in the crowd left, trying to flee before the shooting started. Anneliese pleaded for Lieselotte to leave with her. Camera in hand, her father came to mind. *Had he known the danger he was in during that fateful day?* More than likely, he had. Despite that, he performed his duty. He stayed to capture the moment. And she would, too. Knowing that the right photograph was as powerful a weapon as had ever existed.

West and East Berlin were squares on a chess board. War here meant a global war between the United States and the Soviet Union. It could mean world destruction. Both powers had nuclear weapons. The hydrogen bombs both sides possessed were thousands of times more powerful than the bombs America had dropped on Nagasaki and Hiroshima. An exponential increase in destruction that was unfathomable. If either side launched and targeted East or West Berlin, it wouldn't matter. There'd be nothing left.

The tank standoff lasted sixteen nerve-wracking hours. Lieselotte had been there for thirteen of them. Every minute of those thirteen hours had been the most harrowing of her life. Behind the scenes, the Kennedy administration negotiated with Khrushchev, and on 28 October the Soviet tanks backed down. Followed shortly after by the American tanks. For now, global war had been averted.

As the wall grew, spreading the ninety-six miles along West Berlin, Lieselotte recalled her mother's words—that this relationship could end in heartbreak. No love is without obstacles. But seldom is there an actual wall in the way.

"This came," Sandra said, holding out a letter when Lieselotte walked into their dorm. Her dark blonde hair covered her eyes.

Lieselotte thanked her and took the letter. Someone had opened the envelope. More than likely, the Stasi had upped their efforts in monitoring communication to the West. Looking for those critical of the state. Wolfgang's erratic mix of cursive and print was unmistakable.

Lieselotte,

I write this letter with a heavy heart but strong conviction. I know not when we can see each other again. Perhaps it's for the best. We cannot risk Western spies coming into East Berlin. Ruining all we have built. The equal rights of men and women. The free health care. Locked pricing on goods. Our government is right in creating the anti-fascist barrier. You are in the wrong with your viewpoints. But you can learn. I will keep sending these letters to help you realize the error in your thinking. I believe with these letters, I can rehabilitate you. Please be open to change!

Yours, Wolfgang

Lieselotte gawked at the letter, searching for the cipher. But it was a quick realization that this entire letter was a cipher. Wolfgang would never write these words. He had voiced his complaints about the East frequently. This letter was the complete antithesis of everything he had said. But as she reread the last paragraph, she found the cipher that revealed the entire letter was a cipher.

Letters being read. Reread it all.

Lieselotte grabbed a pen and sheet of paper and went to her work desk to decipher the message. They'd advanced from the third letter of every word to acrostic ciphers—a hidden message formed by taking the first or last letter of each line, paragraph, or sentence. They used drop letter ciphers, capitalizing certain letters that when removed or kept spelled a message. Wolfgang had used a clever mix. It took her half an hour and a full sheet of paper before she finally deciphered it.

I plan to keep my promise to leave. Do not know how. Do not know when. I love you. I know the burden. If you need to end this, I understand.

There was so much to unpack. Mostly the ending. His statement that if she wanted to end this, he would accept it. A rational and thoughtful proposal. But one she never considered. If there had been a time to walk away from Wolfgang, it had long since passed. When she reflected, it had ended the moment they had locked eyes in the movie theater. The second part of the letter she reviewed was his confirmation to leave East Berlin. *How does he propose to do that?* It was an incredibly dangerous undertaking. One that could end in his arrest or even death. Arrest didn't mean a weekend in jail, either. It meant years in prison.

Lieselotte grabbed a new sheet of paper and started her reply, electing for a pencil as she planned out her ciphered response. She needed Wolfgang to know that she couldn't be the reason to risk everything to escape the East. If he was caught, she couldn't live knowing she had been the reason.

It took two hours to write the letter. Writing and erasing, figuring out how to turn the decoded message into a coded cipher. And not just one cipher. The same mix Wolfgang had used. Once finished, she folded it, sealed it in an envelope, and left to send it.

The Wall Grows Higher

More than a week passed before Wolfgang received her letter. The wall's influence now extended to the mail with delays, border controls, and censorship. The envelope looked sealed, but Wolfgang knew he wasn't the first person to read this letter. He had little doubt that Lieselotte wouldn't recognize that his letter had been a cipher. His worry was that she may not catch all the ciphers he'd placed in it. He skimmed through the innocuous text, heading straight to the final sentence.

Decoded.

Breathing a sigh of relief, he reread the letter. He grabbed a pencil and began deciphering. Because she'd followed his logic and structure, he quickly decoded the message.

I want you. Do not risk your life for me. Be careful. Keep me posted. I will do what I can to help.

He couldn't deny he'd hoped for this—for her to want to be with him no matter the adversities. Her blunt "I want you" meant everything. After reading the note he'd scribbled, he set it on fire. It was too risky to keep. He dropped it into the toilet, flushed, and watched the ashes swirl away.

Though some called it the barrier or the divider, it quickly became simply "the Wall." Berlin was an island. Those who once worked in the West for better wages were now jobless or forced into lower-paying careers. Those in the East also had plenty of reasons to be upset with the Wall. They were cut off from family and friends. But even though the list of frustrated people was limitless, the number of people you could trust was few.

Wolfgang wanted to broach the subject of escape with Dietrich and Eckhart, but first, he wanted to talk to his parents. They had lived through the war. He wanted to draw on their experience, so he went to see them.

His father's hair had thinned but stayed dark; his mother's had gone gray—but gracefully. His mother knew far more about his relationship with Lieselotte than his father did. His childhood home didn't look any different. An odd comfort, though he knew it wasn't by choice. His family couldn't afford a new couch or kitchen table. The state paid for housing, but it couldn't afford the upkeep. Once things degraded, they stayed degraded.

"Things are getting worse," Wolfgang said.

His father shrugged. "Things will blow over, they always do."

Wolfgang didn't agree. But he struggled on how to voice it to his father. They had rarely fought. Sitting in the familiarity of the living room, a rush of sadness swooped over Wolfgang at just how different he and his father had become. By asking him to be silent, his father was asking Wolfgang to kill the spark within him—the zeal for life, the dreams, the wishes he still carried, and those yet to come.

"The best you can do is keep your head down. Do what you're asked," his father said.

The words stunned Wolfgang. Shame burned in his chest. *How can he act so complacently? Even cowardly?*

"Even if it goes against what I believe?"

"What do you mean? They're not asking you to do anything illegal. Just stay quiet."

"And if it goes against my happiness?" Wolfgang pressed.

"Happiness? They shouldn't affect your happiness one bit."

"That's exactly my point."

Wolfgang loved his father. He'd always spent time with Wolfgang, taught him, was patient with him. He'd given him the gift of ciphers, which had kept his relationship with Lieselotte alive—a lit ember in a storm. But Wolfgang couldn't accept his kneeling to this oppression. He'd never condemned his father for working for the Nazis. The world could condemn everyone who worked for Hitler, and Wolfgang understood why. The Nazi Party had been architects of evil. But the world didn't understand there wasn't always a choice. Only the illusion of one. His father worked in intelligence, so Wolfgang hadn't had to come to grips with the fact that his father had worked at the camps where millions of people were gassed or shot. He'd been underground, decoding and encoding the Enigma machine or trying to crack English, and later American, codes.

But Wolfgang couldn't help but wonder that if everyone had made a moral stand, things could have been different. There had been attempts on Hitler's life. Most famously, the Von Stauffenberg plotters who smuggled in a briefcase of explosives into the Wolf's Lair. The briefcase was moved at the last second. The thick oak table absorbed the blast, sparing Hitler. All of those involved in the plot were killed. Not the type of ending that instills follow-up acts. But it was this attitude—this unresisting resignation, this eager silence—that allowed evil to go unchecked, unchallenged.

What Wolfgang's father told him to do was to abandon his hopes of being an engineer. Accept that he could never rise above others, no matter how hard he worked. He'd never have pride in what he did. Never feel fulfilled. Never be able to read what he wanted or see which movies he wanted. Listen to what music he wanted. Never travel to where he wanted. Never eat the apple strudel at the Givre Strudel Lieselotte had praised. Never see London or New York City. And most importantly, he'd never be able to love who he wanted to love.

"What about Lieselotte?" he asked.

His father sighed. "I know you care for her. In a different world, I'd tell you to marry her. But that's not the world we live in. There are plenty of women here you could connect with, son."

"If you were told you couldn't marry my mother, would you have listened?"

It was a question Rolf couldn't answer. He hadn't had to make that choice. But his silence spoke volumes. If the powers that be had stated he couldn't marry Wolfgang's mother, his father probably wouldn't have fought for her. An aching sadness crept in. Pity for his father and sorrow for his mother. *Had she ever known what it felt like to be fought for?* Their love was easy. Convenient.

As his parents prepared dinner, the sad realization was clear. Wolfgang couldn't tell them his plan. They would try to talk him out of it. Perhaps his father, thinking he was helping Wolfgang, may even alert the Stasi. His father was a follower. He lacked the courage to make a moral stand. It broke his heart that his father hadn't learned his lesson after the war. That after coming to terms with the horrors his leaders had orchestrated, he hadn't learned to question the status quo and the common narrative. To dig for the truth. His father might argue they weren't killing people. Perhaps. But they were smothering them in shackles.

Each day, the Wall grew—from barbed wire to cinder blocks. Fearmongering ran rampant. The Stasi had arrested two of Wolfgang's colleagues, making a spectacle of it to instill fear and obedience. Wolfgang needed to escape, he just didn't know how.

He wrote letters to Lieselotte, making sure the encoded messages made as much sense as the decoded messages. Each letter took hours, and even then, he worried about mistakes. Sometimes he misspelled words in the cover text just to make the decoded message work.

There wasn't a more watched place on Earth than the Berlin Wall, and there was plenty for Wolfgang to report in his letters. People on both sides cried and yelled. It was pure chaos. On 15 August, East German guard Konrad Schumann leaped over the barbed wire and defected—caught forever in a famous photo.

The barbed wire cut through streets. The young soldiers squeezed their rifles, fearing a riot. All the while, people in the

West screamed and cursed at the guards. Calling them pigs, traitors, and concentration camp guards. The East German government dug up streets to prevent vehicles from being able to plow through the barricade. 100 miles of barbed wire fencing had been raised, including the twenty-seven miles separating West and East Berlin. Wolfgang had monitored the Wall from a safe distance, trying to find the best place to attempt his escape. But as he watched the chaos, it seemed that death was the only possible result.

Lieselotte joined the West Berliners demonstrating against the Wall while West Berlin's Mayor, Willy Brandt, criticized the US for not responding. American President Kennedy had lamented that "a wall is a hell of a lot better than a war." While he denounced the Wall, he tested the borders by sending his vice president, Lyndon B. Johnson, and retired General Lucius D. Clay into Berlin on 19 August.

Before the Wall, public transportation ran through the city. After its creation, rail lines were cut in half, stopping abruptly or bypassing closed stations nicknamed "ghost stations" in the aftermath. While some people attempted to leap over the barbed wire, others jumped out of apartment windows that ran adjacent to the border.

Bernauer Straße became infamous overnight. The street itself was in the West, but the apartment buildings lining it belonged to the East. Escapees could simply climb out a window and drop into freedom.

Wolfgang considered this his best option. But he barely had time to decide that before the East Berlin police put a stop to it. Ida Siekmann was a fifty-eight-year-old nurse who jumped out of her third-floor apartment on 22 August. By which time, the windows and entrances on the lower levels had been sealed and barred. In desperation, people from the upper floors risked life and limb jumping to freedom. The West Berlin fire department waited below Ida's window to catch her with a jumping sheet. But before it was ready, Ida jumped. Gravely injured, she died en route to the hospital.

Soon, any building looking into the West was completely barricaded, guards manning the entrances. It wasn't a viable option for Wolfgang. With hopping over the barbed wire now an obsolete attempt, and the windows of buildings overlooking West Berlin sealed with concrete, Wolfgang contemplated other options.

He considered swimming across the River Spree until, on 24 August, border guards shot and killed twenty-four-year-old Günter Litfin as he swam across.

As 1961 waned, the Wall evolved into a lethal monstrosity. Guard towers sprouted, providing bird's-eye views of the Wall. Dogs paced. The space between the inner and outer walls—a so-called "death strip"—was raked with sand to reveal footprints and impede escapees. Most dangerous of all were the explicit orders for guards to shoot anyone who tried to escape. With each new addition, Wolfgang's dream of freedom felt more implausible, even impossible.

As each day passed, the vice-like feeling in Wolfgang's chest tightened. Each day he failed to come up with a plan, the fewer options remained. Several times, he contemplated making a mad dash for the Wall. Leap for the top and attempt to pull himself over. It was madness, he knew. But every time he neared the Wall, the desire to escape overwhelmed him.

He wrote to Lieselotte, listing the few positives of the East— fixed rent, gender equality—as camouflage. What he really wanted was intel. Perhaps she had heard about weak points or successful escape attempts. Everything was written in cipher. He and Lieselotte had to up their skill level. The Stasi would have expert intelligence officers on their staff.

When Lieselotte read and deciphered the letter, she contemplated. She wanted to help in any way she could. But she needed a foolproof plan if Wolfgang planned to risk his life and liberty for it. The problem was there was no such plan. There was nothing without risk. Any escape plans she heard about meant they were in the past. Meaning if she knew, the Stasi knew. They wouldn't allow someone to escape in the same place or in the same way twice. In her ciphered response, she promised to help however she could, but the decision had to be Wolfgang's.

She headed for the door of her dorm room when Sandra stopped her.

"They won't let that letter through," she said.

Lieselotte paused, staring at the letter gripped in her hands. "I have had others make it through."

Sandra arched her eyebrows as if to say, *if you say so.*

"Why don't you think it will make it through?" Lieselotte asked.

"They know who you are. You need to find someone who will travel into East Berlin and deliver it."

Who? Who would want to venture into East Berlin right now? Risk being stuck there?

"I will take it."

Lieselotte had to look up from the letter in her hands to see that it was her quiet roommate who had spoken those words. They were roommates, but Lieselotte wasn't sure they were friends.

"It's too risky for you," Sandra said. "I doubt the East would allow you in considering who your father was and how vocal you've been."

A chill crawled along her back. *The Stasi know who I am. How? My articles in the newspaper? From the crowds gathered near the Wall?* It struck her then—her first realization that the Stasi had spies in West Berlin.

"I'm quiet. I fly under the radar," Sandra said.

"You would do this for me?"

Sandra shrugged like it wasn't a big deal. "My father lives in East Berlin. I'm going to visit him as much as I can anyway."

Sandra had been fortunate enough that the state accepted her visa request to visit her father.

Lieselotte handed the letter to Sandra, thanked her profusely, and gave her Wolfgang's address. Sandra stated she was traveling into East Berlin that afternoon. Until then, Lieselotte could do nothing but wait. First, she waited for Sandra to leave, which seemed to take an eternity. When she finally left, there was a moment of relief before her body realized there would be no quick answers. She had to wait for Wolfgang to read the letter, decipher, reply, and send out. An unknowable length of time that gnawed at her and sickened her with worry.

Three Must-Haves

In East Berlin, Wolfgang let Dietrich and Eckhart talk him into a few beers at the Copper Cellar. His nerves hadn't settled since the Wall went up, and harboring his secret hadn't helped. He hoped a drink with friends might ease his inner turmoil. Escape attempts had calmed down over the last several weeks after the early onslaught. The shoot-to-kill orders had not been idle. He'd fallen into a despised routine of not seeing Lieselotte. Still, there were moments where her absence and his predicament came to the forefront of his mind—where his laughter faded and his eyes drifted, as though there was no air for him to breathe.

"Wolfgang," Dietrich called.

Apparently, now was one such instance. He'd been in a daze, staring at his beer. *How does that remind me of Lieselotte? Because everything does. Or maybe it's just that every moment seems better with her.*

"Wolfgang," Dietrich said louder.

Wolfgang snapped out of his daze, looking into his friend's soft brown eyes. "Sorry."

"Thinking about Lieselotte?" Eckhart asked, before taking his last sip of beer.

Wolfgang nodded, polishing off his beer, too. He was ready to leave. He wanted a break from overthinking but had brought it with him and ruined the fun his friends were trying to have.

"It sucks," Dietrich said. "I'm sorry."

Wolfgang wanted to talk about the promise he made to Lieselotte on that rainy July night to flee East Berlin, but even among friends, the walls had ears. Every person in here could be an informant. Even if he trusted Eckhart and Dietrich, he didn't know if they shared his desire to flee. And what if they didn't? Telling them could put them in danger. If they joined and failed, they could die. If they stayed and knew, they could be punished as accomplices.

Still, part of him believed he had a better chance alone. Fewer people meant less attention. But then again—if they overpowered a lightly guarded section of the Wall, could numbers be an advantage?

Eckhart rose from the table. "Well, I'm out of here."

Wolfgang followed suit. "Me, too."

Dietrich still had half a beer. "Go ahead. I'm going to stay here. I have nothing else going on."

Eckhart and Wolfgang wished him a good night, then headed for the door. They walked beside each other until Eckhart branched left and Wolfgang continued ahead. East Berlin had no visible homelessness, and at night, it was oddly quiet and deceptively peaceful. Yet even in the quietness of night, he couldn't shake the feeling that every move he made was being watched. Monitored. Critiqued. Judged.

As Wolfgang approached his apartment complex, a figure sat on the stoop. A woman wearing glasses. Nothing more than a silhouette until he crossed the street.

"Sandra?" Wolfgang asked.

She rose from the stoop and stepped toward him. "Good evening, Wolfgang."

Despite attending school in the West, Sandra hadn't adopted Western fashion. She wore a wool coat and Dederon scarf, the cheap East German synthetic, everything in muted shades of gray.

"Good evening."

Already a record for our longest conversation.

If Sandra was here, it was about Lieselotte. And if she waited on his stoop, it probably wasn't good news. He walked toward her, jaw tight and heart racing.

"She's fine. I am visiting my father," Sandra said.

He breathed a sigh of relief. "I didn't know you had family in East Berlin."

"You wouldn't. It's not like we correspond often."

His cheeks flushed with guilt, even though he knew conversations require two people.

"Is there a place where we can get a coffee?" she asked.

He'd been tired even before the two beers. Now, sleep was only a long blink away. He didn't want to walk any further than the required steps to his bedroom. But Sandra had come here. She didn't strike him as traveling to East Berlin to get a cup of coffee. There had to be an ulterior reason. So, he gestured for Sandra to follow.

"Were you from East Berlin?" Wolfgang asked on the walk to the coffee shop.

"Sort of. My parents divorced when I was three. My mother moved to Hamburg. I stayed with her during the school year and stayed in Berlin with my father during the summers."

"You have a visa to see him?"

"I do. My father was a senior planner for the Ministry of Transport. He had a stroke a few months ago, and they've allowed me to visit."

"I'm sorry to hear that," Wolfgang said. Not knowing what else to say about it, he switched the topic to Lieselotte. "How is Lieselotte?"

"Sad. Worried about you. She's vocal."

Wolfgang smiled. Sandra noticed it but didn't share his smile.

"That's the reason you won't be able to see her, and she won't be able to see you," Sandra said.

Blunt, delivered in Sandra's no-fluff way. Wolfgang knew enough about Sandra to realize she meant nothing by it except the delivery of a fact. But he was proud of Lieselotte for expressing her opinion with her voice and her written words. Her strong-mindedness was one of her many qualities he adored.

"Everyone should have the right to voice their opinion," Wolfgang said.

He opened the door to the quaint coffee shop. At this hour, it was vacant. It was doubtful they even had a pot of coffee brewed.

"Yes," Sandra said, pausing before stepping inside. "But there are repercussions for what you say."

The floor was dusty, the tabletops clean but chipped. Like most places, the décor was industrial white and gray. The lone worker stayed behind the counter, preparing for closing, when she asked Wolfgang and Sandra what they would like.

Wolfgang asked for whatever they had on the pot. Sandra agreed. The woman filled two mugs. One sip confirmed it wasn't real coffee. The toasty taste of *Muckefuck*—roasted grains like barley or chicory—was a poor substitute. He hated paying good *Ostmarks* for it.

Sandra drank it, showing no signs of whether she liked or hated it. Then she set the mug down.

"I'm going to use the restroom. It's a long way back. You might want to go, too."

She walked down the short hallway to the restroom. The woman behind the counter finished cleaning and stood waiting, more than likely for the two late guests to leave. Wolfgang gave an apologetic smile, silently promising they'd be on their way soon. Moments later, Sandra stepped out and sat.

"It's open. I'll wait for you."

Wolfgang tried to limit his gawking. No one acted this strange without a reason, not in East Berlin. It wasn't tolerated. Wolfgang rose and went into the lone bathroom. A closet-sized room with a toilet, sink, and towel rack. Resting behind the faucet handles was a letter addressed to Wolfgang. Scribbled on the envelope was a handwriting he didn't recognize, but he surmised it was Sandra's.

In her brisk and blunt way, in sprawling cursive: *Write back. Leave it here.*

Behind the envelope were tri-folded sheets of paper. Wolfgang tore open the envelope and read. Then used a sheet of paper to decipher Lieselotte's message. Anxious, he decoded the best he could, knowing he'd missed a few letters or even a word, but confident he had enough to make sense of it.

Speculation: some sections less fortified—potential Soviet breach points. Drive through. Be safe. Be certain. Do not do this for me.

He considered her advice, then worried about how long he had been in the bathroom. *Has it been seconds or minutes?* He wrote back on the blank sheets of paper, telling her it was a good idea. Writing in cipher had gotten easier, but it still took time. He could screw up a letter or two and not lose the decoded message. But any more than that could alter his intended message. He left his reply behind the sink and flushed Lieselotte's torn letter down the toilet. When he opened the door, Sandra was standing there.

"I'm sorry you aren't feeling well. I need to get going, anyway. It was nice to see you again."

Wolfgang shimmied past her. "I apologize. I hope I don't get you sick."

Ignoring the worker's annoyed stare—or was it watchful?—Wolfgang stepped into the night. The twenty-minute walk gave him time to replay Lieselotte's advice over and over. Whether there were sections of the Wall deliberately weaker seemed like a massive oversight on the East Germans' part, if true. To Wolfgang, that seemed more like West propaganda. Even if unintentional. But sections of the Wall were *unintentionally* weaker because of the amount of barbed wire or cinder blocks available and the terrain itself. Enhancing the Wall was a process.

He created three must-haves. First, a powerful vehicle. It couldn't be the Trabi. The Trabant was made of Duroplast, a plastic-like material, due to the scarcity of steel, which meant it would fold like an accordion against the stone. It was noisy and smoky because of its simplistic two-stroke engine. There were some trucks produced under the state-owned Industrieverband Fahrzeugbau (IFA) that might work. Wolfgang wasn't a car person—but Eckhart was. His father worked at the IFA plant. His brother was a mechanic. *Perhaps one of those trucks could work?*

The second need was the right route. He would have to find a straightaway that allowed him to gain enough speed.

The third must-have was the right section of wall that met a strict requirement. It had to be weak. What that meant, and how to find it, remained unseen. He needed a stretch not heavily fortified. But a weak section of the Wall meant nothing if a platoon manned it.

Wolfgang tried to let those thoughts fade away so he could have a good night's sleep. But it'd been three months since he'd seen Lieselotte. He drifted off to sleep with the comforting knowledge that she would read his letter tonight. And maybe if he was the last thing on her mind before she drifted off to sleep, she'd dream of him.

The Longest Winter

Fall passed into winter. Lieselotte and Wolfgang had kept their correspondence up through Sandra. Even with her acting as courier, they wrote in cipher—first, in case the Stasi searched her, and second, to protect both Sandra and the privacy of their messages.

Wolfgang hadn't acted on his plan to leave the East, and Lieselotte didn't push him. Thinking about what could go wrong made her ill. He claimed he waited for things to settle down, but he admitted the simple truth to her in a letter: he was terrified. Whether she was being kind or honest, she stated it was best to let Wolfgang's presence with the Stasi fade. He hadn't attempted to send a letter to Lieselotte or anyone in the West since November of '61. He was a dependable, hard worker. He remained friends with Dietrich and Eckhart, though he only spoke about surface-level conversations, never detailing his true thoughts and ideas. He still didn't know where their feelings and allegiances lay. But it felt dishonest to even call them friends if he couldn't go to them with his thoughts and problems. And every time they went out for a drink or to a restaurant, there was a roomful of potential Stasi informants. Every glance from a stranger was read and critiqued.

He eavesdropped, paranoid he was being talked about, then realized he was likely causing the same dread he felt. He elected to go for late evening walks to clear his mind. He didn't even trust to voice his thoughts out loud in his own apartment. The thin walls were easy to be overheard through, and the Stasi had installed microphones and listening devices in the homes of thousands. It wouldn't shock Wolfgang if he were one of them. Not being able to voice his thoughts out loud drove him mad. He took to writing instead. Incoherent ramblings poured out—tangled thoughts, no structure, just fragments and tangents. But that didn't matter. It was a release, a desperately needed one. In the end, he burned them all, sending the black ash into his toilet to be flushed away.

The snow had faded, though the cooler temperatures persisted. Wolfgang had to sit all winter with the longing desire to escape. The harsh temperatures and snow and ice would have prevented his plan to drive through the Wall, but that offered little relief. It'd been the longest and loneliest winter of his life. Treptower Park, usually a quiet nature escape stretching along the River Spree, was a muddy mess. Rain and melting snow had muddied the ground.

Wolfgang sat on a bench overlooking the Soviet War Memorial Created in 1949 to honor the 80,000 Soviet soldiers who had died in the Battle of Berlin. Red granite arches, and a wide pathway leading to the massive statue of a soldier holding a child and standing on a broken swastika, flanked the grand entrance.

Wolfgang had no problems with the broken swastika—it had been a symbol of evil. But he longed for a place where the hammer and sickle lay right next to it. He'd asked Dietrich and Eckhart to meet him here. All winter, he'd confided in Lieselotte, detailing his dilemma. To go it alone or invite others. Ultimately, friendship drove Wolfgang's decision. If there was a chance that Dietrich and Eckhart shared his desire to escape, he needed to offer them the opportunity to do so. He rose to meet them as they approached.

"At least it stopped raining," Eckhart said.

"I still think you're crazy for wanting to go out on the water," Dietrich said.

Wolfgang had asked them under the guise of going out on a rowboat. Being out on the Spree would grant them privacy. They strolled past the monument toward the river. It was hardly a nice day, and they had the river mostly to themselves. Even the most spring-hungry Berliners weren't pretending the weather was nice enough for boating. They pushed off from the dock. Once out on the water, Wolfgang pulled in the oars.

"I have something I need to tell you. And it's going to change everything," Wolfgang said.

Silence followed. Wolfgang studied their reactions, then glanced at the clouds where the sun tried to break through. This was another before-and-after moment.

"I am going to escape into West Berlin," Wolfgang said.

Dietrich and Eckhart stayed silent. No doubt weighing what to say, processing what Wolfgang had told them. Dietrich spoke first.

"Wolfgang, that's suicide," he said.

"No. I may die—but it won't be at my hand," Wolfgang said.

Suicide meant choosing death. Wolfgang wanted to live. *God, do I want to live.*

"This is what's been eating at you?" Eckhart asked.

"Since the Wall went up," Wolfgang confirmed.

Eckhart ran his hand through his hair and gazed out at the water. Dietrich stared at Wolfgang, his emotions unreadable.

"Is this all because of Lieselotte?" Dietrich asked.

"No."

The answer came quicker and more truthfully than Wolfgang had expected. Lieselotte was part of the reason—but it ran deeper. He wanted to live somewhere where he could choose where he worked. A place where shelves weren't empty. Where buying an orange didn't feel like a luxury item. Where he could watch and listen to whatever he wanted. Where he could thrive, not just survive.

"Good," Dietrich said. "I love Lieselotte for you. You know I think she's fantastic. But this can't be about her. This can't be about anyone but you."

"I know."

Dietrich nodded, then studied Wolfgang. "So, why are you telling us?"

Eckhart snapped his gaze away from the water to Dietrich. "What's that supposed to mean? We're his best friends."

"I know we are," Dietrich said, keeping his gaze on Wolfgang. "But by telling us, he's risking us ratting him out to the Stasi or making us accomplices."

"I would never rat him out!" Eckhart said.

"Me, neither. And I doubt Wolfgang would risk us being accomplices. So, there's something else here."

Wolfgang hadn't given Dietrich enough credit for how perceptive he was. Eckhart had gotten lost in the gravity of the news while Dietrich had processed it.

Dietrich leaned forward, his eyes narrowing. "I need to know this is coming out of hope. Not despair. If you're doing this because you want to live—because you truly believe there's something better on the other side of that wall—then I'll listen. But if this is out of despair—you've given up ..." He shook his head. "That's not something I can sit back and accept."

Wolfgang let the words sit, but he didn't need time to decide. "I want to live. That's why I'm doing this."

Dietrich studied Wolfgang, accepting his words as truth.

"What about you?" Wolfgang looked between them.

"Do we want to escape?" Eckhart asked.

Wolfgang nodded.

"This is crazy, Wolfgang. I mean, there's so much I hate here. But a lot could go wrong," Eckhart said.

"It could," Wolfgang replied.

He wouldn't try to talk either of them into it. Wouldn't downgrade the severity and risk.

"When are you planning to do this?" Dietrich asked.

"I don't know. But soon. I need to know if you're in or out. It's better to not go over the specifics."

It was better for all parties to keep his escape plan a secret. For Dietrich and Eckhart, should they decide they did not want to risk escaping, the fewer details they knew, the less they needed to lie about.

"And our answer?" Dietrich asked.

"A month," Wolfgang replied.

"How long have you known?" Eckhart asked.

"I told Lieselotte the last time I saw her. Last July."

"Damn. So, you've really thought this through."

"I have."

"It's hard to make a choice and not know the plan," Dietrich said.

"We'll plan it together," Wolfgang said.

They would all be able to have a say in it. Three minds were better than one. They could poke holes in perspective plans. Find the pros and cons of each avenue for escape.

Dietrich looked at the darkening clouds. "We should head back before it rains."

Only the Trusted

Lieselotte read Wolfgang's letter—he had asked Dietrich and Eckhart if they wanted to escape. She'd told Anneliese about his decision to ask Eckhart. Anneliese and Eckhart had an on-again, off-again relationship, never ending it outright. When they were around each other, they were the only two souls in the world. Yet when apart, they drifted back into their separate lives. They hadn't seen each other since before the Wall went up. Though Anneliese never admitted it, Lieselotte knew no other man compared. No one matched Eckhart's larger-than-life personality. Anneliese never looked at another man the way she did at Eckhart.

How do they do that—detach so easily? Lieselotte wished she could. Instead, she worried about Wolfgang all day. All night. Sleep and Wolfgang's letters were her only refuge. But each letter was already outdated—sometimes by weeks, sometimes just hours. By the time she finished deciphering and reading them, everything could have changed.

The West government publicly condemned escape attempts. Nobody wanted to risk an all-out war. Even though the Wall looked drastically different on the West Berlin side, offering her no vantage points of what obstacles lay on the Eastern side, she couldn't sit by. Each evening, she paced the Wall, searching for any sign of weakness. Once spring break began, Anneliese joined her. They set a daily goal of covering five miles every day, taking the bus to a new starting point. They started at ground level, then moved to rooftops of offices, apartments, even private homes when residents allowed.

A weak spot meant nothing if Wolfgang couldn't use it. A crack in the Wall (literal or metaphorical) did no good if on the other side was an impenetrable death strip armed with soldiers and dogs. She needed to help, even if it was an illusion. The high ground offered her a limited glimpse into the East, but not enough for the information to be noteworthy to Wolfgang. He'd have to find the best route to orchestrate his plan. All she could do was tell him what awaited him on the other side of the Wall.

Wolfgang had given his best friends a month to consider their choice. He'd met with them several times during that month outside of work, but none of them broached the subject of escape. Sunshine made it easier to pretend things were fine. But even here in the East, the sun was diminished. Not just in a metaphorical sense, but a literal one. Smog from coal plants, factories, and outdated heating systems made mornings and evenings look overcast—even on clear days. On the worst days, the city took on a muted, yellowish tint. Everything was a reminder—subtle or blunt—of the state in which he lived. He'd long ago taken off those rose-tinted glasses. Once he saw the big flaws, even the little ones became unbearable.

Wolfgang tried not to overanalyze everything Eckhart and Dietrich did or said—it would only drive him mad. Eckhart had been casually seeing a woman from his apartment building named Renate. But he also dated Anneliese the same way, so it didn't seem like she would be a reason to stay. Dietrich was quiet, one to view the party rather than take part in it. He didn't have a girlfriend or anyone he seemed interested in. If Wolfgang had to decide where he thought his friends would land on their decision, he thought Eckhart would say yes to leave. That was based on the loud life his friend wanted to live. But he was also close to his family, so that certainly could sway him into deciding to stay. Dietrich reminded Wolfgang of his own father. Dietrich had the ability to just accept status quos. There was much about the East he disliked, but that itch never drove him wild the way it did Wolfgang. For Wolfgang, it felt like having to claw his own skin off.

On the last Saturday of April, Wolfgang met with Dietrich and Eckhart back on the rowboat on the Spree in Treptower. The weather had changed drastically since the last time they rowed on the water. Warm enough for T-shirts. Boaters filled the Spree, staying far from the border where police boats patrolled. Underneath the water, obstacles hindered any vessel or person trying to cross. There were steel spikes, mesh fences, and nets. Even rumors of underwater mines.

In the West, so many rowboats, canoes, kayaks, and motorboats dotted the water. In the East, they were less common, for the same underlying reasons: fear of escapes, state regulation, and economic limitations.

"It's been a month," Wolfgang said. "I hate to pressure you, but I need an answer."

Eckhart and Dietrich looked at each other, seeing who would answer first. *What if they say no?* He trusted them without reservation, that wasn't what worried him. It was the idea that they'd stay here, and he'd cross alone. That his time with his friends could be drawing to an end. Shame roiled in his gut that he'd once told Lieselotte their friendship was circumstantial. There was no doubt they were his best friends. Maybe it wasn't circumstance but chance.

"I'm in," Eckhart said.

Wolfgang couldn't hide his delight. A smile spread from ear to ear. He exhaled. The weight he'd been carrying since he'd asked them lifted. Well, half lifted. He and Eckhart turned to Dietrich, who leaned back and gazed out at the water.

"I love my parents so much. This," he looked around at the water, the trees, the city behind him, "has been my home," he said "But I'm ready for a change."

A giddiness took hold of them. They burst into smiles and laughter. Such a weight had been lifted from Wolfgang. He wouldn't face this crucible alone. By himself, Wolfgang had his doubts about whether he could succeed. But with his best friends, it seemed preordained. That arrogance of youth that made you feel invincible. The three of them could conquer any obstacle.

"What's your plan?" Eckhart asked. "Please tell me it's not swimming the Spree."

An obvious joking nod to the patrol boats guarding the border. Wolfgang didn't tell them he'd considered it—or that he'd considered just about every other option, however improbable. The idea of swimming across the border seemed so idiotic now that he laughed it off.

"What can you tell me about the trucks at the IFA plant?" Wolfgang asked.

Eckhart's eyebrows curved with confusion. "Why? What do you have in mind?"

"I want to drive through the Wall."

"You want to drive through the Wall?" Eckhart repeated.

Dietrich said nothing. His mouth was too agape for him to speak.

"If it's possible," Wolfgang answered.

Eckhart sat with the information for a few moments. "The IFA S4000-1 has a four-ton capacity," Eckhart said.

"Wait," Dietrich interjected. "We're supposed to buy a truck? And get it, when? In seven years?"

"No. That'll take too long and be too expensive," Wolfgang said.

"The H3A stopped being produced in '57, but they're still everywhere," Eckhart said.

"At a price we can't afford," Wolfgang said.

"So, we steal one?" Dietrich asked, his voice edged with annoyance as Wolfgang and Eckhart dove into specifics while he was still stuck at the "getting a truck" part.

Neither refuted that. To them, it was a simple deduction. But none of them had the courage to say it. Dietrich leaned back. The boat rocked in response.

"Listen, I want to escape, but not at the cost of hurting other people," he said.

"We're not hurting them," Eckhart said.

"Yes, we are. They spent their hard-earned money buying that and stealing it could affect their livelihood. I'm not taking part in that."

Wolfgang hadn't held the same moral stand as Dietrich until he had heard him lay it out. He hadn't considered the lasting ramifications on the people they stole from. The propaganda said that people in the West were selfish, only pursuing their own self-interests, no matter who they hurt along the way. If they did this, they'd prove the propaganda true. Wolfgang's stomach rocked with shame. *Dietrich is right. There is a right way and a wrong way to do this.*

"What if we find a broken-down one from a scrapyard or something?" Wolfgang asked, then turning his attention to Eckhart. "Would you know how to repair it?"

Eckhart considered it. "I mean, I'm a decent mechanic. We'll have to piece the parts together."

Eckhart was the type never to say he wasn't good at something. So, him saying he was decent was probably a stretch. Still better than Wolfgang, who knew nothing about automobiles.

"What about others?" Dietrich asked.

"Others?" Eckhart asked.

Dietrich nodded. "We're not the only ones who want out."

"The more people we invite, the riskier it becomes," Wolfgang replied.

"I know, but the three of us won't be able to repair a car."

That was true. Wolfgang would need to study. His mind worked well without seeing an actual example of what he was learning, but it would take time. A lot of time.

"My brother will go with us. He's a great mechanic. We'll need him," Eckhart said.

This time, Wolfgang believed him. His brother was a great mechanic.

"What about Trude?" Dietrich asked.

"They're both disgruntled. With her being pregnant, they'll want to get into the West, but I doubt she'll go without her best friend."

"Who is that?" Dietrich asked.

"Emilia. She was the maid of honor at their wedding."

"Is she married?"

"I don't know. Why, are you interested?"

Dietrich shook his head with annoyance. "No. I'm wondering how many people. This truck may not fit that many."

"Then we find a truck that will," Wolfgang said. "But we have to keep this to people who we absolutely trust. There are Stasi informants everywhere. Whoever we invite, we're vouching for them on behalf of everyone. Risking the safety of everyone."

Eckhart and Dietrich considered the weight of those words. Just as they had taken a month to decide on escaping, Wolfgang stated the three of them should spend a month deciding on who to invite. Even one mistake—one misplaced trust—meant the Stasi would know. And if they knew, there was no chance of success.

Survival by Subtraction

Lieselotte obsessed every inch of the twenty-seven-mile wall separating West and East Berlin. She pored over newspapers from across the globe, scrutinized grainy black-and-white photographs, clicked through microfilms, and studied city maps deep into the night.

After weeks of tireless research, she narrowed the Wall down to four viable sections: Treptower, with its open spaces near the river; Sonnenallee, Neukölln, and Kreuzberg due to their proximity to industrial areas. The latter three offered more open land for the vehicle to gain the speed necessary to break through.

But these options were all theoretical. She had to consider the intangibles and variables. The number of guards close by, and the diligence of them. Who was there because they were ordered to be, and who was there because they wanted to be? Was there a difference in the number of guards on duty during the day? At night? During the week or the weekend?

There was also the night sky to contend with. A full moon was the best spotlight. She spoke with the university's astronomy professor, requesting a moon-cycle calendar and the year's darkest nights. Then she scouted the guard and military presence at each of the four sections. She observed at every hour—dawn, noon, dusk, and the dead of night. Anneliese joined at times, but for Lieselotte, it had become an obsession. It was what she did every single day. Yes, she was tired. Yes, it was monotonous. Treating this as life-or-death because it was and treating it as an arithmetic problem. Probability and statistics. Which location at which time of day and which day of the week gave Wolfgang the best chance of success?

Her friends enjoyed spring in beer halls or lounging by the lake, while Lieselotte sat beneath dim lamps, research sprawled open, mind racing. She listened to the radio in her dorm room for news.

Volume low, ear pressed against the speaker as Sandra tried to sleep. She went to establishments with televisions so she could watch the evening news. She kept Wolfgang's photo on her as a reminder—of him, of her mission, of every East Berliner who wanted to escape, and her father, another casualty of the oppressive regime. Gazing at his handsome face each morning refilled her resolve. If situations were reversed, he'd be doing the same thing. All their sacrifices would be worth it when he made it over into West Berlin.

Eckhart and Dietrich had spent that month scrutinizing who they would invite. Dietrich knew no one he trusted enough to say yes—or stay silent. Eckhart had settled on his brother, Bastian, and sister-in-law, Trude. But he hadn't asked him yet. There was a chance he'd say no, tell Eckhart how stupid he was. It would take some coaxing. Eckhart wanted his brother and sister-in-law and their unborn child to have the best life, but there was also an ulterior motive. They needed Bastian's mechanical skills.

The next morning, Wolfgang had just finished his breakfast when there was a knock on his door. He checked his watch. It was considerably early for company. His stomach churned. *Is it the Stasi?* A flicker of relief—*they wouldn't knock. Or would they?*

He opened the door. Dietrich and Eckhart stood there. They didn't say anything—only nodded. None of them trusted this as a secure setting. Together, they took the bus to Treptower.

"Bastian and Trude are in," Eckhart said.

Relief then excitement washed over Wolfgang. They would finally go from talking about planning to planning. But with that change, fear gripped his veins with its icy fingers.

"My brother also has a place to find the IFA truck. An old salvage yard. We can go there this afternoon," Eckhart said.

"During the daylight?" Dietrich asked.

"Less suspicious than going in the middle of the night. It's just a salvage yard."

True, but here, everything was questioned. A new kind of SS had emerged in Germany: Study and Scrutinize. Not only by the Stasi, but by your neighbors, family, and friends. Where even silence was suspect.

The three met Eckhart's brother and sister-in-law at a restaurant and ordered *Jägerschnitzel*, East German-style that subbed the veal or pork for processed sausage. Eckhart's brother Bastian was five years older than him, with a thicker frame, thinning hair, but the same eyes and smile. His wife, Trude, had her leather brown hair done up in a bun. She was cute, not strikingly beautiful, with olive green eyes and thin lips. She rested her hand on her stomach, just now showing a bump.

After introductions and lunch, they hiked to the salvage yard. It was a massive area with defunct cars, buses, trucks, piles of wiring and tubing from buildings. The East German regime was in dire need of manufacturing, so nothing was left to waste. Every morsel was mined.

All around blowtorches hissed, hammers clanked, and saws screeched as they sliced through metal. The air was a harsh medley of rusted metal, oil, grease, and gasoline. Enough chemicals in the air to feel a buzz. Trude hadn't come along; this was no place for a pregnant woman. It seemed at any moment one of the giant heaps of parts could collapse.

Bastian slapped the hood of a defunct truck. The color of paint had faded so severely that Wolfgang couldn't even guess what color it had been. But the color was the least of his concerns. There was no windshield. It was missing its doors. There were no tires. The wheelbase rested on slabs of wood to keep it from sinking into the ground. Springs punctured through the torn seating. It was filled with dust, leaves, and twigs. More than likely, this hunk of junk was home to a nest of rats. All visible at a quick glance. *What does it look like under the engine?*

"What the hell is this hunk of junk?" Eckhart asked.

"The hunk of junk that will get us through the Wall," Bastian replied.

"Through the Wall? This thing can't even roll downhill."

"Needs some work," Bastian admitted.

"*Some* work?"

Wolfgang and Dietrich circled the truck, letting the two brothers banter. They both exchanged a glance that said they were on Eckhart's side. This truck dreamed of one day being a piece of shit.

Bastian lifted the hood. The truck groaned, squealing for a merciful death. All four huddled to gaze at what lay under the hood. Wolfgang didn't need to research to know there should be something there. Words like engine and carburetor came to mind.

"Does this thing run on hopes and prayers?" Eckhart asked.

Bastian rolled his eyes, then slammed the hood. "Again, it needs work. If you can find a truck that's ready to go, great. Where is it, Eckhart? Is it parked at your apartment? At Mom and Dad's? Didn't think so. So shut your damn mouth!"

"I told you we needed a truck. Did I need to specify it having four fucking wheels and an engine?"

The two brothers spewed curse words. The next escalation wouldn't be a fist fight but an old-fashioned wrestling match.

Wolfgang stepped between them. "So, how do we get the parts we need?"

Bastian looked around the scrapyard as if the answer was obvious. "We hunt."

It was hard not to get dejected at that moment. There were hundreds of scrap cars, all waiting to be torn apart so the metal could be repurposed into something useful. Any vehicles that needed minor work would have been repaired and sold back into circulation. There were millions of items here. And Wolfgang didn't even know what the hell he was looking for.

"I know nothing about automobiles," Dietrich said with a hint of an apologetic tone in his voice.

"Same," Wolfgang said, deciding to not make Dietrich feel bad. After all, his reading hadn't prepared him for this scavenger hunt.

"Don't worry. Neither does shit head over here," Bastian said.

"The hell I don't. You taught me everything you know," Eckhart said.

"No, I taught you everything *you* know."

"Can you tell us what you need?" Wolfgang asked, cutting through the bickering. He understood the dynamic between the two brothers, but it didn't stop it from being annoying.

"There're probably a few course catalogues from when I was in school I could dig up. They will have pictures, diagrams, that sort of thing," Bastian said.

"That'd be great," Wolfgang said. "I've done a bit of reading, but pictures would be helpful."

Bastian put his hand on the hood of the car. "There's another thing I need to tell you all. Trude's best friend is coming with us."

"How many people can this thing hold?" Wolfgang asked.

"The way it is now? Five. Maybe six," Bastian replied.

"Okay, then we're already full," Dietrich said.

"We need space for Emilia and Franco," Bastian said. "And maybe more."

Wolfgang's pulse quickened. *Maybe more? Who?*

Eckhart sighed. "*Mensch*, man. Is she going to invite her entire kindergarten class?"

Bastian ignored his brother. Sensing that Wolfgang was the leader de facto, he kept his gaze on him.

"You know secrecy is paramount," Wolfgang said.

Bastian nodded. "They've been friends longer than the three of you."

Wolfgang sighed. He was losing control of this circus. It wasn't worth getting into an argument over this. No one wanted to be told they were trusting untrustworthy people.

"You said we can fit five or six the way it is now. What does that mean?" Wolfgang asked.

"We could take the back off. Make it a flatbed. Then? We could fit twenty," Bastian said.

"Twenty people? That's too many," Eckhart said, shaking his head.

Dietrich bit his lip. Wolfgang knew Dietrich was all for helping people, but there needed to be an element of surprise with this escape attempt. Twenty people was a mighty risk. During the war, there had been the slogan *loose lips sink ships!* That still held true.

"It's a numbers game," Bastian said.

"What are you saying?" Wolfgang asked.

"The more people we have, the greater the chance that some of us make it. Survival by subtraction."

Wolfgang hated thinking that way. That this was a move to increase the likelihood of his own escape by adding more people. More frantic people the Stasi or VoPo or soldiers would be presented with the chance to arrest. *Or am I increasing someone else's chances of escape and increasing the probability of my own arrest?*

"If this goes well, we won't have to worry about that," Dietrich said. "We're planning on driving this thing through the Wall."

Calling it a "thing" was generous. It wasn't fair to automobiles across the globe to give this heap the same name.

"I agree with you that we need people we can trust," Bastian said. "But we also need money. If we can't find what we need here, we'll need to buy it. If it comes down to it, I know some people who may have the parts we need."

"Do you trust them?" Eckhart asked.

Bastian hesitated. All the answer the group needed. "That's a road we travel down if need be."

Eckhart exhaled, trying to limit his annoyance. "The people Emilia and Franco want to invite. Do you trust them?"

"Me? No. But they do."

"Well, that's reassuring," Eckhart said sarcastically.

"I don't trust Dietrich. I don't trust Wolfgang. No offense. I don't know you. I trust Eckhart. Eckhart trusts you. That's the math I'm using."

Wolfgang considered it, then nodded. A simple way of looking at it. Clean. Concise.

As they left the junkyard, they discussed the next course of action. Bastian would find the diagrams and pictures he thought he had, so that Wolfgang and Dietrich would have a better understanding of the parts they'd be searching for. Bastian and Eckhart would start repairing the truck. Trude, not wanting to be unhelpful, volunteered to host dinners once a week and supply lunches on the Saturdays the group would spend at the junkyard.

If the Stasi questioned them at any point, the story was that Bastian, his brother, and his brother's friends wanted to repair a vehicle for Bastian to have for his pregnant wife. Repairing and rebuilding a shell of a truck was a daunting task. But the idea of having to lie to the Stasi and get away with it was the most formidable task Wolfgang could think of. One he didn't think they could pull off.

His Name Was Peter Fechter

By 17 August, summer had become routine—relentless sun, restless thoughts. That Friday, Wolfgang met Dietrich and Eckhart at Treptower, searching for a secluded section to go for a walk.

They spent summer rebuilding the truck. Wolfgang had studied automotive engineering, but it had been tricky. The Stasi catalogued and scrutinized every book he read, forcing him to sift through state-approved titles to mask his real reasoning. But the fear persisted. Fear of arrest. Of Stasi prisons. Of dying.

They walked from Treptower to Zimmerstraße, where their conversation ended out of fear of being overheard. Zimmerstraße ran parallel to Checkpoint Charlie and was heavily patrolled and monitored. They headed toward the Copper Cellar for a beer or two. It was doubtful it would take the edge off, but Wolfgang would give it a try.

Then it happened.

Two young men sprinted toward the Wall and scrambled up. Wolfgang, Dietrich, and Eckhart froze. They hadn't witnessed an escape attempt in a year—especially not one so brazen, in broad daylight, near one of the most fortified sections of the border.

Gunfire cracked before their shock settled. One man—Helmut Kulbeik—cleared the Wall. The second—Peter Fechter—wasn't so lucky. Bullets pierced through the air, into the ground, into the Wall, and into his pelvis. He screamed out in agony on the death strip, bleeding into the scorched sand.

In full view of both East and West Berlin. His cries heard by everyone nearby. Wolfgang and his friends stared—horrified and helpless. Each imagined himself in Peter's place—bleeding, begging, and ignored. Western soldiers watched, powerless to act apart from throwing bandages. Any intervention risked igniting global war, even nuclear conflict.

The East guards stood by in their watchtowers, making no attempt to help their fellow citizen. As the shock subsided, the silence ceased. People on both sides of the Wall demanded action.

Peter writhed in the sand, screaming for help as the scorching sun burned his body. The minutes ticked by, each one an eternity of excruciating pain. Each minute, his cries grew weaker. Dietrich tried to pull Wolfgang and Eckhart away, but they couldn't move. Horror rooted them in place, the scene too magnetic to leave. After fifty agonizing minutes, Peter Fechter succumbed to his injuries. The Wall had claimed another life—the twenty-seventh.

It did them no good to see how likely this result could be for them. But what were they supposed to do? Continue on their way to the pub and drink beer? Try to talk over Peter's screams? Dozens of others watched, daring reprimand from the Stasi and VoPo, until East Berlin soldiers dragged Peter's corpse away from the Wall. Sobs from both sides of the Wall filled the silent afternoon.

Peter Fechter was only eighteen years old.

Wolfgang followed Eckhart and Dietrich to the pub. Dietrich ordered the first round. Other patrons mumbled and whispered about what had happened. The news spread rapidly. For some, they heard the news and moved on. Others focused on it, trying to make sense of what they had seen or heard. Some said nothing, knowing their words weren't safe.

Wolfgang couldn't process what he wanted to here. Couldn't say what needed to be said. So, he drank his beer in a few gulps and rose to leave.

"We need to talk," Wolfgang said.

It was all he would say at the pub, prompting Dietrich and Eckhart to follow him. Wolfgang stormed toward the Spree, the other two struggling to keep up. Wolfgang gazed at the sunset reflecting on the majestic water.

"I think we need to reconsider this," Dietrich said before Wolfgang spoke his mind.

"You're out?" Eckhart asked.

Dietrich demurred, shifting his feet and his gaze. "We just watched someone die doing what we're thinking about doing."

"We knew it was a risk."

"Yes, but we saw it. That could have been us. There's a great chance that if we try it, that's our fate. Is it worth us risking our lives?"

Eckhart nodded in grim concession. Dietrich had a point. Witnessing the brutal, harrowing death had shifted this prospective escape into the realm of reality.

Wolfgang stared at the river, trying to process everything that had happened. "They killed him." The screams echoed in his ears. His body still on edge from the crack of the gunshots. "They killed him for trying to leave. Our government killed its own citizen."

Eckhart and Dietrich listened to him, not wanting to interrupt his emotional tirade.

"East Berlin isn't simply flawed. It's cruel. It's dangerous. They care nothing for us," Wolfgang said.

"You're not scared? After what we just saw?" Dietrich asked.

"I'm terrified. But I'm more terrified if I stay here. If we stay here, we know what our lives will be. It's a period. Fact. Definitive. Over there," he pointed to where the Wall loomed in the unseeable distance. "Over there, it's a question mark. An exclamation point. That man died fighting for freedom. He knew we get one chance at life—and he refused to spend it in a cage. Dying wasn't the worst outcome. Staying here was."

Wolfgang let his two friends consider his words, his resolve. Giving them time to find their own. Fechter's death had only stoked his fire to escape even more.

"I'm still in. We've come so far," Eckhart said.

Dietrich nodded, struggling to find his voice. Emotion clogged whatever words he wanted to say. "I want you to know if it comes to one of us bleeding out in no-man's-land, I won't leave you," Dietrich said. "If it's me ... you have my blessing to run and keep going."

"No. I'm not leaving either of you. We're in this together," Wolfgang said.

Wolfgang and Dietrich turned their gaze to Eckhart.

"To hell with you—I'm running," Eckhart said with a crooked grin. "But I have to be honest, my brother's priority is his wife and their unborn child. We can't expect that promise from them, and they shouldn't expect it from you two."

Wolfgang nodded, understanding where Bastian's loyalty lay. If they had a chance to escape, they would seize it.

Back at his apartment, Wolfgang wrote to Lieselotte, even though he was unsure when Sandra could deliver the letter. But he needed to talk to her. Needed to get his tumultuous thoughts on paper. To free them before they rioted.

He'd sharpened his skills—writing now came faster, like a second language. He wrote about Peter Fechter. A life cut short by a bullet and a border. Tomorrow, his face would be all over the newspapers in the West. In the East, they'd spin the story—that he was a Western spy—or more than likely, not even mention him. With their silence denying that it had even happened. By the time Lieselotte read this letter, she would know as much as he did. Even more, given the facts disclosed in the West. But he needed her to know that this hadn't deterred him. His desire was to escape. He signed the last part in an uncoded message. Even if intercepted, he didn't want to hide it.

With all my love,

Wolfgang.

Pine and *Riesling*

Peter Fechter's death devastated Lieselotte—not just for the man himself, but because every image of Fechter in the newspapers might as well have been Wolfgang. His death added weight to Wolfgang's planned escape. She pored over Wolfgang's letter; his resolve seemed stronger than ever. The next letter detailed adding others into the escape attempt. He voiced his concerns about the numbers and the plan they had in place. She shared his worry, selfishly wanting Wolfgang's safety. But also wanting as many people as possible who wished to escape to have the option to do so. What unnerved her the most was that Wolfgang didn't know the new recruits.

As fall arrived with early nights and chilly winds, she feared her scouting was useless. It was already months' old information. Any perceived weakness in the Wall could be repaired by the time the truck was drivable. But rushing the escape wasn't an option.

For a long time, the letters had sufficed—they were all they had, their only option. But now, they weren't enough. She needed to see Wolfgang. *But how? He's not allowed to go West; I won't be allowed to go into the East.*

The answer came as she scoured maps of Berlin inside the Freie Universität Berlin library. One map showed Berlin's sewer system, including a tunnel that ran beneath the Wall. There had been a few escape attempts using the sewers shortly after the Wall's creation. The East Germans would have sealed them off with grates or bars. Nevertheless, she could see Wolfgang.

She wrote the letter in cipher and gave it to Sandra to carry into East Berlin, wishing she could send a copy of the sewer map for Wolfgang, but knowing that was far too risky. Instead, she had to hope that he understood. She had set the meeting for Christmas

Eve at 11 p.m. That gave Sandra a couple of weeks to deliver the letter, and about a month to return with his reply.

As November came and went, the weather grew fouler. Colder. Meaner. Snow fell in mid-December and temperatures plummeted below freezing. Her mother had wanted her to return home for Christmas, but she told her she would stay on campus. Keeping the truth from her for her own well-being. If she knew about her proposed rendezvous with Wolfgang, it'd cause her nothing but sleepless nights and a nervous stomach.

While festive lights and holiday decorations adorned the campus, most students had left for the holidays, including Sandra, who was in the East at her father's. Anneliese was with her brother and parents.

On Christmas Eve, Lieselotte listened to Christmas music on her transistor radio in her dorm room before seeing a showing of the newly released *The Treasure of the Silver Lake* at the movie theater. Despite the scattered crowds, she felt utterly alone— unaffected by the holiday buzz.

At 9:30, she dressed in a thick sweater, a wool coat, tapered trousers, and old flat leather boots. She slipped on her gloves and scarf on her way out into the frigid air. As she passed one of the many Christmas trees around campus, she plucked a handful of needles and placed them in her pocket.

To no surprise, the streets were barren. Only a few cars drove by. Most people were nestled around kitchen tables or in living rooms, playing games, listening to Christmas music. The young children were already in bed. *How many people were lamenting the absence of family and friends living in East Berlin?*

Lieselotte had rehearsed the sewer route a dozen times. She climbed down the storm drain, ensuring her feet touched the bottom—and that she could still lift herself out. The air was foul— a rank stew of dampness, decay, and filth. Each breath brought a new assault. The water was high enough that it rose above her boots. She tried not to think about how disgusting this water was.

But this trek would be worth every sloshing step and every gag-inducing smell. She'd be able to see Wolfgang, for the first time in over a year.

The main sewer veered left and then rose to a smaller branch. Lieselotte dug out the map of the sewer she had copied using carbon paper. She had to continue ahead, then turn right, follow the straightaway, before taking a sharp left that led to an overflow outlet. That's where Wolfgang was to meet her.

Lieselotte stepped onto the catwalk to avoid the deeper section of the sewer. When the smells got particularly rancid, she pressed the pine tree needles to her nose, breathing in the festive smell of Christmas. When she took the sharp left and approached the overflow outlet, the silhouette of a man waited for her.

"Lieselotte."

The voice she had longed to hear. She nearly wept at the sound of her name on his lips. She dashed up onto the overflow outlet and jutted her fingers through heavy-duty iron bars separating them. Even though they were covered in rust and corrosion, they were embedded into the tunnel walls with concrete and metal brackets. Impenetrable.

"Wolfgang ... God, I've missed you."

Only now—seeing him, saying those words—did she realize how much.

"I know. Me, too."

Only their fingertips could make it through the bars. Both rested their foreheads against the cold iron, trying to get as close to one another as possible. She wanted to stay that way. Feeling the exhales of his soft breaths and the caress of his fingertips. But they didn't have unlimited time, so she took a step back to take him in.

"How is the plan going?" she asked.

Wolfgang hesitated. He didn't want to worry her, but honesty mattered more. Being here, in front of her, even if separated by the bars, was more than he had ever hoped. A Christmas miracle. And my God, did it reiterate his desire to leave. He was more than half-inclined to attempt to pry the bars apart again, even though he already knew they wouldn't budge. He'd tried the moment he arrived. Only powerful tools could cut through them, and anything louder than their whispers would be heard.

"We're searching for parts, but it's challenging," Wolfgang answered.

"If you had to guess completion percentage?" she asked.

Wolfgang considered his answer. "Seventy percent. Maybe."

Lieselotte did her best to hide her disappointment. "And the others Bastian and Trude invited?"

"I don't know much about them. We have twelve total now."

"And you're aiming for twenty?"

"That's the max." Wolfgang tried to get his fingers further through the bars to wrap them around hers. "I know what you're thinking, but we have to trust each other." He explained Bastian's math about trusting one person who trusts another person.

Lieselotte didn't correct the flawed logic—trust isn't transferable. Loyalty isn't a common denominator.

He explained their progress in greater detail than he could do in a ciphered letter. They had found the truck bed and Bastian and Eckhart had stored it near the truck, deciding it was smartest and safest to install that last. The moment they put the truck bed on, the cover story that this was a vehicle for a family vanished. They still hadn't found an engine, but the tires, spark plugs, and carburetor had depleted their money. An engine would be the most expensive and the hardest to come by. It would be sold at black-market prices, which is why they needed to invite more people in on the escape attempt.

"I can smuggle you more money. Ask Sandra to deliver it. Bit by bit, so it doesn't draw scrutiny," Lieselotte said.

"I can't ask for your money, Lieselotte."

"You didn't. It's a gift." She fished into her pockets and removed her *Deutschmarks*. Their buying power was exponentially higher than Wolfgang's *Ostmarks*.

"I can't accept this …"

But she rolled the money up and fished it through the bars. "You can. And you will."

Wolfgang nodded, cheeks burning with shame at needing to accept this—but also grateful. She was risking everything. Without this, it would take months, maybe a year longer for the group to acquire enough money. Force them to expand their group and lower their standards.

"We will pay you back," Wolfgang assured her.

"When do you think you'll be ready?" she asked.

Wolfgang sat on the question, thinking it over. "If we get the engine, we can be ready as soon as Bastian puts it in. Any changes to the Wall that you can see?"

She shook her head, but the nervous bite of her lip betrayed her answer.

"What is it?" he asked.

"It's just … each day that passes, they will reinforce the Wall. Make it thicker. Taller. More guards. More dogs. More guns. More towers. More searchlights."

"I know."

Lieselotte removed a chocolate bar from her pocket and broke it into smaller pieces and slid a chunk through the bars. Wolfgang hadn't had real chocolate since his visit into West Berlin over two years ago. Real West German chocolate—rich in sugar, cocoa, and milk powder—was nearly impossible to come by in the East, where artificial sweeteners and fillers were used.

Wolfgang closed his eyes in ecstasy when he bit into it. "This is amazing."

"I brought more. For Eckhart and Dietrich. Anneliese brought this for Eckhart." She held up an orange.

Wolfgang smiled. Eckhart's favorite fruit. She had to get creative to squeeze the orange through. In the lower right-hand corner, a piece of concrete had broken off. Parts of the rind scraped away as she squeezed it through.

After Wolfgang finished the chocolate, Lieselotte removed her final gift. Two paper cups and a bottle of *Riesling*.

"My mother and father used to share a bottle of *Riesling* every Christmas. I want to continue their tradition with you."

She poured two cups and slid one through the crack. For a few quiet minutes, they sipped together—pretending the world above didn't exist. They talked of life, not escape. Of memories, not plans. They talked about that Christmas all those years ago, when Rolf had taught them how to use ciphers. Wolfgang talked about his family's tradition of singing carols on Christmas Eve. Like the Dickens novel, they revisited the past, discussed the present, and dreamed of what lay ahead. Words were their touch. And then, as their time together neared its end, the Wall had to be discussed once more.

"Do you have a best guess where we should target?" Wolfgang asked.

"I narrowed it down to Treptower, Sonnenallee, Neukölln, and Kreuzberg."

"Yes, your letter stated that. But what does your gut tell you?"

Lieselotte hesitated to answer. There was so much pressure in choosing. So much at stake. But through his glasses, his eyes longed for her input. The fact he valued it in a legitimate life-or-death situation was a level of trust few lovers ever experience.

"Kreuzberg," she answered. "It's industrial—less of a military presence. There's enough open space for you to get to the necessary speed to drive through the Wall."

Wolfgang sensed her nervousness. The pressure weighing on her, the worry roiling in her gut. He smiled, trying to alleviate it. "Kreuzberg it is."

"I don't think it's going to work, Wolfgang." She paused, hating the look her words caused. "I'm worried you can't drive through it. Not anymore."

Wolfgang considered her words. "We need a contingency plan."

"Ladders," she said. "If the truck can't make it through, you climb over."

Wolfgang nodded, smirking. "Either we go through it or over it." He checked his watch. "We need to get going."

Lieselotte stepped toward the bars, trying to get as close to him as she could. Trying to feel even the faintest brush of his lips. To feel even the whisper of his breath. But it was a frustrating and futile endeavor.

"You'll get back alright?" Wolfgang asked.

She nodded. "And you?"

He nodded, too. But neither moved. Staring at each other, not knowing when the next time they would see each other would be. This meeting was a gamble. If the Stasi caught Wolfgang in the sewer, imprisonment was certain—if not worse. What rational reason would he have for being down here other than trying to escape? He couldn't risk anything to put him further in the Stasi crosshairs. This was a onetime thing. As much as he loved this, needed this, it couldn't happen again.

With unblinking eyes, they gazed at each other. The way people gaze at a breathtaking painting. Trying to understand how something could be so beautiful. Contemplating how it came to be. Taking every line, every curve to memory. They had few photographs of each other, and though they looked at them every morning and every night, they did not do each other justice. Photographs would never measure up, never mimic, never match.

"I'll see you soon," Lieselotte said.

A wistful smile curved on his lips. "See you soon."

"Maybe you'll get those eyes for Christmas this year."

Wolfgang laughed. "Maybe."

And then she turned to leave. Wolfgang fought the urge to call after her. Already, the desire to see her once more overcame him. But this would be the closest to her he would get until he made it through the Wall.

The Eve of Freedom

Wolfgang awoke Christmas morning with a renewed sense of purpose. The life he desired had revealed itself the night before, like a vision from the Ghost of Christmas Future. The following day, he and the others returned to the junkyard. Wolfgang handed Bastian Lieselotte's money.

"Where did you get this?" he asked.

"My girlfriend."

Dietrich and Eckhart exchanged a look of disbelief as Bastian pocketed the money before anyone else could see.

"Will this get us an engine?" Wolfgang asked.

"Oh, yes," Bastian said. "I'll talk down what I can. Is this all for the truck?"

Wolfgang nodded.

"Just make sure this thing can steamroll through that fucking wall," Eckhart said.

Bastian smiled, but Wolfgang didn't share it.

"Lieselotte has her doubts about us driving through the Wall," Wolfgang said. "It's become more fortified than when I hatched this plan."

"Does she expect us not to try?" Eckhart asked.

Wolfgang shook his head, then explained the contingency plan of ladders.

Bastian considered it and nodded. "Smart. More chances for success."

It took only a day for Bastian to find an engine and he, with the others looking on, assembled it that very day. After, Bastian started the truck for the first time. It was hardly a massive accomplishment, but just hearing the engine turn over and rumble to life was cause for celebration. It sputtered and died after fifteen seconds, but for a fleeting moment, the truck had tasted power.

Dietrich and Eckhart acquired five twelve-foot ladders. Repaired any broken steps and tested their weight.

The first successful test-drive occurred on 30 December. They drove it out of the junkyard. The first test passed: the truck drove. It handled. It turned. It accelerated. It braked. But puttering along wasn't the speed and force they needed to break through the Wall. How fast could this Frankenstein's-Monster-of-a-truck go?

"How fast do you think we need to be going?" Bastian asked.

Wolfgang had considered it, done the calculations. Tried to account for as many variables as he could.

"At least fifty to sixty-five kilometers per hour. Eighty is safer. But if there's rebar, we might face deflection."

"Deflection? What's that?" Eckhart asked.

"The Wall hits back."

No one asked for details. The silence that followed said everything—their minds could conjure enough.

Wolfgang asked Bastian to organize a meeting with everybody on 31 December at Treptower. It was time to put faces to the names of those who would escape.

Wolfgang, Dietrich, and Eckhart were first to arrive. It was an absolutely frigid day. Bundled up, the three men stamped their feet and hugged their arms to their chests for warmth. Bastian and Trude arrived next, along with Franco and Emilia. Franco had the swagger of someone used to being noticed—dark eyes, thick slicked-back hair, and a newsboy cap tilted just enough to be stylish yet proper. He looked like he could charm his way out of anything with just a smirk. Emilia was striking in a quieter way. Her rich, chestnut hair cascaded over her shoulders, and her figure turned heads without trying. They'd met in Berlin while Franco was on vacation. One look at her and it was obvious why he had never made it back to Italy. Trude handled the introductions, a warm smile on her face.

A couple in their sixties gingerly approached next. Conrad and Fresa Köning. They looked just as nervous to meet Wolfgang and the others as they were to meet them.

"The moon is in a favorable position," Conrad said.

"Unless you want to see the stars," Wolfgang replied.

Both parties released the nervous tension they'd had. Next to arrive were two identical twin sisters, Johanna and Thersea Fischer. They were in their late twenties and strikingly beautiful.

"Holy hell," Eckhart muttered.

"Don't," Bastian warned.

"What?"

"Don't hit on them, or you'll convince them to stay in East Berlin."

Johanna stepped in front of her timid sister. She whispered the secret phrase, and Eckhart repeated it before Wolfgang could.

"Is this everyone?" Johanna asked.

"No, we are waiting on a few more," Trude answered.

"Thank you for letting us join," she said.

Theresa kept her eyes on the ground, arms crossed tightly over her chest. Her shoulders flinched at every sound. This wasn't the twitchy anxiety of an informant, but a woman who'd been battered and broken.

Everyone had their reasons for escaping. But Wolfgang couldn't help but wonder if for the Fischer sisters, it wasn't East Berlin they needed to flee—but someone in it.

The last to arrive were Matthias and Katrin Schneider, in their mid-forties, flanked by their seventeen-year-old son, Lukas, and fourteen-year-old daughter Annalena. Matthias whispered the secret phrase, and Wolfgang repeated it. With everyone present, Wolfgang spoke.

"We go on the 2nd," he said.

"Two days?" Dietrich asked.

"We're ready. The truck's ready. I'm done waiting." He didn't look to see their reactions. "We meet outside the junkyard at nine sharp. We'll have the truck parked out front and covered."

"If you're late, there's no waiting," Eckhart said.

"Do not tell anyone goodbye. It's too risky. And I don't mean just a permanent goodbye. I mean any visits to people you wouldn't normally visit," Wolfgang said.

"Do not pack a bag," Bastian added. "People take notice of people with suitcases or bags."

"Only what you can fit in a purse or in your pockets," Wolfgang said.

He knew what he was asking. For him, all his familial possessions were at his parents' house. Maybe they could stash a few photographs into a purse. Anything larger would have to be left behind. And no matter what anyone says, that would be a loss. The loss of lineage.

"And if things go wrong? We surrender, eh?" Franco asked.

"That's for all of you to decide," Wolfgang said.

For Wolfgang, if there was any chance to run and make it, he would take it. But he had vowed to share the same fate as Dietrich and Eckhart. The larger group was one of varying allegiances.

Johanna pulled Wolfgang aside, eyes darting toward the others.

"Did Trude or Emilia say anything about us—my sister and I?" she asked.

Wolfgang shook his head.

She chewed her lip, hesitating. "My sister needs to get away. Her husband …" Her voice broke off.

Wolfgang gave a sympathetic nod, sparing her the pain of spelling it out. "I understand."

"Please," Johanna whispered. "Make sure she gets out."

He gave a silent promise with his eyes, and she rejoined her sister. Then the groups of strangers dispersed. This would be the longest two days of their lives. How was anyone supposed to sleep? Go to work and act normal? Wolfgang's mother could always read when something was wrong. Said it was painted all over his face. He couldn't call in sick to work, as that would bring attention. Wolfgang didn't miss work.

He wrote a letter to Lieselotte and met Sandra at her father's house on New Year's Day. All the details of the escape—time, location, and date—were encoded in that message. He knew Lieselotte would be waiting on the other side of the Wall.

Those two days crept by painfully slowly. With no work on New Year's, he had nothing to do but go over every possible scenario of his pending escape. It was a blessing to go to work the next day. It at least offered a relief from the worry. The manual labor required Wolfgang to focus on the task at hand. But once his shift ended, he found himself pacing his living room. He couldn't sit still. He barely slept those nights. Tossing and turning. Staring at the ceiling. Body, mind, spirit—all were exhausted.

In a few hours, they'd be in the truck speeding toward the Wall. The nerves and excitement were at a level Wolfgang had never experienced. He had no idea how to process them. *Why the hell did I say 9 p.m.? How can I wait that long?*

Wolfgang paced the living room, nerves sending him to the bathroom repeatedly. He vomited on three more occasions before it was time to leave. The only items he took were his photographs of Lieselotte and his parents. Over the last year, he'd brought any sentimental or valuable items to his parents' house. Every glance was a goodbye. He took a last look and then flipped the light switch and stepped out.

It was a misty, foggy Wednesday night. A below-freezing temperature with few pedestrians out and about. Hands in his pockets, Wolfgang walked to the junkyard, trying to stay calm as each vehicle passed. Trying to walk deliberately but not rushed. Fighting the urge to run. It was hard to stay calm when you could literally die in a few hours' time. He drew Lieselotte's picture from his pocket. It was the lone photograph of the two of them together. Arms wrapped around each other. Smiling. Beaming in the summer sun. He pocketed the picture and headed across the street toward the meeting point. The truck was parked on the side of the road, a canopy tarp stretched over the flatbed. Wolfgang was ten minutes early. Discreetly, he glanced around for any approaching figures, any people hiding in the shadows.

Over the course of the next five minutes, hopeful escapees trickled in. Eckhart and Dietrich approached from down the street. Bastian, Trude, Emilia, and Franco. Conrad and Fresa. Matthias and Katrin Schneider and their children, Lukas and Annalena. Then the twins Johanna and Theresa Fischer. Even though he'd only met them once, hope etched along Theresa's face in a way that had been absent upon that first meeting.

In twenty minutes, Wolfgang would either be free, captured, or dead. Any of those outcomes made his body throb. The adrenaline rush was unlike anything he'd experienced. Though far from over, the escape already brought quiet smiles among the group. They'd made it this far. Collectively, they'd agreed on Bastian driving. Wolfgang and Eckhart would sit up front, as it was the most dangerous place in the vehicle. Trude, ready to give birth any day, would be in the back, shielded by Franco and Dietrich.

The moon was a waxing crescent—just a faint silver sliver blurred by mist and fog. Perfect conditions. After breaking through the Wall, they'd drink and laugh, howl at the moon, scream at the stars. Tonight, Wolfgang would sleep in Lieselotte's arms. The thought stirred something deep inside him—warm and electric.

"We're all here. Let's go!" Wolfgang said.

"Yes, we are all here," came a voice from the fog.

Boots clacked against the street. Inside the truck, soldiers ripped the flatbed canopy aside and leapt down from the benches, merging with troops closing in from all directions. Submachine guns aimed at Wolfgang and the other escapees.

The man who'd spoken stepped out from the shadows, allowing the streetlight to bask him in its light. An eerie fog billowed at his feet. The smile on his face chilled Wolfgang to the bone.

"*Herr* Kirschke," Schwarzfuchs said. "Did you really think you could outsmart us? We have eyes and ears everywhere. Arrest them all."

With brute force, the soldiers threw them to the ground, no discrimination to the men or women.

"My wife is pregnant!" Bastian shouted.

A soldier clocked Bastian across the head with his weapon. Eckhart tried to wrestle free to help his brother, but the guards overpowered and shackled him. Wolfgang stared in stunned disbelief before he was slammed to the hard street. Filled with shock and horror. *This isn't happening. I'm having a nightmare. I just have to find evidence of the dream.* But there was none. Because this wasn't a nightmare, this was reality.

All their planning—Schwarzfuchs and the Stasi knew. Somebody had tipped them. *Who?* They'd handcuffed everyone in the group. Everything had happened too fast to scan the group to look for any signs of guilt, of betrayal. Army trucks rumbled in. Wolfgang didn't need to see his watch to know they had arrived precisely at nine. They knew every last detail about this plan. *How could I have been so arrogant to think I could outsmart them?*

The guards yanked Wolfgang and the others to their feet, putting black cloth bags over their heads, and threw them into the back of the trucks.

"Who is in here with me?" Wolfgang called out.

"Shut up! Do not speak!" a guard ordered, smacking the barrel of his gun across Wolfgang's temple. Pain split across his skull like lightning.

The trucks thundered down the streets of East Berlin to an unknown destination. Hope had been a mistake. He'd let it bewitch his senses. Now, Wolfgang no longer just felt like a prisoner. He was one.

Stillness at the Wall

Lieselotte and Anneliese waited near the Wall in Kreuzberg, flanked by tenement buildings and overgrown lots. They carried flashlights but left them turned off, unwilling to attract attention from the border guards in the East. When Sandra had handed her Wolfgang's letter, a firework-burst of excitement and dread exploded in Lieselotte's chest. *The escape date—could it be real?* She'd double-checked her decoding. It was real.

"It's nine," Lieselotte said, her mouth bone dry.

Anneliese squeezed Lieselotte's hand. According to the letter, Wolfgang and the others would leave at 9 p.m. with a twenty-four-minute drive to the Wall. Right now, Wolfgang was in that truck, on his way to her. She tried to keep the negative thoughts from creeping in as she clung to Anneliese's arm, her legs threatening to buckle.

"It's okay, Lieselotte," Anneliese said.

Time crawled. By 9:10, her nerves churned bile into her throat. Tonight, she might share a bed with Wolfgang—wake to his arm around her. At 9:20, she squeezed Anneliese's hand.

Then 9:23. Less than sixty seconds and a roaring truck should be barreling toward the Wall. But 9:24 came, and still no sound.

"Don't worry. Twenty-four minutes was a best guess," Anneliese said.

Yes, it had only been a guess—with too many variables: traffic, fog, checkpoints, bad roads, and increased patrols near the checkpoints. Perhaps they had gotten off to a late start. Even though Wolfgang had said nine sharp with no waiting, would they have left without everyone?

9:30. The thrill curdled into dread. They were ten minutes late.

"Don't worry," Anneliese said.

Her friend meant well, but it was too late—worry had already consumed her. Anneliese knew that, but what else could she say?

9:44. Twenty minutes late. No low growl of an approaching engine. No headlights breaking through the fog. From where they stood, the other side of the Wall was in view. There was nothing. No activity whatsoever. When 10:24 came, Lieselotte could feel Anneliese watching her. Waiting for her to come to a conclusion she already had.

At 10:54, an hour and a half after they were supposed to plow through the Wall, Anneliese rested a hand on Lieselotte's shoulder.

"We have to go," she said.

"No. They're just running behind. That's all. We have to be here when they break through."

"They're not coming, Lieselotte."

Lieselotte wrenched away. "Don't say that! Don't give up on them!"

"Something happened. They're not coming."

Anneliese grabbed Lieselotte's flailing arms and held her until she calmed. Tears streamed down Lieselotte's face, blurring her vision. Anneliese loosened her grip, and the moment she did so, Lieselotte sprinted for the Wall.

"What are you doing?!" Anneliese yelled, running after her.

Grief possessed Lieselotte. She stumbled toward the Wall, wild and aimless, like a wounded animal. Anneliese tackled her to the ground, pinning her down.

"It's okay! It's okay!" she repeated.

Lieselotte stopped struggling, her fight gone. Anneliese loosened her grip, no longer a captor, but a comforter.

Lieselotte cried until there were no more tears left to cry. As Anneliese guided her away from the Wall, questions circled like wolves. *What had gone wrong? Had they changed the date? Had the Stasi found out? What happened to the others Wolfgang had invited?* But the most pressing—and the one she couldn't answer—kept returning: *If the Stasi had found them, were they captured ... or killed?*

The Submarine

The truck groaned to a halt. The engine cut off. Boots hit the ground, circling. Wolfgang, blinded by the black bag over his head, couldn't tell how many. He listened to footsteps leaving the truck. But telling who was a soldier and who was a prisoner was impossible. A hand gripped his shoulder and steered him forward. The footfalls shifted from concrete thuds to tile clacks. *We're inside.* No breeze, no wind. The stench hit him—stale air, disinfectant, cigarette smoke, and damp concrete. It clung to his tongue.

They ushered Wolfgang through a long hallway of some kind, then down a flight of stairs. Wolfgang wanted to linger on each step, but the hand on his shoulder kept pushing him forward. *They didn't care if I fall.* Down and down—an unending flight of stairs. When the soldier suddenly shoved him forward, Wolfgang stumbled, bracing for a fall, but he hit solid ground instead. A final push sent him into a wall. A door slammed shut with a resounding slam.

Wolfgang crept along the wall, his restrained hands behind his back reaching, trying to determine how big this room was. It was a cell of some kind. Depressingly small. He wanted to get this damn black cloth bag off his head so he could see, but it was securely in place. He brushed against what felt like a metal bed, a chair, and a toilet. He had to urinate terribly, but he had no way of getting his pants undone.

He shuffled heel to toe, counting each step. Eleven and a half inches per foot—give or take. Eight feet on each side, maybe less. Eighty square feet, max. He climbed onto the toilet, bracing himself against the wall. His head was still short of the ceiling. Seven feet, then. The size made sense but it didn't help. A claustrophobically small cell. The walls were too close. No space to breathe.

Wolfgang sat on the bed, waiting for someone to come into the cell. He waited and waited. But no one came. With his sense of vision removed, he'd hoped his other senses, especially his hearing, would enhance. But he heard nothing from outside the cell. It was as quiet as space. The only sounds were the sturdy drip of a pipe and the squeal of the mattress springs. And how he wished his sense of smell hadn't grown. The room reeked. A horrid blend of old sweat, stale urine, and musk.

With no sight and no sound to help keep track of the minutes and the hours, time lost all meaning. However much time had passed, it was too long to hold his pee any longer. He rose and went to the corner and relieved himself. Blindfolded and hands cuffed behind his back, he couldn't unbutton his pants. Warmth soaked his trousers. Shame followed. And then, helplessness. He slumped to the floor and sobbed. But that only made everything worse because he couldn't wipe his tears. The bag clung to his wet face, suffocating him with every panicked breath. Each struggled breath dragged the bag tighter into his face. *This is it. The end.* His body knew.

He gasped and gasped for breath, until his overwhelmed brain shut down and he fell asleep on the hard concrete floor. But that bliss lasted seconds before the cell door clanged open and someone heaved Wolfgang to his feet.

"Hello! Please tell me where I am?" Wolfgang asked.

But the hands under his elbows were gone, and the door slammed shut again. *What's going on?! Where are the others?!* Wolfgang stumbled to the bed. The shock of being dragged to his feet subsided, and he drifted off once more, only to be hauled upright again. Every time he dozed off, someone or multiple someones jarred him awake.

They slapped him, dragged him off the bed, screamed at him. When Wolfgang reached a point of exhaustion that would have required the guards to constantly wake him, they incorporated blaring radios, alarms, and shrieking whistles. Then came the warning growls of dogs reverberating around the cell. Wolfgang's muscles clenched, bracing for the attack. Only later did he realize they were recordings, playing on a loop.

At last, two guards stormed into the room and dragged him out of his cell. Even with his blindfold, he sensed light. The two guards dragged him down the hallway into another room. One guard unlaced his boots, while the other uncuffed his hands. Wolfgang was too weak and disorientated to fight. The guards stripped him and then shoved him onto a metal chair. Only then did they remove the black bag over his head and tear his glasses off.

"Where am I?" Wolfgang uttered, so dehydrated he could barely form the words.

The two soldiers said nothing. They stared ahead, postures as rigid as boards.

"Please tell me where I am," Wolfgang pleaded, trying to stop the quiver in his voice.

But again, no answer.

Wolfgang sat there, naked, on the cold steel chair, struggling to see. After so long in the dark, the sudden light stabbed at his eyes. And after so long in silence, the hum of the lights sounded like a thousand mosquitos buzzing in his ears.

He had no idea how far below ground he was. His body fought on two fronts. Fighting off both hypothermia and exhaustion. The room was freezing. Each breath visible. At last, the door creaked open. Schwarzfuchs stepped into the room, a manila folder tucked under his arm. He sat across from Wolfgang but didn't acknowledge him. Instead, he opened the folder and leafed through the documents inside with clinical calm. Satisfied, he looked up and leered.

"Where am I?" Wolfgang asked.

"You are at the Berlin-Hohenschönhausen Stasi Prison. Known more simply as the Hohenschönhausen Prison. Although, there is a colloquial moniker for this place. Do you know what it is?"

Wolfgang struggled to nod—so weak it felt like his head was a boulder. "The Submarine."

Wolfgang had heard the horror stories of this place. It wasn't even supposed to exist. It wasn't on any map. Nicknamed "the Submarine" because of its dark, windowless cells known as U-Boot-Zellen. No lights. No fresh air. And its incredible ability to inflict claustrophobia.

"I have granted you one question, and I have answered your question truthfully and fully. Do you agree?" Schwarzfuchs asked.

Wolfgang nodded, looking around the barren room. Dull-gray painted walls. Stale air, tinged with sweat and cigarette smoke. The two guards behind them looked like menacing silhouettes as the lone overhead light failed to even illuminate their faces.

"This is a verbal conversation, *Herr* Kirschke," Schwarzfuchs said.

"Yes."

"Yes?"

"Yes, I agree."

"Wonderful. Now I will ask you questions, and you will show me the same courtesy by answering truthfully and fully." Schwarzfuchs straightened his papers before continuing. "How did you acquire the money to purchase the truck engine?"

The question hit like a blow. *They know. Or are they bluffing? How does he know that?*

"We split the cost," Wolfgang said.

Schwarzfuchs sighed, disappointed at the lie. "We had an agreement. That was not the truth. How did you get the *Deutschmarks* you used to purchase the truck engine?"

"I don't know what you're talking about."

"Your friends have told us everything. Why submit yourself to unnecessary torment? Just tell us what we already know. Confirm what your friends have already told us."

Wolfgang stayed silent. They wouldn't have told him.

Would they?

Schwarzfuchs picked up the thick stack of papers. "This is their testimony. 476 pages worth. Do you know which of your friends broke first? I do."

"You're lying."

Schwarzfuchs chuckled. "Why would I bother? This is your chance, *Herr* Kirschke. Confirm what the others have told us, perhaps what they were not privy to, and we can reduce your sentence. You will not survive this place."

Wolfgang bit the inside of his cheek. This was a nightmare. A recurring one. One with the same room. Same smell. Same face across the table. *Is this a loop? Has time fractured?*

"You were going to kill to escape," Schwarzfuchs said.

"No!" Wolfgang shouted.

"Then explain the knife and pistol we found in the vehicle you were going to escape in."

Wolfgang's face scrunched. "What? There was no knife or gun."

"Every member of your group confirmed that you were prepared to kill to escape."

Wolfgang shook his head adamantly. "No … no … no!"

"It's all right here," Schwarzfuchs said, lifting the stack of 476 pages.

"I didn't have a knife or a gun! I didn't plan on killing anybody! I don't know what you're talking about!"

"No?" Schwarzfuchs considered it. "Very well."

He signaled for the guards, and without a word, they grabbed Wolfgang from under his armpits and dragged him out of the chair.

"Where are you taking me?! Where are the others?!" Wolfgang shouted.

The guards manhandled him down the stairs and into the basement. He tried fighting but had no strength. He was lightheaded, feeling disconnected from his own body. He didn't know when he last ate, or the last time he had a drink of water.

"Please!" Wolfgang shouted.

He didn't know what he was trying to stop. What they planned to do to him. They shoved him into a cell and slammed the door. Goosebumps spread over his nude flesh. The frigid air clung to him. To his horror, a water nozzle groaned. Arctic water surged through the pipes, cascading out into his cell like a waterfall, splattering onto his feet. He gasped at the sheer chill and stumbled to the cell door, banging on it, begging for the water to be shut off.

The water blasted in, relentless. It swallowed the floor, lapping over his feet. He rose onto his toes, searching for height in a room with none. No bunk. No chair. No toilet. Nothing but rising ice. It didn't care for his screams. It poured in without mercy, up to his ankles now. His chest spasmed with every breath. Teeth chattered. Panic clawed at his chest. His heart thundering in his ribs to escape. But there was no escape.

How long will they let this water run? Will they drown me in here? He wouldn't survive long enough to drown. He'd freeze to death first.

But then the water slowed to a trickle before stopping, pooling up to his shins. He'd lost feeling in his feet. He cried out for help with a quivering voice. But no help came. No saviors sauntered out of the shadows. Wolfgang shuffled to the corner, using the two walls to help support his weight. Maybe this was the plan—not to kill him, but to erase him. Drown out any hope he still had.

How long have I been in here? The pitch blackness only added to his terror. He felt his eyes drifting shut. He was fading fast. No longer aware of how freezing he was.

Then the sound of a pump woke him. The water level lowered. *Thank God.* Once emptied, the door opened. Two guards stormed in, grabbed Wolfgang, and carried him out of the cell. His frozen feet and legs were incapable of walking. The guards dragged him, his feet sliding, back into the interrogation room and onto that ruthless, ice-cold chair. Then they stood like sentries at the back of the wall. *Are they different guards? Or the same ones? Is this the same room?* Wolfgang questioned the veracity of everything. Some unknown amount of time later, Schwarzfuchs stepped back in.

"H-how l-long wa-was I-I in there?" Wolfgang stuttered.

"You look cold," Schwarzfuchs commented, ignoring Wolfgang's question.

Schwarzfuchs consulted his files once again, a steaming mug of coffee beside him. The thought of holding that hot mug overwhelmed Wolfgang. To feel the heat of the coffee course through his body. Schwarzfuchs raised the mug and sipped.

"Oh, it's stifling! I'll have to wait for it to cool." He set the mug down and then raised his hands in mock confusion. "Where was I? Oh, yes. The money. Where did you get it? Answer me, and I shall give you a warm blanket. Some hot soup. How does that sound?"

He didn't answer. Couldn't. The promise of warmth was enough to cry over. But there was no way he'd give up Lieselotte's name. Even if she was safe in West Berlin. *What if they have agents over there? But what can I give them that will sound truthful?*

"I traded my father's war medal to a collector in West Berlin," he said.

"What medal?"

"I don't know what it was called."

"You do know I can have my men break into your parents' home and validate your statement? Do you wish that?"

Wolfgang shook his head, nearly sobbing at his complete defeat.

Schwarzfuchs sighed. "*Herr* Kirschke, this game must come to an end. I am doing everything I can to keep you alive, but my power is reaching its limit." He sifted through his manila folder and removed a photo. The contents of which made him cast a sorrowful frown. He set it down in front of Wolfgang. It was a photograph of a man being led to a work camp.

"Conrad Köning. A member of your little group, yes? His fate is the mines. Given his age, and lack of physical prowess, I would guess the state gets less than a year of satisfactory labor from him. But from you?" he tsked. "A big, strapping young man such as yourself? Decades."

What is real? What is fake? Schwarzfuchs's expression never changed. Truth or lie, his face never twitched.

Schwarzfuchs rounded the table and laid a cold hand on Wolfgang's shoulder. He bent close, his mouth near Wolfgang's ear. "The clock ticks, *Herr* Kirschke."

Wolfgang couldn't fight the exhaustion. His eyes grew heavy, impossible to keep open. But then the chair flew backward and stopped, hovering on its back legs.

What just happened? Wasn't I in my cell? Now I'm back in the interrogation room?

Or did I never leave?

"Stay with me, *Herr* Kirschke," Schwarzfuchs said.

He listed off questions, naming off the members of the group, asking how Wolfgang knew them. He saw no harm in answering part of that truthfully—they already had them in custody.

Schwarzfuchs drank his coffee, the whole while deliberately making a spectacle of it—sighing with satisfaction, gasping at how scalding it was. How long the interrogation went, Wolfgang had no idea.

The questions came like punches—easily seen jabs to vicious hooks: Who helped you? Who in your family knew about this escape? Did you have help from the West? What was your route? Why that section of the Wall? Why that time? Why that date? Why? Why? Why?

Hadn't he asked these already?

What color was the truck? What did you eat that day? Where did you hide the knife? Questions delivered so fast and demanding, Wolfgang lost recollection of what he knew and what he didn't.

"What color shoes were you wearing?"

"Black," Wolfgang said. *Right?*

The questions made no sense, seemingly random. But there was a reason behind them—most likely to gauge his truthfulness.

"Here's what I don't understand, *Herr* Kirschke. What the others are incapable of telling me. You had the opportunity to escape, yet you hesitated. Why?"

"What?" Wolfgang asked.

"You had the opportunity to escape. You were in the truck, yet you didn't drive. Which tells me your heart wasn't in it. You knew the mistake you would be making."

Wolfgang closed his eyes and shook his head, trying to shake the thousands of conflicting thoughts multiplying and destroying each other.

125

Even in his deprived state, Wolfgang knew there had to be a method to the madness. These were bluffs to create confusion, contradiction, and coercion. *Right?*

His voice was hoarse from talking, his throat raw. His body ached from hours in the cold, hard chair. But they offered no water. No relief.

"Please stop," Wolfgang said.

"Only you can stop this. My hands are tied," Schwarzfuchs said.

Wolfgang closed his eyes, but he couldn't escape. No matter how hard he shook his head or wished or prayed.

"Now, the money you acquired for the truck engine," Schwarzfuchs said, returning to his initial question. "I grow cold and tired of asking. You received this from Lieselotte Reisinger, did you not?"

Wolfgang shook his head. "No."

"You lie."

"No."

"When is the last time you saw *Frau* Reisinger?"

Wolfgang considered it. He knew the answer. Knew the answer down to the last day, hour, and minute. But that was before he'd been put inside here. He still didn't know if he'd been in prison for hours, days, or weeks. *Or was it far longer than that?*

"In West Berlin before the Wall was built," Wolfgang said.

The struggle to keep his eyes open was a Herculean task. All the Earth's gravity wrenched them shut. But every time his blink lasted just a fraction longer than normal, one of the guards tipped his chair back. Screamed at him. Threatened to hit him with their batons.

"You know, don't you? That worried roiling in your gut. It's telling you that I know you're lying. You should heed that warning."

"I wrote her letters. That's all."

"How did you get these letters to her?"

Wolfgang hesitated with his answer. Lying was hard enough for him when well-rested. In this inebriated, deprived state, lies came slow.

"Pl—please. Water," Wolfgang said.

His chapped lips peeled open. His tongue felt like a piece of rock. Schwarzfuchs stared at Wolfgang and then motioned to a guard. The guard left the room and returned with a glass and pitcher of water. Schwarzfuchs poured a glass.

"All you have to do is tell me every person involved. The people who smuggled your letters, the people who sold you the parts for the truck, who gave you the money for it. Just confirm the names we have, so that no innocent people become responsible for these crimes."

Wolfgang's mouth was so dry he could barely open it. Hardly speak. His voice soft and hoarse—little more than a grumble.

"Later, then," Schwarzfuchs said.

He held out the glass of water to the side and made a dramatic show of emptying it onto the floor.

The guards dragged Wolfgang out of the room and back into his cell—the one with a bunk and toilet. Slamming the door shut with a resounding thud. Wolfgang stumbled to the metal bed and curled atop it, trying to warm himself.

Sleep came instantly. Some indistinguishable length of time later, the door opened. A guard slid a tray of food across the floor. Wolfgang crawled toward it—a chunk of bread with a faint smearing of jam, a hard-boiled egg, and a tin cup of water. He grabbed the water first, drinking it as carefully as he could, but even the cup felt like a cannon ball in his trembling hand. Never had water tasted so grand. He tore into the bread and egg next, alternating between the two.

With food finally in his stomach, he had to use the toilet, only to find there was no handle to flush. They decided when filth stayed and when it left—when he ate, when he drank, and when and if he slept. They controlled everything. Wolfgang had power over nothing. The stench of the unflushed toilet lingered. Each time he urinated, the stench grew. When the guard delivered his supper of a piece of bread some hours later, he begged them to flush the toilet. They ignored the request.

Wolfgang tried to keep tabs on how many times they fed him. He deduced they fed him three meals a day. Breakfast usually consisted of bread and tea. Lunch was a small bowl of gruel or soup. Dinner was a paltry piece of bread. They dragged him to the interrogation room a dozen times. Asked the same questions over and over. *Or were they new? Schwarzfuchs should show signs of annoyance, anger even, if he'd asked them several times before, right?*

They finally gave Wolfgang a uniform. It hung on him like drapes, but having clothing was a small victory—a shred of dignity, a flicker of civility restored after being dragged around naked. However, there was a downside. The material of the long-sleeved button-up shirts and loose-fitting trousers were made of rough cotton, designed to itch and irritate—and they certainly did.

The door clanged open, and two guards hauled him out and brought him into an interrogation room. Schwarzfuchs was already in the room, smoking a cigarette.

"*Herr* Kirschke, today is a very special day. Do you know what day it is?" he asked.

Wolfgang shook his head and mumbled no. *Of course I don't know.* He hadn't seen a clock since arriving here—hadn't seen outside, didn't even know if it was day or night.

"Today is 2 May. The anniversary of the end of the Patriotic War. The defeat of fascism by the diligent workers and heroic soldiers of socialism," Schwarzfuchs said.

The ending of his words had trailed off for Wolfgang. He hadn't heard past 2 May. *Has it really been that long? Has it only been that long?*

"Shall we begin again, *Herr* Kirschke?" Schwarzfuchs asked.

The questions came out in rapid succession. He asked the same questions, interspersed, to see if Wolfgang's answers changed. Chiseling away at Wolfgang, waiting for him to break—to give up whoever he could, and invent whoever he must. Standing in water, forced awake, stripped naked, food and water withheld—it could all end if he spoke those names. They burned on the tip of his tongue, but he kept his mouth shut. He'd never forgive himself if he gave a single name—real or fabricated—not even to save his life.

At the conclusion of the interrogation, the guards hauled Wolfgang out. But they didn't return him to his normal cell. It was a different one. Thankfully, not the one that flooded.

"This isn't my cell," Wolfgang said.

They didn't care. But for Wolfgang, it was oddly emotional. That cell had been his home. That was his bed. His toilet. It was all he had. Tears fell unchecked. After switching cells, the interrogations stopped. Wolfgang didn't leave the cell. He had food, water, and time. Time to reflect. To think about every action that had led to him being in this cell. The thousands of questions Schwarzfuchs had asked. Then a nagging, gnawing question at the center of it all. The heartbreaking, incontrovertible truth that someone had betrayed them. *But who?* As he went over the list of names, he kept returning to one. A name that broke his heart. When presented with time and no outside distractions, a person reaches a level of retrospection that is almost supernatural. Memories long ago forgotten bloomed in that fertile garden of thought.

A muffled sound carried through a broken pipe along the ground. *Rats scurrying?* Wolfgang went to the back corner of the cell to listen. *What was that?* Then a voice carried through the pipe. Warped as it spooled through. The first words he'd heard since those spoken by Schwarzfuchs—however long ago that was.

Somebody was speaking to him.

Head, Heart, and Gut

The weeks after the failed escape attempt shattered Lieselotte. Anneliese tried to comfort her, but it didn't help. All she wanted was to go back home to her parents' house ... her mother's house. To curl up in her mother's lap as if she were a little girl again.

She took the train to Leverkusen without calling ahead. Her mother opened the door with a smile—but it faltered when she saw her daughter's face. Without Lieselotte saying a word, her mother pulled her into a hug and stroked her hair.

"What's wrong, *Liebes*?" she asked.

"It's Wolfgang," Lieselotte said.

It was all she could manage. Inside, she curled up on the couch while her mother poured her a glass of milk.

"Take your time," her mother said.

Lieselotte blurted it all out, fearing if she paused, she'd cry. Explaining it all, avoiding looking at her mother's face for a reaction.

Lieselotte stayed the rest of the winter break. Sleeping so late, her mother had to yank open the curtains to get her out of bed. She trailed her mother from room to room, offering help where she could. She rehashed the same conversations. Yet her mother listened as if hearing them for the first time. Her patience was endless, her intuition precise. She knew when to coax, when to challenge, when to remind Lieselotte of the life she still wanted. Having to return to Freie was brutal. The train ride back to Berlin was a hollow reflection of her grief. Not just for Wolfgang, but for leaving her mother once more, and for how returning home always tore open the gaping wound her father had left behind.

When Lieselotte returned to Berlin, she heard the news: American president John F. Kennedy would speak in West Berlin on 26 June 1963. *Will Kennedy announce drastic change in Berlin?* She and Anneliese joined hundreds of thousands at Rudolph Wilde Platz to hear Kennedy speak. She'd never seen so many people packed into one square—faces alight with hope and nervous excitement. Shoulder to shoulder, backs to chests, people craned their necks and rose onto their toes for a glimpse. Kennedy stood on the platform and addressed the raucous crowd, ending his epic speech with the instantly famous "Ich bin ein Berliner." It was a show of support not just for West Berlin but a condemnation of East Germany. It's estimated that as many as 450,000 people stood to hear the American president speak. Those in the East listened, too—gathering near the Wall or risking arrest by bending their antennas to hear his words on the radio.

Lieselotte clung to the hope that maybe America would finally act. Tear down the cursed wall. Declare that every Berliner, every person around the world, had the natural right to be free and that suppression of freedom would be met with force. And just maybe, in the coming weeks, Wolfgang would walk across the rubble of the collapsed wall.

As summer trickled by, Anneliese tried to get Lieselotte to return to her normal life. She was compassionate but never pitied her. Forced her to go grocery shopping, for a walk, and get some sun.

It was nearing the end of August. Her final year of university would start soon, and she still knew nothing of Wolfgang's fate. Before classes started, she spent a week with her mother—helping her in the garden and listening to stories about her father.

"I'm sick with worry. With dread. It doesn't let up," she told her mother.

Her mother reached over and squeezed her hands. "I know. I'm so sorry I can't make this better."

She wanted it to be like when she was a child, and her mother could make everything right. But that had ended with her father's death. She hadn't been able to make that better. To diminish that pain, lessen that loss. At least with her father, she knew. He hadn't gone into the East and never returned.

"No word from the West government?" her mother asked.

Lieselotte shook her head. "They have little information on arrests in the East. Even less if they are not West Berlin citizens."

"You know what your grandmother would tell you to do?"

Lieselotte shook her head. She lost her grandmother soon after that first Christmas with Wolfgang.

"She'd tell you to sit in a quiet room and drown out all noise and listen to three things."

"What three things?"

"Your head. Your heart. And your gut."

Lieselotte thought on that wisdom, considering it. "My heart tells me he's alive—because I don't know what I'll do if he isn't."

Her mother smiled softly. She'd had to come to terms with losing her soul's counterpart. "Your head?"

"That he's gone. He was killed."

Her heart quivered as the betrayal left her lips, her voice trembling with the weight of it.

She couldn't trust her heart. It was too foolish, too lovesick to reason with. But nor could she trust her head. That was the pessimist in her—always expecting the worst.

"And your gut?" her mother asked.

"It tells me he's alive."

God in the Pipe

*D*id I imagine the voice? Was it a rat? Or worse—a ghost? How long
have I been here? Has my mind snapped? Wolfgang stared into the
broken pipe. *Nothing.* He pressed his ear closer.

"Yes, I'm talking to you in the cell," the voice said.

Since arriving at Hohenschönhausen, only Schwarzfuchs had
spoken to him. The guards communicated in gestures, training him
like an animal—beneath even dogs and horses.

"Who are you?" Wolfgang asked.

"Friedemann Langer. Father Friedemann Langer," the voice
said.

"You're a priest?" Wolfgang asked.

A chuckle came through the broken pipe. "Start of a joke, isn't
it? A priest walks into a prison."

Wolfgang chuckled back. It certainly was.

"What's your name, son?"

Father Langer had a deep, soothing voice. A voice that
belonged on the radio—ironically fitting, given how Wolfgang now
heard him.

"Wolfgang Kirschke."

"Pleasure to meet you, Wolfgang."

"I wish I could say the same."

They both snickered but stopped themselves. Not wanting the
guards to hear them. He asked Wolfgang what accused crime
brought him to Hohenschönhausen. Wolfgang appreciated Father
Langer's use of "accused." There were plenty of people in this

prison accused of crimes they hadn't committed, but Wolfgang wasn't one of them. He should keep his guard up, stay silent. The Stasi planted spies in these cells, false confidants who won trust only to pass it along. But Wolfgang couldn't. He had held out against Schwarzfuchs, but he'd been alone for so long. Craved interaction. If a priest—a man who swore to uphold the ideals of Christ—betrayed him, and they had somehow planted this broken pipe, then so be it.

"I am guilty," Wolfgang said, then explained the failed escape. That he had been part of a group and the attempt had been his idea. And he told Father Langer the most troubling bit: that someone in their group betrayed them.

"They knew we were coming. They were waiting in the truck," Wolfgang said. "And I know who betrayed us."

"Who?" Father Langer asked.

"Dietrich."

"How do you know?"

This cell had given him nothing to do but think of all the hundreds, maybe thousands, of questions the Stasi had asked. Hardly any of them had been about Dietrich. They had asked about Trude and Bastian and Emilia and Franco. The Fischer sisters and the Schneiders. Conrad and Fresa. Eckhart and Lieselotte. Each name was a face, a memory of how he had failed them. But anytime they mentioned Dietrich, it was a secondary subject. Never the object of the sentence.

"I'm sorry," Father Langer said. "You're angry."

"Damn right I am angry. He was my best friend."

"Anger is a necessary step."

Wolfgang glanced at the pipe, confused. "It is? Aren't you supposed to say something else? Like, anything else?"

135

Father Langer chuckled again. It was a hearty, soothing laugh. "We mustn't let anger blind us. But it is only human to feel it. I will say this, and it may make you angry with me. I have seen many people pushed to make terrible decisions."

"What do you mean?"

"The Stasi have information on people that they use to their advantage. To coerce and blackmail people into becoming their informants. If they say no, they find themselves here."

"What type of information?"

"Personal. A wide array of things. People who are homosexuals. Jews. Catholics. Adulterers. Or they are offered the promise of advancement for their children."

"That doesn't make it right. They've asked me the same questions a million times and I haven't given up anybody."

"And that is admirable, Wolfgang. Not every person shares your conviction."

"What about you? What did they say you did?"

"I, like you, am guilty of my accusations. The Stasi wished for me to exploit confessionals. To entice my parishioners to reveal their sins for the state's gains."

"What did you tell them?"

"I told them what any Catholic would. To go to hell."

Wolfgang chuckled. "So, you're a man of conviction, too."

"I try."

If what Father Langer said was true, it was admirable that he wouldn't break his oath. No matter if he was a priest or not. He wouldn't betray the trust of those who had given him it.

"I have a weird request," Wolfgang said. "Can you tell me what you look like?"

"Not used to the confession through the screen?" Father Langer quipped.

He told Wolfgang he was fifty-two years old. A tall man with thin gray hair, a beard, and dark blue eyes and admitted to having gained weight. He asked Wolfgang to do the same.

"It's hard to believe it's May," Wolfgang said after.

"May?"

"Well, who knows? I guess it could be June by now."

"My dear boy, it's December."

"What?"

"December."

Wolfgang considered it. *Would Schwarzfuchs lie? Of course he would. But why?*

"December of?" Wolfgang asked.

"'63."

"How do you know this?" Wolfgang asked.

"I am granted a bit of exercise outside. There's snow on the ground."

So, Schwarzfuchs had lied about the date. To make me question my reality?

"I haven't had a trial," Wolfgang said.

"There won't be one."

"So, what happens to me?"

"I'm sorry, son. I don't know."

The weight of it was too much. Suffocation clung to him; the air abandoned him.

"How do you survive this place?" Wolfgang asked.

"I'm not alone in here, for one."

"You have a cellmate?"

"You could say that. I'm talking about God. My Lord and Savior Jesus Christ. I pray to Him as much as I can. It keeps my mind sane. Talking to someone else helps."

The Stasi interrogations had ended, replaced by the dull rhythm of prison life. Wolfgang saw no other prisoners, only guards. Wolfgang hadn't seen the outside since his arrest. He hadn't breathed fresh air or felt the sun on his face. The stale urine smell of the cells went unnoticed now. This cell was his home. He knew every crack, chip, and protrusion on the concrete walls. Time truly was meaningless. Though he tried to keep track of the meals, the guards would sometimes rearrange the order of what was breakfast and what was dinner. Sometimes, they'd skip a meal. All to rattle Wolfgang. His only saving grace was communicating with Father Langer.

He was a friend. A confidant. Wolfgang spoke about Dietrich often. Every time he thought his anger had waned, the realization of the hell he was in reignited it. He had asked Father Langer about the others in his group, but Father Langer had no news to share. The broken pipe was a link between their cells only.

How are the others? Are they in this prison or another? Or are they free? What about Bastian and Trude's baby? What will they do with it once she has it? Let Trude raise it in prison? Or give it to a loyal couple of the state? The thought of Bastian and Trude having their child ripped from their arms was beyond heartbreaking.

Father Langer never forced his religion on Wolfgang, but he heard the priest pray every morning and every night and before every meal. Wolfgang's grandparents had been Lutheran—his father, too, until advancing in the Nazi Party meant abandoning devotion to God and giving it to Hitler and his party. Wolfgang knew about Jesus, recognized names like Noah and Moses. But beyond that, religion was an abstract thing. Like characters and a plot from a book he hadn't read.

"Do you think you could teach me?" Wolfgang asked.

"I could. From the beginning?" Father Langer asked.

"Unless you have to get going," Wolfgang quipped.

Father Langer's hearty laugh echoed in the broken pipe. *Where would I be without him?* So, they started with the Book of Genesis. Father Langer knew some chapters and verses by heart, and others he knew enough to paraphrase. Working his way through the Old Testament and enjoying the lessons just as much as Wolfgang. Father Langer was meant to spread the word of God. To take the mysteries of faith and make them understandable in everyday life.

Some unknowable number of days later, after learning about Ecclesiastes, the guards opened his door and motioned for him to follow. To his utter shock but delighted surprise, Wolfgang followed them outside. An unfathomably intense sun blinded him. Wolfgang shielded his eyes. He'd grown so pale and gaunt, feeling like a creature who had stumbled out of a cave.

"Fifteen minutes," the guard said.

The sun caressed his skin. A forgotten warmth. A memory of freedom. A promise that everything would be alright. With how hot it was outside, he had to guess it was summer. Over a year and a half had gone by since his arrest. *Or has it been longer?*

Wolfgang had no energy to run, either for pleasure or escape. He walked, but his legs were brittle, his body weak. So, he lay on the ground, overwhelmed by how deeply he had missed the sun. It was the feeling of the first warm spring day multiplied. Because even during the coldest winters, Wolfgang had seen the sun. But if he slept, the guards would shake and slap him awake. Even if they didn't, sleeping would make the fifteen minutes vanish. He had to stay awake. Be cognizant of every second of this gift.

But a shadow blocked out the sun. Wolfgang looked up. Schwarzfuchs loomed over him.

"*Herr* Kirschke," Schwarzfuchs said.

Wolfgang struggled to his feet.

"The sun is glorious, isn't it?" Schwarzfuchs asked rhetorically, then nodded. Enough preamble. "I normally would not reveal this information, as you are neither kin nor spouse."

Wolfgang's face contorted with worry.

"Your paramour, *Frau* Lieselotte Reisinger, was killed," Schwarzfuchs said.

From behind his back, he brought out a manila envelope and flipped it open. A cutout section of the *Tagesspiegel*, a major West Berlin newspaper, had a type-written page paper-clipped to it. He unclipped the newspaper and handed it to Wolfgang.

The date of the newspaper was 14 July 1964. *Is this today's paper? Yesterday's? Last month's?* The headline screamed: *American bomb misfires. Destroys University building.* A picture showed a heap of rubble. Behind it, a building missing half its side. Schwarzfuchs plucked it away before Wolfgang could finish reading.

"The Americans are fortunate their bomb misfired in West Berlin. They had aimed to drop it in East Berlin. Of course, they will not admit to this. They are stating it was an unfortunate military accident." Schwarzfuchs sifted through his papers and removed a sheet displaying a list of typed names. A casualty report. "It's quite a list, but scroll to the fourteenth entry."

Wolfgang's eyes scrolled through the list of names. Freezing on the name on line fourteen.

Lieselotte Reisinger.

"You're lying …" Wolfgang said.

Schwarzfuchs said nothing. He handed over a second newspaper clipping—an obituary. Lieselotte's face smiled in the grainy print.

Wolfgang's breath caught in his throat. "No …"

"I have presented you with the facts. Accept them. Refute them. It does not change their existence. I believe your exercise period has ended."

He motioned for the guards. With long strides, they approached Wolfgang, snatching him by the elbows.

"Why would you tell me this? You've given me no information," Wolfgang said. "This is bullshit! All of this! Nothing but lies!"

"Perhaps I'm being cruel. Or perhaps I'm trying to show you that the West is far from perfect," Schwarzfuchs said.

"Please, tell me you're lying!" Wolfgang called out.

But Schwarzfuchs turned away from him. Wolfgang screamed after him as the guards dragged him back inside. He tried wrestling free, but he was too thin, too weak. The guards shoved him into his cell, clanging the door shut. Darkness swallowed him.

Wolfgang sobbed into his mattress. It was a lie. It had to be. *If the Americans had dropped a bomb, that news would have spread like wildfire.*

But maybe it had. *How would I hear about it?* No sounds from the outside world made their way into his cell. For all he knew, Eckhart, Bastian, Trude, and the others were all dead. Or they were rotting in cells right next to him.

"Wolfgang," Father Langer called out. "What's wrong?"

"Lieselotte is dead."

Father Langer replied, but right now, Wolfgang didn't want to talk about it. Talk about anything. He couldn't do this anymore. He couldn't stay in this prison a moment longer. He needed to end it.

But how? There was nothing to hang himself from or with. No mirror to shatter to slit his wrists. Even if there had been, the guards were always watching. Every moment of every day. They'd never let him kill himself. There would be no escaping this hell.

No Cipher. No Closure.

Lieselotte reread old letters, even though she knew she shouldn't. Maybe someday—years or decades from now—she could read them and smile. But not now. Now, they only tore at fresh scabs. She'd asked Sandra to inquire about Wolfgang during one of her trips to the East, but Sandra, ever blunt, refused. "Too dangerous," she said. "I won't risk my father." She had stopped by his apartment, though. New tenants had moved in.

There were no answers, only questions. To ease the pain, Lieselotte dove into her studies. By spring, she'd graduated and landed a job at the West Berlin office of an American affiliate of the Associated Press. At first, she was dismissed as a pretty face, an errand girl. But she fought and proved she belonged. *Liberty for all*, she realized, *isn't handed to you. You have to fight for it.*

Just months after Kennedy's speech in Berlin, he was assassinated on 22 November. Rumors flew—were the Soviets involved? If so, it would mean war. Lieselotte mourned for Mrs. Kennedy. A new president had stepped in. His gaze was not in Berlin, but rather on the jungles of Vietnam. A place most couldn't find on a map. The world had turned its attention elsewhere.

For months, checking the mail brought a nauseating mix of hope and dread. As the hour approached, she'd sometimes race to the bathroom to vomit. But eventually, even that stopped. No letters came. Then, in June 1964, an envelope from the East arrived. Goosebumps rose. *If not from Wolfgang, then who?* She opened the letter with trembling hands. She gasped. The sporadic shift from cursive to print was unmistakably his. Her lips twitched into a disbelieving laugh. This was a dream. It had to be.

Lieselotte,

I am sorry I didn't write sooner. My escape failed. I was arrested, tried, and sentenced to a labor camp near the Polish border. This is hard to write, but I met someone. Adaline—the daughter of the farmer I work for. We're engaged. I never meant to hurt you. I hope this letter brings you closure—knowing I'm alive. I'll always remember you.

Go find your someone,

Wolfgang

She stood motionless, scouring it for ciphers. First the obvious ones, then the obscure. Nothing. No message. Only coincidences. Every letter they'd exchanged since childhood had carried a code. Her mother's voice echoed in her mind: *Trust your brain. Your heart. Your gut.* Her heart whispered that Wolfgang would never do this. Their love had been real. Love fades, yes—but this didn't fit. He had dreams he couldn't pursue in the East. He'd made that clear. Their relationship was a bonus, not the motive.

Her gut screamed: *This isn't him.*

But her verdict needed all three: mind, heart, and gut.

The Stasi had confiscated many of their letters. A handwriting expert could mimic Wolfgang's writing, but they hadn't known about the ciphers. This letter was a forgery. And if someone went through this much trouble to fake it, then Wolfgang must be alive.

He is alive!

Time Is at an End

Since Schwarzfuchs told him of Lieselotte's death, Wolfgang had vanished into his own thoughts. He teetered between belief and doubt. Sure, Schwarzfuchs had documentation. But this was the Stasi—deception was their craft. Wolfgang thought about the photograph in the newspaper. It was the same photograph he had had of her in his pocket the night of the arrest. One of the few possessions he was taking with him into West Berlin. *What are the odds of that being the same photo used? But how long was I able to look at that newspaper clipping before Schwarzfuchs plucked it out of my hands? Seconds?* Plus, the newspaper's graininess removed clarity and resolution. *Was it the same photo? Or one that just looked similar?*

He offered his contemplation to Father Langer. The priest listened, but he offered no answers. How could he? He thought about Dietrich's betrayal, and what Father Langer had said—that sometimes people were bullied or forced into spying and betraying their loved ones. *To hell with those excuses. We get to choose how we react.* Schwarzfuchs had wanted Wolfgang to betray Lieselotte and others who may have knowingly or unknowingly aided in their escape. But he hadn't. He didn't break. That pride was something he'd carry to his last breath.

Trapped in this small cell, his mind drifted into unbidden memories, both real and imagined. Moments with Lieselotte became a sanctuary—places he could retreat to and feel like he was with her again. In her bed. On the walking trails. On the beach. Feel her soft hands caressing his head, running her fingers through his hair. What was truth and what was fiction was lost in the fog of his mind.

But he also disappeared into moments with Eckhart and Dietrich. At the pubs, beaches, and restaurants. The way Dietrich's eyes lingered on people. Always watching. Always listening. *But was there more to it? Certain people? Certain genders?* Every man feels a flicker of doubt and competitiveness when an attractive man enters a room—an instinctive sizing up. It's primitive. Innate. Buried in our DNA. But for Dietrich, it extended beyond that. His gaze lingered longer. It wasn't eyeing up a potential adversary or ally. It was the way Eckhart scanned a crowd for a woman. Ranking them in terms of desirability.

Had the signs been there all along? Dietrich had never told Wolfgang he was gay. Never hinted at it. Never even made a comment that suggested as much. And if it had not been for this prison and the unreachable levels of retrospection it offered, Wolfgang would never have seen it. But now that he had, he knew it was true. Dietrich was a gay man. A criminal offense in most places in the world, including in East Berlin. If he'd been arrested in the throes of love with another man, it was all the Stasi needed. Dietrich could either become an informant for them, or he could spend his life in prison or at a hard labor camp.

Though it made him feel like a terrible friend for not noticing, for making Dietrich think he couldn't divulge this secret to his two best friends, Wolfgang couldn't forgive him. Dietrich could have refused to become an informant. At the very least, informed only on strangers. But he had aided in their escape plans. Wolfgang thought about the promise Dietrich had made. To share the same fate as Eckhart and Wolfgang.

The cell door clanged open. Two guards motioned for him to follow. They sat him in the cold metal chair inside the interrogation room. He'd been kept in darkness for weeks, and the fluorescent lights assaulted his eyes. Schwarzfuchs sat across the table, a blazing aura.

"*Herr* Kirschke. How have you been doing?" he asked.

"When is my trial? What is my sentence?"

"Have you processed your grief with the young woman's death?" Schwarzfuchs asked, ignoring Wolfgang's question.

"There is no grief to process. You're lying. It's a ruse. Besides, I told you, I have not spoken to her since before the Wall came up."

Schwarzfuchs gave a slow, deliberate nod. "We both know that's a lie. I have nothing to gain from reporting the death of a West Berliner. I offered you the knowledge so you could accept your fate behind these walls. To end your foolish ideas to leave East Germany. To illustrate the West aren't the saints you hold them to be. Think of a future you may still yet see if you change your ways. Your beliefs. Your thinking. You were once a bright engineering student, before you were corrupted. There is still a chance for you to have a life. We will talk again in the future."

Future. A deliberately vague word—meant to torment, to warp hope into dread.

The guards dragged him back into his cell. They alternated between keeping the lights on for days at a time and keeping it dark. Right now, the lights were on. Blinding and bright, just as they were in the interrogation room. Illuminating the decrepit cell. Wolfgang ate his gruel for supper and then sat in the corner to converse with Father Langer.

He listened to the sage priest pray, joining in with the appropriately placed "Amen." He told him about this interrogation with Schwarzfuchs and his mention of Lieselotte.

"You seem much more certain about her fate than you had been before," Father Langer commented.

"I prayed on it. Prayed to God for some sort of clarity."

"I don't want to spoil it, but God does not always speak in ways we can hear or understand."

"The photograph they used in her obituary. I believe it's the same one I had in my pocket when they arrested me."

He heard the smile in Father Langer's voice. "You've kept a sharp mind in here, my friend."

"I am still not sure you're even real," Wolfgang said. "Maybe I created you—maybe my mind split."

"I have to admit I've considered that, too."

"But I guess it doesn't matter. You're real to me." Wolfgang rested his arms on his knees. "Sometimes, I disappear into my mind—into this life with Lieselotte that never was. Memories, but they're not my memories because they've never happened. Like events in the future. They're so real …"

"The mind is an incredible thing, Wolfgang."

They continued into their Bible studies. They'd left the Old Testament behind and advanced into the New. Reviewing the key figures and events and how they applied to life. For Wolfgang, the prison had tried to destroy his mind, break his heart, and atrophy his body. But it failed. For inside this submarine prison, they'd placed him in a cell with a broken pipe. And they had placed Father Langer in the cell beside him. There was no one else in the world who could have kept Wolfgang sane the way Father Langer had. Not only that, but he had helped Wolfgang temper his hatred of Dietrich. He was working on forgiveness. Father Langer stated that hate is a necessary step in the process of grief. But to hold onto it is to forge an anchor you can't move on from. A cancer that destroys us and everyone around us. Without Father Langer, Wolfgang would have stayed fixated on his betrayal. Relived every moment. Trying to change the past by changing the decisions he made, the friendship he'd formed. Rewriting the past a hundred ways. But none of that did any good. He couldn't change it.

He prayed. For Lieselotte. For his parents. For the others whose fates he'd never know. The prayers offered no answers, but they helped his spirit. He thought about his parents. About how disappointed his father would be with him. This was exactly what his father had warned him about. If he could have just been content, none of this would have happened.

Not having any more books of the Bible to learn was a massive loss. His lessons with Father Langer were the only thing he had had to look forward to.

The cell creaked open. Normally, light flooded into the dark room. But instead, the harsh light from his room spilled into the hallway.

The guard motioned with a come-hither fashion with his finger. Wolfgang followed them to the interrogation room. He expected to see Schwarzfuchs sitting in his seat. But he wasn't. The room was vacant. His clothes were on the seat. Clothes he hadn't seen since he had tried to escape. His dark pair of trousers and his thick wool pullover and jacket. His black work boots. And most heavenly, his glasses.

The sight of them hit him like a gut punch. How could mere clothes make him cry? For longer than he knew, this prison uniform had been all he'd known. And he had been grateful for it, because before that he had been naked for days. Weeks. Maybe even months. But these clothes were proof that he had existed outside this place. Mementos, historical artifacts from the night everything changed. Another before and after moment.

"What's going on?" Wolfgang asked.

"Dress," the guard said.

Wolfgang slipped on his boxer shorts, then his trousers. They were far too baggy now. He knew he had lost weight, but he was drowning in these clothes. He looked like a child swallowed up by his father's clothes. At least his boots fit. His glasses were askew on his face and the lenses too caked with grime to see clearly. He turned to the guard.

"Follow me," the guard commanded.

Wolfgang followed, dread mounting.

"Where are you taking me?"

Silence, as expected. Prior to his incarceration, he'd heard murmurings that prisoners were often transferred to other prisons. Like Leipzig or Dresden, where they were killed by a single shot to the back of the head. For others, it marked the start of their hard labor. *Am I being transferred to work? Or being sent to my execution?*

Wolfgang followed the guard to a section of the building he had been to only once: the night he first arrived. The corridor was narrow and dimly lit. The guard pushed open the thick metal door. Brutal winds attacked them in the chilly afternoon.

Schwarzfuchs had his back to the prison, gazing out at the barbed wire fencing and watchtowers. He turned around and leered. "*Herr* Kirschke, your time at Hohenschönhausen has come to an end."

Released Into a Cage

Wolfgang stopped walking and gazed at Schwarzfuchs.

"Come with me," Schwarzfuchs said.

Wolfgang hesitated. When the guards advanced, he moved, still expecting a bullet in the back of the head. Flanked by the two guards, Wolfgang followed Schwarzfuchs to a Wartburg 311, a larger, more robust car than the Trabant.

Schwarzfuchs opened the rear passenger side door. "Get in."

Wolfgang didn't have a choice, but he wouldn't have chosen differently if he had. The alternative was to go back inside the prison. Wherever the car led, it was somewhere new—even if it was to his execution. Feeling, seeing the sun, even in its diminished state, was enough for him to know, to accept, that he'd rather die than go back to that dark, dank cell.

He sat in the middle while the two guards sat on either side. Schwarzfuchs drove. The car rumbled past the gates, leaving the prison behind. It offered Wolfgang his first glimpse at the prison he'd been trapped in for God only knew how long. It was bleak and utilitarian, like so much of East Germany. Surrounded by high, barbed-wire-topped walls. Guard towers dotted along the fence line of the massive brick-and-concrete prison. But before he could take it all in, a guard shoved his head forward.

"Where are you taking me?" Wolfgang asked, even though he knew he wouldn't get an answer.

"Tell me about the man in the cell beside you," Schwarzfuchs said.

"What man?" Wolfgang asked.

Schwarzfuchs flicked his gaze to the rearview mirror, holding it on Wolfgang for a moment before returning it to the road.

He didn't answer Wolfgang's question, nor did he ask any more of his own. The drive was rather quick, roughly five miles before he stopped the car in front of the Berlin Wall. The buildings hadn't changed, but the Wall had—steel-reinforced concrete now replaced the early cinder blocks. It was over ten feet tall now and had never been more intimidating. An impenetrable barrier.

Schwarzfuchs stepped out of the car as the guards dragged Wolfgang out beside him. Schwarzfuchs paused to admire the Wall. Behind him, guards paced, and German Shepherds and Belgian Malinois sniffed. Watchtowers loomed overhead.

"You have lied to me from the beginning to the end," Schwarzfuchs said. "Pretending you do not know the man in the cell next to yours. I will find out how you communicated with him."

Wolfgang would say nothing about his friend, the man who had kept him sane.

"Friedemann Langer has secured your release."

Wolfgang stayed silent, trying not to let Schwarzfuchs destroy his mind any more than he had. *This is a lie. Father Langer is a prisoner. How could he secure my release?*

Schwarzfuchs didn't turn around to gaze at Wolfgang while he spoke. He kept his hands behind his back, his body rigid. "I can see your brain spinning from here." Now he turned. For the first time since Wolfgang had known him, Schwarzfuchs looked disturbed, not in control. And how that irritated the Stasi agent to no end.

"It appears your priest was a Western spy. I will be honest with you, *Herr* Kirschke. Our East German government makes choices for the good of its people. Of all its people. While I personally would see you in a cell until I know you have been rehabilitated, the state requires a different use from you. You have been sold."

"Sold?"

"Yes, flesh for cash. Just like the Americans did with the Negros."

"Who has bought me?"

"The West German government."

This is a game. A mental torture of sorts. There is no way this is true.

"You are a free man," Schwarzfuchs said.

Wolfgang didn't move. He couldn't. If this was another lie, his sanity wouldn't survive it.

"What are you waiting for? Go!" Schwarzfuchs said.

That crack in Schwarzfuchs's control was still there—different now, but Wolfgang couldn't say how. A man who had lost his plaything. Trying to conceal his rage.

To hell with this. Wolfgang was *this* close to the border. Something that seemed impossible just this morning. Something beyond wishing, desiring, and even dreaming. There was no way he could pass up this chance. He approached Checkpoint Charlie. The wind groaned, mournful and low, as if he were walking toward a haunted cemetery.

"Oh, one moment, *Herr* Kirschke," Schwarzfuchs called out.

Wolfgang stopped. *This is where he reveals his trick.* He turned slowly at the sound of Schwarzfuchs's boots clacking on the pavement. The Stasi officer held out his passport.

"You will need this," he said.

Wolfgang took it. Before Schwarzfuchs could call out again, Wolfgang demanded his weak legs to power him as fast as they were able. At the checkpoint, he held out his passport for the guard to approve.

"You cannot access West Berlin," the guard said, thrusting Wolfgang's passport back into his chest.

Wolfgang grunted—even that little push hurt. He turned to Schwarzfuchs, unsure why. *For an explanation? Help?*

"I'm afraid I may have misinformed you, *Herr* Kirschke. While the priest and the West may have bought your freedom, I deem the amount paid not worthy of letting you leave East Germany. Look down at your feet." When Wolfgang didn't, Schwarzfuchs shoved his head down. It was the first time he'd laid a hand on him. His torture was psychological, not physical. Wolfgang stared at the space between his boots and Schwarzfuchs's.

"This is the closest you will get to West Berlin." He released Wolfgang's head, then straightened his uniform. "I am an honorable man, so I will not return you to prison where you belong. Your crime has been bought and paid for but not forgotten." Schwarzfuchs leaned closer, his breath a mix of cigarettes and mint as it crested over Wolfgang's face. "Know this. Everything you do, we see. Everything you say, we hear. Everything you write, we read. Our eyes and ears are everywhere. And be sure, *Herr* Kirschke, that the next time you break the law, no amount of money from those *Bonner* will buy your freedom. You will die in prison." He removed a letter from his coat pocket. "Now that our game has come to an end, I will tell you that your precious little girlfriend is alive. But I do not believe she is still your girlfriend after reading the letter you wrote her."

There was too much to process at once. Foremost: Lieselotte was alive. That hope he'd clung to in the cells—that fragile, immaculate, wondrous thing—hadn't been false. The mental anguish, the wafting of whether she was alive or dead, had been soul-crushing.

"What letter? I didn't write anything."

Schwarzfuchs removed a folded letter and handed it to Wolfgang. He skimmed it. The handwriting was his—only it wasn't. He spotted the tells, tiny flaws that betrayed the forgery.

Would anyone else notice them? Most likely not. The words written—about a labor camp and falling in love—were ones he never would have written. Wolfgang hid his smile. This letter was another failure. How he wanted to prove it to Schwarzfuchs. To see his calm facade break with anger. But to do so, he'd have to tell them how he knew, and he wouldn't give up the secret of his encoded messages.

"I'm sure she was quite heartbroken reading it," Schwarzfuchs said. "You can keep that." Schwarzfuchs marched back to his car and opened the door. "Until we see each other again! And I assure you, we shall see each other again!"

He got into the Wartburg with the two guards and drove away, leaving Wolfgang at Checkpoint Charlie in front of the Wall with nothing but a useless passport. Being this close, the temptation to make a run for it consumed him. He could tackle the guard, try to sprint—but he wouldn't get far. He didn't know if he *could* run. His legs hadn't stretched in months—they might buckle beneath him. A permanent hunger gurgled in his stomach and sleep was a dream. *Do I even still have a home? Or has the state taken my apartment?* But all those things were second to the one question he needed answering. A question that had haunted him since 2 January 1963.

What is the date?

Beyond the Wall, through Checkpoint Charlie, West Berlin shimmered like a beacon. A sight he never thought he'd see again. He lumbered away from it toward a small kiosk selling newspapers. He grabbed one, scanning for the date.

22 November 1964.

That couldn't be. He'd lost twenty-three months. The prime of his life. Yet, it had *only* been twenty-three months. It seemed impossible. Some of those days alone had felt like twenty-three months. He hadn't seen his reflection—couldn't know how much or how little he had aged. They had routinely shaved his face and head. He had no idea what he even looked like anymore.

But he couldn't contemplate that anymore. Lieselotte was alive, and he needed to get word to her. *Is there any chance she believed that letter?* No, she never would have. This letter didn't contain any ciphers because the Stasi hadn't known about them. In his arrogance, Schwarzfuchs thought he had destroyed their relationship. Maybe Lieselotte had moved on, but it wouldn't have been because of this letter. If anything, Schwarzfuchs had just let Lieselotte know he was alive.

But how can I reach her? Does Sandra still cross into East Berlin? Now that he was free, he needed to see what had happened to Eckhart and Bastian. All the others. But that had to be tomorrow's goal. Right now, he needed to know where he would be sleeping. Needed to get a meal and something to drink.

Wolfgang returned to his apartment building and put his key into the lock, trying to get it to turn. But it wouldn't. He tugged on the door handle with no success.

"Can I help you?"

A man holding a bag of groceries approached.

"This is my apartment," Wolfgang said.

"The hell it is!" the man yelled, taking an offensive step forward.

"When?"

"When what?"

"When did you move in?"

"I've been living here for almost two years! Now get the hell away from my door!"

Almost two years. Just after his arrest. He'd been erased so quickly.

Wolfgang wasn't a confrontational person by nature, and in this depleted physical state, he wouldn't win a fight. But he wanted to stand his ground. He had expected to lose his possessions when he made it into the West. But he hadn't made it into the West.

"My things," Wolfgang said.

"Everything in that apartment is mine. Now get out of here before I call the police!"

Wolfgang left without apologizing. He didn't need the police called on him. He went back outside. With no place to sleep for the night, he curled up on a bench. He had never been more aware of the bitter winds. Schwarzfuchs had left him nothing. He'd left him in a different kind of prison. Now, instead of a cell inside, protected from the elements, he was exposed to them. Instead of three meals, paltry to say the least, he had no food.

The following morning, he set out for answers to what had happened to Eckhart and Bastian. *What will I do if I see Dietrich?* He went to Eckhart's apartment and knocked on the door, hopeful that his friend would answer the door. But he didn't. It was an older man in his sixties. Wolfgang asked if he knew where the previous tenant had moved. The man shook his head and closed the door.

Next stop was Bastian's house. He had little hope. And sure enough, a stranger opened the door—a woman in her early thirties.

"Do you know where the couple who owned this house went?" Wolfgang asked.

Shame spread across her face. "There was a woman a few months ago who came here claiming this was her house."

His chest filled with joy. *Trude made it out. At least someone had.* "Trude?" Wolfgang asked.

"I believe that was her name. I ended up driving her to her mother's house."

"Do you remember where this house was?"

She nodded. "Would you like me to take you there?"

"You would do that?"

"Of course. I feel terrible for all this."

Wolfgang thanked her, feeling her look him over. His frail frame. His gaunt face. She introduced herself as Lisbeth. Wolfgang stated his name. Her lingering stare depleted his self-esteem.

"Sorry, it's just … can you see? Those glasses are cracked and as cloudy as milk."

"Not really," Wolfgang admitted.

"I work at an eye doctor's office. Let's get you a new pair."

"I have no money."

While healthcare was state-provided, ex-prisoners were often given minimal support. The Stasi ensured political prisoners struggled to find housing and employment. Schwarzfuchs wouldn't have made an exception for Wolfgang.

"We can work something out."

She drove Wolfgang to the clinic. Inside, they had a wall of glasses. As he looked at the limited designs, she asked what his prescription was. Wolfgang shrugged. So, Lisbeth gave him an eye exam.

"I can clean up your existing lenses—that should give you some relief. As for the new lenses, I'll place the order right away," she said after.

The frames were thick black plastic. Once he slid them on, the world displayed itself in a clarity he'd long forgotten. But it was far from perfect. His eyes had worsened considerably inside Hohenschönhausen. Without his corrective frames, his eyesight had degraded.

"How long until they arrive?" Wolfgang asked.

"Normally, weeks, sometimes months. I have a friend I can call—maybe he can get them sooner." Lisbeth said.

Wolfgang smiled in gratitude.

"Let's get you to your friend," she said.

"What about the cost of the glasses?"

"Don't worry about that."

Wolfgang refuted, but Lisbeth wouldn't hear about it. She filled the drive pointing out houses, cars, and people. All to make him not feel pitiful about not having money to pay for his glasses. Less than ten minutes later, she pulled into a driveway.

"This is the one," she said.

The building was a prefabricated boxy design of *Plattenbau* blocks of concrete erected in the postwar. Before Wolfgang stepped out, Lizbeth reached into her purse and removed a few *Ostmarks.*

"I'm sorry I can't give more. But please see you get yourself some food," she said with a sad smile.

Wolfgang wanted to refuse, but the truth was he was starved. Seeing his emaciated frame while trying on his glasses had terrified him. He looked on the verge of death. As if the Stasi knew exactly how many calories he had needed to stay alive. He missed supper last night. He wasn't sure if he could skip another meal.

"You have been so kind," Wolfgang said.

Lizbeth smiled. Wolfgang stepped out of the rattling Trabant and tried to show his thanks with his smile as she backed out of the driveway and drove away.

Wolfgang walked to the front door and knocked. Waiting to see who answered the door. *What is my next course of action if Trude isn't here? Ask the owners if they know where she is? And if not? Then what?*

A woman in her fifties answered the door, big, lush eyelashes batting at him as she studied Wolfgang for recognition.

"Can I help you?" she asked.

"Hi. I was told that Trude Kleppelstein might be staying here."

"Who is asking?"

"My name is Wolfgang Kirschke. We are friends."

It was the simplest answer. But they were more than that. Over the course of the months of planning and rebuilding the truck, Wolfgang, Eckhart, Bastian, Trude, Emilia, and Franco had become family. There was another name who belonged on that list, but Wolfgang didn't want to think of him right now.

"Just a moment," she said, then turned away and called out for Trude.

Seconds later, Trude stood in the doorway. Lines etched her face, bags drooping under her eyes, but that friendly gleam in them remained. Her jaw dropped when she saw Wolfgang. She threw herself at him, wrapping him in a hug.

"Oh my God!" she cried.

Wolfgang returned the hug, and she led him into the living room without letting go.

"How are you here?" she asked.

Where to start? How far back? He elected to start with stopping at her former house.

"When did you get out of prison?" she asked.

"Yesterday. You?"

"A while ago. I was inside for eighteen months."

Wolfgang hesitated. Trude had been pregnant when they had tried to escape. A quick glance around the room showed no signs of a toddler.

"Your child?" he asked, sheepishly.

Her eyes welled with tears. "They took my baby. Gave him away."

Wolfgang clenched his eyes shut, imagining the horror of what Trude and Bastian had been through. For Trude to have to give birth alone in one of those depressing cells. To have a stranger pry her baby from her breast. It was a pain only she could fathom.

"I'm so sorry. For all this."

She reached for his hand and squeezed it. "None of this was your fault. We all chose."

"Any update on the others? Eckhart? Bastian?"

"Bastian is in a hard labor camp. Eckhart was just released yesterday morning."

Wolfgang beamed when he heard Eckhart was out. "Where is he?"

"At his parents'. Should we go see him now?"

"Absolutely."

But as they headed toward the door, Trude took in Wolfgang's appearance for the first time. At least without tears blurring her vision.

"You need a meal first," she said.

Trude returned with a sandwich for Wolfgang and a glass of milk. He destroyed the sandwich in a few bites, gulping the milk down as if it were oxygen. It was far and away the best meal he'd had since 2 January 1963. Trude borrowed her mother's Trabant. On the way to her in-laws, Wolfgang asked if she had seen Dietrich.

"No. Not since that night."

There was no clarification. 2 January 1963 would always be that night. The night everything changed.

Wolfgang hesitated, but in doing so, knew that Trude would question why he had paused in such a way.

"What is it?" she asked.

"It was him, Trude. Dietrich betrayed us."

She sat with that information. For her, the betrayal was different. There was a degree of separation from trusting Dietrich. She trusted Bastian, who trusted Eckhart, who trusted Dietrich. It wasn't the shock it was for Wolfgang, and the shock it would be for Eckhart. For her, it was nothing but anger. At what Dietrich had caused. The abduction of her baby, her husband in a hard labor camp in another country, and her own imprisonment. No matter if she didn't say it, it was Wolfgang and Eckhart's trust that caused this.

She collected herself and drove to Eckhart's parents. Trude knocked on the door of their home and then entered.

"Eckhart! There's someone here to see you!" she called, doing a masterful job hiding her emotions.

Eckhart emerged from the kitchen, a glass of water in his hand. He stopped. Then, in a fluid motion, he set his glass on the nightstand and rushed at Wolfgang. The two men met in a forceful hug. Looking each other over, neither saying what they were thinking: how terrible the other looked.

"When did you get out?" Eckhart asked.

"Just yesterday. You?"

"Me, too."

"How?"

Eckhart shrugged. "My freedom was bought. Negotiated by a priest."

Wolfgang's lip quivered. His only regret about leaving Hohenschönhausen was that he hadn't been able to have a proper goodbye with Father Langer. Wolfgang had no idea that Father Langer had remembered the names he'd listed. Remembered everything Wolfgang had told him. And somehow, he'd smuggled a list of names for the West German government to buy. Wolfgang had unknowingly vetted Eckhart. Father Langer knew he wasn't an East German spy. Of course, his ideal result was that Wolfgang and the others were released into the West, but being out of that hell was a tremendous gift.

The two friends sat at the kitchen table, revealing their experiences in the Submarine. It was unbelievable to know that their cells were directly across from each other. They discussed the interrogations they underwent, the food, the torment, and the lack of sleep. All that while he had wondered about Eckhart, and he was less than twenty feet away. The guards had done a masterful job at making the prisoners feel isolated. As if they were the only people there.

Eckhart shifted the conversation. "They were waiting for us, Wolfgang. Someone betrayed us."

Wolfgang and Trude glanced at each other. Trude stood and went into the living room, granting Wolfgang and Eckhart privacy. If he were Trude, he'd be yelling. Her stoicism was heartbreaking—and it didn't go unnoticed.

"What is it?" Eckhart asked.

There was no easy way to say it. Wolfgang had rehearsed this moment a hundred times, yet part of him never believed it would come.

"It was Dietrich."

Eckhart hesitated only because he had waited for Wolfgang to explain what he was talking about. Because they had been talking about the person who had betrayed them and there was no way that was Dietrich. "What? No. Never."

Wolfgang respected the instinct to defend his friend—the flash of anger in Eckhart's eyes said everything. But after Wolfgang remained silent, Eckhart asked why he thought that. Wolfgang explained. During the interrogations, they'd barely asked about Dietrich. Whereas Schwarzfuchs wanted information on everyone in the group, he had rarely asked about Dietrich.

Eckhart was silent. No doubt trying to replay his own interrogations and all the events Wolfgang had described. He paced the length of the kitchen table. He paused, gripping the back of a chair—then smacked it across the kitchen.

"I'll kill him! Do you know what he's done?! Where Bastian is?! What happened to my nephew?!" Eckhart yelled.

Wolfgang rose. It seemed wrong, insensitive to stay seated. "I do know," he said softly. "And I'm sorry."

Eckhart breathed slowly, biting his lip to stifle his anger. "So, now what?"

Wolfgang shrugged. *Where should we start? A place to live? A job? Our next meal?* But for Wolfgang, there was something else he needed to do first. "I need to get word to Lieselotte."

Eckhart thought on it. "It'll be tough. With the East cracking down, there are fewer people willing to help."

Wolfgang couldn't blame anyone who refused to help. Especially now. They were enemies of the state. All it took for arrest was a whisper. Unsubstantiated accusations could send people to prison.

The telephone rang. Eckhart ignored it, but it kept ringing. He stormed across the room to answer. His face softened at the voice on the other end. He lowered the phone and shouted for Trude. She hurried into the kitchen.

"What is it?" she asked.

"… it's for you."

Concerned, she took the phone. "Hello?" Her voice barely rose above a whisper.

When the person on the phone spoke, Trude broke down, sobbing so hard she would have collapsed to the floor if Eckhart hadn't caught her. But it was clear they were good tears. She clung to the receiver as though it would bring her closer to the person on the other end. Even when the line had gone silent, she couldn't let go. Eckhart gingerly freed the phone from her hands and placed it onto the receiver.

"What's going on?" Wolfgang asked.

"That was Bastian," Eckhart said.

"His freedom's been purchased! He's coming home!" Trude exclaimed.

Trude looked ready to hug anyone in her orbit, and right now, that was only Eckhart and Wolfgang. Sobbing and smiling, she clung to both men. The last twenty-three months had left them scarred, broken in places unseen. But today was a good day— where all those scars and breaks could be put aside.

Wolfgang stayed for dinner, though it didn't take much to fill him—his stomach had shrunk in prison. But when Eckhart's mother served lemon cake, he didn't hesitate.

The mood was so euphoric, he hated to have to break it. He had answers on Eckhart, Trude, and Bastian. But there were others in their group. People who had placed their trust in him.

"Have you heard from Emilia and Franco?" he asked.

Trude beamed. "Emilia got out around the same time I did. Franco ... they interrogated him a lot since he's a foreigner. They released him after nine months."

"That's fantastic," Wolfgang said. "And the others? The Fischer sisters? Conrad and Fresa? The Schneiders?"

Trude folded her hands. Her jovial spirit drained, her smile fading into something hollow.

"Johanna and Theresa couldn't go on," she said softly.

"Couldn't go on?" Eckhart blinked, confused. "What does that mean?"

Wolfgang's gut turned—he knew what it meant but prayed he was wrong.

"After Theresa was released, they returned her to her husband. She knew what he would do. She went into the bathroom and slit her wrists in the bathtub. Once Johanna found out … she followed her sister. She couldn't live in a world without her."

Silence slammed into the room.

Eckhart stared blankly. Wolfgang lowered his gaze, Johanna's whispered plea replaying in his mind: *Please, make sure she gets out.* He had promised her and now he could never rectify that broken promise. He was afraid to ask about the others. But he had to.

"Conrad died at a hard labor camp," Trude stated. "Fresa is out. She's … absolutely gutted. Lukas and Annalena Schneider were put into state-run homes. The Stasi deemed them innocent. Their parents took full blame. I'm not sure where they are."

Wolfgang had feared he'd ruin the mood and had—but it deserved to be ruined. *Why celebrate when so many others couldn't?*

Without a place to stay, Eckhart's parents insisted Wolfgang stay there. He slept on the couch but slept horribly, wrestling with the day's highs and lows. Thoughts of those beautiful sisters and their tragic fate consumed him. A part of him couldn't help but feel responsible.

But he also knew he had a decision to make. He was homeless. Jobless. If he were to stay in East Berlin, he'd have to find both a place to live and a job. Eckhart's parents couldn't support him even if they were willing. But did he want to try to make a life here in the East? Accept the die that had been cast? *My dreams have caused more problems than blessings. Could I toe the line? Work when told to work? Eat when told to eat? Think what I'm told to think?* He'd done it at Hohenschönhausen. He'd survived the silence, the obedience, the void of joy, and the daily surrender of self. *Could I live like that again? For the rest of my life? Could I choose that fate?*

Escape or Die Trying

Wolfgang didn't need the night to decide—he wasn't staying in East Berlin. Even if Lieselotte had moved on, she was just one of many reasons.

As the first rays of sun trickled through the closed blinds, Wolfgang abandoned trying to get any more sleep. He crept into the kitchen for a pen and paper. Once he found them, he wrote his first letter to Lieselotte in almost two years.

He was rusty writing the ciphers, and it took him longer than he had hoped. But he still finished before the others woke up. He scribbled a note for Eckhart, explaining he would stop by later, and set off for Sandra's father's house. If she had kept her routine, she should be visiting him today. He doubted she'd be willing to smuggle the letter to Lieselotte, but he'd rather have it should she say yes. At the very least, she could tell Lieselotte that he was alive.

He waited at the café across from her father's building all morning—through lunch and into the afternoon. Waiting might have driven him mad—if not for the months spent in Hohenschönhausen. The café's smells, sounds, and colors overwhelmed in the best way. Yet with no money—except for a coffee bought with Trude's spare change—those sights and smells became pure anguish.

Finally, around four, Sandra approached her father's house. Wolfgang jogged across the street, calling her name. Her eyes lit up when she recognized him.

"Wolfgang?"

He smiled and leaned in for a hug. She didn't pull away, but she wasn't looking for one—not even a handshake.

"How?" she asked.

Wolfgang gave her the abridged version of his incarceration and freedom. "Can you tell Lieselotte I'm okay?"

"Of course."

"How is she?" He hoped she'd understand all that he was asking. Not just how her mood was, where she was living and working, but if she had moved on from him.

"She graduated last May. She works for an American news company and lives with her friend Anneliese."

"That's wonderful. Is she … seeing anyone?" he was forced to ask.

Sandra shook her head then shrugged. "Not that I know of. We haven't kept in touch that well. But she was heartbroken. She received this letter from you, or at least it said it was from you."

"It wasn't me."

"Oh, she knew that. I don't know how, but she did."

Wolfgang smiled, a rare flicker of warmth rising through the numbness. "Of course she did." He paused, delaying what he didn't want to ask her, but needed to. "Can you deliver a letter?"

She shook her head, having no trouble declining his request. "It's too risky for me. I need to be able to see my father. They'll stop me at the border, now that we've talked."

Wolfgang knew that was true. Schwarzfuchs had promised as much. The idea that right now, someone was watching them, unnerved him.

"I understand. Would you be willing to give her a message for me?"

He'd have to code the message. Even then, it was still a risk. He wanted to trust Sandra—but he'd trusted Dietrich once, too. And that had cost him and so many others dearly.

Sandra hesitated. "Sure."

"Some evenings eclipse yesterday. Over unlit alleys, trains cross hurried roads. In snowfall, twilight meets amber skies."

Sandra gawked. "Umm, what?"

Wolfgang repeated it. It took four tries before she got it right. There was a good chance she wouldn't get it right when she repeated it to Lieselotte. *If she misses a word or words, will Lieselotte understand?*

"It's a poem I wrote for her," Wolfgang said.

Not quite the truth. Not quite a lie.

She arched her eyebrows in an *okay* way. Wolfgang thanked her and left her to give Sandra her treasured time with her father. He returned to Eckhart's parents' house, doing all he could to earn his keep. He helped with housework, washed and dried dishes with Eckhart. Tried to keep everyone calm as they waited for Bastian's return. Trude had baked a cake for him, and his mother had made his favorite meal, *Sauerbraten*. Eckhart and Wolfgang drove to the train station in Eckhart's parents' Trabant.

They leaned on the hood, waiting for the train. All the people waiting for the trains would ultimately head in one direction: East.

The train Bastian was supposed to be on pulled into the station, squealing to a stop.

"I don't want to stay in East Berlin," Eckhart said.

"Me, neither," Wolfgang said, relieved he hadn't had to bring it up.

"I also don't want to go back to prison."

Wolfgang gave a short, pained laugh—more of a breath than a sound. "Nor I."

"Next time, I'm getting over that wall. Or I die trying." He turned to look at Wolfgang.

Its meaning was clear. Eckhart's attempt would be all-in. If Wolfgang wasn't prepared to die, he had to find and develop his own plan. But there was no need. Wolfgang had no desire to be taken alive. Patrick Henry's words echoed: "Give me liberty or give me death!" Nearly two centuries later, a new generation of a different nation had taken up that creed.

"Escape or die trying," Wolfgang said.

Eckhart nodded, then watched for his brother. Bastian stood out in the crowd as he scouted for his ride. Eckhart waved. Bastian hurried toward them. Bastian had always been bulky, but now he'd lost all his muscle—a shell of the man Wolfgang remembered. His face had weathered and wrinkled, looking a decade older since Wolfgang had last seen him.

Eckhart and Bastian embraced like never before. Their bickering often made it seem like they hated each other, like fists might fly—but this hug revealed the depths of their love. In time, they'd return to that antagonistic competitiveness—one always rooted in love. But right now, neither wanted to break that hug.

Wolfgang stood a short distance away, unsure if he belonged. When they broke away, Bastian hugged him—catching Wolfgang off guard.

"Get me home, boys," Bastian ordered.

Wolfgang offered the passenger seat to Bastian, but he declined, stating he wanted to sprawl out in the back. On the short drive to his parents' house, Bastian asked the same questions Eckhart and Wolfgang had discussed days ago.

Everyone had a reason to hate Dietrich. But for Bastian and Trude, his betrayal had cost them their child. *If Bastian found out that it was Dietrich, would it be beyond the realm of realistic possibility that he would kill him?*

Bastian didn't mention his child, and Wolfgang didn't dare broach the subject. Eckhart refrained from telling Bastian the truth about Dietrich. Not out of forgiveness for what Dietrich had done and not to save his life, but to keep Bastian out of prison. He was wise enough to know that if Bastian found out, he would kill Dietrich. *And who could blame him?*

The plan had been to surprise Bastian when he walked into the house, but Trude couldn't wait that long. She rushed out the door, throwing herself into his arms before he could get out of the car. A tangle of limbs clattered against the car door. Kissing. Feeling. Crying. Bastian wanted to carry her into the house, but he lacked the strength. Instead, they held each other as they walked toward the house.

Inside, his mother and father hugged him. But Bastian had eyes on the modest spread, and everyone agreed questions could wait until he filled his stomach. He ate and ate and ate, talked a bit, and then kept eating.

"Do you have updates on any of the others?" Eckhart asked him.

Bastian's mood shifted. His eyes lowered to the table. "They sent Conrad and Matthias to the uranium mines."

Everyone at the table lowered their heads in a moment of silence. Bastian was fortunate he hadn't been sent there. It was one of the most grueling jobs. Prisoners were forced into radioactive mines, contributing to the Soviet nuclear program. Most died within months from radiation poisoning, collapsed lungs, and exhaustion.

"You three were in Hohenschönhausen?" Bastian asked Eckhart.

"Us three?" Eckhart asked.

Bastian nodded as he forked a piece of cake into his mouth. "Yes. You, Wolfgang, and Dietrich."

"Yes, that's right," Eckhart said.

"Is Dietrich out?"

Eckhart looked to Wolfgang for help.

"We haven't seen him yet," Wolfgang said.

Eckhart didn't chance a glance at Trude, knowing his brother would pick up on it. A loaded moment followed, one where it was unclear if Trude would tell the truth. She knew it—carried that burden. But Trude knew her husband—and the wrath the truth would unleash.

Bastian's energy depleted rapidly. No surprise. He thanked everyone, and he and Trude disappeared upstairs.

"Let's go for a drink," Eckhart suggested to Wolfgang.

Wolfgang followed Eckhart outside. They could have taken the Trabi, but both were more than willing to walk in the brisk air. They'd never take that for granted again. Besides, the Trabant was notoriously bad in cold weather. After twenty-three months in an eight-square-foot cell, the neighborhood felt like the size of a country.

They went to the Copper Cellar—the pub they had frequented with Dietrich. *Did Eckhart bring us here hoping to see Dietrich? And if we see him, what does he plan on doing? What will I do??*

But fortunately, Wolfgang didn't have to find out, because Dietrich wasn't there. The beer sat heavy in his stomach, and after one stein, they strolled along the Spree.

"It's hard to shake that place," Eckhart said.

He didn't need to explain it. Wolfgang knew exactly what he meant.

"I cried flushing the toilet," Eckhart said, laughing through the emotion that sentence caused.

"I know. Last night, I woke and saw a silhouette in the kitchen. I thought I was back in that cell—a guard watching me sleep. Then I realized it was your dad."

Flipping a light switch, flushing a toilet, choosing when to eat, when to sleep. In prison, they had had power over nothing. Control over nothing. But it was the paranoia that was so hard to shake. The thought that everything they said was being heard.

"And I worry …" Eckhart said, trailing off before he had finished.

"Worry about what?" Wolfgang gently pressed.

"If the person I was before is still there. Or is it just this empty, scared version of him?"

"I feel that, too. I worry that I won't be the person Lieselotte fell in love with." Wolfgang paused. "I don't know if we can be who we were before. But if we don't try, if we don't fight to reclaim them, then they win. And you know what?"

"What?"

"Fuck them. They don't get to win. Not in everything. They can try to break us, scare us, intimidate us, but they don't get to change us."

"Fuck them," Eckhart said, and for the first time, Wolfgang felt something shift. Not fear—something stronger. A hardened resolve.

Some Evenings Eclipse Yesterday

Lieselotte hadn't spoken to Sandra since their dorm days—not even the usual promise to stay in touch. So, when Sandra showed up at her door, Lieselotte was stunned. *Did I give her the address? Or has she tracked me down another way?*

Sandra entered with stiff shoulders and wary eyes, like she expected to be interrogated.

"I saw Wolfgang," she said with no pretense. No emotion behind those words.

"What?" Lieselotte gasped.

Sandra detailed the conversation she'd had. "Then he said a poem."

"A poem?"

"Yes. *Some evenings eclipse yesterday. Over unlit alleys, trains cross hurried roads. In snowfall, twilight meets amber skies.*"

Lieselotte blinked. "Wait—can you say it again?"

She dashed to the kitchen for a pen and asked Sandra to repeat it. After, Lieselotte asked a dozen follow-up questions. How did he look? Where was he living? Did he say what had happened?

"He looked exhausted. Rail thin. Beaten down. His eyes were sad."

Each word struck Lieselotte like a blow. But that last sentence shattered her. *His eyes were sad.* They'd never looked sad before. They'd always gleamed with joy, with mischief, with a zest for life. A curiosity of the world around him.

Lieselotte thanked Sandra for telling her, offering her something to drink. To stay and catch up. But she declined. As Sandra left, a strange sadness swept over Lieselotte. Sandra had helped her, risked couriering their letters. She had been the vessel that kept her relationship with Wolfgang alive. Above all, she'd been loyal—and they'd never truly been friends.

Afterward, she sat at the kitchen table reading Wolfgang's "poem." She read it a half dozen times—silently and out loud. Years of reading Wolfgang's hidden messages kicked in.

SEE YOU AT CHRISTMAS.

The same time and place from when we met Christmas Eve 1962.

Though the idea of seeing him sent a current of electricity through her body, it also cast a rock of worry in her gut. *Isn't it too soon to risk a visit?*

But as November gave way to December, each day her excitement grew. The way a child's excitement grows as Christmas approaches. December blurred by. Work became a fog. Sleep came in fragments. Only walks with Anneliese and her camera brought clarity. Anneliese listened, gave feedback, but her eyes filled with worry that Lieselotte would once again have her heart broken. That she'd be standing there waiting and, once again, he wouldn't come. There was nothing Anneliese could say that Lieselotte hadn't considered.

On Christmas Eve, she spent the day with Anneliese's family. She had plans to travel to her mother's on Christmas Day afternoon. The wholesome family, conversations, and games would be a much-needed distraction.

At nine she left, stopping at her apartment for her bag and to change her shoes. It was below freezing and foggy, giving the Christmas Eve night a menacing tone. As she gazed upon the storm drain, it had almost a mythical presence to it. Like the wardrobe leading to Narnia. She climbed down. Then went straight, followed by a right, another straightaway, before taking the sharp left leading to the overflow outlet.

But there was no silhouette waiting for her. No voice whispering her name.

No. This isn't happening again. No. Please. No.

Is this a repeat of 2 January 1963? How long will I stand and foolishly wait? An hour? Two? Until dawn?

But the sharp splatter of boots cutting through the water carried from beyond the grates.

Wolfgang.

They both lunged, fingers clawing for purchase through the bars. The rust was gone—replaced with stronger steel, fresh bolts, and concrete. When her fingertip grazed his cheek, she choked back a sob.

He's real.

He stared at her as if afraid she might vanish. Taking her in. This moment seemed impossible.

"Tell me everything," she said.

"I will. But first, let me look at you." He stared into her eyes and she into his. "I saw you every single day. It felt so real … but standing here, I realize my imagination never even came close."

Lieselotte smiled, then drew two glasses and a bottle of *Riesling* from her bag.

"Christmas tradition," she whispered.

Wolfgang smiled. She poured them carefully, sliding one toward the bars and slipping a straw into Wolfgang's so it could fit through the screen. The small crack she had been able to fit the glass through last time had been sealed. Between sips of *Riesling*, Wolfgang shared fragments from after prison—the incredible gift of his new glasses that had just arrived—and during prison—what he could piece together from the fog. Father Langer. The cell beside him holding Eckhart. Bastian and Trude's stolen child. But not that fateful night in January. Not yet. He knew she would ask. But every time he had to tell the truth about Dietrich's betrayal, it destroyed him all over again.

"What happened that night, Wolfgang?"

"It was Dietrich."

He told her everything. She couldn't believe it. It showed in her eyes. *How can Sandra possess so much loyalty and courage, yet one of my best friends lack it?*

"The Stasi must have something on him," Lieselotte said.

Wolfgang nodded. "He's gay."

She understood how that could make a person turn desperate. It wasn't just societal suicide, it was imprisonment. That injustice wasn't just in East Germany, but all over the world.

"And you? Tell me everything," Wolfgang said.

As she listed off all that had happened since 2 January 1963, even in the dark, the sadness in his eyes was visible. All the memories and moments she had experienced that he wished he could have been there for. All the memories and moments they should have had together.

She detailed her job, the progress she'd made and the respect she'd garnered. Her job had brought her back to Paris, and she'd stopped at the Givre Strudel.

"I have been thinking, Wolfgang. About us …"

Wolfgang readied himself the best he could for the news he had expected to hear. It was only natural that she had moved on. It'd been so long. He'd vanished without a trace. She was a beautiful woman with a brilliant mind. Of course, she'd found someone new.

"I don't want to be apart from you. Not a moment longer," she said.

He gasped with relief. It wasn't what he had expected. For how righteous he wanted to be, every cell in his body longed to be with her.

"I want to move to the East," she said.

Wolfgang recoiled. "No … no. You can't. You can't give up everything for me, Lieselotte."

"It's the only way."

"I'm not content staying here. Eckhart and I … we're trying again."

Lieselotte gripped the grate with her fingertips, rising onto her tippy toes to see him better. "Have you seen the Wall? Every weak point I thought I had found has been reinforced. The Wall is thicker. Taller. Stronger. More guards. More deterrents in place. You'll never make it through, never make it over."

Emotion curdled in her throat at the thought of him risking it again. The prospect of him even thinking about escaping terrified her. *What if he is caught again?* They wouldn't send him to prison. They'd either send him to a hard labor camp to work until he died or would execute him.

"Then we go under it," Wolfgang whispered. The idea revealed itself like a cipher.

She stepped back, eyes widening. "Under it? A tunnel?"

Wolfgang nodded, resolve stirring. "Yes. Exactly that. A tunnel."

"That would take months. Maybe even years."

Wolfgang gave a grave nod. Yes, it would. If it were just him and Eckhart, it would take longer than that. They'd have primitive supplies. Nothing but a shovel. So many dangers and variables to even consider them all.

"We'll ask Bastian and Trude," Wolfgang said.

"Be careful with who you trust," she said.

"We need people to help dig."

"Yes, but what if Dietrich wasn't the only spy?"

She hated to say those words, but they were words Wolfgang had considered. Those twenty-three months in Hohenschönhausen had given him time to consider everything.

"Bastian and Trude, we can trust. They took their child. Emilia and Franco, too."

Lieselotte considered it, thinking it over. "What if I help?"

"Help? How? You can't cross into the East. Even if you could, I wouldn't let you risk that."

"No, not in the East. In the West. If I help dig. There are so many people who want to help. We could … I don't know. Meet in the middle?"

Wolfgang thought on it. "We'd have to line it up perfectly. And I mean perfectly."

Lieselotte smirked. "Good thing you're an engineer."

Wolfgang smiled back. Seeing her smile meant everything. "I don't think I can risk meeting you here again. I will need to lie low."

"Agreed. As much as I love seeing you, this is the last time."

Silence followed. The finality of it—the unknown length of time it implied—settled like a weight between them. They searched every space in the grate, desperate to touch, to kiss. But like the Wall above, it held strong. Unyielding.

"How will we coordinate this? I don't know if Sandra is willing," Lieselotte said.

They traded ideas, only to find flaws in every one. Writing a note in a bottle and throwing it over the Wall. Wolfgang would have to get close to the Wall to throw something over. The VoPos might arrest him, especially if they saw him throw something. They considered trying to find a contact who transferred into West and East Berlin, but they quickly shut that down as it meant putting trust in a potential stranger. Given Wolfgang's arrest, the Stasi would never allow contact with anyone in the West. Mail was out of the question.

"Flashlight signals?" Lieselotte asked.

"We'd have to keep it simple."

"Coordinates," she said.

He nodded. "Where can we both see the light?"

"By the Spree, near the woods for you. Treptower? I don't need to worry about being concealed."

"Treptower works."

"Okay. When?"

"1st March."

Lieselotte didn't reply. March was so far away.

"I know," Wolfgang said. "But the ground's frozen, anyway. Eckhart and I need time—to recruit, to find a place to live, to work. We can't rush any of it."

"No, I know. 1st March, 10 p.m." Lieselotte sensed it was getting late. "You need to get going."

"I know, but I don't want to."

Foreheads resting on the cold grate, they closed their eyes. Willing the grate to vanish. But when they opened their eyes, it was just as unpassable as it had been.

Wolfgang stepped back from the grate, eyes fixed on Lieselotte. "I let open vivid eyes yearn over you. Forever."

Lieselotte gazed as Wolfgang disappeared into the shadows and decoded his final message.

I Let Open Vivid Eyes Yearn Over You. Forever.

I love you forever.

Difficult, Not Impossible

After seeing her, Wolfgang knew one thing for certain: he had to get out of East Berlin. The idea of staying here for any length of time made a different kind of claustrophobia set in—worse than the prison.

Wolfgang and Eckhart needed to find jobs and a place to live. They couldn't expect Eckhart's parents to feed and house them. Wolfgang was leery of visiting his parents. He didn't want to have the conversation with his father about conformity.

Work was nearly impossible to find. Most employers blacklisted anyone with a subversive past. Those who hired them offered only soul-crushing, hard labor. After a dozen rejections, Wolfgang and Eckhart finally found nighttime jobs at a cemetery.

The same stigma followed them into the housing market. To save money, they moved into a small apartment in the Lichtenberg district, an area filled with aging, neglected buildings. Theirs was an *Altbau*. It was in poor disrepair—cracked walls, peeling wallpaper, and unreliable heat. Water stains blotted the ceiling. A single lightbulb hung in the living room, casting a yellow hue on the drab furniture and scuffed linoleum. It was a modest improvement from their cells at Hohenschönhausen.

Their duties at the cemetery comprised patrolling for trespassers, clearing debris, inspecting headstones, maintaining paths—and, most unsettling, digging graves. Apart from that last task, Wolfgang didn't loathe the work. Maybe because he knew it was temporary. The constant reminder of death was all around them. An omen from the Stasi of what awaited should they not toe the line.

Eckhart spent a lot of time at his parents' house or the apartment Bastian and Trude had moved into. They always invited Wolfgang, and sometimes he'd tag along, but most often, he politely declined. He had trouble staying inside his dark, cramped apartment. After twenty-three months of solitary confinement, he wanted to spend as much time as possible outdoors. He needed the crisp winter air to burn his nostrils and fill his lungs.

On a Saturday afternoon walk, he approached Treptower when a voice called out his name. He didn't turn to look. He knew who had spoken. Wolfgang bit the inside of his lip and turned. Dietrich rushed up and hugged him. *Judas betrayed with a kiss—Dietrich a hug.* Wolfgang's body went rigid, a cold revulsion creeping down his spine.

"When did you get out?" he asked.

As if he didn't know. *How can he lie so easily? Look me in the eye, make all those promises, and show nothing?* No shame. No hesitation. No guilt.

Wolfgang told him, trying to keep emotion out of his voice. Trying to sound normal, whatever that sounded like. But what Wolfgang had sounded like before his sentence in prison, he couldn't remember. He was a changed man. *How could I not be?*

"I was released, too. They told me West Germany bought my freedom—but didn't pay enough for me to be allowed to leave," Dietrich said.

Wolfgang bit his lip harder, ignoring the pain and taste of blood. Dietrich, who had over two years to reflect on what he'd done, had decided to lie.

Wolfgang couldn't speak. He kept his hands clenched in his pocket.

"We were betrayed, Wolfgang," he said. "How else would they have been there?"

Internally, Wolfgang was ready to explode. A tear-filled rage that had reduced his inner monologue to two questions: *How could you do this? Why would you do this?*

But he couldn't let Dietrich know—not yet. The Stasi had sent him to keep tabs. If Wolfgang ousted him, then the Stasi would send someone else. Someone Wolfgang didn't know. This was an advantage. He couldn't let his anger or thirst for revenge squander it.

"That's the only explanation," Wolfgang said.

"Do you have any idea who?"

For the first time, Dietrich's tell appeared. The physical cue he was lying. It was the fraction of a second glance down at the ground when he lied. *Had that tell always been there? Or can I only spot it now that I know the truth?*

Wolfgang shook his head. "It could have been anyone."

"Have you heard from the others?" Dietrich asked.

More than likely the Stasi had alerted Dietrich that Wolfgang, Eckhart, and the others had been freed. Told him that Eckhart and Wolfgang worked and lived together.

So, Wolfgang told him—about the long prison sentences, about Bastian and Trude's child, about Conrad's death, the Fischer suicides, the Schneider family. The price they all paid. He watched Dietrich's face for any flicker of remorse. And it was there. He looked horrified and saddened at everything he heard. *But is that pure sorrow? Is it tainted with guilt? Or is he acting?* He'd hidden his sexuality from the world, mastered showing only what he had wanted to show. *Is he doing that now?* Wolfgang went silent, letting Dietrich stew with all that suffering he had caused.

"So, what's next?" Dietrich asked.

"What do you mean?"

Dietrich looked around, then stepped closer to Wolfgang. "I still want out. Don't you?"

Wolfgang scrutinized everything Dietrich did. Had he taken a step closer because he was bugged? Because someone was listening—waiting for proof that Wolfgang hadn't reformed? Or was it a tool to disarm Wolfgang? Make him feel safe?

Wolfgang shook his head. "No. It was foolish to try. It cost me two years of my life."

"Wait? You're done? How can that be? You were so adamant about escaping."

He wanted to scream, "That was before you ratted me out!" But he withheld. He collected himself. "Listen, Dietrich. My time in there, it made me do a lot of thinking. I have qualms, but nothing I'm willing to rot in prison for. I have to accept."

"Accept what?"

"That twenty years ago, two superpowers drew a line through Germany—and I ended up on the wrong side."

"What about Lieselotte?"

Wolfgang curled his hand into a fist. Thankfully, it stayed hidden in his pocket. Dietrich had told Schwarzfuchs and the Stasi everything about Wolfgang and Lieselotte. Put her at risk. It was how Schwarzfuchs knew she had given him the money. And if Lieselotte had come to East Berlin, she would have been arrested for it.

"I'll always love her. But fate has steered us different ways," Wolfgang stated.

Dietrich shook his head, fighting his disappointment. *Is he acting disappointed, or is he truly disappointed because he has nothing to report to the Stasi?* Sure, his previous efforts led to the arrest of fourteen people. Granted him some honors and privileges with the Stasi. Maybe no longer just an informal collaborator, but now a "Special Purpose Informant"—someone with enemy contact. Maybe even awarded the *Medaille für Treue Dienste*, the East German medal for loyal service. If Dietrich didn't deliver new information, information the Stasi deemed useful, he would find himself in a prison cell, too.

When you make a deal with the devil, the devil always wins. And Dietrich had shaken his hand with both eyes open.

"And the others? Eckhart? He's content?" Dietrich asked.

"As far as I know, yes."

Dietrich nodded, realizing this conversation had run its course. "Tell him I'm out. I'd love to reconnect with you both. Get a beer, yeah?"

"Sounds great."

They exchanged addresses. Wolfgang didn't care—Dietrich knowing meant nothing. The Stasi already did.

"It's great to see you," Dietrich said before he turned and headed out of the park.

Wolfgang elected to keep his run-in with Dietrich to himself. Eckhart's decision regarding Dietrich was to forget his existence. He didn't talk about the arrest anymore. Didn't talk about any of the thousands of memories the three of them had had. Though he had wanted that to be true, there was no way to erase all that. That pain, hurt, and betrayal still ate at him—no matter how deeply he tried to bury it.

As January's freeze gave way to February's false spring, Wolfgang broached the subject with Eckhart he and Lieselotte had discussed on Christmas Eve. The timing seemed right after a month of job-and-apartment searching. The cemetery was eerie and quiet, apart from the wind whistling through the trees. As if a cemetery needed any help to be creepy.

He and Eckhart toiled, digging a grave. They'd been at it for a while, but were only halfway to the standard six-foot depth. Wolfgang rested, the gloves doing little to stop blisters spreading along the palms of his hands. He was both sweating and freezing.

"I have an idea," Wolfgang said.

187

"Yeah, what's that?" Eckhart asked, still shoveling. "Split the cost of a bulldozer?"

"On how to escape."

Eckhart stopped shoveling and faced Wolfgang. Seeing how fortified the Wall had grown had demoralized him. The sheer size of it. The looming height. The armed guards, the watchtowers, the menacing dogs, and the harsh spotlights. And the unsubstantiated rumors of what lay on the other side of the Wall in the area known as no-man's-land. Rumors of land mines and the menacing "Stalin's Lawn"—a long strip of nails to greet anyone who made it over the Wall. Meant to cripple escapees on impact.

"What is it?" Eckhart asked.

"A tunnel," Wolfgang said.

"A tunnel?" Eckhart repeated, his voice filled with incredulity. "Wolfgang, do you know how long it takes us to dig a single grave?"

"I do."

"Okay. Then multiply that by, like, a million."

"It won't be quick. It won't be easy. But it'll be worth it. We either dig or rot away here. Do this for fifty years."

Eckhart considered it, and even that terrified him. It didn't take much contemplation to come up with a dozen things that could go wrong.

"You've seen the Wall," Wolfgang said. "It's a monster now. There's no driving a truck through that anymore. They'll have tire strips. They've limited the amount of straightaways leading to the Wall to prevent vehicles from being able to reach high speeds. It's reinforced with steel. Guard towers."

Eckhart rubbed at his chin. "Can't go through it. Can't go over it."

"Exactly. All those dangers will be above."

"But you and me. That could take years. I don't want to wait that long. I can't wait that long."

"Me, neither. It's why we need more people."

Eckhart gave him a look of disbelief and pity. Like Wolfgang was a naïve child. "If we can't trust our best friend, how can we trust anybody?"

Though he hadn't used Dietrich's name, it was the first time he'd mentioned him in months.

"Because there are people out there who are just as desperate as us."

"And there are people who are pretending to be."

That was true. Wolfgang couldn't refute that.

"What about Bastian and Trude?" Wolfgang asked.

Eckhart shrugged. "I don't know. I think they're still holding out hope that they can find their …"

He didn't finish. As he neared the end of that sentence, his voice had given out. Wolfgang wouldn't make him finish it.

"There's a spot for them, if they want it," Wolfgang said. "Lieselotte is going to help dig."

Eckhart scrunched his forehead. "What? How?"

"In the West. With Anneliese and others. They'll have more manpower, better supplies."

"And meet up in the middle? That sounds impossible."

Wolfgang smiled. "Difficult. Not impossible."

"And how do we coordinate that? Not like we can call her."

Wolfgang explained the 1 March meeting and using Morse code signaled by flashlights to designate coordinates.

"Damn, you've made a compelling case," Eckhart said with a smile.

"There's a lot to do before we dig. We need to find an abandoned building."

"To dig through the floor. Can't dig a hole out in the street."

"Exactly."

"Fuck it. I'm in."

Eckhart held out his hand to shake. Wolfgang shook it.

"We take this to the grave," Eckhart quipped.

Wolfgang chuckled. A little dark humor was good for the soul.

"What about the others? From before?" Eckhart asked.

Wolfgang shrugged. "Maybe Fresa. The Schneiders won't leave without their children."

"We know the Stasi are watching us. That means they're watching them. The more of the group we invite, the more attention we draw. It's dangerous to meet with them. Bastian and Trude … that's my family. It makes sense I would see them. But the others?"

"Emilia and Franco. They're in."

Eckhart nodded in agreement.

Way back before they had tried to escape, they had understood that within their group of fifteen, there were subgroups with their own loyalties. The same was true now. It was too dangerous to offer any of the others in the group a second chance at escape.

"But that poses a brand-new set of problems," Wolfgang said. "Everyone in that group, except for *him*, proved to be trustworthy.

Now we have to risk it again. The idea of gambling on the wrong option terrifies me."

"It should," Eckhart said. "If we choose wrong, we're fucked."

Permission Not Required

After many sleepless nights replaying her promise to Wolfgang, Lieselotte finally settled on an idea—either madness or brilliance—and one her boss would have to judge. Tom Jackson, an American with prematurely graying hair and a clean-shaven face, had been living in West Berlin since the Wall had gone up. The Associated Press had wanted boots on the ground in the most watched city in the world. Lieselotte had made a minor name for herself. Tom had liked a few of her photographs and thought her prose showed promise.

The layout of the Associated Press building was broken into two main areas: the main newsroom and the telecommunications area. Telephones rang. Typewriters clacked. People moved at a frenetic pace. Tom's office was in a glass-walled room. Lieselotte knocked on the door.

"Miss Reisinger, come in," he said in English. He spoke a bit of German, but Lieselotte communicated in his native tongue.

He didn't rise from his desk, the top of which was cluttered with papers, an ashtray filled with cigarette butts, and a telephone. The room reeked of cigarettes and whiskey—his antidote to deadlines, Cold War anxiety, and existential dread. He had an open-door policy; but he was an incredibly busy man. So, she had to make this count.

"What can I do for you?" he asked.

"I have a story idea," she said.

"Okay …" he said, holding the word.

"I want to document a tunnel escape from East Berlin."

Tom sat up in his chair, ending his multitasking. "Document how?"

"Photograph it. Write about it. Exclusive interviews after. Obviously, nothing can go to print until after the escape."

"How do you plan on documenting it? I doubt they'd allow you into East Berlin. Even if they did, aiding in an escape could land you in prison."

"I help dig here in West Berlin," she said.

Tom nodded to shut the door. She did so.

"You know the West Berlin government doesn't condone aiding in escape attempts," Tom said.

"I do."

"But you don't give a shit."

"None whatsoever."

Tom smiled. Exactly what he looked for in a reporter. Someone who chased the story.

"Is this personal?"

She could lie. She should. But she knew she'd fail. Tom had a great bullshit detector. He knew when a reporter truly had a story or if they had just said they had one to save their ass.

"Yes."

"That's not a good mix."

"I know. My father warned me. He was a photographer, too—said our job is to watch like a bird on a wire."

"Exactly."

"My father was killed in Berlin in 1953. During the protests. This was personal for me long before today. My boyfriend is in East Berlin. The Stasi arrested him in January 1963. They held him in prison without a trial for two years. And do you know what he said the moment he was released? That he wanted to try again."

Tom considered it. "I assume because you're telling me about this, you want something from the A.P.?"

"We'll need supplies—tools, food, manpower. I want the A.P. to fund it."

Tom huffed. "Quite the set of balls on you, Miss."

Lieselotte smirked. "Picture the headlines. And the photographs."

"I'm kind of imagining the lawsuits right now. Not to mention how pissed off Mayor Brandt will be."

Lieselotte noted the picture of Tom and his family on the wall behind him. His wife and children. All smiles and love.

"If she were on the other side, what would you do?" she asked.

Tom didn't hesitate. "The same thing you're doing."

"It's not just my boyfriend. There are thousands of people trapped over there, desperate to break free. I want to show the grime, the sweat, the dirt. The lengths people are willing to go through to leave East Germany. Those photographs will do more damage to communism than any bomb can. It's how they lose, and we win."

Tom studied her, weighing his choice. "Alright, we have a deal. But I assure you this is mutual assured destruction. We both go down. Think of that. For me, I go back to America. Get a job selling beer at Green Bay Packers games. For you, it's the end of your journalism career."

"I understand the risks and I accept them."

"Very well."

Tom stood and offered his hand. Lieselotte shook it.

It had gone better than she had hoped. The rest of the day took forever. Now that she had secured the funds, every second felt wasted. She ached to plunge a shovel into the earth. A ceremonial first step of sorts. But she had to wait until 1 March and her across-the-Spree meeting with Wolfgang.

At five, she left the office to meet Anneliese at the Ku'damm. Anneliese had grown to love American food—particularly burgers and fries, so she had elected to meet at Rosie's Diner—the same counter where Lieselotte and Wolfgang had first crossed from friends to something more.

"So, you said you had big news?" Anneliese said, rather annoyed that Lieselotte hadn't just come out with it.

"Oh, right. Sorry," Lieselotte said, before detailing her meeting with Tom.

"Are you serious?"

Lieselotte nodded, unable and unwilling to hide her smile.

Anneliese returned it and leaned toward her. "I want in! What do we do?"

"We need to be selective. There will be plenty who want to help, but the Stasi will have agents here in the West. Trying to learn of escape plans."

"Stasi? Here? In the West?"

"Of course. It's smart," Lieselotte answered. Send young adults into crowds of protestors to learn about escape attempts, identify subversive people, and gathering spots for illegal activities.

Anneliese's eyes flicked to the other tables. Scrutinizing the other patrons, wondering if there was a spy in their midst right now.

"We need to find a location to dig. A defunct, abandoned building," Lieselotte said.

"Or permission from the homeowner to dig up their basement."

True. Though Lieselotte didn't want to rely on someone's blessing to destroy their home. There were many sympathetic people to the plight of East Germans, but that sympathy had a limit. Usually right around destruction of personal property.

They stayed for dinner, ordered cheeseburgers and fries, and left once the baskets held nothing but grease-stained paper.

"Did Wolfgang say how Eckhart is doing?" Anneliese asked.

"He's as adamant about leaving as Wolfgang."

That made Anneliese smile. "No news on his nephew?"

Lieselotte shook her head.

"That's so terribly sad," Anneliese said.

They strolled Ku'damm, never taking for granted the freedom they had here in the West. It was the vibrant heart of the city. The embodiment of resilience, of prosperity, of capitalism.

"So, do we look for a spot?" Anneliese asked.

"It'll be much harder for them to find one, so we will have to wait until they give us the coordinates. Then we'll look based on that."

Anneliese nodded, but it was clear she, too, was not a fan of waiting. "My brother and his friends can help us."

"Do you trust them?

"Trust my brother's friends? Not at all." She laughed. "But in this, yes."

"When can we meet with them?" Lieselotte asked.

"Well, the little shit is out tonight. At a beer hall not far from here."

"You want to go now?"

"What's that saying? No time like the present." She cast a devious smirk.

Lieselotte rolled her eyes, then followed Anneliese. Music—both German and American—wafted out of clubs. Then, a short walk later, the sound of raucous laughter burst out from inside a beer hall. Wooden beams crisscrossed a low ceiling above long, worn tables and sturdy benches. The air was a pleasant blend of tobacco smoke, yeasty beer, and fried potatoes and meats. A steady hum of conversation, interjected with fits of laughter, clinking *steins*, and the scrape of knives and forks on plates rose through the room.

Anneliese's brother looked like his sister, having the same vibrant blond hair and striking blue eyes, but with a sharp, masculine jawline. His eyes lit up—then fell into a scowl, as if the record had scratched mid-party. Anneliese approached him. She grabbed his *stein* of beer and took a swig. His friends gawked at the two attractive women, as if he had summoned them to his side.

"What the hell are you doing here?" he asked.

"Same as you. Enjoying the night," his sister replied.

"Well, like, can you enjoy it somewhere else?"

"Well, like, am I embarrassing you in front of your lady friends? Oh, wait. There's none here."

"Ha. Ha. Ha."

"Hey, Petyr," Lieselotte said.

Petyr gave Lieselotte a quick smile, then scowled when his eyes flicked back to his sister.

"We're here because I asked to see you. All of you, actually," Lieselotte said, scanning the five men at the table and realizing she knew none of them.

"Don't be rude," Anneliese said to Petyr. "Tell us who your friends are."

Petyr sighed and introduced them: Mikael, Rory, Johan, George, and Hansel. They all had similar hair styles—Beatle-style mop tops—popular among the counterculture youth. They were dressed in turtlenecks or sweaters and straight-cut jeans, except Rory, who wore a military surplus jacket. George tapped a rhythm on the table with his fingers, creating his own soundtrack. Mikael adjusted his glasses and nodded politely, his posture more serious than the others. Johan towered over them, but stood with shoulders sunken inward, like he felt guilty for taking up so much space. Hansel fiddled with his change, glancing nervously at the two attractive women.

Lieselotte smiled politely, then addressed them. "My boyfriend and a small group of East Berliners are going to dig a tunnel to try to escape. I am going to help them by digging a tunnel here in West Berlin that connects with theirs."

She paused, noticing how their shoulders slumped at "boyfriend" and stiffened again at "escape." Though no one said it, their eyes made quick glances at Petyr, as if to say, *What the hell have you gotten us into?*

"What I am asking," Lieselotte continued, "is for help digging the tunnel."

The men looked at each other, hoping one of them would say what they were all thinking. Even Petyr shot a glare at his sister for coming to his friends with such a request.

"Imagine we were on the other side," Anneliese said. "Desperate. Risking our lives. Wouldn't you hope someone, somewhere, chose courage over comfort—even if there was nothing in it for them?"

Petyr leaned on the table, considering it.

"Have you been at any of the protests?" Lieselotte asked them. "At Bernauer Straße or Checkpoint Charlie or the Brandenburg Gate?"

The men nodded—some timidly, others proudly.

"This is your chance to make a difference. You can hold your signs and shout slogans until your voice is hoarse. But this ... this will make a real difference."

"Where are you digging?" Petyr asked.

"To be determined."

"Can you give us ... them time to think it over?" Petyr asked.

"No," Anneliese shot back.

"No?"

"If you won't help, we need to find people who will," Anneliese said. "The clock is ticking. Every moment counts. Every day an escape gets more difficult, encroaching further toward becoming impossible. They tried once before. They were arrested and spent twenty-three months in prison, and they're ready, willing to risk another chance. What are you willing to risk?"

The men exchanged uneasy glances. It was quite the sight to see bulky grown men intimidated by a woman. Anneliese was a lioness, and they would hear her roar.

"You're a pain in the ass," Petyr said.

"But you love me anyway," Anneliese said.

Petyr smirked. "Something like that." He puffed. "Alright, I'm in."

Rory raised his beer. "First women to talk to me in weeks, and it's to dig a tunnel. What a boost to my ego. I'm in."

Hansel looked around, waiting to join the majority. George tapped a rhythm on the table, then paused, like the start of a song. "The times really are changing, huh?" he said. "I'm in."

"I could shout for change until my voice gives out, or I could pick up a shovel," Mikael said.

Johan, the tallest of the group, shyly nodded. Then Hansel raised his hand, as if waiting for permission to speak. Anneliese nodded to do so.

"I'm in," he whispered.

"Just don't expect us to whistle while we work," Rory said.

"You are pretty short," George said.

"What? You're like half an inch taller than me," Rory said.

"Great. I'll be in touch with the details," Anneliese said, squeezing Petyr's cheek. She tore off a piece of the pretzel on his plate. Lieselotte gave a sheepish smile, a silent apology for his sister's brashness.

As they stepped outside, buttoning their coats, she turned to her best friend, smiling. "You are quite scary."

"The Dead Won't Talk"

Wolfgang and Eckhart stopped by Bastian and Trude's cramped apartment in Prenzlauer Berg. Like their own place, it lacked a private toilet or bath—only a shared toilet on the floor and a bathtub in the basement. So often, Wolfgang, caked in dirt and sweat, just wanted to clean or relax in a hot bath, only to find a long line.

Bastian struggled to find work and was still recovering from the back-breaking labor of the work camp. Wolfgang often wondered what was worse—wasting away in a cell or working until your body gave out under an open sky.

Trude found work at a state-run laundry serving hospitals and military barracks. The air was thick and hot from steaming presses. The wages were pitiful. She could trust no one. Each person who stopped in could be an informant. But she had no choice.

She greeted Wolfgang and Eckhart with a hug and poured them glasses of water. Bastian came from out of their bedroom, groaning.

"It's early for a visit. Are you expecting breakfast?" he asked.

"Wanted to know if you two wanted to go for a walk. Sun's out for once," Eckhart said.

Even under a sky that could generously be called partly cloudy, Bastian knew there was a reason. He and Trude understood—whatever Eckhart and Wolfgang had to say, they couldn't say it here. Their apartment was certainly bugged.

Trude bundled up in her coat and scarf and joined her husband in following Eckhart and Wolfgang outside. Snow and slush blanketed the ground.

Bastian led them to Berlin's oldest park, Volkspark Friedrichshain, with its winding paths and the Märchenbrunnen— an idyllic fountain lined with sculptures from *Grimms' Fairy Tales* like Hansel and Gretel, Sleeping Beauty, and Little Red Riding Hood. Because it was a less-than-halcyon day, there were few people around.

"So," Bastian said, sitting on the ledge of the fountain.

Eckhart nodded for Wolfgang to speak.

"Eckhart and I are going to try again," he said.

Just hearing that made Trude bring her hand to her mouth in horror. Bastian shook his head in frustration.

"I know," Wolfgang said, "but we've thought this through."

"Yeah? You've thought this through?" Bastian snapped his head up. "You want to end up in a cell again? If that happens, you don't get out. Or maybe you get sixteen-hour days out in a field! There're no magic priests. Not twice," Bastian said.

"We won't get arrested," Eckhart said.

"Yeah? I didn't plan on getting arrested last time, either," Bastian said.

"It's freedom or death," Wolfgang said.

Bastian's shoulders slumped. He saw the resolve in their eyes— his little brother and his best friend weren't bluffing.

"I know you have a reason to stay here," Eckhart said.

No one needed it to be explained further. They had more reason to stay than most.

"It's not that I don't want to get out of here ... God, do I want to." Bastian's voice caught at the end when he found Trude's eyes.

"It's impossible now," she whispered.

"Impossible? No. Improbable? Yes," Wolfgang said.

"We have a good plan. A better plan than even last time," Eckhart added.

Bastian and Trude studied each other to see what they were thinking. Should they even entertain this idea, or had it cost them too much already? They exchanged a look. That was enough.

"Let's hear it," Bastian said.

Wolfgang explained the tunnel, and the help Lieselotte had promised.

"That'll take forever," Bastian said.

Eckhart agreed. "It'll take a shit ton of time. It's why we need more people."

"We misplaced our trust last time, and it cost us," Bastian said.

Eckhart, Wolfgang, and Trude avoided eye contact. They knew who had ratted them out. Bastian did not.

"Only Emilia and Franco can come," Eckhart said.

Trude's expression flickered with sadness. Bastian understood why.

"If we meet with the old group, the number of eyes on us will triple, Trude," Bastian said.

"You'll coordinate," Wolfgang told Trude. "You've been best friends with Emilia since you were three. It won't be odd for you two to talk. But Eckhart and I can't."

"Makes sense," Trude said.

"So, we have two weeks to decide on a location?" Bastian asked.

"It's our goal," Wolfgang said.

If they couldn't find a suitable location, they'd have to postpone that date. But Wolfgang didn't want to. That thought crippled him, filled him with a throbbing tightness in his chest.

"So, we need to find a place where we can dig a tunnel that the Stasi won't find out about. Carry out all that dirt and dispose of it with no one knowing anything about it. Simple enough," Bastian quipped.

"Oh, piss off. We know it's tough," Eckhart said.

"Please don't fight," Trude said.

"No one's fighting," Bastian said. "Just telling my brother he's being an idiot."

Eckhart scoffed. "If you're so smart, find a place!"

Bastian threw his hands up. "Sure. Maybe if we find a place filled with deaf and blind people, then no one will see or hear what we're doing!"

Wolfgang stared, unblinking. "Wait. That's it."

But the two brothers still cursed each other with Trude powerless to stop the quarrel. Their fighting would eventually end and they'd hug it out. But Wolfgang didn't have time for that.

"That's it!" he shouted.

Bastian and Eckhart stopped and looked at Wolfgang, almost offended that he had raised his voice.

"You're right," Bastian said. "I'm sorry, Eckhart."

"Oh, shut up. I started it. I'm sorry," Eckhart said.

Jeez, are they going to fight about who has the right to apologize?

"No," Wolfgang said. "I don't mean that's it. I mean *that's it!*"

When an idea hits, it's hard to contain the excitement long enough to explain it.

"You said the deaf and blind. That they wouldn't be able to hear or see what we're doing," Wolfgang said.

"I don't know if there is a place like that …" Eckhart said, now looking concerned.

"No. But there is a place where the people can't hear or see what we're doing."

"Where?" Trude asked.

"The cemetery."

Wolfgang did not receive the reaction he'd hoped for. No awe, no lightbulb moment—just blank stares.

"No one is around at night," Wolfgang said, looking for Eckhart to back him up on that.

But he only gave a noncommittal shrug. "That's true, but the cemetery is like four blocks from the Wall."

"So, you what? Start digging a grave and just don't stop?" Bastian asked.

Wolfgang shook his head. "A mausoleum. Many are kept locked."

"What about all the dirt?" Trude asked.

"We bury it," Wolfgang said.

It was all the pitch he had at the moment. All the details would have to come later. He let them weigh the idea in loaded silence.

"It's not a bad idea. But damn, that's a long way," Bastian said.

"No doubt," Wolfgang said.

"Okay, Wolfgang. Engineer this for us," Eckhart asked. "Distance. Depth. Number of hours."

Wolfgang considered it, going over it in his head, ignoring the pressure of the three of them watching him think.

The soil near the Wall was a mix of sand, clay, and gravel. Nearer to the Spree, the ground was looser, sandier, making it easier to dig but more prone to collapse. Contrast that to other areas where the ground was a denser clay, making it harder to dig through but less likely to collapse.

"We take about three hours to dig a six-foot grave. To go under the Wall, we'd need at least sixteen feet deep, maybe more, with wooden beams for support. And if we dig one meter wide by one high, we're looking at half a year. Closer to a year, realistically."

A year. Wolfgang swallowed hard. *Can I last that long—knowing that tomorrow is promised to no one?*

"And that's figuring us working eight to ten hours a day every day. No breaks," Eckhart said. "Which we won't be able to do. So, it's definitely closer to a year."

No one had wanted that to be the answer. They wanted something in weeks or days, even though they knew that was not feasible. But the thought of having to dig a tunnel for at least a year was an incredible weight. Every day they dug was another day for the Stasi to find out. Another day for the eyes and ears of their unlimited informants to watch, to listen. Another day away from Lieselotte. Another day his soul eroded in silence.

The Devil's Bargain

An eerie silence clung to the cemetery at night. The graves lay bare, nothing but dirt or mud. Eternal Peace Cemetery held over 6,000 graves and fifty mausoleums. Wolfgang and Eckhart had taken a new route to work, passing within a hundred feet of the Wall before veering toward the cemetery. Wolfgang estimated the distance between wall and Eternal Peace entrance at 1,500 feet.

Eckhart used his key to unlock the padlock on a mausoleum. The chain clattered to the ground. He shouldered the heavy door open; it groaned against the stone.

A dozen crypts lined the corridor, six on either side. The family name etched in the stone archway spelled, *Von Haven Stein.* Wolfgang examined the red marble crypts, noting the names and dates.

"This is where we dig," Eckhart said.

"What about family that comes to pay their respects?" Wolfgang asked.

How would I feel if someone disturbed the resting place of one of my relatives?

"Look at the dates. They've been dead a hundred years. All this dust? No one visits," Eckhart said.

The dust burned Wolfgang's lungs, his eyes watering as a sneeze tore through him. Still, the risk nagged at him. *What if someone comes to pay their respects, only to find the floor dug up?* But nowhere was truly safe—they just had to pick the least dangerous spot, and this was it.

"My idea is we move this marble sarcophagus to dig into the earth," Eckhart said.

"And push it back to hide it?" Wolfgang finished.

"Exactly. It's heavy as shit, though."

Wolfgang surveyed the cramped crypt. Even with just the two of them, space was tight. Adding more hands would only make it worse. The tunnel would be worse still—claustrophobic, suffocating. Maybe they could rig some kind of pulley or bucket chain system to move the dirt out faster.

Excitement surged—they had a location. That alone felt like a victory. But the next step—digging—smothered the thrill. It would be grueling. The mausoleum stood another 500 feet beyond the entrance, pushing the total distance to nearly 2,000 feet. Half a kilometer of dirt to move. In secret.

"If Lieselotte and Anneliese handle most of the digging, that'd help," Eckhart said.

Yes—but the work would be brutal. Suffocating, dangerous. A single mistake could mean a cave-in. *What if Lieselotte gets hurt? Or worse—what if she dies down there? How could I use flashlights to tell her of this risk? The plan, the distance?*

"I need to see her again," Wolfgang said.

"It's too dangerous. For you and her. You know that."

"I have an idea, but it's the dumbest one I've ever had."

Eckhart rolled his eyes. "Great start. Let's hear it."

"I ask Schwarzfuchs for permission."

Eckhart scoffed. Unsure whether to laugh or call Wolfgang stupid. He waited for Wolfgang to elaborate, but when he didn't, he spoke. "Why would he let you?"

"I don't know. I could try to play to his humanity."

"His humanity? He doesn't have any."

"I'll tell him it's to say goodbye. He'll agree to that."

"What? Why?"

"Because he'll want to watch me suffer."

At that, Eckhart saw the rationale in the ask. It wasn't out of a favor for Wolfgang or sympathy. Schwarzfuchs would see an opportunity for the fresh scabs of heartbreak to be ripped open once again. Another form of psychological torment to unleash.

"Okay, even if he agrees, there'll be Stasi agents all around you. It's not like you can talk about any of this," Eckhart reasoned.

"We have our own way of communicating," Wolfgang said.

He'd never told anyone about the ciphers. It was something between him and Lieselotte. He could speak to her in cipher. Or figure that part out if Schwarzfuchs agreed, which even though he told Eckhart he would, he had doubts.

The following morning, Wolfgang approached the Wall. The whole air felt different. Thicker. Colder. Charged with tension.

Two VoPos, one holding the lead of a German Shepherd, marched toward him. The dog snapped its jaws. Wolfgang stopped and lifted his hands.

"Papers!" they shouted.

"I'm not looking to cross. I need to speak with *Hauptmann* Schwarzfuchs," Wolfgang said.

"He is not here," a guard said.

"Can you tell me where to find him?"

"He'll find you."

It's all the guard would say. Wolfgang knew to try to get more information from them would be a futile attempt. It would only aggravate them. So, he refrained and walked away, feeling defeated. The idea that Schwarzfuchs would find him sent an arctic shiver down his spine. He'd summoned the devil—and the devil would answer.

Once he returned to his apartment, he wrote on a scrap piece of paper: *Schwarzfuchs will find me*. He held it up for Eckhart to read and then tore it into three dozen pieces and washed them down the sink.

Neither trusted that their apartment wasn't bugged, so Eckhart was limited to showing his shock with bulging eyes. As they ate dinner, they half expected a knock on the door and to see Schwarzfuchs behind it. But he didn't come that night or the following day. Nor the day that followed.

The anxiety became all-consuming. Wolfgang flinched at shadows, expected Schwarzfuchs around every corner, behind every door. The bastard knew exactly what this suspense would do to him—how dread could be its own kind of punishment.

After four days, Wolfgang doubted the VoPo had forwarded the message. The guards had never asked Wolfgang for his papers. But of course, someone or someones had watched Wolfgang approach the Wall—maybe even Dietrich.

On Friday, Eckhart went to his parents' house for a family dinner. He assured Wolfgang he was invited, but they had done more than enough for him. Instead, he went to the market to pick up his rations of food.

He unlocked the apartment door and stepped inside. He froze. A man sat in the shadows on his couch, puffing on a cigarette.

"*Herr* Kirschke," he said.

Schwarzfuchs rose and tugged the pull chain of the light, turning on the lone lightbulb in the room and casting a muted yellow hue. Wolfgang carried the groceries to the kitchen.

"I understand you were looking for me," Schwarzfuchs said.

Schwarzfuchs looked around the room, as if he hadn't ransacked it. Though maybe he hadn't. Maybe someone else had. Or they already knew everything because Wolfgang had been watched since the moment he was released from prison.

"I see you have acclimated back into life quite well," Schwarzfuchs commented.

"Yes. I am grateful for the second chance," Wolfgang said.

"An unearned second chance."

Wolfgang let the insult pass, refusing the bait. "I am asking for a favor."

Schwarzfuchs laughed, all venom and smoke. "You feel you have earned my favor?"

"No. But I ask it anyway."

Schwarzfuchs respected Wolfgang's honesty and prompted him to continue with a wave of his hand. He lit a fresh Karo cigarette.

"I would like to say goodbye to Lieselotte. Properly. I'm told the state sometimes allows separated family members to see each other at Friedrichstraße."

"Even if that were true, she is not your family. Not even your wife. Not even your girlfriend."

"No, but she meant something to me. I just want the chance to give a final goodbye. It's the closure I need to embrace life here in the East."

Schwarzfuchs puffed his cigarette, holding the presence of a man who looked as though this was his home and Wolfgang was the unexpected, unwelcomed guest.

"Why should I do this?" Schwarzfuchs asked.

"I was foolish to do what I did. It cost me everything. It's time to put that all behind me. I do that with closure. The East needs loyal citizens."

211

Schwarzfuchs laughed. "Please tell me that's not the best you've got."

"This gives you control. You dictate how this plays out. You stand there. Watch. Listen."

"You'd owe me."

"I would."

"And how would you repay that debt?"

"I won't spy on anyone." Wolfgang cut to the chase, knowing what Schwarzfuchs was hinting at.

"Then you have no currency."

"My currency is that I am a cog in the machine. A worker. A body."

Schwarzfuchs took a long drag of his cigarette, growing tired of the conversation.

"*Frau* Reisinger corrupted you severely. How do I know she will not corrupt you again? The space between a woman's thighs has corrupted stronger men than you."

"If she does, you get to throw me in prison for good. I know that intrigues you."

Schwarzfuchs smirked. "You would wager your life?"

"Please."

Schwarzfuchs crossed into the kitchen, opened a drawer, and retrieved a pencil. A shiver ran down Wolfgang's spine: he knew exactly where Wolfgang kept them.

"I can be reasonable when dealing with a reasonable man," he said. "Write to her. Date. Time. Location. I will see that the letter gets to her."

Wolfgang took the pencil, hesitating. There was no way she would believe he had sent a letter if it did not contain a cipher. It was how she had known the letter the Stasi had sent was a fake. But writing with Schwarzfuchs looming over his shoulder was the real challenge. He had to write a cipher, but if it was too bizarre of a sentence, he would comment on it. Schwarzfuchs was cunning. He would figure it out.

"Do you need help writing?" Schwarzfuchs asked.

The hint in his voice was overtly bored. Worried that he would change his mind at any moment, Wolfgang brought the pencil to the paper and wrote. He fought the trembling in his hand. Every word was a risk. But she had to know it was him. He wrote for Lieselotte to meet him on 1 March at 6 p.m. That the Stasi had permitted it. His cipher, when decoded, said, *It's real.*

He handed the sheet of paper to Schwarzfuchs. He read the letter, glancing up at Wolfgang after every paragraph. Studying both the words and the writer. Critiquing with overt skepticism. Wolfgang steadied his emotions, kept eye contact.

"Remember this, *Herr* Kirschke. The state rewards its loyal comrades," he said, waving the letter before pocketing it. He headed for the door, then paused. "You are in my debt now. And I will collect." Schwarzfuchs stepped out and closed the door behind him. Dread growled in Wolfgang's stomach. He'd not only called the devil, he'd made a deal with him.

The Palace of Tears

Lieselotte stared at the letter—the handwriting unmistakably Wolfgang's. She decoded his cipher: *It's real.* But how had he gotten it out—unredacted? That meant the Stasi had read and approved it. 1 March. It was the date they had set to finalize the location. Something must have come up—too complex for Morse code and flashlights. With the Stasi watching, speaking freely was impossible. Wolfgang would've known that. They'd need to speak in cipher. She no longer needed a pencil and paper to decode, but speaking naturally in cipher would test her limits.

As February waned, Lieselotte prepared for the meeting at Friedrichstraße. Anneliese warned her about venturing into East Berlin, fearing her arrest. Lieselotte tried to quell those fears, mentioning the presence of West Berlin police and custom officers, but truth be told, she had those same fears. The letter stated Wolfgang wanted to say goodbye. That part she knew was a lie. She had to play the part of a woman mostly moved on, looking only for that final bit of closure.

Friedrichstraße Station, made of steel and glass, was a major hub between West and East. Nervous travelers stood in lines, watched by the ever-present guards. As Lieselotte approached the terminal, Wolfgang waited for her. Her pulse quickened. Guards strolled the length of the terminal, listening and watching as people said tearful goodbyes. History called it the Palace of Tears.

Every part of her ached to sprint to Wolfgang, to bury herself in his arms, stroke his hair, feel his lips. But she couldn't. Instead, she had to settle for a cold handshake. He shook her hand, his thumb brushing hers.

"*Fraulein,*" said a Stasi officer in a tailored uniform, his smile all teeth, no warmth. "I'm *Hauptmann* Schwarzfuchs. I have been instrumental in rehabilitating *Herr* Kirschke."

Lieselotte gave him a quick glance. Nothing more. No smile. No nod. No handshake.

"You look well," Wolfgang said.

"Thank you. You are well, I hope?" Lieselotte asked.

"Yes. The state has been most generous in allowing me a second chance. I was foolish." Each word rehearsed. A performance for his captor.

Lieselotte forced a smile but wiped it clean. The Stasi knew who she was. Knew that she was adamantly against them. To smile as if she had agreed Wolfgang was foolish to try to escape was against her character and sure to raise suspicion.

"Please, speak as though I'm not here," Schwarzfuchs said.

Impossible.

"So, are you working?" Wolfgang asked.

"I am a photographer and journalist for the Associated Press in West Berlin. And you?"

"I am a caretaker at Eternal Peace, a cemetery close by."

"Do you like it?"

"Very much. I work with Eckhart. Just the two of us. Not a soul more. Though you feel as though the dead are still there. Demanding reverence and respect."

Lieselotte took the words to memory. If he said these words, then they had meaning. She forced a polite nod, but one that displayed a lack of interest and a sense of urgency. Pretending she wanted to leave.

"Well, I hope you have a great spring. Summer. Autumn." He gave a strained laugh. "A great Christmas, too, I guess. Maybe you'll get a gift you least expect. Maybe I'll finally get those new eyes."

Lieselotte smiled, sadness in her eyes. "Yes, maybe."

"Things didn't work out the way I planned. I think we met in the middle of our own stories. You know, walking the grounds, gazing at all those graves, I always wonder what their stories were. But they're lost, like the leaves falling off the giant beech tree above them."

"Graves can't tell their stories," Lieselotte said softly. "But they're where all stories end."

"Or a mausoleum. Though, I suppose the destination is the same."

"One minute," Schwarzfuchs called out.

Wolfgang wanted to spend those sixty seconds gazing at her. *How can I pretend I have gotten closure? How could I ever move on from her?*

Lieselotte met his eyes—so warm once, sparkling with joy, now clouded with pain. His smile faltered, then vanished. Something inside him dimmed. Day by day, his soul died. She wanted to hold him, run her fingers through his hair—but all she could offer was a hollow, distant hug. One where their bodies didn't touch, only the hands on each other's backs.

All around them, people said goodbyes. Some of these would be for the last time. Maybe it was their last time. If she didn't focus, she'd let that thought destroy her. She had to tune out the soft cries and stifled sobs around her—or risk falling apart.

"I'll miss your poetry," Wolfgang said. "Vitriol of night, horrific and violent endeavors need solemn tranquility. Effulgent imagination necessitates."

"*Frau* Reisinger," Schwarzfuchs said, "it's time for you to go back to where you belong."

"Yes, it is," Lieselotte snapped back, not giving him the satisfaction of looking at him. He was a fly she brushed away. "Goodbye, Wolfgang."

"Goodbye, Lieselotte."

Leaving without one last look—like she had in the sewers, where a minute longer became ten—gutted her. She bit her lip and rushed to West Berlin crossing, her heels clacking against the gray tiles as she added her own tears to the Palace of Tears.

A Sketch of What Might Have Been

The waves of her hair rippled as she strode away. Schwarzfuchs stepped beside Wolfgang, also watching her vanish back into West Berlin—but while Wolfgang looked on with longing, Schwarzfuchs studied her like a predator.

"Rest easy, *Herr* Kirschke. That woman will have no trouble finding men to fill the gap between her legs," he said.

Wolfgang said nothing. He knew better than to show frustration; Schwarzfuchs would only feed on it.

She was gone again. *How many times can I endure this—watching her walk away?* This had to be the last time. He couldn't keep betraying his heart like this, and he couldn't be this close to the Wall—it was too tempting, too intoxicating. It had a maddening effect, amplifying every desperate impulse. That's why so many people risked death trying to cross it: the ravenous idea of freedom overpowered reason.

"Well, did you find the closure you were looking for?" Schwarzfuchs asked.

Wolfgang turned away from the checkpoint, trying to reduce its power over him. "I believe so."

"Well, I think it's best to go over all the scenarios. For how else can you have closure if you have not considered everything?" Schwarzfuchs stated.

From his leather coat, Schwarzfuchs pulled out a folded page, keeping the contents hidden.

"I had one of our artists sketch what your son might look like."

He handed it to Wolfgang—a child, only five. Dark, wavy hair. A smile full of baby teeth. Lieselotte's blue eyes, but Wolfgang's face.

"And a daughter," Schwarzfuchs added, offering another sketch. This child had Wolfgang's eye color and glasses, just like him.

So lifelike it made Wolfgang feel as if he gazed upon children he'd lost. He had expected Schwarzfuchs to instill pain. He knew the only reason he had allowed this meeting was for the torment he could wreak. But this … this was something Wolfgang hadn't expected. He'd overestimated his humanity and underestimated his cruelness.

"What would you have named these children?" Schwarzfuchs asked.

Wolfgang tried blinking away the tears. But he wasn't in control of his emotions. They were in control of him. A mix of despair and grief with a tinge of anger he worried would grow and dwarf the others. This meeting had been necessary. He had spoken to Lieselotte, tried to reveal his plan to her innocuously. He'd been able to hug her—not the way he wanted to. This hug had to be distant and cold. He had wanted to pull her close, shield her so that nothing in this world could ever harm her. But it was still a hug. He'd felt her hands on his back. Breathed in the alluring scent of her hair. Saw the brilliance of the blue of her eyes he treasured.

Schwarzfuchs grabbed the two drawings from Wolfgang. "Closure is important indeed, *Herr* Kirschke. I wonder what her real children will look like, don't you?"

Schwarzfuchs removed a lighter and held it over the pages. Wolfgang's initial reaction was to reach for those pages. To save them from being destroyed. They were only sketches. Yet in Hohenschönhausen, they'd been more than drawings. When he had disappeared into the recesses of his mind, he had seen those children. He stopped himself from reaching for the sketches, but the slight movement betrayed how deeply it had cut him. Wolfgang could do nothing but watch the flames consume the paper, the black shards floating away.

Schwarzfuchs brought his face inches from Wolfgang's. So close that their noses nearly touched. "I do not think you have found closure, *Herr* Kirschke. Do you wish to run after her?" he taunted. "Go ahead. See how close you can get. Perhaps there is a miracle awaiting you."

"My life is in East Berlin," Wolfgang said.

He turned and left the platform.

"You are in my debt!" Schwarzfuchs shouted after him.

Wolfgang returned to his apartment in a daze. His meeting with Lieselotte had sucked everything from him. Left him weak and depleted. The frustration of being trapped in East Berlin consumed him. Escape felt impossibly far—2,000-some feet of earth to dig through.

He tried to think rationally. His goal of escape needed to be broken down into smaller goals, and those smaller goals into even smaller goals until it was a shovelful of dirt by shovelful of dirt. When Eckhart returned to the apartment, he asked Wolfgang how it had gone. Wolfgang told him everything, including about the drawings Schwarzfuchs had shown him. He'd never broken down in front of Eckhart before. But he didn't have the will or care to fight the emotion weakening his voice.

"That demented bastard," Eckhart said. "I'm sorry."

Wolfgang nodded, eyes pleading for Eckhart to move on.

"Do you think she understood your message?" Eckhart asked.

"Yes," Wolfgang said. "She'll know what to do."

Eckhart sighed with relief. "Well, then I guess it's time to get started."

Wolfgang nodded. It was time to get started. Time to confirm who was on board.

Eckhart had stopped at Bastian and Trude's, showing them a note that told them to come to Treptower on Saturday the 9th at 4 p.m. Trude had forwarded the message to Emilia and Franco.

Wolfgang hadn't seen Emilia and Franco since the failed escape attempt. They shared brief greetings. Then they followed one of the less traveled walking paths. Bastian and Franco branched out on opposite ends, so they could signal for Wolfgang to stop speaking if someone approached around the winding curves.

Trude had told Emilia, who had undoubtedly told Franco about Dietrich's betrayal. Thankfully, as it removed any reasonable questions about trust they otherwise would have had.

Wolfgang brought them up to speed about the tunnel, its location, distance, and Lieselotte's help in the West. Emilia and Franco processed what they had been told.

"This is our best option?" Emilia asked.

Wolfgang hated the question but understood why she asked it. "As far as I can see, yes. But that's for you to decide. If you want to find another way, I understand. But I've seen the Wall, and I don't foresee any way through it or over it."

Emilia looked at her husband before speaking, silently communicating her answer to him. "Count us in."

"How many of us are there?" Franco asked.

"What you see right now," Eckhart answered.

"Anyone you bring in has to be someone you trust with your life," Bastian warned. "If you screw that up, everyone pays." He held up a hand. "Shh. Someone's coming."

A half minute later, a middle-aged couple rounded the curve. Wolfgang and the others were happy for the distraction. Now the guilty looks on their faces could be chalked up to the two people walking by, not the fact they all knew who had betrayed them.

"We need to prioritize those who can help us with the tunnel," Wolfgang said, after Franco gave the all clear that the couple was out of earshot. "If there are those we want to give a chance at escape who aren't able to dig the tunnel, we keep it a secret until the last moment. This is our last chance."

He didn't tell them of his oath with Eckhart to die in the attempt. There would be no more Stasi prisons for them. If the others couldn't face that choice, they had to make peace with spending the rest of their lives in a cell.

"None of us will get a chance to escape a third time," Eckhart reiterated.

"What about Dietrich?" Bastian asked.

Wolfgang waited for Eckhart to answer, but he hesitated. Keeping this from his brother was in his best interest, but it was still a lie.

"He doesn't want to risk it," Wolfgang said. "Prison changed him."

Eckhart thanked Wolfgang with his eyes.

The plan would unravel if Bastian found out the truth. Despite Berlin's size, Bastian and Dietrich might still cross paths, especially with Dietrich wanting to reconnect with Eckhart. At some point, Eckhart and Wolfgang would have to tell Bastian but also remind him during his blinding rage that to act on that anger would jeopardize everyone.

"We begin tonight," Wolfgang said.

"How long do we think this will take?" Franco asked.

"My goal is Christmas," Wolfgang answered.

"Christmas? You said it would take a year," Bastian said.

"I said it *could* take a year. But I'm not waiting that long. I'll calculate how much we need to dig each day to make it work."

There was much skepticism. Only natural. But at one point, every single accomplishment in the history of mankind seemed impossible. Backed into a corner, desperation became their most powerful weapon. There was no backup plan. Failure was not an option. It would drive every shovel that tore through the earth.

Terms of Freedom

L ieselotte left the Palace of Tears, her heart heavy, an aching in her bones. Once out of the Stasi agent's sight, tears streamed down her cheeks.

Anneliese waited for her on the other side of the border and hugged her when she crossed, then asked how it had gone. Lieselotte gave a brief rundown during their hurried walk to a café. She waited until she could recount everything Wolfgang had said.

At the café, Anneliese ordered two *Pharisäsers*—strong coffee with a shot of rum and topped with whipped cream. Lieselotte asked for a pen and scribbled down everything Wolfgang had said and decoded it.

"Wolfgang and Eckhart plan to dig their tunnel at Eternal Peace Cemetery, about four blocks from the Wall. He wants the tunnel to be finished on Christmas," Lieselotte whispered.

The unexpected Christmas gift he'd mentioned.

"Christmas? That's only … nine months away," Anneliese exclaimed.

The waitress set their cups of *Pharisäser* before them. Lieselotte returned Anneliese's pen.

"We need to see a map of the cemetery," Lieselotte said.

They drank, riding the buzz of alcohol and caffeine. After, they rushed to the State Library of Berlin. Inside, massive shelves towered, housing thousands upon thousands of books and documents. Long wooden tables stretched across the hall, occupied by people reading or researching.

Lieselotte scoured the shelves for documents and maps of East Berlin. She found one and spread it open across a vacant table.

Anneliese pointed out Eternal Peace Cemetery on the map. Lieselotte traced her finger back to where the Wall loomed.

"According to what I found, that's a rather large cemetery? Where exactly is he digging?" Anneliese asked.

Lieselotte repeated Wolfgang's poem. *Vitriol of night, horrific and violent endeavors need solemn tranquility. Effulgent imagination necessitates.* "Von Haven Stein. It must be a mausoleum," she added, remembering Wolfgang's clarification.

All around them, people perused the shelves for their next great read. Here, Lieselotte and Anneliese were out in the open, investigating how to dig a tunnel. They didn't need to do it secretly. Wolfgang and Eckhart didn't have that luxury.

Since this map was printed before the Wall's creation, it didn't show it, but Lieselotte knew its location. She had memorized it when Wolfgang planned his previous escape. But Anneliese couldn't visualize the Wall. Didn't know every street. So, Lieselotte used a pencil to draw in the line representing the Wall.

Lieselotte tasked Anneliese with finding a copy of the public record listing of Eternal Peace Cemetery, while she continued to study the map. Wolfgang's estimate of four city blocks had been fairly accurate. The shortest distance to the Wall was 1,476 feet.

Anneliese returned with an armful of documents and maps. "I need more alcohol and caffeine."

Lieselotte couldn't have asked for a better person to help sift through the mountain of documents. Anneliese had interned as a research assistant at a law firm before being hired full-time.

Anneliese had found urban planning documents and records pertaining to both West and East Berlin, and those when it had been one city. Historical and governmental documents, cadastral and topographical maps.

Anneliese was right—they needed more alcohol and caffeine. This would take hours. As the afternoon faded into evening, the library emptied. Half an hour before closing, they were the only two seated at tables. The librarian closest to them kept glaring at the mound of material at their table, worrying she'd have to stay late to return it all.

"Here," Anneliese said. "Plot number 10A-7M."

She explained that **10** designated the section or block of graves. **A** indicated the area within that section. **7** was the row, and **M** distinguished it as a mausoleum. Anneliese used that information to find the mausoleum on the plot map. She marked it with an X. Lieselotte converted the distance from mausoleum to entrance at 514 feet.

"2,064 feet to the Wall," Lieselotte uttered.

"We need to find something as close to the Wall as possible," Anneliese said. She drew a line with her fingers. "Everything outside this is a no-go. Otherwise, we'll have to dig at an angle to meet their tunnel."

They categorized streets as acceptable, favorable, or most desirable—those offering a direct path to the Von Haven Stein mausoleum. Lieselotte and Anneliese decided to resume the search the following day. They met at half past four in the afternoon in front of a bagel shop, each grabbing a bagel to eat on their way. There were few buildings inside the area they had dubbed the most desirable. Most were businesses—a tailor, a bakery, a grocery store. It was easier to dig here in the West than the threat Wolfgang and the others faced in the East, but that didn't mean Lieselotte had clear rein to start tearing the street up. They needed to dig inside a building to keep it hidden.

"Any vacant buildings?" Anneliese asked.

Of course, there were some in West Berlin. No economy is immune to defunct businesses. Certainly there were less than in the East, but in this desired area there weren't any. Which left Lieselotte with two options: move on and find a different place to dig; or stay and ask the shop owners' permission to dig up their basement. Both choices were less than ideal. Finding a different location meant they had to dig longer and figure out how to dig at the proper angle to the Von Haven Stein mausoleum. The longer they had to dig, the more likely it was that they would not meet that Christmas deadline. But staying in this area also presented the likelihood that not only would the shop owners deny her request to destroy their basement, but of word getting out. Family dinner talk consisting of, "You'll never believe what someone asked me."

She voiced her frustration to Anneliese, looking for her input.

"I say we ask them. An unasked question is always a no," Anneliese said.

That was true, but what if we ask the wrong person? Has Wolfgang's ordeal, Dietrich's betrayal, and the omnipresent Stasi eroded my faith in others? Their influence seeped through the Wall like an invisible gas—silent, odorless, and inescapable.

"You're right. We ask but only after we've vetted them out. We can't risk this getting back to the Stasi," Lieselotte said.

There were three possible buildings. The first was the tailor shop, owned by an elderly couple. The second, a bakery owned by a man in his forties who had his seven children working for him. And the third, a grocery store owned by a woman in her early sixties. Anneliese and Lieselotte had learned much about the buildings to understand the layout. All three buildings would suffice. And after watching and listening—how the tailor spoke kindly of families split by the Wall, the baker let slip too many negative opinions of the East, and the way the grocer kept her head down and to herself—to feel enough of a hunch they could ask. But they could never know for certain.

They had stopped into each business under harmless guises—a hemming of a dress, picking up a freshly baked loaf of bread, and a bag full of groceries—to rank the people based on appearance and friendliness for the likelihood they would say yes. The woman who owned the grocery store looked incapable of a smile. The wrinkles came not from smiling, but decades of scowling, which put her in last place.

Each time they stopped into these businesses, they stayed a little longer. Lieselotte would let a comment about "ration cards in the East" hang in the air and wait for reactions. At the tailors, Ernest tapped the newspaper with a snort—another article about a family torn apart—while Berduna blinked back tears. In the bakery, Karl muttered to a customer about having to close up his bakery in the East due to extreme rationing and fleeing to the West. The grocer, however, gave nothing but a nod or a clipped *thank you*.

Lieselotte combed through the AP's extensive resources and old clippings, while Anneliese checked registrations. Karl's defection story held. The tailors and grocer had long been West Berliners.

A single wrong word to the wrong person and Wolfgang would never see daylight again.

They had ranked Ernest and Berduna first. Aiding in the tunnel would be less of a risk, with no children involved. Karl the baker was certainly a better candidate than the scowling grocery store owner, but with so many children, there was much for him to consider. Digging a tunnel beneath his bakery was hardly sanitary. Nor would a tunnel beneath a grocery store. The austere woman who owned the grocery store was the biggest question mark, her thoughts shielded away behind silence.

Lieselotte and Anneliese entered the quaint tailor shop. The first floor of the two-story building was their shop, with their home presumably above. It was quiet inside. The woman greeted them with a genial smile. Suits and dresses adorned the walls. Near the back of the store was a wooden platform where all the measurements were taken.

At the sound of the entrance bell, Ernest, the old tailor, stepped out from the back room.

"Back again? Was there something wrong with the dress?" he asked.

"No, the dress fits perfectly. We're here to discuss something sensitive," Lieselotte said.

Their sales smiles slipped away. Caution settled over their demeanors.

"Which is?" Berduna asked.

Lieselotte explained the predicament of Wolfgang and the others—keeping their names and her relationship to them redacted. Ernest and Berduna listened, waiting for how this would involve them.

"They are planning to escape. And we need a place to help them."

"Help them how?" Berduna asked.

But Ernest shook his head before Lieselotte could even answer. "We are not interested in getting involved. I hate the East. I want nothing to do with them. But they have spies here. I want no trouble. You would be wise to do the same."

Berduna didn't look on board; she seemed more willing to hear more. But once her husband had refused, she asked no more questions.

"We do wish you luck," Berduna said.

Lieselotte thanked them, and she and Anneliese stepped outside. They had thought this genial old couple had been their best bet.

"Do you think they would have said yes with more information?" Lieselotte asked.

Anneliese shook her head. "No. And we can't give away too much. I don't blame them, though. They're old. They have lived through so much. They just want peace."

Of course they did. That's all everyone wanted. Peace and freedom. They were fortunate to be on this side of the Wall. That when they had bought this shop, however many years or decades ago, that fate unfolded the way it did with them on the right side. But Anneliese's point was more than fair. These people were in their seventies, had lived through two World Wars and years of unfathomable hardship.

Their next stop was *Lauer's Bakery*. Karl Lauer had a round, cheerful demeanor, and a body suggesting a fondness for his own baked goods. The shop smelled heavenly. A display case housed donuts, croissants, fresh loaves of bread, and cinnamon rolls.

Lauer's Bakery hung in black letters on a white sign behind the counter. Anneliese had established a rapport with him when she mentioned she had once eaten at a *Lauer's Bakery* in Chicago. Karl had beamed, stating it was his great uncle's bakery. Apart from the bread, Lieselotte and Anneliese had returned for the *kringle*.

"Two slices of blueberry cheese *kringle*?" Karl asked, remembering their order.

"You know me, Karl—this is how I fight communism."

Karl smiled. "If that worked, I'd catapult *kringle* over the Wall."

He placed two heaping slices of *kringle* onto plates.

"What if we didn't want to use something to go over the Wall, but underneath," Anneliese said.

"What do you mean?"

Anneliese gave the abridged, redacted version of their plan.

"Listen, I feel for them, I do. I was blessed to get out of there before the Wall came up. But we're not supposed to get involved. This place," he looked around, "it's how I support my family. I can't risk that. I'm sorry."

Anneliese forced a smile and removed the necessary money to pay for the *kringles*, but Karl shook his head.

"It's on the house," he said.

The two women thanked him and left. It appeared they would have to expand their search to beyond the favorable section. *What if no one on the list, even the adequate locations, says yes? Then what?*

"One more to check," Anneliese said.

"The scowling old woman?" Lieselotte asked. "She's the scariest woman I've ever seen."

"Agreed. But an unasked question is—"

"Always no. Yeah, I got it."

Anneliese wrapped her arm around Lieselotte. "Have faith, friend."

They walked into the small grocery store. The tiled floor was immaculately clean. Every item was pulled forward, labels facing out with meticulous detail. Shoppers, pushing carts or holding baskets, strolled up and down the half dozen aisles. Shelves were stocked with canned vegetables, boxes of rice, and bags of potatoes. Produce stands displayed apples, bananas, and oranges. Beef, chicken, turkey, and pork packed meat cases. No stores like this existed in East Germany.

Lieselotte and Anneliese approached the young woman behind the lone checkout counter and asked for the owner. The cashier looked nervous to even point to where the owner was, raising a finger to hip level only and pointing to the stairwell at the back of the store leading up to an office with a glass window. Lieselotte thanked her and trekked through the store and up the stairs. She knocked and waited.

Lieselotte glanced at Anneliese, silently asking if she'd heard a reply. Anneliese shrugged, then nodded for her to go. Deciding it was pathetic how nervous she was, Lieselotte opened the door and stepped inside.

"Excuse me," she announced.

An older woman, her hair a curly mess of gray, held up a skeletal finger in warning. "Did you hear me say you could enter?"

"I couldn't hear through the door," Lieselotte replied.

The woman ignored the reply and returned to writing. Her desk was organized yet cluttered, telling Lieselotte the woman hated having so much on her desk. She appeared to be filling out order forms and payrolls.

While she waited, Lieselotte discreetly looked about the space, realizing quickly it was more than an office. It was roughly the size of an apartment, with all the furnishings—a couch, a bed in the back, a small kitchen, and bathroom.

When the old woman had finished writing, she looked up and appraised her two visitors. Her fierce glare was capable of melting steel.

"How may I help you?" she asked.

Lieselotte waited for Anneliese to take this one, staying silent until it was blatantly obvious her friend's bravado would not extend into this office. Something that terrified Lieselotte, as Anneliese was never afraid to speak loud and freely. Lieselotte introduced herself and Anneliese, first names only.

"We need after-hour access to a basement for ... construction," Anneliese added.

From their research, they knew the woman's name was Elfriede Winterstein—but the stern woman hadn't revealed that. She sat ruler straight. Never had sitting looked more uncomfortable.

"And how does this involve me?" Mrs. Winterstein asked.

"The escape plan requires a place here in West Berlin," Lieselotte said.

"Why?" Short, blunt, and accusatory. It screamed, *get to the point*. She had been unaffected by the story of Wolfgang and the others. They had been right to rank her last. They shouldn't have even

232

spoken with her. This was nothing but a waste of time. They should have started scouting the next set of locations.

"My dear, if you expect my help, you cannot keep me in the dark. Nor will I allow you to treat me as if I'm deaf, dumb, and blind. I assure you, I am none of those things," Mrs. Winterstein said.

"It's needed to get past the Wall," Anneliese offered.

Lieselotte appreciated the help, but that comment wasn't going to calm Mrs. Winterstein's growing irritation.

"The Wall is a monster. Impenetrable. Unscalable. You would be best to tell your boyfriend and the others that," she said.

They were a second away from losing her audience. Her eyes had shifted back to the work on her desk needing to be completed. Food to be ordered, schedules to be made, payrolls to be paid, taxes to be filed.

"They're not going over the Wall or through it. They're going under it," Lieselotte said.

That reclaimed Mrs. Winterstein's attention. Her gaze had locked onto Lieselotte. For the first time, she noticed Mrs. Winterstein's beautiful blue eyes. Eyes the color of a lake during summer.

"And you wish to what? Tunnel through my basement?" she asked.

"Yes."

She would say no, maybe even curse them out. But Lieselotte would stand her ground until she answered. Mrs. Winterstein was silent, surveying Lieselotte. She had a tremendous presence. A person of power who commanded a room. Time obeyed her.

"I have conditions," Mrs. Winterstein stated. "The digging must not compromise my store's sanitation and must occur outside business hours."

Lieselotte didn't dare look at Anneliese, feeling as if this were a ploy, or something so fragile that she couldn't look away and risk it vanishing.

"You're … you're offering to help?" she asked.

Mrs. Winterstein shook her head. "No."

There it was. The clarification Lieselotte had needed. Clearly, she had missed something before.

"No?" Lieselotte asked.

"No. I will not assist with the digging. But you may use my basement for your tunnel."

Gratitude surged through Lieselotte. She rushed forward to hug Mrs. Winterstein but caught herself, quickly realizing that wasn't a smart move.

"If I see any dirty footprints on my floor, I will wage hell. I know the exact count of every product I have on my shelves. If I find out you or your group have been stealing from me, I will have you arrested. I am offering you help. I trust you won't make me regret it."

"No, of course not. Thank you so much! You have no idea how much this means. Can I ask why?"

Mrs. Winterstein gazed into Lieselotte's eyes. Then her magnificent blue eyes darted to the door, and the meaning was clear. The meeting was over. Relief washed over Lieselotte; they had secured a location for the tunnel—a pivotal step toward freedom.

Unhallowed Ground

Wolfgang told the others to arrive at the cemetery at nine—well after dark. They were to take separate routes and abort if they suspected a tail. The goal was to work until 3:30 a.m. and vanish long before the landscapers arrived.

Wolfgang and Eckhart arrived at seven. They scanned trees, crypts, and tombstones for anything resembling surveillance. In two frantic hours, they crammed in twelve hours of labor. At nine, Bastian and Trude approached the main entrance. Emilia and Franco waited by the rear gate.

"Did anyone see you coming?" Eckhart asked.

"Sure, people saw us walking. So what?" Bastian replied.

"So what?!"

"Enough!" Trude hissed. "We're risking our lives, so stop bickering like children!"

It was a whisper shout, but both brothers took the point. Wolfgang led them to the Von Haven Stein mausoleum. Eckhart unlocked the door and heaved it open.

"Going to need more than a shovel," Trude said, staring at the concrete floor.

"First, we need to get this out of the way," Bastian said, kicking the sarcophagus.

The four men pressed against the massive tomb—first with hands, then backs—but it didn't budge.

"Holy shit," Eckhart whispered.

Trude and Emilia joined in as best they could. It was challenging to find enough room for everyone to put their full weight behind it. But the crypt barely moved. The only evidence that they had made any progress was the groaning sound as the marble scraped against the concrete.

"I have an idea," Wolfgang said.

He rushed off, Eckhart chasing behind him, wanting to know what the idea was. Eternal Peace had an IFA H3A work truck; its gray color concealed by dirt and rust. Wolfgang drove to the edge of the crypt. Fortunately, a walkway led to the crypt, so they didn't have to worry about accidentally destroying any tombstones or desecrating any graves. Wolfgang hopped out and hooked four heavy-duty ratchet straps to the truck.

"Secure those around the tomb," Wolfgang said.

Franco and Bastian wrapped them around the tomb, securing them into place.

"Okay, test it out!" Bastian said over the rumble of the truck.

Wolfgang gave the truck some gas. The engine roared. The straps went taut with a threatening creak.

"Looks good! Keep going!" Bastian shouted over the rumble, motioning with his hand.

Wolfgang pushed harder on the pedal. The tomb scraped along the floor, protected from cracking by an old canvas bag they'd secured under it. Once they moved half the sarcophagus's length, Bastian waved for Wolfgang to stop.

Wolfgang killed the engine and shut the lights off. Then the group stood in the crypt surveying the invisible spot on the floor that served as their X. Wolfgang took out chalk and a tape measure from his pocket. Kneeling, he drew a three-foot-wide chalk circle.

"We need to keep it this size to distribute the tomb's weight and avoid collapse," Wolfgang explained.

For some, the small size of that circle would instill claustrophobia. But Wolfgang had gone over the numbers. Safety first. Quickness second. Comfort third.

"We dig at an angle until we reach our tunneling depth," Wolfgang said.

"Why at an angle?" Emilia asked, not combative but curious.

"Structural stability, easier entry and exit, and easier for dirt removal."

Franco removed a chisel and rubber mallet from his work bag. He hesitated, then handed them to Wolfgang.

"The first strike, it should be yours," he said, his Italian accent giving the words a quiet dignity.

Wolfgang looked to the others for argument, but everyone encouraged him to be the first. He crouched and positioned the chisel in the center of the chalk circle and paused. One swing would turn their scheme into a full-blown escape attempt.

He took a breath and swung the mallet. The crack reverberated in his hands, the sound echoing around the desolate tomb, sounding like the groans of the disturbed dead.

He hammered for twenty minutes as the others watched in silence. Then he passed the hammer and chisel to Eckhart, beginning the rotation—everyone, including the women, took their turn against the concrete. After a full rotation, their strength began to fray. They cut shifts to ten minutes. Then five.

They traded turns, each swing less powerful than the one before it. Muscles sore and hands aching until the concrete finally cracked hours later. It was clear what they were thinking: this plan was insane. Six hours for twelve inches of concrete. To tunnel over 2,000 feet in a year was impossible.

"We need to push the tomb back in place," Eckhart said.

Wolfgang grabbed two metal bars that had a flat, shovel-like blade on the end. They were normally used to help loosen soil or wedge between heavy objects to make it easier to lift, which was their intended purpose now.

"Trude, Emilia, in the truck are metal rollers," Wolfgang said. "Place them in front of the tomb. Once it's lifted, slide the rollers underneath."

"Essentially giving the tomb wheels," Franco said.

Wolfgang nodded. Franco clapped him on the back, grinning.

Two men to a pole, they wrenched down. The tomb lifted. Trude and Emilia slid the rollers into place and then gave the all clear. All that remained was to add more rollers until they had pushed the sarcophagus back into place.

Afterward, they gathered the bits of concrete and swept away the dust. Then the two couples went home—in opposite directions. It was a rather unsanctimonious first night.

Wolfgang had his doubts that they would return the following night. But they arrived at nine—not a complaint to be heard from any of them. Using the metal bars and rollers made moving the thousand-pound tomb much easier, and with the concrete out of the way, shovel struck soil.

After a night of digging, they'd created a forty-five-degree decline of five feet. They placed the dirt atop graves, spreading thin layers across weather-worn sites, hoping it went without suspicion.

"I estimated that from this mausoleum to the Wall is roughly 2,000 feet," Wolfgang said. "Which means we're down to 1,995 feet."

Five feet may seem like nothing, but they no longer had to dig 2,000 feet. The first goal had been accomplished. Now came the time to improve—dig faster, smarter, quieter. Every night mattered. Each inch forward brought him closer to being the unexpected Christmas gift he'd promised Lieselotte.

Grave Decisions/Requiem for the Nameless

Lieselotte and Anneliese arrived at Mrs. Winterstein's store five minutes early. They had little time to wonder if she'd changed her mind—at precisely 9:15, she unlocked the door. She refused to keep the door unlocked, stating that no matter what the sign out front said, people would still try to come in and shop after hours. Lieselotte and Anneliese tried small talk, but Mrs. Winterstein clearly didn't enjoy it. She had no problem with silence. Nearly fifteen awkward-silence-filled minutes later, fists rapped against the glass door.

"If he leaves so much as a smudge on the glass with those ogre knuckles, he'll be cleaning it," Mrs. Winterstein snapped, heading to the door.

"Oh, hello," Petyr said, not expecting to meet Mrs. Winterstein.

"What's on your wrist?" Mrs. Winterstein asked.

Petyr blinked. "A mole?"

Anneliese sighed. "She means your watch, *Dummkopf.* How can you be late?"

"Oh, well … I don't know." Petyr shrugged.

Mrs. Winterstein gawked from the men to the women. "You know, they sent a chimpanzee into space."

Lieselotte and Anneliese smiled—and perhaps, just perhaps, Mrs. Winterstein's lips twitched in response.

Mikael. Rory. Johan. George. Hansel. Lieselotte never quite believed they'd show up. Yet here they were.

"Would you please show us the basement again, Mrs. Winterstein?" Lieselotte asked.

"This way," Mrs. Winterstein said.

The others followed her as she walked down the dairy cooler stocked with milk, cheese, and eggs, and into a back room. Pallets of product covered the concrete floor. The freezer was to the left. She turned into a small break room and unlocked a door with a bronze key. Lieselotte and Anneliese had followed her down here once before, but this time she unlocked the door for all of them, flipped the light switch, and descended the staircase.

The ceilings were only six and a half feet, more than enough height for Lieselotte and Anneliese, but a few of Petyr's friends hovered over the six-foot mark.

Lieselotte consulted the compass dangling from her neck to ensure which direction to dig.

"This is the wall you want," Mrs. Winterstein said, putting her hand on the eastern wall. Lieselotte thanked her. "So, what's your plan to get rid of all the dirt?" Mrs. Winterstein asked.

A question Lieselotte had expected but still didn't have an answer for. Disappointment flashed across Mrs. Winterstein's face at Lieselotte's hesitation. Looking as if Lieselotte had already broken her word.

"We'll think of something, I promise," Lieselotte meekly offered.

"Is there any underground access to the outside from here?" Petyr asked, looking around. It didn't take much of a scan.

"No," Mrs. Winterstein snapped.

That posed a problem. Lieselotte had no idea how many pounds of dirt they would have. The only way out of this area was up the stairs. Quite the trek.

"I have dumpsters in the back of the store. They're emptied on Tuesdays, Thursdays, and Saturdays," Mrs. Winterstein said. "You can use those until you come up with a better idea. I'll be in my office, so when you are finished, knock on my door. Wait for me to answer. I repeat, wait for me to answer, and I will see you out. Understood?"

Lieselotte nodded and thanked her again.

"Excuse me, but do you have a bathroom?" Johan asked.

It was odd to see the burly, tall man so timid around the older woman.

"Dig yourself a hole," Mrs. Winterstein said.

Then she went up the steps, leaving them standing around. Looks passed among one another, waiting for the plan to be revealed. For Petyr and his friends, they simply knew they were digging a tunnel. Lieselotte had imagined this moment—eager and excited to begin. Yet now, standing at the threshold of the plan she'd dreamed of, spent so many hours planning for, all the preparation scattered like leaves in the wind. *Where am I supposed to start?*

"We should probably look at the map," Anneliese offered with an encouraging nod.

"Right, yes, thank you," Lieselotte said. She slung her rucksack off her shoulder and drew out a few copies of the maps she and Anneliese had scoured over, along with a ruler and pencil.

"This is the cemetery Wolfgang and the others are starting from," she said, pointing to Eternal Peace Cemetery on the map. "From our location here," another point of the map, "we are 664 feet from the Wall. Bringing the total distance to 2,728 feet from where we stand to the Von Haven Stein mausoleum."

Their motivation evaporated. *What had they expected? One night of digging?* She took a deep, discreet breath. Everyone here was a volunteer. She had to keep that at the forefront of her thoughts.

"Are we meeting halfway?" Mikael asked.

Lieselotte shrugged. "I don't know how that will shape up. We are both just working as fast as we can. But understand, we have fewer obstacles on our side. Everything they do is in secret, with little manpower and few supplies. Risking imprisonment and death every single day—"

"We should be ashamed of ourselves if they dig half," Anneliese cut in.

"Okay, we'll need some good supplies," Petyr said, tapping the thick concrete wall. "My good looks aren't cracking this sucker open."

"What do you need for supplies?" Anneliese asked, biting back a retort.

George stepped beside Petyr, running his fingers across the cold wall. He tapped it, like testing the resonance of a drum. "This concrete won't go silently into the night. We need to get our hands on a hammer drill. Some crowbars, pry bars, a sledgehammer."

"It'll be dark as hell in there," Rory added. "We'll need light."

"Lamps?" Petyr asked.

"No, the light of Eärendil," Rory said, deadpan. "Yes, lamps."

"We'll want spare batteries … and spares for the spare," Hansel said.

Anneliese raised her brow—it seemed like overkill. "Okay."

"I can bring some, too," Hansel uttered.

"This tunnel will have to be deep, so we'll need to reinforce with beams," Johan said.

"Are you able to get these tools?" Lieselotte asked Petyr.

"I'm sure we can round up the sledgehammer and crowbars from family," Petyr said. "The hammer drill may cost us."

"I can pay for it," Lieselotte said.

She didn't explain—only Anneliese knew about the Associated Press funds. But the others didn't ask. Maybe they didn't want to know.

"I have a list of items, too," Lieselotte said, pulling the folded sheet from her pocket. She read off the items: trowels, garden spades, augers, buckets, pails, rope, gloves, and flashlights. All thanks to the research she and Anneliese had done—reading and calling several companies for their "hypothetical" input.

"So, we have our marching orders," Anneliese said. "We return tomorrow at nine o'clock."

"Nine? Why earlier?" Petyr asked.

"Then maybe you'll actually be on time."

She waved her brother and his friends toward the stairs. Before joining them, Lieselotte removed her camera and snapped a picture of the concrete wall and then the map. Documenting day one of the tunnel.

The following day at work, she asked Tom for the cash he had promised. He nodded for her to close the door and take a seat.

"Before I fork out the dough—American slang, by the way," he added with a smirk, "I need something. Some outline. Some plan. Some *thing*."

Lieselotte dug into her rucksack and removed the map she had shown the others the previous night. She showed it to Tom, pointing out the two starting points.

"They're digging in a cemetery?" he asked incredulously. "Jesus. That's ... dark." He sifted through the documents. "Distance?"

"2,728 feet."

Tom looked up. An expression of shock at the number he'd just heard. "That's almost a kilometer."

"Exactly. Which is why we need to start now."

He blinked at the map again. "Wait—you're digging from a grocery store?"

"Yes."

She lost Tom to the documents she'd put together, including the list of supplies.

"What about airflow?" Tom asked.

"What do you mean?"

"There won't be much oxygen in there."

"What about hand-operated air pumps?"

Tom shrugged. "Sure, that would work, but seems like a waste of a body. Buy electrical fans and a portable generator." He paused. "I mean, that's what I would do if I was actively involved in this, which I'm not."

Lieselotte smiled. "Involved in what?"

Tom smirked. "You learn quickly." He reached into his desk drawer and removed a stack of *Deutschmarks*. "Keep detailed receipts."

"I will. Thank you."

She took the cash and finished her daily tasks before meeting Anneliese for supper. Afterward, they made their way through several hardware stores, careful to buy only one or two items from each to avoid suspicion. By the end of the evening, they had crossed off nearly everything on the list—lamps, sledgehammers, chisels, shovels, and buckets—along with the newest additions: portable generators and electric fans. They loaded the haul into the back of Petyr's truck.

"What's all this? Digging a tunnel?" Petyr quipped.

"Shut up, *Dummkopf*," Anneliese said, laughing.

Days blurred together. Weeks passed in the same grueling rhythm. Wolfgang worked Monday to Saturday. Sleeping during the day. Working at night. Digging the tunnel in the middle of his shift. The most nerve-wracking day had been the first morning when the day shift had arrived. Wolfgang couldn't help but divert his eyes to see what they had forgotten to clean up that would damn them. His stomach was nothing but nerves that prevented him from eating and sleeping. He had the feeling that "today" would be the day the distant relatives of the Von Haven Steins would decide to visit their familial crypt. He couldn't sleep when he returned to his apartment, thinking at any moment the Stasi would come crashing in. That someone had found something. That someone or someones were watching him. That it was a game to let Wolfgang and the others dig a tunnel they'd never get to use. There was no shaking that anxiety. That perpetual state of fear he existed under. It made eating a task. Food wasn't pleasurable anymore; it was fuel.

They'd carved an eighteen-foot slope for the tunnel entrance. Now they had to devise a quicker, more efficient way to remove buckets of dirt than carrying them one at a time or passing them like an assembly line. So, Wolfgang devised a simple pulley system to hoist the buckets out. Trude and Emilia manned the pulley. Two men were in the tunnel shoveling out the soil into the buckets, and the other two emptied them, tossing the dirt onto fresh graves or in the bushes. But once they ran out of fresh graves, they refilled empty pots of soil kept in the groundskeeping shack. Once the shack was stocked, they filled Franco's truck bed with extra bags he could sell on the side for some added cash.

It had taken weeks to dig those eighteen feet. They were still so far away from their goal. But this was a turning point. The entrance was complete. Now it was time to dig the tunnel. At one point, just breaking through the concrete seemed impossible.

Since Wolfgang had had the ceremonial first strike on the concrete floor, he let Eckhart break ground on the tunnel first. But after they filled that first bucket, the excitement faded quickly.

By the time Sundays rolled around, Wolfgang slept all day. Exhausted didn't begin to cover it. His hands had blistered and then calloused over. His back and shoulders ached. It took Trude stopping over at their apartment and wrestling them awake to get them to go to her place for a home-cooked meal.

"We have news," Bastian said, seated at the head of the table.

He and Trude had done their best to make the dilapidated apartment their home—albeit a temporary home—but like Wolfgang and Eckhart, they had had to start over. Because of the clandestine nature of their previous escape attempt, they had left all their possessions. The state had claimed every item—every dishcloth, every pair of socks. Destroyed any photographs or mementos left behind.

"Is this news coming in the mail?" Eckhart kidded when no one spoke.

Trude laced the fingers of one hand with Bastian's and with the other rubbed her belly. "I am pregnant!"

She showed no signs of pregnancy yet, but Wolfgang didn't doubt she would try to conceal that as long as possible. He understood how bittersweet this moment was. *Joyous for certain, but how could they not think about the child stolen from them? Not fear that the same fate could await this unborn child?*

"She'll need to limit her physical excursions," Bastian said with a smile.

Wolfgang congratulated them, but Eckhart just tapped his spoon against the table. Wolfgang wanted to nudge him, but knew better than to intervene in their complex relationship.

"Something wrong?" Bastian asked his brother.

"Well, not exactly a great time to get pregnant," Eckhart said.

"It wasn't planned."

Wolfgang cheated a glance at Trude. Her joyful smile was frozen in place, but her eyes held no joy.

Eckhart gave a short, humorless laugh. "Right. Because there aren't ways to not get pregnant."

"What the hell is your problem?" Bastian said.

"You've created a useless person. No offense, Trude."

How Trude wasn't supposed to take offense to that Wolfgang didn't know. He only hoped Eckhart didn't look to him for support. Though Eckhart lacked tact, Wolfgang understood the message he was trying to deliver. This was not a great time for Trude to be pregnant. Not only did it limit the tasks she could aid in, she would also be well into her third trimester when they crawled through the tunnel. There was even a chance she could have the baby by the time the tunnel was ready to go.

"You're a piece of shit," Bastian said.

"If I knocked up a girl, you'd be saying the same thing to me!" Eckhart yelled.

"She isn't some girl! She is my wife!"

"Why would you want to do this?"

"Do what?"

"Risk having your child taken again! Why? Why couldn't you wait? I don't want another nephew or niece of mine taken!"

Eckhart's rage morphed into sobs so quickly it left Wolfgang confused. Eckhart's chest heaved up and down. Bastian rose from his table. It was unclear if he stormed toward Eckhart to clobber him. But he didn't. He wrapped his brother in a hug.

Trude stood by, biting her lip, trying to let the two brothers have their moment. But Wolfgang rose and crossed to her. He rubbed her shoulder before stepping into the kitchen.

For Eckhart, he'd never truly grieved the loss of his nephew. He'd heard the news and had been devastated. But the moment had never come where he truly grieved. Maybe it had been denial. This irrational hope or belief that the child would be returned, or they would find him. Or maybe his mind had protected him from the pain just like Wolfgang's had by creating a fictional life. Protected him by removing the memory. As if it had never happened. But that wasn't true. Eckhart had been living with all that sadness.

After the moment passed, they ate supper. The emotional catharsis had drained them, so they called it an early night. Trude offered them a ride home, but Eckhart declined, stating he wanted to walk. Wolfgang longed to get home and sleep, but since Eckhart wanted to walk, he joined him out of obligation.

An awkward silence hovered. It seemed Eckhart both wanted to talk about what had happened and wanted to let it go. Wolfgang wanted to mention it but didn't know how to broach the subject.

"Does he know?" Eckhart asked.

"Does *who* know *what?*" Wolfgang replied, cautious not to sound annoyed.

"Dietrich. Does he know I'll never see my nephew? Never even know what he looked like? Does he know Bastian never even got to hold him? Never took his tiny hand in his?"

Wolfgang had no answer. But that wasn't the point. All Eckhart needed was for him to listen.

"You know Trude didn't get to see him? She said the moment she gave birth, and they cut the umbilical cord, they took him away. Never even saw his face."

"It's awful, Eckhart. The damage he's caused ... I can't even believe," Wolfgang said.

Eckhart rubbed his eyes and took a deep breath, then cleared his throat. "So, Anneliese still holding out for me?"

They both laughed.

"Not exactly getting a lot of updates on this side of the Wall," Wolfgang quipped.

"You can be the best man at our wedding."

"Wedding? What happened to cool and casual?"

"Well, we've been fighting this thing for too long. I figured it's about time."

He smiled. Wolfgang returned it. A moment of shame traveled through Wolfgang for ever thinking that Eckhart hadn't been a great friend. Sure, time and circumstance had kept them in orbit, but friendship is about more than shared interests. Engineering bored the ever-loving daylights out of Eckhart, and he enjoyed partying to a degree Wolfgang loathed. It's easy to find someone to drink with, to have a casual conversation. But Eckhart had been a true friend. Loyal. And what quality can we desire in a friend more than that? A friend who fights for you in a room you're not in— like Eckhart, who hadn't said a word in prison, even when they held something over him. The promise, even if untruthful, of returning his nephew if he would just tell the truth.

For so long, Wolfgang had focused on everything he didn't have here in East Berlin. But he hadn't appreciated what he did have. A loyal best friend whose family had taken him in as an adopted son. Bastian. Trude. Emilia. Franco. They'd all proven their loyalty to him, too. Knowing they had his back empowered him. If things went wrong during this attempt, they wouldn't flee. They would stay with him, and he would stay with them.

Wolfgang spent what little free time he had designing the tunnel. Knowing the risk, he burned every blueprint and sketch— memorizing the dimensions and designs until they were engrained in his mind. And those drawings and calculations had confirmed they had a problem. A very serious problem.

When the others arrived, this time at ten, to keep mixing up patterns, Wolfgang addressed them.

"We need to place support beams every three to four feet," Wolfgang said.

"How many do we need?" Trude asked.

"Each frame needs a crossbeam and two supports. So, we're talking 1,500 to 2,000 pieces."

"What type of wood?" Emilia asked Franco, the resident carpenter.

"Ideally? Oak or beech. But that will be hard to come by. Pine or spruce is cheaper and easier to find."

"2,000 beams?" Eckhart asked, ignoring everything else that had been said.

"Well, I know of a way to reduce that," Wolfgang said. "We use a triangle design."

"How many beams for each one, then?" Eckhart asked.

"Three."

"Three? I'm not good at mathematics, but doesn't three equal three?"

Wolfgang smirked. "Triangles handle weight better—the most stable shape under pressure. We could space them every five or six feet—cuts the total in half."

Franco knew the problem before the others caught on. "We cannot buy so much wood without someone noticing."

Wolfgang agreed with a nod.

"Even if we all buy some?" Bastian asked.

"It's too risky. If they look into our names, they'll place us as a group," Trude said.

"Okay, so if we can't get that much wood, what's the worst-case scenario with getting skimpy with the support beams?" Eckhart asked.

Wolfgang took a deep breath. "The tunnel collapses and buries us eighteen feet down. Maybe an air pocket gives you a few extra minutes—if the weight doesn't crush you first—and you slowly suffocate to death."

Eckhart gawked at Wolfgang. "Death. That's all you needed to say."

"So, we're damned?" Emilia asked. "We either abandon the plan or we take the risk of a horrible death?"

"I have an idea to get more wood. But I don't like it," Wolfgang said.

In fact, it sickened him. The others looked at him, worried expressions on their faces.

"What is it?" Bastian asked.

"We dig up coffins," Wolfgang said.

Silence. Their revulsion mirrored his own.

"I don't like the idea of desecrating graves," Bastian said.

"I don't think Wolfgang is doing it for kicks, *Bastian*," Eckhart said.

"Listen. I hate it, too, but these people aren't here anymore—they're in heaven," Wolfgang said.

"Their souls may have moved on—but their rotting bodies are still here," Bastian said.

Eckhart had no smart retort for his brother. It was a valid point.

"Give me another possible resolution. Please. Something that won't bring attention from the Stasi," Wolfgang said.

They considered other options—cutting trees in a forest, stealing lumber at night. *But how could we do those things and someone not see them?* And in East Berlin, you had to assume everyone was an informant.

Bastian sighed. "Tell us what you have in mind."

"We need to focus on key aspects," Wolfgang said. "One, we need to target older graves."

"Like how old?" Eckhart asked.

"The older, the better. Less chance of visitors and the greater the odds that there's not much left in the coffin."

He let the others use their imagination of what that was.

"If we dig up graves, the other workers will notice," Trude said.

Wolfgang nodded. "Yes, but there are plenty of graves here that don't have grass."

"Right. The giant beech tree in the southwest corner. All those graves are just dirt," Eckhart said.

"So then, what do we do?" Franco asked.

"We search the graves in the southwest corner under the giant beech tree for ones from the 1800s."

The others processed what Wolfgang had said in silence. It sounded awful. But seeing, smelling, and touching would be far worse. Emilia gagged as she contemplated it.

Trude crossed her arms, trying to stop herself from shivering. "If there's no other way."

"If you'd give your life for liberty, wouldn't you give your grave, too?" Eckhart asked.

Bastian nodded and squeezed his brother's shoulder.

"Can we continue tonight without having to …" Emilia trailed off.

"Without having to dig up a grave?" Eckhart finished for her.

"Yes. That."

"Yes, tonight. But we need time to repurpose the wood we find," Wolfgang said.

"That, I can do," Franco said.

So, it was settled that they would dig the tunnel tonight and tomorrow they would excavate their support beams. They had decided on that terminology. Treating it like an archaeological project.

When Wolfgang crawled into bed that morning, he thought of Father Langer. *Where is he? Is he safe? What would he think of our plan?* If only he could speak with him again. Just hearing Father Langer's voice had instilled comfort and strength. *What would he say now, about digging up the dead?*

Ever since Father Langer introduced him to the Bible, Wolfgang had flirted with prayer—drawn to its quiet promise of comfort. He recalled the passages Father Langer had gone through, trying to recall one that came to mind that could offer comfort during this arduous task ahead. He had trouble falling asleep and then trouble staying asleep.

Tomorrow, he would have to dig up a grave. He and Eckhart had dug dozens of fresh graves. Never dug an occupied one up. They'd have to remove whatever remained of the body. It was hard to contemplate that.

The following night, Eckhart vomited before they left their apartment. Right now, it was out of guilt, shame, and remorse. All psychological. Later, it would be a guttural physical response. An abhorrent repulsion to the very air they breathed. They headed to work, having to tell the day workers that Eckhart had a case of food poisoning he was getting over.

After the dayshift workers left, Wolfgang and Eckhart used the remaining daylight to begin their search. They paced the southwest corner of the cemetery. The great beech bloomed in the late spring, keeping the graves below its massive sprawl hidden from sunlight. The dirt was old and brittle. Wolfgang and Eckhart walked among the crumbling tombstones, squinting at faded dates and eroded names.

When he could make out a name, emotion leveled him. At a moment in time, every one of these graves was new, caked in a mound of fresh dirt. Loved ones gathered around here to say their final goodbyes. In the throes of life's greatest pain. Some returned to remember. Fewer came each year—until no one did. Until the mourners, too, had joined the dead. Death is the cruel reminder of how little time we're given.

Wolfgang turned away before Eckhart saw tears in his eyes. Not that he would have made fun of him for it, but he didn't need to see the way this tore his soul apart. *Is freedom worth this?*

When the others arrived, they gathered in front of an indistinguishable grave. In some ways, not knowing a name or date made it easier. But in other ways, it felt as though they couldn't truly honor the person.

"If it's okay, I'd like to say a prayer before we begin," Wolfgang said.

Trude reached for his hand. "That would be wonderful."

"It's from the Book of Revelation. I don't remember the chapter. I might misquote it."

"There are no wrong prayers," Emilia whispered.

Wolfgang and the others bowed their heads and folded their hands in prayer. "*And God shall wipe away all the tears from their eyes; and there shall be no more death, neither sorrow, nor crying, neither shall there be any more pain: for the former world has passed away.*"

"Amen," the group recited.

Trude and Emilia sniffled, the air around the group heavy.

"Here," Trude said, holding out a handful of handkerchiefs. "For the smell."

"Woah," Eckhart said after taking a whiff. "What is that? It smells amazing."

"I soaked them in clove and cinnamon," Trude said. "I have some lavender oil, and if things get terrible, some vinegar."

"Vinegar? That'll make me puke," Eckhart said.

Bastian tied his white handkerchief around his face, concealing his mouth and nose. "Trust me, little brother. Vinegar is going to smell like roses compared to this."

After they fastened the handkerchiefs, the men stabbed their shovels into the dirt. Heaving it away, trying to dig as fast as they could. Powering through the dirt that had been untouched for over a hundred years. One foot down. Two. Three. Taking a quick breather. Four. Five. And finally six.

"We're close," Bastian said.

Eckhart's next shovel struck the wooden casket. Carefully, they dug around the coffin. Once they had enough space to stand beside the coffin, they stopped digging. They stared, in somewhat disbelief, at the coffin, then looked at each other. It seemed they were waiting for someone to act. Since this and the tunnel itself were Wolfgang's ideas, he felt compelled to be that someone.

He jammed the shovel into the crease and pried. The lid stuck—then gave suddenly, groaning like a dying breath. The others lifted the lid and slid it onto its side. Fetid air escaped. The men grimaced, holding their breath for as long as they could.

The person inside the casket was nothing but bones and a few strands of frayed fabric. Wolfgang needed to breathe. He sipped the air, hoping the clove and cinnamon would overpower that fetidness of death. Fortunately, in this state of advanced decay, the foulest of smells had long ago dissipated.

"Be careful not to hit him," Wolfgang said.

They worked breaking apart the coffin in the cramped space. The wood had held up remarkably well. There were only a few areas that had rotted. Franco and Bastian hoisted the lid out of the grave as Eckhart and Wolfgang broke the sides down.

Franco and Bastian lifted themselves out of the hole and then reached down for the chunks of wood. Once the sides were off, Eckhart and Wolfgang hesitated on the best approach to get to the bottom of the coffin. The skeleton was too degraded for them to lift it and remove the wooden bottom. If they did that, it would collapse into a heap of bones.

"I think we slide it," Wolfgang said.

"Yes, let's just hurry," Eckhart said.

With caution, they shimmied the board away. Bastian and Franco took it and then lifted Eckhart out of the grave.

Wolfgang stared at the skeleton. Into the skull, where the person's eyes once dwelled. Whether this had been a man or a woman, black or white, Jew or Gentile was impossible to tell. There is no more powerful confirmation of the pointlessness of divide than gazing upon the bones of the long-ago deceased.

"Thank you," Wolfgang whispered.

Franco and Bastian helped him out of the grave. Trude and Emilia carried the wood away while the men refilled the grave. Wolfgang surveyed it then spread some of the older dirt around the grave so that it matched. While Franco and Emilia worked at repurposing the wood, Eckhart and Wolfgang crawled back into the tunnel and dug.

Trude, not wanting to be without value, was always around with a canteen of water. Always insisting they stay hydrated and to take breaks when they needed them. Only the muffled hammering of wooden beams, the scrape of shovels, and the creak of the pulley lifting dirt disturbed the still night.

"The first beam, *sí!*" Franco cried.

Eckhart and Wolfgang grabbed it and secured it in place. Then the second—wedging it tight before hammering the nails home. When the first horizontal crossbeam was secured, the tunnel went from looking like something children had dug, to something complex. To something that might actually work.

"See this?" Wolfgang said to Eckhart. "The hypotenuse of the triangle supports the vertical weight, and the shape helps distribute the load among all three points."

Eckhart put his hand on Wolfgang's shoulder. "It's hard to breathe down here and I won't understand any of this. Don't risk your life for it." Then he rushed toward the tunnel opening and called to the others, "You need to see this!"

He crawled out; Wolfgang followed. Franco and Emilia climbed down first. Their laughter and excitement careened out of the hole. Franco smacked his lips against hers; her delighted cries rang out as he twirled her around. Bastian and Trude went down next.

"It's wonderful!" she exclaimed.

Once everyone gathered around the tunnel entrance, they stared into the hole, taking a moment to consider all they had accomplished.

"This is going to work," Bastian said.

"Fucking right it is!" Eckhart said.

"We have to celebrate," Trude said. "I know we still have so much to do. But we have support beams!"

The others laughed.

"For all we know, Lieselotte and the others are ten feet from us," Bastian said.

It was easy to get lost in that wishful thinking. How incredible that would be! There were still so many nights to go. So many more feet to dig, hundreds of thousands of buckets to empty. But they had made progress.

As they always did, Wolfgang's thoughts turned to Lieselotte. *How is her part of the tunnel fairing? How many of the 2,000 feet remain? Where has she dug and how many feet has that added?* And more importantly, *How many days does that distance equate to?*

The Grave Mistake

Summer dampened their spirits. Though Wolfgang and Eckhart's hours remained the same, the long daylight meant Trude, Emilia, Franco, and Bastian had to wait until nearly 10:30 to arrive. Even after sunset, it still felt like working in an oven. They knew the tunnel wouldn't be finished yet, but facing another summer in East Berlin devastated them.

By Wolfgang's measurements, they had dug ninety-seven feet of tunnel. To create the support beams, they had had to dig up fourteen graves. Each time was unbearable—a task that ravaged mind, body, and soul.

Instead of shouting, they rigged a bell to the nearest support beam outside the tunnel. When those inside the tunnel were needed, someone pulled the cord up top, and the bell rang. Normally, it was to signify the change in work. But the bell rang now even though Wolfgang and Eckhart weren't due for their change for another forty-three minutes. This ringing bell meant they had run out of wood. Wolfgang and Eckhart exchanged disheartened glances in the narrow space of the tunnel.

They crawled out of the tunnel. Trude handed them a canteen of water. Sweat stung Wolfgang's eyes. He and Eckhart doused their heads at the water pump adjacent to the entrance building. Then they grabbed their shovels and joined Bastian and Franco, who had already begun digging.

The air reeked of their sweat and body odor. This was his life now: work, sleep, repeat. *How I wish I was at a beach with Lieselotte.*

Once they reached the coffin below, Trude handed out scented handkerchiefs. The four men secured them around their faces and then worked at opening the casket.

The moment it freed, a miasma attacked them—thick, putrid air that burned their throats and stung their eyes. So horrid it pierced right through the alluring scent of cinnamon and clove. Wolfgang and Eckhart recoiled from the casket and vomited. The acidic, chunky puke clogged their handkerchiefs. Bastian and Franco turned away, clutching their fists to their mouths.

The person in the casket wasn't a skeleton. There was still an appalling amount of flesh clinging to its bones. Its eyeballs had liquefied, leaving sunken sockets. A black, swollen blob of a tongue lolled between its teeth. Yet somehow, the tux looked almost wearable, as if freshly dry-cleaned. Its hands still bore remnants of dried skin, curling the fingers into clawlike shapes. It was the most horrifying thing Wolfgang had ever seen.

"What is it?" Trude called from above.

"Don't look down here!" Bastian yelled.

But then the sound of Emilia's retching carried down into the pit. The smell had gusted out of the grave, tainting the air above it.

"We have to hurry! If that smell stains the air, people will ask questions!" Wolfgang said.

Bastian and Franco lifted the lid out of the grave, and Eckhart and Wolfgang worked at breaking the sides apart. Wolfgang tried to take sips of air through his mouth, but even then, the smell assaulted him. He heaved and gagged before puking again.

When the left side of the coffin broke free, the corpse stumbled out, landing on Wolfgang and Eckhart's feet, coating their boots in grave wax.

"Shit!" Eckhart said, kicking him off.

"Easy. This is a person," Wolfgang reminded.

"Take this fucking wood, Bastian!"

Too loud. Someone might hear.

After Bastian and Franco had taken it, they helped Eckhart and Wolfgang out of the hole.

"Here," Trude said, thrusting a small ointment bottle toward them. "Breath that."

Wolfgang took it and sniffed. A strong smell of lavender filled his nostrils. He passed it to Eckhart, who huffed it.

"Who picked this grave?" Eckhart asked, toweling the grave wax off his boots.

"That was me," Franco said.

"What was the date on the tombstone?" Wolfgang asked.

"1858."

Wolfgang looked at the tombstone. The date had faded some, but that second number wasn't an 8.

"This says 1958."

"You've got to be kidding," Eckhart muttered.

"*Mi dispiace* … I didn't realize," Franco said.

"You should have asked for a second opinion," Bastian said.

"He said he was sorry," Emilia said.

"Sorry means shit!" Eckhart said. "That was a rotting body!"

Wolfgang scrutinized the tombstone, looking for the full date. 17 July 1958.

"We could have a problem," Wolfgang said.

He hadn't raised his voice, but the others heard the worry in it.

"What?" Bastian asked.

"He died on the 17th of July. If he still has family living …"

"That means they may visit in mere days," Trude said.

Panic spread—raised voices, half-formed accusations, chaos. What they should do, what they shouldn't do. How to rectify this mistake and what might make it worse.

"Quiet!" Wolfgang said as loud as he dared. "Right now, we need to cover this grave up. That's step one. Until that's done, we don't speculate on what ifs."

"Wolfgang's right," Trude said.

It was far from the end of the argument, but at least a pause. Their shoveling was much more aggressive. Wolfgang struggled to hide his irritation. He'd told them all to be careful with the dates. Slipups and mistakes happen. But in this scenario, they needed to be perfect. They couldn't rely on luck, as errors could be costly. He'd gone over the criteria: southwest corner, dirt-covered graves from the 1800s.

As he shoveled the dirt back into the grave, he glanced at the tombstone. *Do I see a 9 because it is there—or because I know it is?*

At least covering the grave accomplished two things. One, the most pressing, burying the body. Second, physical activity has a way of reducing anger. Anger is a flash fire. It can last only so long. By the time they had finished covering the grave and applying older dirt to match the graves beside it, tempers had faded.

"Trude, Emilia," Wolfgang said. "This area smells awful. Can you try to do something about it?"

"I have some oils I think could help with the smell a bit," Trude said.

"Perfect."

"And if someone comes to visit the grave?" Franco asked.

"Worrying won't accomplish anything. I, for one, do not want to call tonight a loss. So, I say we continue working," Wolfgang said. "If the smell is still bad in the morning, we'll say we found a rotting animal."

The three men nodded and returned to work. Franco worked on creating support beams at the entrance of the tunnel to help minimize sound and visibility, while Eckhart and Bastian returned to the tunnel. Whether Bastian wanted to give Wolfgang a break, or worried his temper would cause him to lash out at Franco, Wolfgang couldn't say.

So, while Trude and Emilia spread oils around the grave to help conceal the smell, Wolfgang joined Franco in creating the support beams.

"I'm terribly sorry," Franco said.

"It happens."

"Eh, tell me, what's worse? To be betrayed or be caught because someone was stupid?"

"Betrayed."

No hesitation on Wolfgang's part. Stupidity was an innocent act. Certainly frustrating, but betrayal was a frustration entirely different. A shocking pain.

Franco nodded with appreciation, then stenciled the shape of the support beams. After, he and Wolfgang sawed through them and hammered them together into the required thickness.

Wolfgang and Franco hadn't ever really had a conversation. In the tunnel, it was too exhausting to spend effort speaking. Bastian or Emilia usually helped Franco with the beams. And outside of the tunnel, they didn't see each other. It was safer that way. But he always struck Wolfgang as a kind man and had proven himself trustworthy. The only criticism Wolfgang had of him, apart from his stupid mistake, was that he was overly innocent. Too naïve. *After all, who the hell moves into East Berlin?*

But can I criticize him for that? If Lieselotte were here in East Berlin and I was in a free country, would I have stayed away? Or be a moth to the flame, no matter if it engulfed me?

"We'll need a way to bring oxygen into the tunnel," Wolfgang said.

"Eh, why?" Franco asked.

"It's going to build up with carbon dioxide."

"So, how do we fix that?"

"Ideally, we'd run fans on generators."

"Eh, we aren't in an ideal situation." Franco cast a dashing smile.

"Far from it. But we could use lime."

"Lime—like the fruit?"

Wolfgang shook his head, holding three pieces of the casket steady for Franco to nail together. "No. Slaked lime. It'll help absorb the carbon dioxide."

"And where do we find that?"

Wolfgang waited until Franco finished hammering before answering. "That's the trouble. I don't know. And to buy the amounts we need …"

"Would draw attention. You have an answer. I can see it in your eyes."

"We could rig a manual fan and a rubber hose. Build crude ductwork. At night, we separate the fan from the ductwork, coil that in the tunnel."

"I can get rubber tubing," Emilia said.

Wolfgang hadn't noticed her come down. Trude had stayed up top—always someone to keep a look out.

"We have a hand-crank fan, too," Franco said.

Bastian and Eckhart told Franco they were ready for the next support beam. Franco and Wolfgang carried it to the end of the tunnel and secured it in place. When they climbed out of the tunnel, Trude had lit incense candles placed in the crypt tombs.

"For the musty smell," she said.

"Great idea."

As the others left, Wolfgang and Eckhart took a final walk around the Von Haven Stein mausoleum to make sure everything had been put away and hidden. Eckhart locked the door and tugged on the padlock to make sure it was secure. Then they examined the grave, looking for anything that would reveal they had dug it up. But Wolfgang knew the longer they stared at it, the more evidence they would find. So, he ushered Eckhart away.

But after returning home, his mind raced. He cursed himself for not checking every inch of that grave for evidence of disturbance. Because he hadn't, his mind crafted fallacies. Disturbances so glaringly obvious, any rational person would know it was fake. The Stasi couldn't be blamed for his anxiety and paranoia, but they had weaponized it. Implanted a self-destruct deep inside his brain that was almost impossible to shut off.

Three days. The length of the time they'd have to wait to see if the deceased would have guests visiting. It shouldn't matter. *Will anyone be able to tell the grave had been disturbed?* They'd spread fresh dirt on the surrounding graves. But Wolfgang couldn't think rationally. Couldn't shake the feeling that they'd left some damning piece of evidence. This was just another day, another chance for the Stasi to catch them. And each day that passed, that likelihood increased.

Shovels and Coordinates

Mikael and Hansel raised their sledgehammers, aiming at the chalk-drawn rectangle Lieselotte had marked. She snapped a photo with her father's camera to mark the first day of digging. The sledgehammers smashed against the concrete wall, their blows deafening—yet the hammer drill was even louder. Johan drilled through while Hansel followed with his hammer, breaking apart chunks that tumbled to their feet. George, Rory, and Petyr scooped the rubble into buckets and wheeled them upstairs. Using the drill to bore holes, then wedges and chisels to create fractures, the team breached the ten-inch-thick wall in two and a half hours.

"First shovel should be yours," Anneliese said, raising a shovel for Lieselotte to take.

Anneliese readied Lieselotte's camera and snapped the photo of her stabbing her shovel into the wall of dirt. No one in the group had known what to expect. They'd gone into this with a certain level of realism. But they'd hoped that after a few shovelfuls, the tunnel would take shape. Instead, they faced the grim reality that this would be a hell of an undertaking.

As the night wore on, Lieselotte reminded herself of their advantages over Wolfgang's team. Though the West Berlin government might intervene, they faced no risk of imprisonment or death. They had electric power tools, ergonomic shovels, generator-powered fans, and wooden support beams crafted for tunnel work. They had to leverage these tools to carry the lion's share of the effort.

The team paired off—two digging, two loading wheelbarrows, and two carrying dirt up. Soon it was clear the space was too cramped for everyone at once. Shifts would work better, but Mrs. Winterstein forbade digging during business hours. *Could we work unnoticed?* Shoveling was quiet, but electric tools were deafening.

Even here in West Berlin, neighbors might hear grinding and wonder. Someone might complain, or worse, report the noises. They could only risk the power tools while still far from the Wall. Once they neared it, the danger of being heard—and betrayed— was too great. Mrs. Winterstein had her cover story prepared: she was expanding the basement for extra storage.

"My shoppers know better than to meddle in my business," she said.

Before Lieselotte presented the idea to the team, she ran it by Anneliese.

"Mrs. Winterstein will need to approve," Anneliese said.

"I know. But I wanted to see if you could pick holes in any of my arguments."

Anneliese shook her head but shrugged. "That doesn't mean she won't."

Bringing Anneliese along felt childish—but Lieselotte did, anyway. While the men cleaned up, the two women climbed the stairs to Mrs. Winterstein's office, knocked, and waited.

Entering uninvited risked Mrs. Winterstein throwing them out and rescinding the deal. It was one of her few hard rules. Yet if Mrs. Winterstein had invited them in, lingering outside would surely annoy her. It was a damned-if-you-do, damned-if-you-don't moment. So, Lieselotte decided to enter while simultaneously stating her presence. Mrs. Winterstein was at her desk, though it was clear she hadn't been there long. She wore a nightgown under a thick bathrobe.

"Done for the night?" Mrs. Winterstein asked.

"Yes, ma'am. But I wanted to run something past you," Lieselotte said.

"Are you wanting to change the terms of our agreement?"

Lieselotte explained the situation—how having too many people at one time hindered progress. By structuring their time and manpower more efficiently, they could double their output and finish in fewer days.

"And if I hear you? Or worse, my customers hear you? What then?"

"You tell us, and we stop."

Even in a bathrobe, with her hair in a bun, Mrs. Winterstein intimidated Lieselotte. But she also fiercely respected her. Lieselotte worked among men and tried demanding respect through appearance, but true authority came from presence. Mrs. Winterstein had it in spades.

"Very well," Mrs. Winterstein said. Lieselotte thanked her. "Thank me by walking down those steps so I can shoo you and your lot out my door."

There was a charm behind her words, and she wouldn't let Lieselotte know if she was serious or not, but Lieselotte was finding out that was half the fun.

By late July, their shift rotation had pushed the tunnel past 500 feet. Oaken beams braced the tunnel, securing the earth around them. Petyr had had no trouble acquiring the lumber. The generators powered fans that kept air circulating. Johan and George had strung electrical lines throughout the tunnel, placing lightbulbs every six feet.

At the Associated Press, Lieselotte showed Tom the photos: Mikael and Hansel wielding sledgehammers; Johan at the drill; she and Anneliese shoveling; Petyr, Rory, and George hauling buckets of dirt. Dirt-streaked faces glistening with sweat.

Tom nodded, impressed. "Wow. These are powerful images, Lieselotte." He placed the photos back in her manila folder. "Are you past the Wall?"

"Not yet. 664 feet puts us past the Wall into the East. We're at 514 feet."

"No idea how far the other team is?"

Team. Like this was a race. But for Tom, it sort of was. He planned to capture the event (after the fact) to the whole world. It was only natural he viewed it as teams and a match. But maybe that made it easier for him. When dealing with deep subjects, you had to make it less life-or-death, diminish the stakes, so you could exist in that world long term.

"No. I have had no correspondence with Wolfgang," Lieselotte said.

"So, how do you know your tunnels will intersect?" Tom asked.

"We're using a compass."

"But there are more variables than direction. Depth, for one."

"I know. But I don't know how to get in contact with him."

"Fishing for ideas?"

Lieselotte shook her head. "Unless I go into East Berlin myself, I can't think of any sure way."

"I could give some thought to trying to get you a press pass into the East, but given your vocal condemnation of the government, I don't think you'd be approved."

He smiled at that. Lieselotte returned it.

"No, I do not think so, either."

"But I would be. The GDR is showing off new high-rises—part of their National Construction Program. They want to gloat about their 'workers' paradise.'"

Lieselotte paused, unsure of what he was saying. "You would be allowed to go freely?"

"I would have a *minder* following me around. Government-assigned—someone to watch my every move. But I could get a few moments to speak freely."

"How would this work?"

"Well, let's say you happened to write the exact coordinates and depth of your tunnel, the distance covered. I might walk into the pub where your boyfriend drinks, strike up a conversation, and slip him the note."

"You'd do that?"

"These photos, Lieselotte," he said, holding them up, "are powerful. Imagine the world seeing Wolfgang and the others crawling to freedom."

"Is it just about the story?"

"It's always about the story. But the people are the story—their struggles, their triumphs. Sharing these stories keeps them from fading into history."

Lieselotte wrote down the address of the Copper Cellar pub, telling Tom that Wolfgang and Eckhart went for a beer every Friday before work. If Tom was willing to stay for a few rounds, he'd have a high probability of running into him.

After work, Lieselotte took over digging for Rory and Johan. With everyone present, she explained she had a source who could pass the exact depth of the tunnel and precise coordinates to Wolfgang so that their tunnels could line up.

"Will your source find out how far they've gotten?" Petyr asked.

"I'm not sure. I hope so. I can't thank you enough—you've given so much time."

And they'd never complained or asked for anything.

Rory and Johan went home. Lieselotte and Anneliese crouched through the tunnel, driving their shovels into the dirt and loading trays for Petyr and Mikael to haul out with a pulley. Though lit, the tunnel's depths pressed in claustrophobically—like a worm burrowing through earth. A cave-in could happen at any moment. But they'd taken every precaution they could.

But right now, that wasn't on her mind. Right now, it was on the note she had placed on Tom's desk for his trip into East Berlin and his rendezvous with Wolfgang.

The Man with the Note

Three days. Even in sleep, Wolfgang obsessed over the grave. He and Eckhart inspected it the day after. *The earth showed clear signs of disturbance, but who would suspect it had been exhumed? And even if someone does—who would imagine it was to dig a tunnel?* Wolfgang should worry more about the crypt hiding the tunnel. That was the real danger. If a distant Von Haven Stein died and wished to be interred in the familial mausoleum, there'd be dozens of people inside.

With that shift in focus, the anxiety about the grave faded, latching onto the crypt instead. Making it feel as though he had made some deal with the devil and forgotten to examine the details. Schwarzfuchs's threat also echoed in his mind: *Everything you do, we see. Everything you say, we hear. Everything you write, we read. Our eyes and ears are everywhere.* The words were scripture—sacred to the Stasi, a curse for everyone else.

Or was it not a threat, but a promise? An undeniable fact? The paranoia Hohenschönhausen instilled was slow to fade—maybe it never would.

On that third day, Wolfgang and Eckhart arrived at work, waiting for Stasi agents to swarm them. But none did. They waited for questions from the day shift. But none came.

After the debacle of the 17 July 1958 grave, they were much more careful with the graves they dug up. Always having a second set of eyes validate. It was morbid how quickly they became used to digging up graves. *How can I ever tell Lieselotte about this?* Though he got used to the smells and sights, it still split his soul to desecrate a person's final resting spot. He recited the prayer from the Book of Revelation before digging and memorized the names (those of which they could decipher on the tombstones). Thanking them for aiding in their quest for freedom.

Wolfgang and Eckhart used vacation on a Friday. They all had agreed they needed a day off from digging. It took a lot of convincing for Wolfgang to accept. Eckhart had wanted to go out for a few beers at the Copper Cellar. So many people inside the pub were familiar. People who hadn't changed. Who still sat in the same spot drinking the same type of beer. The only change was physical. Fatter. Grayer. Older.

They sipped their beers and scanned the pub. The dim lights and cigarette smoke clouded the room, making it hard to see. But through the veil of smoke and shadows, a face from their past sat across the bar. The moment they dreaded had finally arrived.

Dietrich was across the bar with a group of friends. His gaze found Wolfgang and Eckhart, his eyes lighting up. *How could they light up like that? With such joy when he knew what he had done? What he'd caused?*

Dietrich crossed the room toward them, smiling as if nothing had happened.

"Are you going to be okay?" Wolfgang whispered to Eckhart.

"I don't know."

Wolfgang sensed Eckhart's body tense. His muscles flexing, his neck veins surging.

Dietrich slid into a seat at their table. "Where have you guys been?" he asked.

Wolfgang bit the inside of his lip. Recalling every single reason he wanted to escape into the West. He needed to remember them. That's what was at stake if he lost his cool.

"Working. Not much else," Wolfgang said, forcing casualness.

But he'd never been an actor. That was Dietrich's gift.

"I saw your parents," Dietrich said to Eckhart. "You're working at a cemetery now?"

Eckhart nodded. Wolfgang slid his foot over and gave Eckhart a little tap: he'd have to do better than this to not cause suspicion.

"Leaves me dead tired," Eckhart muttered.

Dietrich grinned. "Still the same dry humor. I've missed you two."

"Where have you been?" Wolfgang asked, deciding it was beyond either of his or Eckhart's acting skills to say they missed him, too.

"I am at a cereal plant now."

Dietrich went into the specifics. Details that frankly Wolfgang never would have been interested in. Add Dietrich's betrayal into the mix, and Wolfgang could hardly bear the sound of his voice, let alone his life updates. *How much money did the Stasi pay you to betray us? Thirty pieces of silver?*

"I'll get us another round," Dietrich said, rising to go to the bar. He stopped and took in the moment. "Damn, it's been way too long."

He went to the bar, leaving Wolfgang and Eckhart to their almost finished beers.

"Do you need to leave?" Wolfgang asked.

"I should bash his head in," Eckhart said.

"The Stasi will have asked him to keep tabs on us. If they think he can't, they'll infiltrate with someone else."

"That doesn't mean we'll divulge any secrets to them."

"No. But we don't know what they have on any of us. What they could try to force us to do. I'd rather know who to watch out for. Wouldn't you?"

Eckhart scowled. "He's not the only one."

True. The Stasi wouldn't rely solely on one informant. *Who knew how many they had in this bar? Maybe the day workers at the cemetery were informants. Our next-door neighbors.*

Dietrich returned with three pints of *pilsners* and slid one to each of them.

"Are you still planning on getting out of here?" Dietrich whispered, leaning close to them.

"Yes," Eckhart said. "Leaving and going to bed."

"No, that's not what I mean."

Eckhart took a hearty swig of his *pilsner*, needing to conceal his look of disgust. "Leave Berlin?"

Dietrich looked around again, seemingly for informants. Acting, masterfully, as if he wasn't one of them.

"No. I'm not that dumb anymore. I learned my lesson."

"What, you're happy and content here?"

"Happy?" Eckhart shrugged. "Content? No. But I've got no desire to end up back in prison."

Dietrich leaned back. *Is that a look of worry on his face? Is he losing favor with his Stasi masters?*

"So, you both are just ..." he didn't finish. Didn't know how to. "I want out." His voice was steady, maybe too steady. His eyes didn't darken, didn't waver. They held Wolfgang with a clarity that might've seemed sincere.

Might've.

Wolfgang brought the crisp, slightly bitter beverage to his lips. "I get it. But you'll have to find someone else."

Dietrich shook his head, annoyed. "We all suffered. But you wanted out so badly. What changed?"

"Twenty-three months in a prison. No sense of day or night. Kept awake for what must've been a week straight," Eckhart said. "And when I finally got out, discovering they took my nephew!"

Wolfgang steadied him with a look, before turning to Dietrich.

"And you?" Wolfgang asked. "You were locked up, too. Didn't it change you?"

For the briefest moment, Dietrich's gaze faltered—then steadied again.

"I can't live here anymore. Prison only made me realize that even more."

Eckhart glared at Dietrich. Wolfgang didn't know how to stifle Eckhart's growing anger. If he acted, maybe Dietrich would realize they knew. But if he didn't stop him, there was a chance that this ended with Dietrich lying on the floor with a broken nose and blood dripping down his face.

And … maybe that's how this should end. Should Dietrich's betrayal go unpunished? He deserves a swollen eye. A split lip. But if we did, would the Stasi imprison us? Would this fall under one of Schwarzfuchs's reasons for throwing me in prison forever?

But the heated moment paused when a man appeared beside their table. Graying at the temples, wearing a fedora and a sharp suit. He wasn't just from the West. He was American.

"Wolfgang Kirschke?" the man asked.

Wolfgang looked to Eckhart, then Dietrich—neither had an answer as to who this was. Hopefully, Dietrich noticed the shock on his face and the uncertainty in his eyes. That Wolfgang had no knowledge of this American.

"I'm Tom Jackson from the Associated Press," he said in rough German. "Lieselotte Reisinger is on my staff. That stern-looking fellow over my shoulder is my *minder*."

Wolfgang couldn't hide his surprise. *What is he doing here?* Nothing he said would be safe with the human tape recorder at the table. Nor the Stasi agent tasked with following him around.

"She used to have a photograph of the two of you on her desk. That's how I recognized you."

Dietrich studied Wolfgang; Eckhart studied Dietrich, trying to see what Dietrich thought about an American journalist coming up to them.

"Nice to meet you," Wolfgang said.

They shook hands, and Tom nodded toward a spot at the table. Wolfgang nodded the okay, even though he knew he should refuse. His eyes darted about the pub, trying to see who among the patrons was noting this interaction. But no matter. There was a Stasi informant tailing the American and one right beside him, able to hear everything being said.

"I'm in the East covering a story, wanted to get a beer. Funny how small the world can be."

Wolfgang nodded, not sure what to say. Tom's eyes glanced at Eckhart and Dietrich for enough time for Wolfgang to understand he wanted an introduction. Wolfgang made them.

"Gentlemen. Nice to meet you. I can get the next round," Tom said.

"How is Lieselotte?" Dietrich asked.

"Oh, she's fantastic. Great eye for photography. Her framing. Her timing. It's impressive. She's been doing a bit of journalism as well and really making strides with it," Tom said.

"Are you two still talking?" Dietrich asked Wolfgang.

Wolfgang shook his head. "No. Not for a while. I spoke with her a few months ago to say goodbye."

Dietrich more than likely knew about that meeting at the Palace of Tears, as Schwarzfuchs would have notified him, so that he could know whether that had truly been goodbye.

"She's been seeing a young man. Or at least that's the gossip around the office," Tom said.

His eyes only met Wolfgang's for a millisecond, but it was enough time for Wolfgang to know. Tom was privy to their plan. He wanted Wolfgang to know that last part was all bullshit.

Tom shoved a few bills into Dietrich's hand. "Would you mind getting us another round while I head to the bathroom?"

It was less of a question than it was an order. No doubt, Dietrich wanted to stay put, so he didn't miss anything. But he reluctantly rose from his seat and headed to the bar. Tom rose, too, shielding Dietrich's viewpoint of them with his back.

"Go into the stall after me," Tom whispered.

Then he ventured to the bathroom—his *minder* following him and standing outside the door. Dietrich was back with the beers before Tom. Wolfgang still had beer left. He couldn't finish it, let alone start another.

Tom sighed when he sat down. "Man, East beer just flows right through me. I'm afraid I've broken the seal," Tom said, then added with a grin, "that's an American phrase."

"Well, I think I have to break my seal, too," Wolfgang said.

"Once you do, you'll be going all night," Tom said.

Wolfgang rose. His legs felt weak—a mixture of all the beer he'd drank so quickly and the anticipation of what he would find in the bathroom.

The bathroom was like any pub bathroom around the world—a reminder of how disgusting human beings could be. Men with terrible aim, splattering urine on the floor, forcing the next man to stand further back and adding his own mess. The air had a permanent stench of stale piss and spilled beer. Wolfgang went into the lone stall and locked it. Turning around and surveying … what? The toilet? Was there something hidden? Or had he misunderstood?

There was nothing on the top of the toilet tank. Nothing on the toilet paper roll holder. He crouched, mindful not to touch anything as he scanned around. At the back of the toilet, resting on the curved pipe disappearing into the wall, was a tiny note that looked as though it had been folded a dozen times.

Deciding it would take too long to read it in here, he kept it folded. Instead of slipping it into his trouser pocket, he removed his boot and placed the note inside, then slid his boot back on. He stepped out of the bathroom and returned to the table but didn't sit.

"I think I am going to head home," Wolfgang said.

Tom glanced at his watch. "Holy smokes. Yes, I should go, too. Gentlemen, thanks for the company."

Dietrich watched Tom and his *minder* leave—his beer half full. Wolfgang hadn't touched his latest refill. Eckhart's was nearly empty.

"You're leaving?" Dietrich asked.

"I'm tired," Wolfgang said.

"I should get going, too," Eckhart said.

Dietrich wasn't going to be successful in persuading them to stay, so he accepted his defeat. "It was great seeing you guys again. Let's keep in touch better."

"Definitely," Wolfgang said.

Eckhart forced a nod.

"If something changes, or I find another way, I'll let you guys know. Us three. In it together, right?" Dietrich asked.

Recalling the pledge they'd made not to leave one of them behind—that they would risk death or imprisonment to help each other cross—took audacity.

"Right," Wolfgang said. But the words came out choked. It wasn't anger that caused his voice to quiver, but the pain of Dietrich's betrayal.

Another moment where the scab was yanked off. Where the pain came back in full swing. They had made a promise. The whole while Dietrich had known he had been betraying them, revealing their plans to the Stasi. That promise hadn't been made lightly. For Wolfgang, it had been true. He wouldn't have turned away from his friends. If it had come down to staying with Eckhart and Dietrich or abandoning them for freedom, he would have stayed. Would have died bleeding out in no-man's-land with them.

Wolfgang turned before Dietrich could see the emotion on his face. If he did, he'd realize Wolfgang knew he was the one who had betrayed them.

Wolfgang guided Eckhart outside first, so that if Eckhart had a change of heart and wanted to deck Dietrich, he could intervene.

"That *Scheißkerl*!" Eckhart said when they were outside and down the street.

"I think we need to keep him closer," Wolfgang said.

Eckhart turned to him. "Are you blitzed?"

Yes, he was. He'd drank too much. But this wasn't a drunken thought. To keep the Stasi content, they needed to keep their number one informant in the loop. Especially now that Wolfgang had had an American journalist visit him. Wolfgang explained that to Eckhart.

"What the hell was that about, anyway?" Eckhart asked, regarding Tom Jackson.

"He left me a note," Wolfgang said.

"What's it say?"

Wolfgang shrugged. "Too dangerous to open there. Lieselotte sent him. I know it."

Eckhart didn't ask any more questions. It was a pleasant summer night with plenty of people out for drinks. It was far too foolish to continue talking about the note out here. The fresh air and walk helped Wolfgang sober up, but he didn't think he'd be in the clear to wake up without a pounding headache.

Once inside their apartment, Wolfgang removed his boots and unfolded the note. Eckhart tried reading over his shoulder. To him, it was useless. Sure, he was happy for Wolfgang to get a letter from Lieselotte, but why would she send her American boss with this note of seemingly inconsequential information?

Wolfgang grabbed a piece of paper and a pencil and jotted: *It's a cipher.*

Eckhart's face scrunched in confusion and a nod that asked, *What does it say?*

Wolfgang deciphered the note in his mind, piecing together the words, then wrote it for Eckhart to read.

514 feet into the tunnel. Depth of 22 feet. Digging to Lat 24 degrees. Long 16. Started at 14 Flecke drive—664 feet from wall.

Eckhart's eyes lit up: *Holy shit.*

Wolfgang did the calculations. Their team was at 249 feet. 763 feet total. According to her letter, Lieselotte had started 664 feet away from the Wall. So, she hadn't crossed under it yet, but they were close.

Over a quarter of the way, Wolfgang wrote.

Eckhart dipped his head back in excitement then scribbled: *I'll tell Bastian and Trude tomorrow.*

Lieselotte had promised she would help dig, and she had. As Wolfgang lay in bed, he couldn't help but smile at her resolve, moved by the depth of her loyalty. She was digging through the earth to get to him.

All In

Lieselotte arrived at the office early to develop her tunnel photographs. She used both her father's old Leica, and the Associated Press's modern Nokia. The black-and-white images carried dramatic power. But the color photographs made it real—this was happening now. It wasn't some distant event in the pages of history. A reminder that change could still make a difference. Using her father's camera made her feel closer to him, as if continuing the work he'd begun documenting East Berlin's suffering during the 1953 uprising—which was still occurring now in 1965.

After she had developed her photographs, she worked on her article about the growing conflict in the obscure jungles of Vietnam. American president Lyndon B. Johnson had increased his efforts there. It had become the coveted place on the chessboard. An attempt to stop communism from taking over—fearing that if one domino fell, they all would. Lieselotte had heard of Vietnam before because of the French colonial conflict—but, shockingly, many of her American colleagues hadn't. Thousands of young men were being sent to a place they couldn't even find on a map. Coming home crippled or disabled or not coming home at all. Wasn't being able to find it on a map the least that their fellow Americans could do? The Cold War's gaze had shifted from Berlin, but the battle remained the same: people yearning to be free.

She typed away on her IBM Selectric typewriter, ever mindful of her phrasing and spelling, to avoid dreaded correction tape or sacrificing the entire line with X's. The office had the distinct, lively sound of clacking typewriters and ringing phones, with two dozen different conversations occurring at the same time.

Once Tom entered his office, Lieselotte darted inside before his secretary could give him the rundown of his schedule or hang up his fedora and coat on the rack.

"Good morning," she said.

Tom nodded for her to shut the door. She did so, trying to shut it gently, but with her jitters, the blinds on the door rattled.

"I saw him," Tom said.

"Is he okay? How's everything going? Have they made good progress?"

"Whoa, slow down. One question at a time. Let me get a sip of coffee and a cigarette."

He lit a Marlboro and took a few therapeutic puffs along with a swig of coffee that had surely burned his throat. Then he told Lieselotte about his meetup with Wolfgang, Eckhart, and Dietrich.

"He was with Dietrich?" she asked. *Why?*

"That was the name Wolfgang said."

"You didn't say anything about the tunnel with him around, did you?" she asked.

Oh, no. If Dietrich had overheard anything, that meant he'd tell the Stasi. They wouldn't wait to arrest them like last time. Just building the tunnel would be enough evidence to throw them in prison forever. Brandish them traitors. Maybe even seek the death penalty.

"Calm down. I didn't say anything about the tunnel," Tom said. He slid his cup of coffee over, offering her a sip.

"I'm okay."

"It's Irish coffee—go on, take a sip."

Lieselotte didn't know what that meant, but she took a sip and swallowed. Not expecting her esophagus to flare up as the liquid passed down. Apparently, Tom liked his coffee with a punch.

"Did Wolfgang say anything? Any sign of how far they've come?" Lieselotte asked.

Tom took a big sip of his coffee, sighing with satisfaction. If she had taken a gulp that big, she'd be drunk and would've burnt her throat.

"No. It wasn't safe."

"But the note?"

"Delivered."

Lieselotte nodded, frustration and questions twisting in her chest. *How much ground have they covered?* She hadn't promised Anneliese and the others any concrete information. Still, they knew the meeting was happening and would want an update. They had given so much time and effort, it would have been nice to know how much longer they would have to keep going.

"Sorry I couldn't find out more," Tom said.

"No—I appreciate you doing this."

"You'll need me again. Once you get close. Review your daily totals with your team. How much ground you're covering. It's a fair assumption they're going slower. Secrecy and stealth require caution. Caution means slow."

Lieselotte wanted to ask more questions and repeat the ones she had asked. Thinking if she asked them multiple times, the answers would change. That he would have more details. But she knew they wouldn't. So, she thanked him silently once more, this time with a smile, then headed back to work and her story about the war escalating in Vietnam.

When she arrived at the grocery store, Mrs. Winterstein acknowledged her with only a nod. That was fine with Lieselotte. She wasn't in the mood for her bluntness. Sometimes strong people fail to see that not everyone possesses their strength. Mrs. Winterstein would see the sadness in her eyes. The perpetual worry that was eroding her youth. Maybe she wouldn't have commented on it. But chances were, she would—annoyed by what she saw as weakness.

Some days, the weight of the world suffocated—it didn't sneer or scold. It simply threw its weight atop her, silent and indifferent. And today was one of those days.

Petyr, Hansel, Rory, and Johan were on duty. The first two were inside the tunnel while the others loaded the dirt into the corner, waiting to remove it once the store closed. They were caked in dirt and sweat.

"What's wrong?" Petyr asked Lieselotte.

"Nothing." She tried to force a smile. Even though she couldn't see it, she knew it was a puny attempt.

Once Anneliese, Mikael, and George arrived, she asked the others to join her so she could tell them about Tom's trip into the East and his successful delivery of her note.

"But we don't know how far they've dug?" George asked.

She shook her head. "I'm sorry." Their chests deflated and shoulders sagged. "We've been digging for a while. I know how much I've asked of you. You all have your own lives to live and you're spending your free time here."

"This isn't charity," Anneliese said. "This isn't even about helping people across the world. These are our people. Children we grew up with. But because someone drew an arbitrary line, it separated us into the lucky and the unlucky."

"We keep digging," Petyr said. "We have better tools over here. Can cover more ground than they can."

"What are your thoughts on recruiting more people?" Mikael asked.

"And work around the clock?" Lieselotte asked.

"Yeah, night shifters," Rory said, lifting his shirt to wipe his face. "I'm more of a nestled-in-bed-by-ten kind of revolutionary—but you know, I'll do it in the name of freedom."

A round of nods followed at the suggestion of twenty-four shifts.

"We're aiming to be finished before the end of the year. For that to happen, we need to put in more time," Petyr said.

"I hate that I have to agree with my *Dummkopf* brother," Anneliese teased. "But he's right."

"We can't sacrifice quality for quantity," Mikael said. Lieselotte nodded—that was a shared concern. "Bring in too many inexperienced hands, and we're not digging a tunnel—we're building a burial chamber."

Hansel blanched. "That could happen?"

George ran his fingers through his hair—finally getting to that front man's length. "Of course that could happen, but it won't. Tell them, Johan."

Johan looked pained to have to speak. "We need to reinforce the tunnel. Thick beams. Proper bracing. Better safe than sorry."

"We can train them," Anneliese said. "Problem solved. Twenty-four-hour coverage."

"I don't know if Mrs. Winterstein will go for it."

"No offense to her," Petyr said. "But if she's in, she needs to be all in."

Lieselotte considered his comment and told them she would talk to her before she left in the morning. They said goodbye to Petyr, Hansel, Rory, and Johan and got to work. Listening to the radio as they dug—George always finding the best station. American pop songs came through the static before being swallowed up in the tunnel. Mikael and George laid the support beams that Johan slung across his back like twigs. The two women kept tearing into the mound of earth in front of them—sweat streaking their foreheads.

When the shift was over, Lieselotte wiped herself off as best she could, including the bottoms of her shoes, so as not to leave dirty footprints on Mrs. Winterstein's freshly cleaned floors. Anneliese had offered to go with her, but Lieselotte declined. She needed to stand on her own—courageous and clear-eyed. Talking to Mrs. Winterstein required not a fraction of the courage Wolfgang and the others had to possess every moment.

She knocked on the door and waited for permission to enter. It didn't take long—no more second-guessing. Mrs. Winterstein had grown used to the routine, and she woke before the knock on the door. She was in her nightgown and bathrobe, grabbing her keys and heading for the door.

"May I speak with you?" Lieselotte asked.

"You're changing the terms of our agreement again."

"I am." No point in denying. The key to any relationship is to not be the one constantly asking something of the other person. A give and take. A balance. But Lieselotte had only taken and offered nothing. That had to change. "Our goal is to be finished by the end of the year, but we're not proceeding at the pace we need to be. If we come across any rock, that could put us behind schedule even further. Every day is a day the Stasi could discover their tunnel."

"What are you proposing?" Mrs. Winterstein asked.

"We recruit more people and work around the clock."

"No peace the whole day?" Mrs. Winterstein asked, her tone incredulous.

"I know I keep changing our terms. And you're getting nothing from us. We'll clean your floors every night and stock your shelves."

Mrs. Winterstein tugged her bathrobe tight, irritated. "Fine. Sweep the floors. Mop the floors. Fill the dairy coolers. Stock the shelves. Rotate the old product to the front."

"Deal."

"Is he worth it?"

It was the first time Mrs. Winterstein had asked for any information about those in the East. About Wolfgang.

"Yes. But I'm not doing it because I love him."

Mrs. Winterstein's jaw slacked. "Then whatever are you doing it for?"

"Because everyone deserves the freedoms we have."

Mrs. Winterstein scoffed. "The whole world is filled with places with no freedoms, dear. Do not be so naïve to think this is unique to Berlin."

"I'm not naïve," Lieselotte shot back. Perhaps a bit too forcefully, because it took Mrs. Winterstein by surprise. The sureness in her voice. The confidence. "The world's full of injustice. China. Vietnam. Cuba. Africa. I can't fix all that. But I can help people less than a mile from me. And that matters."

For the first time, Mrs. Winterstein looked upon Lieselotte not as an immature, lovesick young woman, but as a driven woman who saw injustice and tried to right it.

Mrs. Winterstein gave permission to dig twenty-four hours a day. Now Lieselotte needed to find the bodies to do so.

Confession at the Wall

Talking to Trude wasn't easy—especially without Bastian discovering Dietrich's role. Eckhart and Wolfgang had stopped by the next day. As Trude's pregnancy advanced, Bastian took over grocery shopping. Once he returned, they'd share the news Lieselotte had passed along.

Trude made apple cider—less sweet and watered down from fewer apples and less sugar, but the gesture was appreciated.

"You're going to hang out with Dietrich … so he can report to the Stasi?" Trude asked, the water running as a safeguard against hidden microphones.

"Yes. Let him see everything we're doing," Wolfgang said.

"Well, not everything. Nothing about the you-know-what," Eckhart clarified.

"Because if he's not spying and reporting on us, someone else is?" Trude asked.

Wolfgang knew Dietrich wasn't the only one. Trude had someone watching her—so did Bastian, Franco, and Emilia. And those watchers had watchers. That was the Stasi's power: infinite informants, infinite paranoia.

"That's right," Wolfgang said.

"Bastian cannot know about Dietrich," Eckhart said.

The front door opened, and Bastian called out, "I'm home."

"Darling, Eckhart and Wolfgang are here!" she called back.

Bastian came into the kitchen, setting a cloth bag onto the table and then kissing Trude on the cheek and giving her growing belly a rub.

"What's going on?" he asked Wolfgang and Eckhart.

Wolfgang handed him the same note Eckhart and Trude had read, explaining the progress Lieselotte had made in the West. Bastian's eyes widened and a grin spread on his face.

Wolfgang and Eckhart stayed for lunch. Trude prepared *sauerkraut*; Bastian grilled *bratwurst*. The four of them drinking beer as the sausages grilled, enjoying the last few weeks of summer sun.

After they had lunch, Wolfgang and Eckhart left. Dietrich had invited them to go onto the water on a paddleboat. They had agreed to go. The chilled breeze on the water reminded them that the warm weather of July and August wouldn't be returning for a long time. Dietrich talked about work, recalling the memories before their arrest. No matter how hard he tried, there would be no new memories of the three of them. Just these fake ones for appearances only. Hollow and meaningless. Wolfgang and Eckhart had explained their distance to the lingering effects of prison.

After they docked, they went out for drinks. Dietrich introduced them to a group of women their age. Beautiful and attractive. Alcohol came in every vessel—shot glasses, cocktail glasses, pint glasses, *steins*, and boots. The odor inside the beer hall was an unpleasant mix of stale beer, sweat, and fried potatoes. Wolfgang and Eckhart excused themselves to go to the bathroom.

"It's a trap," Wolfgang whispered, checking under the stalls. "The drinks. The women. It's all bait."

Eckhart wasn't normally a mean drunk. He was a drunk who lost his inhibitions. But around Dietrich, that meant he'd become mean.

"I can think of worse forms of torture," Eckhart quipped.

"We can't trust anyone," Wolfgang said.

"I don't have to trust someone to sleep with them," Eckhart said with a smirk. "But seriously. He thinks you and Lieselotte are long done. If you want him to believe that, you need to show him something."

"I'm not cheating on Lieselotte."

Absolutely not. Even if she may understand why he did, that wasn't something he was willing to do.

"I'm not saying you have to. But you can't look like they're carrying the Black Plague."

"Or like they're Stasi informants?"

"Or that, too."

They went to the sink and washed their hands. The door swung open.

"Thought you two were hiding out in here," Dietrich said.

"No, just pissing out three gallons of beer, asshole," Eckhart said.

It hadn't been uncommon for Eckhart to swear at Dietrich, so it was a nice pass for him to call him a vulgar name without it causing suspicion.

Eckhart stepped out of the bathroom, but Dietrich blocked Wolfgang with a hand to the chest.

"Is this all too soon?" he asked.

Wolfgang stiffened. "Is what?"

"Larna cuts my hair. I told her about you and Eckhart. Her friend Esmeralda thinks you're handsome. But if you're still in love with Lieselotte, I can tell her for you."

"No, I'm fine. Lieselotte's been out of my life for a long time."

Dietrich shook his head. "Come on. Be truthful. You still love her. That's okay."

Be truthful? *The audacity.* Wolfgang mentally counted every reason he wanted to escape to the West like tally marks, trying to calm himself.

"She was my first love. She'll always hold a place. But I'm not hung up on her. I'd just rather not talk about her," Wolfgang said.

"What's changed between us?" Dietrich asked.

"What do you mean?"

"You and Eckhart walk like you're on eggshells around me."

Wolfgang exhaled hard. He should tell him off. Tell him everything. That he knew it was he who had betrayed them all. But he couldn't do that to the others.

"Not all of us came out of prison whole," Wolfgang settled for.

If the sadness on Dietrich's face was fake, it was masterful. A forgery not even an expert could spot. Wolfgang hoped it was fake. It was easier to hate Dietrich. To know that he was conflicted or pressured into being an informant didn't help the rage he felt. It made the whole situation much more complex. Anger doesn't like complex, moral ambiguousness. It wants clear-cut, black and white.

Maybe he should ask which of the women Dietrich was planning on flirting with. But oddly, he didn't want to out his friend's sexuality like that. There was still a part of Wolfgang that felt like a terrible friend that he hadn't picked up on it sooner. Hadn't asked him. Hadn't told him it wouldn't have mattered if he was gay. *Would it have changed anything for Dietrich?* Maybe he felt distant—like they'd never been real friends. After all, friends share secrets. But that didn't excuse the betrayal.

Wolfgang stepped out of the bathroom and joined the others. He took a sip of his beer; the massive boot blocking his face gave him time to hide his emotions. He had a role to play. He wouldn't cheat on Lieselotte. But that didn't mean he couldn't talk with Esmeralda.

When Dietrich came out of the bathroom, Wolfgang was already deep in conversation with her. Smiling. Looking into her eyes, listening to everything she said, as if it was a gripping thriller. Eckhart hadn't narrowed in on one woman. He was a man who fed on attention bestowed upon him by his female counterparts. He was charming and funny. Not afraid of a little self-deprecation to get a laugh.

Wolfgang needed to proceed with caution. Having had too much alcohol to trust his words, he stayed silent. It wasn't like he'd blurt out he was digging a tunnel. But would he give away some nugget of useful information that Dietrich and maybe some of these women could divulge to the Stasi that would allow them to deduce the tunnel?

Eckhart's choice of which woman he would end up with was chosen for him. Glenda, a tall blonde, had grabbed him by the shirt on the group's walk to the next pub and pulled him into the alleyway.

Wolfgang kept to the street side, subtly resisting any pull toward an alley. He played it cool but tightened his core—ready if she tried to drag him away for a private embrace.

Eckhart and Glenda met them at the next bar. Her cheeks were flushed, and she giggled with her friends. Eckhart was a little quieter with his actions. He dunked a piece of the Bavarian pretzel into beer cheese and took a bite.

As the women had to come to grips with the brutal reality of how drunk they were, they decided to leave once Tina vomited in the bathroom. She came out disheveled and crying.

"We have to do this again," Esmeralda said.

Wolfgang smiled. "Sounds great."

She bit her lip as she walked away—undeniably gorgeous. In another life, he might have followed her home. Asked for her number. But that was impossible. He'd met Lieselotte. And ever since he was a young boy, he'd developed a connection with her that could never be duplicated. She was in full color. Everyone else was in grainy black and white. It would have been easier for him if he hadn't. *Would I have been content here? Would Esmeralda or a similar woman be able to talk me out of fanciful dreams and ground me in reality? Convince me it was neither brutal nor unfair, it was the simple truth of our lives? Would it have offset a job I hated?* No, it wouldn't have. *Lieselotte was just the face my hopes and dreams have taken on.*

The massive pretzel, fresh air, and water had sobered Wolfgang to a manageable buzz. He'd have a headache in the morning, no doubt, but he felt good about avoiding a sloshing stomach.

"Can we go for a walk?" Dietrich asked.

"It's late," Eckhart said.

"You work nights. This is early," Dietrich said.

"Well, I don't work drunk."

"Please?"

Wolfgang refrained from scoffing. *Please?* He tried to remember how he might've answered before the failed escape. *Would I have agreed to go even if I didn't want to?*

But maybe Wolfgang felt as though he owed Dietrich something. Maybe friendship wasn't about what you did or didn't do. Wolfgang hadn't been the close friend Dietrich had needed. Neither had Dietrich, but Father Langer's lessons were all about treating people the way you wanted to be treated.

"Sure," Wolfgang said.

Dietrich nodded his thanks. As they walked, Wolfgang waited for him to speak. To say something. But he appeared content to just enjoy the September night. A night cool enough to escape summer's heat but not yet brushed by autumn's chill. He only stopped walking once the Wall was a stone's throw away. Spotlights illuminated the menacing wall. A challenge to those wishing to escape: *We dare you to try.* VoPos patrolled along the

Wall, armed with machine guns and accompanied by dogs. Wolfgang didn't like being so close to the Wall. Especially at night.

"Why don't we head back?" Wolfgang suggested.

"Yeah, I'm tired," Eckhart agreed.

"I know you know," Dietrich said.

His back was to them, his eyes on the Wall. But he found what courage he had and turned to face them.

"Know we know what?" Eckhart asked.

Wolfgang couldn't play dumb. There was no menace in Dietrich's eyes. No hint he was a predator that had caught prey. No, there was relief in his eyes.

Dietrich's voice wavered, but he didn't look away. "You know it was me who betrayed you."

"I don't know what you're talking about," Eckhart said.

"Don't. I know it. Please, let's just come clean," Dietrich pleaded.

Wolfgang stepped forward before Eckhart could. Whatever suppressed anger Wolfgang felt was a fraction of Eckhart's.

"We trusted you. You promised us you wouldn't leave us. That we'd share the same fate," Wolfgang said.

"I did."

"You fucking betrayed us!" Eckhart said, the words spitting out of his mouth. "They took my nephew! Theresa and Johanna killed themselves! Conrad died at that labor camp! The Schneiders lost their children!" Eckhart grabbed Dietrich by his shirt, balling it into his fists. Wolfgang tried to pull him away. Dietrich didn't fight it. "I never even got to see him! Bastian never got to hold his son!" His head and grip fell. He sobbed, his chest heaving.

Wolfgang pulled Eckhart away from Dietrich, holding him up because his grief was all-consuming.

"I never wanted that," Dietrich said.

"You should have thought of the consequences before you ratted us out," Wolfgang said.

"Why? Why did you do it?" Eckhart asked.

"I know why," Wolfgang said.

Eckhart's sobbing stopped as he looked at Wolfgang, pleading to know why Wolfgang hadn't told him. *Because it wasn't my secret to tell.* Dietrich met Wolfgang's eyes. A glimmer of hope in them that Wolfgang truly knew why.

"Why?" Dietrich asked.

"They had something on you. Your choice was to become an informant or go to prison."

Dietrich looked disappointed, hoping Wolfgang knew more. His eyes pleaded for Wolfgang to end the lie he'd carried his whole life.

"You love men," Wolfgang said.

Eckhart looked at Dietrich for an explanation. As if Wolfgang had lost his mind. But Dietrich didn't deny it.

"You're a homosexual? You never said anything," Eckhart said.

"I didn't know how to," Dietrich said.

"How about, 'I'm gay'?" Eckhart said.

"Would that have worked?"

Eckhart hesitated. Wolfgang had gone through that contemplation in the cells. It was too hard to examine his viewpoint from before his incarceration. If he would have cared then. But after spending those months in prison, a person's bedroom preferences were the last thing he cared about.

"I don't know," Eckhart said.

Dietrich smiled through his pain. "I appreciate your truthfulness."

"Why tell us now?" Wolfgang asked. "When did you find out we knew?"

"The first time I saw you, Wolfgang. I could tell in your eyes," Dietrich replied.

"When did you start informing?" Wolfgang asked.

"A year and a half before we planned our escape."

"Tell us why."

Dietrich hesitated, not deciding if he would tell them, but mentally preparing to do so. To verbally acknowledge the person he had become. "I was seeing a man. A barber at the same place Larna works at. He was the first man I'd been with. We kept it secret … or so I thought. But he hadn't been so secretive in the past. The Stasi had arrested him. They wanted names. He gave up mine. Schwarzfuchs came to my apartment with armed guards. He gave me a choice. Life in prison or become his rat."

Wolfgang and Eckhart listened. Even after all he'd done, it still hurt to watch someone they once cared for suffer.

"Did you love him?" Wolfgang asked.

"I did," Dietrich said. "For the first time in my life, I could be me. All of me. When I was arrested, I was so afraid."

Wolfgang knew that fear. Thinking about it sucked his breath away.

"I think about our escape a lot. What we'd be doing if we'd made it over. I lost everything and cost you everything," Dietrich said.

Both Wolfgang and Eckhart stayed silent. There was no argument; he had cost them everything, including time—the most precious commodity in the world, the only currency without a known balance.

Dietrich's face had gone pale. "But—God, I didn't know what else to do." He drew a breath. "Freedom doesn't exist for people like me—not here, not on the other side of that wall. But I wanted you to know that I'm sorry. I chose wrong. I never should have gone through with it. I regret it. But there's no taking it back. No undoing it."

"No, there isn't," Eckhart said.

"Thank you for being my friend. It's my greatest regret that I ruined that. Thank you for letting me apologize."

Dietrich turned before Wolfgang could even decide how he wanted to end this conversation. A final goodbye? A final curse? An uneasiness took hold of Wolfgang's stomach. The feeling that something bad was about to happen.

And it did.

Without warning, Dietrich sprinted toward the Wall. Wolfgang and Eckhart stepped forward, their minds not working in conjunction with their bodies. *What the hell is he doing?!*

The dogs barked, yanking their leashes taut and gaining the attention of their masters. The guards shouted for Dietrich to stop. Watchtower spotlights swung toward him, engulfing him in their harsh light.

Wolfgang and Eckhart shouted Dietrich's name. But Dietrich ignored their pleas, ignored the guards' warnings. He leaped toward the Wall, his feet trying to scale up the smooth stone.

A shot cracked through the night like a whip. Dietrich fell from the Wall. A splattering of blood dripped down the gray stone. Dietrich lay sprawled on his back, eyes open, blood pooling around him.

299

Wolfgang moved to charge forward, but Eckhart grabbed him by the arm. The dogs turned their attention away from the dead man to the new threats.

"Stay back!" the guards shouted, aiming their guns at Wolfgang and Eckhart.

Shock drowned out the danger. Wolfgang only wanted to reach Dietrich, to make sense of what had happened. As if seeing him more clearly might offer answers. His heart demanded he get closer, and his body responded, ignoring his brain's rational pleas to stay still. Eckhart clamped on and the two spiraled to the ground.

Screaming filled Wolfgang's ears—his own, though he didn't realize it at first. Eckhart wrapped his arms around him. Wolfgang's glasses had been knocked askew. Maybe a gift from God, so he didn't see Dietrich's body. But he put them back on. He had to see.

"He's gone," Eckhart said. "He's … gone."

Though Eckhart didn't sob the way Wolfgang had, emotion shook his voice. For the first time since Dietrich's betrayal, they could remember the friend he'd been.

His death hadn't solved anything. It hadn't rectified anything. Forgiveness was no longer possible. Mercy had missed its chance. And yet, grief tugged at Wolfgang—not just for the person Dietrich had been, but for the future he'd thrown away.

"We need to go," Eckhart said.

Wolfgang's breath caught—there was still time to run. It was dark, with little chance the guards had seen their faces. But then the guards released the leads of the German Shepherds. The dogs, ears pinned back, charged. Daring them to run. Circling them, snarling teeth and dripping saliva. Snapping the air. The guards threw Wolfgang and Eckhart to the ground, and once again, Wolfgang was in handcuffs.

On Our Own

The black bag came off. Blinding fluorescent lights attacked Wolfgang. He squinted, unable to shield his eyes with his hands because they were handcuffed behind him. When the harshness of the light faded, Wolfgang took in the empty room. He was alone. No clocks. No windows. No way to tell how long he'd waited. *Is this the same room as before?* His body thought so. Fear flashed through him. He was back inside Hohenschönhausen.

Finally, the door opened. He didn't have a moment's question of who it would be. Schwarzfuchs, accompanied by two armed guards, stepped into the room.

"*Herr* Kirschke, we meet again," he said. He sat at the steel table, a massive folder in his hands. He flipped it open and sprawled the documents in front of him. "Let's start with your version of events," Schwarzfuchs said, his tone calm but unreadable.

"We've done nothing wrong," Wolfgang said.

"Why do you feel the need to tell me that?"

"Because I'm in handcuffs."

"Our brave border guards said you were beside yourself. We handcuffed you for your safety. It would have been a terrible shame that in your grief, you struck one of our guards."

Sure. More likely, the guard was reprimanded for taking that possibility away. *The state requires you to take a fist to the face.*

"Do you wish for me to tell you what I've been told? Maybe that will help your tied tongue," Schwarzfuchs said.

There was no point wasting breath arguing. Schwarzfuchs would twist whatever he said.

"Three known defectors, previously arrested for an escape attempt, reconnect. They take a rowboat out on the Spree, then imbibe in beverages at a beer hall. *Pilsners*, to be exact. So many witnesses stated they saw you imbibe copious amounts of alcohol. Then you take a long walk toward the Wall. Then one of the three attempts to scale it." He paused. "Those are all undeniable facts; would you like to refute them?"

Wolfgang shook his head. Then remembered the rules: Everything was recorded. Audial responses only. "No."

"I think in your drunken state, the three of you discussed your desire to escape. The alcohol you fiendishly drank lowered your inhibitions, perhaps removed them entirely, and your desire became a need. Unanimously, you decide to test the fates and try to escape. But only one of you possessed the courage to follow through. The other two succumbed to cowardice."

Wolfgang shook his head. "Not at all."

"No?" Schwarzfuchs said, leaning back in his chair. "Enlighten me."

Wolfgang hesitated. "Dietrich admitted to us—that he was the one who betrayed us."

"Us?" Schwarzfuchs interjected, looking for more information.

"Eckhart and I."

"Eckhart Kleppelstein?" Schwarzfuchs asked. Wolfgang confirmed. Schwarzfuchs waved his hand. "Continue."

"Dietrich admitted to us he was the one who had betrayed us when we had tried to escape."

"Did you know before?"

Wolfgang shook his head. "No."

"No?"

"I wondered. But I didn't know for sure."

That part was technically true. He had been confident it had been him, but until Dietrich had admitted it, it had only ever been a strong guess. It was a convenient half-truth.

"Why did he tell you?"

"You'd have to ask him."

"I cannot ask him. He's dead. His body is being cremated as we speak."

That sentence hit Wolfgang like a club to the gut. Dietrich was dead. Not even his body remained. How was that possible? He was alive just hours ago.

"I can only speculate," Wolfgang said.

"Then speculate." His normally relaxed tone had turned sharp.

"Guilt. For betraying his friends."

"Are you planning an escape?"

The question Wolfgang had waited to be asked. What this whole ruse was about.

"No. I don't have a desire to end up back in prison."

"Yet, here you are." Schwarzfuchs smiled.

Wolfgang scoffed. "Yet, here I am. But I did nothing wrong."

"I could argue you were waiting to see if your friend was successful before attempting the escape yourself."

"No. He asked us to go for a walk. I had no idea what he was planning."

He held Schwarzfuchs's glare. *Let him look. There's no lie to find.* It was the truth. During his previous interrogations, Wolfgang was always trying to hide the truth. Now, he had nothing to lie about— except for the escape.

"Why should I believe you?" Schwarzfuchs asked.

"I know you have people watching me. Watching the people I interact with." Schwarzfuchs didn't confirm or refute. He only glared at Wolfgang with calm intensity. A tea kettle close to boiling. "You don't have to say yes. I know it's true," Wolfgang said. "You threatened me with that fact when you released me from prison."

"I know that your friend's brother Bastian Kleppelstein and his wife Trude Kleppelstein, nee Holdenbrücke, leave their home in the evening."

"That's odd?" Wolfgang asked, with just a bit too much sarcasm. Schwarzfuchs shot him a warning look.

"Where do they go?" the Stasi agent asked.

Wolfgang shrugged. "I don't know. I work nights."

"But you go to their apartment."

"I do. Eckhart is my best friend. That's his brother."

"Why so many visits?"

"They're family."

He almost said it was because of Trude's pregnancy, and Eckhart just wanted to help. But he bit it back. Surely, they knew already, but if they didn't, he'd never be the one to tell them. Not after what they had done to their first child.

"They've been seen heading toward Eternal Peace Cemetery," Schwarzfuchs said.

A cold chill ran along Wolfgang's flesh. He couldn't react. He couldn't let his body betray him with the reddening of his skin, or a nervous swallow, or diverting his eyes. This news had to mean nothing to him.

"Sometimes Trude brings supper," Wolfgang said, careful to keep his voice flat and steady.

"Is that so?"

"She doesn't think Eckhart and I eat enough."

Schwarzfuchs smiled. "Do you think you have a chance at this chess match, *Herr* Kirschke? I play with a board full of queens. You? Nothing but pawns." Wolfgang stayed silent, knowing that he had to stay calm. He steadied his breathing. In slow, out slower. "You are up to something," Schwarzfuchs said.

"Like you said, you have eyes and ears everywhere. If I was doing something, you would know," Wolfgang said.

Schwarzfuchs gathered his papers and placed them back inside the folder. "A word of caution, *Herr* Kirschke. This chess match between us ends in one inevitable way: checkmate. No matter how many moves it takes, remember that. Checkmate."

Schwarzfuchs rose and headed to the door.

"What about Dietrich?" Wolfgang asked.

"What of him?"

"Will you give his remains to his parents?"

"They will be notified of their son's treachery."

"He was your informant. Does that not garner him any respect?"

Schwarzfuchs turned to look at Wolfgang. A smug look on his handsome face. "I have no idea what you are talking about."

The guards yanked Wolfgang from the chair and shoved the black bag over his head.

"Where are you taking me?!" Wolfgang asked.

He didn't expect an answer, but he had to ask. *Am I being released—or returned to a cell?*

A gust of wind pierced the bag. Wolfgang used the extra air to calm his breathing. Trying to suppress flashbacks of that cell. He was ecstatic to be outside, but was it only temporary?

The guards pushed him into the back seat of a Wartburg and slammed the door shut. The engine came to life. Wolfgang tried to keep track of the turns, but he didn't doubt they were turning to disorientate him. Make retracing his steps impossible. Not that Wolfgang had any desire to do that. Going back to Stasi headquarters or the Submarine were the last places he wanted to go. Then the car stopped. The engine shut off. He waited. For someone to open the door or speak. But no one did. All part of their psychological game.

Finally, the door opened, and someone dragged Wolfgang out of the Wartburg. They unlocked his handcuffs first, then removed the bag. He was back at the Wall, at the very spot where he had been thrown to the ground. The dogs remembered his scent and were on high alert.

Did the pool of blood remain, or had they cleaned it up? Without the spotlights illuminating the ground, it was impossible to tell. Wolfgang assumed they would have left it. What greater deterrent for future escape attempts than to see the result of the last person trying to do so? But then again, East Germany and their Soviet puppet masters had a lie to sell. The Wall was for the safety of its citizens. Hard to sell that lie with bloodstains on *your* side of the Wall.

Wolfgang turned from the menacing wall and trudged home. *Where is Eckhart?* Wolfgang contemplated waiting out on the stoop for him but headed inside. Hoping he had been released before him. When he turned the handle to his apartment, a force on the other side of the door did the same. Eckhart pulled Wolfgang inside.

"Jesus, you had me worried!" he said.

"When did you get home?" Wolfgang asked.

"About half an hour ago."

Wolfgang grabbed a single sheet of paper for him and Eckhart. A single sheet, as writing on pads left indentations for purveying eyes to decipher. They shared what had happened, reviewing the questions they'd been asked and their answers.

Wolfgang underlined a section: *They know Trude and Bastian have been going to the cemetery.*

Eckhart scribbled one word across the page: *Fuck.*

Yes, a succinctly put recap of their situation.

They'll send more people to watch us now.

Eckhart wrote back: *What about the tunnel?*

Wolfgang shook his head. He didn't have an answer. The Stasi were onto them. They had known they were being watched, so why did this disturb him as much as it did? This was all contemplation he'd have to do later. Right now, all the shock of the night had worn off. He'd depleted his body's adrenaline supply and now he was beyond exhausted.

When they woke the following morning, Wolfgang stated they needed to stop by Bastian's. Trude greeted them the way she always did, with a welcoming smile and warm hug, and an offer of something to drink.

Eckhart cut to the chase with little preamble. Starting with Dietrich's death. This part they spoke out loud. It was normal to share life-changing news.

"I'm sorry," Bastian said. "I know he was a good friend to you both."

Trude's sorrow wasn't as overt as Bastian's. She knew the truth. Knew what Dietrich had cost everyone at the table. None more than Bastian and herself. But it would be out of character if she didn't comment on it, so she offered her condolences, too.

"I was thinking, maybe we could go out on the water one last time this season," Eckhart said, then slid a note across the table.

More to say.

Trude and Bastian pretended well, as if they hadn't read the note. They grabbed their coats and followed Wolfgang and Eckhart outside and strolled to Treptower. The skies were clear and the temperature mild, resulting in a gorgeous fall day. The world once again displayed its impartiality to their trials and tribulations. Once at Treptower, away from the informants and hidden microphones, Bastian spoke.

"I don't get it," he said. "You said he didn't want to escape. That he didn't want to risk it. Why try going over the Wall like that? It's mad."

Eckhart glanced at Wolfgang—Wolfgang hoped Bastian hadn't noticed it.

"He just … snapped," Eckhart said.

"There's more, though," Wolfgang said. He divulged that he and Eckhart had been arrested, and Schwarzfuchs's concerning comments.

"He knows you two visit us at the cemetery," Wolfgang said.

Trude looked sick. Whether consciously or unconsciously, she protectively rubbed her stomach.

"Fuck!" Bastian said, using the same word his brother had used to describe the situation.

Trude's voice was small but firm. "We have to stop the tunnel. At least for now."

"What?" Eckhart said. "After all that work?"

"They are onto us!" Trude said with a sternness in her voice Wolfgang had never heard. But there was also a fear-induced quiver.

Eckhart shook his head slowly. "We're just … giving up?"

Bastian looked at Trude. A silent communication taking place between them. "I can't risk what happened last time happening again."

Eckhart wanted to fight that decision. But he couldn't. Because he didn't want them to risk that happening again, either.

"It's for the best you don't go to the cemetery," Wolfgang agreed. "You'll need to tell Franco and Emilia."

"They won't want to stop," Trude said.

"They have to. If you two are being watched, it means they're being watched, too," Wolfgang said. "Schwarzfuchs knows. He just doesn't want to play his full hand."

"We're never getting out of here," Trude said.

That sentence destroyed her. Bastian wrapped his arms around her, consoling her.

"It's not safe for you to come to the cemetery, but that doesn't mean Eckhart and I can't continue with it," Wolfgang said.

"You two dig on your own?" Bastian asked.

Certainly not an ideal situation. It also meant that their portion of the tunnel completion would take a serious hit. With only having two people, it meant they could no longer have two people dig, two people empty, two people work on the support beams. Have sets of eyes scanning the cemetery fence for watching eyes.

"You'd still let us come if we can't help?" Trude asked.

"Of course," Eckhart said, beating Wolfgang to it. "You're family."

"What about Franco and Emilia?" Bastian asked.

"We'd never turn them away," Wolfgang said. "They're as much a part of this as we are. The most help any of you can offer right now is to stay away."

They returned to Trude and Bastian's, and Wolfgang and Eckhart stayed for lunch. The goodbye was bittersweet. It would have to be the final visit for quite a while. At least for Wolfgang. Trude promised to relay the message to Emilia later that day. Eckhart and Wolfgang walked the mile back to their apartment, enjoying the brisk air.

"With the two of us, we're not going to get much done," Eckhart said, every word drenched and dragged down in defeat.

Wolfgang nodded. Still, he would do something. Trying not to think of the Christmas Eve date they had set. Knowing if Lieselotte in the West didn't make up for their lack of production, there was no chance they could meet it. At the rate the two of them could dig, remove the dirt, dig up graves for lumber, fashion support beams, and install support beams—they weren't looking at three months of digging. They were looking at three years.

"We have to put our faith in Lieselotte," Wolfgang said. "And pray that she has better luck than us."

Scars and Soil

Their improved efficiency wasn't just because of more hands—it came from keeping everyone fresh. No one worked beyond the point of fatigue. Once someone became tired, they switched to a less demanding task. Lieselotte and Anneliese had recruited former Freie Universität Berlin classmates they knew had been vocal about the East. They knew the risk—one of them could be a Stasi informant. Those agreeing to help did so with the understanding they would know next to nothing. Only Petyr and his friends knew the details—Anneliese had sworn them to secrecy under penalty of what she termed "blunt-force castration."

Lieselotte was there. If she wasn't working at the Associated Press, she was at the tunnel. Arriving early. Staying late. She wanted to prove she'd never ask more than she gave—a mark of a true leader. She ignored Anneliese's pleas to go home and sleep. Sleep could happen later.

Near midnight, Petyr shouted into the tunnel that Mrs. Winterstein wanted to see her. She crawled out of the tunnel, brushed off the dirt, and wiped her shoes with a rag.

"A word," Mrs. Winterstein said from the bottom step. It was as close to the tunnel as she got. Then she turned and went back upstairs.

Lieselotte wiped her face clean. By the time she got up the stairs to the main level, Mrs. Winterstein was halfway up the stairs to her office/apartment. At the top of the stairs, she knocked on the door, listening for permission to enter. Then she did so.

"Yes?" Lieselotte asked, mustering as much patience as she could.

She knew she was only here because of Mrs. Winterstein's blessing, but she didn't want to waste time on something that didn't matter. There was no time for trivial snide comments or even looks of condescension.

"You are exhausted," Mrs. Winterstein said.

Lieselotte shook her head. "No, I'm okay."

"That was not a question. It was a comment stemmed in incontrovertible fact."

"It's hard work," Lieselotte conceded, giving her the quick victory. Arguing about her exhaustion level was a waste of time. Let her deliver her critique and move on.

"Rest on the couch," Mrs. Winterstein said.

"No, really, I'm fine. There's so much work to do."

"And it is being done."

"Thank you, but I can manage."

She turned toward the door, forcing herself to walk, not run. Her hand reached for the handle.

"If you do not rest, I am revoking my permission. I'll call the police. The government will come. And the tunnel will be closed."

Lieselotte turned toward her. Stared at her. *Is this an idle bluff? But when have I ever known Mrs. Winterstein to joke, to threaten?* Those weren't skills she possessed, or if she had them, they weren't skills she used.

"I will not stand by and watch you work yourself to death. If you continue at this rate, you'll end up in the hospital," Mrs. Winterstein said.

"Please, just let me keep working."

"I'm doing what everyone down there should be doing. You need rest."

"Those in the East don't have the luxury of rest."

Mrs. Winterstein conceded that point with a nod. But even that frustrated Lieselotte. She never looked fazed by anything that happened. There was no morale blow after a temporary defeat.

"That is true. But would your boyfriend want you to work in such a reckless manner?" Mrs. Winterstein asked.

Lieselotte could say he would. That he would say to push through and forward no matter what. Rest later. Keep digging. But that would cast Wolfgang in a poor light. And she wouldn't do that. Because the truth was he would ask that she stop. Never order. But he would beg her to take care of herself.

"And when is the last time you ate?" Mrs. Winterstein asked.

Again, shamefully, Lieselotte's first instinct was to lie. To say she had eaten just before coming here, or at lunch. But Mrs. Winterstein would ask what, and Lieselotte was too exhausted to think of a lie.

"Oh, for heaven's sake," Mrs. Winterstein said, whipping her bathrobe tighter around herself. "Lay down and rest. I will make you something to eat."

Lieselotte wanted to refute, to politely decline, but she didn't have enough energy to fight. Knowing that Mrs. Winterstein's threat to call the police wasn't idle, she approached the couch.

"Hold up. You look like a badger. Let me at least throw a sheet down," Mrs. Winterstein said.

She crouched beneath her bed and drew out an extra pair of white sheets. She sprawled it over the couch. Lieselotte had only been in here briefly and always addressed Mrs. Winterstein from in front of her desk. But now that Mrs. Winterstein walked about the area, she felt able to look around. There was the bed she had seen before, but in front of that was a small kitchenette. A fridge, stove, and a table barely big enough for two. A narrow hallway led to a bathroom and shower. A lone wooden dresser stood near the bed.

313

How had this cramped space become her home? Lieselotte had seen the number of people who shopped at the grocery store. Surely business was good enough that she could have a home of her own. At least an apartment.

Lieselotte sat on the couch as Mrs. Winterstein left. The couch was old, but at that moment, she couldn't remember anything more comfortable. She lay down, and every muscle, every tendon, throbbed in relief. She planned to sleep only briefly—wake when Mrs. Winterstein came back.

But when she woke, Mrs. Winterstein was in bed. The panic set in about how long she had slept. Her eyes darted to the clock behind Mrs. Winterstein's desk. She'd slept three and a half hours. But that couldn't be right. She'd only rested her eyes. But then she noted the carrots, celery, and broccoli. Thick French bread, buttery and warm, with romaine lettuce, roast beef, and cheese. She'd slept through Mrs. Winterstein making her a snack. Lieselotte scarfed the sandwich down and drank the glass of milk.

She wanted to get back to work but feared if she did without Mrs. Winterstein's blessing, she'd follow through on her threat. Instead, she cleared her throat—subtle, but purposeful.

"Three and a half hours isn't enough for a night's sleep but more than enough for a nap," Mrs. Winterstein said. "Go back to work."

"Thank you for the meal. It was gracious of you."

Lieselotte headed for the door, but hesitated. *Will there ever be a better time to ask Mrs. Winterstein about her life? How she had ended up living in this confined space?* Lieselotte had seen her every day for months, yet still knew so little about her.

"If you don't ask, I'll have been mistaken about the courage I thought you possessed," Mrs. Winterstein said.

Lieselotte turned to face her. She sat in her bed now, no longer laying.

"Why do you live up here?" Lieselotte asked, sounding more blunt than she intended.

Mrs. Winterstein rose and tightened her bathrobe belt. It was the only tick she possessed. Something she did when she was frustrated, angry, or annoyed. Or was it the safety she thought it brought?

"This wasn't my store," Mrs. Winterstein said.

She paused. Lieselotte reclaimed a seat on the couch—a polite but pointed move. She didn't want to rush Mrs. Winterstein, but she expected an answer. And Mrs. Winterstein respected confidence. She dragged the chair from behind her desk and positioned it in front of the couch.

"It belonged to my husband's father. My in-laws ran the store before giving it to my husband's older brother. But he was killed in the Great War. So, it fell to my husband, Manfred."

"When did he pass?" Lieselotte asked.

"He killed himself toward the end of the Second World War, when Germany's defeat became clear. Took cyanide like some of the other cowards. Wanted me to take that way out, too. But I wouldn't. Now ask the question you need to ask."

"Were you Nazis?" Lieselotte asked.

"Yes, we were. I was a Nazi."

Lieselotte had never heard someone so brazenly declare that before. Certainly, there was a mass of people who were still devoted to Hitler and the Nazi Party. Behind closed doors, they praise the leader he was. The radical changes he brought. Some knew about the Holocaust—some considered it necessary, others a terrible smear on an otherwise "great" record. And then there were the deniers who thought the Allies had fabricated the story.

As for Mrs. Winterstein being a Nazi, Lieselotte didn't know what to say. Which category did she fall into? One of the blind fools who raised their arms in salutes and who had no idea of the man and radical and genocidal policies they were supporting? Or had she known what the Nazi Party stood for? And agreed with it?

"I see your mind racing," Mrs. Winterstein said. "I didn't know about the camps, if that's what you're thinking. I had no love for Jews. But I hadn't started with hate."

Hadn't started with hate. That had changed. The propaganda had turned her against Jews.

"But I grew to believe everything I was told to believe. That anyone who didn't think like me was a dangerous enemy. That it was necessary to limit these people from owning businesses, from being allowed into the same places as me, from being a part of our society in any way. It was too dangerous." Mrs. Winterstein paused. "So, when my coward husband would rather die than take responsibility for his choices, he left me with this store and his name."

"Accepting responsibility ... that must have been ..."

What is the word to finish that sentence? Horrible? Deserved? Warranted? Awful?

"Do you know what they did to us German women after the war?"

Lieselotte had heard the stories—the mass rape, the silence that followed. Over 400,000 children were born after the war. How many were born of rape? No one could say. But it felt unfair to nod and say that she knew what Mrs. Winterstein went through. That diminished her experience, and she wouldn't do that.

"I heard, but I do not pretend to know," Lieselotte said.

"They raped us en masse. Lined up one after the other like a soup kitchen. They sheared our hair like sheep. Spat on us. Urinated on us. But all those things could be washed away. Hair would regrow. So, they gave me something that I couldn't hide."

Mrs. Winterstein unclenched her hand, releasing the robe closed around her neck. Something Lieselotte had taken as assurance for absolute modesty. She spread the robe, exposing her sternum. In the pale-yellow light, Lieselotte could make out a scar. A swastika covered from the bottom of her throat to the start of her cleavage.

Lieselotte gasped. "That's horrible!"

"It was deserved."

Lieselotte sighed. She could refute that, but she didn't. Her journalistic integrity meant she stayed unbiased. But that wasn't the reason. It was because she wasn't sure she disagreed. *If I were Jewish, how would I feel if I had lost someone in the camps?*

Mrs. Winterstein closed her bathrobe, sealing it tight with a hard yank of her belt.

"They took my house. This store had shut down in '43. No one could afford groceries. Heavy rationing. Once the war ended, I moved in here. Started from the ground up. I could have moved out. The store's been successful." She paused. "This is my prison. And it's far better than I deserve." A loaded silence took hold. "You once asked me why I agreed to help you," Mrs. Winterstein said. Lieselotte had. On that first day, Mrs. Winterstein hadn't answered. "You once wrote that their way isn't wrong, and ours isn't right, but people should have the freedom to choose."

Lieselotte had written that in a column for the Freie student newspaper. Her most celebrated article. The one that convinced Tom to allow her to write as well as photograph.

"I will never again feign to know what's best for people. That is dangerous rhetoric. I too believe people should have the freedom to choose. I want to be on the right side of history this time."

Lieselotte only nodded, knowing Mrs. Winterstein wasn't looking for, nor did she want words of encouragement, forgiveness, or gratitude. She wanted to be acknowledged as a woman of strength by a woman of strength. And that's what Lieselotte gave her.

Over the course of the next few weeks, Lieselotte discovered she slept better on Mrs. Winterstein's couch than she did in her bed. Most likely due to a myriad of reasons. First being the proximity to the tunnel. She was just a couple of flights of stairs away as opposed to blocks away. Second, it seemed when she intended not to sleep is when she could sleep. It was only in her own bed that sleep evaded her. And third, there was a calming presence around Mrs. Winterstein. She was like a beacon of strength that Lieselotte could draw from.

Lieselotte kept meticulous notes on the tunnel's progress, documenting how many feet they covered each day and recalculating their daily average. She photographed the progress—both with her father's black-and-white camera and the colored Nokia one. But something troubled her. They were at 1,314 feet. Wolfgang, with fewer resources and people, should have at least made it halfway. Yet there were no signs—no sounds. Nothing.

"Something's wrong," Lieselotte said.

Only Anneliese was beside her. Petyr and his friends were in the tunnel.

"Relax. Don't get in your head again," Anneliese said.

She was certainly guilty of overthinking. But this felt real—even if she had nothing to prove it. There was no point worrying the others. She could bear this alone. But she needed to find out what was happening. *Could Tom go across once more? And if he can't, what am I prepared to do?* November was in full swing. The end of the year was only a measly six weeks away. At this rate, her unexpected Christmas gift wouldn't arrive in time. Maybe it never would.

The Grave for the Unforgiven

Dietrich hadn't intended to cause more problems for Wolfgang and the others. Wolfgang was sure of that. His actions had been those of a desperate man. But whether it was intentional or unintentional, the result was the same. Wolfgang and Eckhart knew it would be much harder and more time-consuming to dig without the others, but it wasn't until Eckhart unlocked and opened the Von Haven Stein mausoleum that they realized just how much. Moving the tomb on rollers was far harder. With no lookout, they paused every few seconds, spooked by wind and phantom footsteps on fallen leaves.

Only one could dig while the other manned the pulley and kept watch. They also had their work tasks to complete. If they didn't complete them, they would be reprimanded. *What if we are fired?* They'd have to sneak into the cemetery, which was trespassing. Possibly even breaking and entering. Enough for the Stasi to imprison them for decades.

"We can't do this," Eckhart said.

There was no complaining in his voice. It was delivered as the fact it was. The two of them could not dig this tunnel.

"No, we can't," Wolfgang agreed.

It was too risky to invite the others back here. They were being watched. Their hopes lay with Lieselotte in the West. *What if she isn't able to continue, either?* They had spent so much time and effort digging the tunnel. It was all or nothing. *And what if it has all been for nothing?*

The prospect of that was too devastating to consider. *If this tunnel fails, what will I do next?* Though Eckhart said nothing, Wolfgang knew his friend was considering the same thing. Would they move onto the next plan? Or would this finally break their spirits?

"I'm going to use the toilet," Eckhart said.

He needed a moment alone. Wolfgang stared at the tunnel entrance—it looked less like a passage and more like a grave. It was poetic, cruelly so, that his dream of making it to the West had died in a cemetery.

Wolfgang disassembled the pulley system and let the bucket roll into the dirt some fifteen feet below. He started to remove the rollers but stopped.

What was that?

A sound—indistinct, but real. Most likely his imagination running rampant now that he was doing something forbidden with no one to look out. No different from all those phantom noises they'd heard earlier.

But then he heard it again. A voice. Not just a voice, but voices.

Oh, shit!

Wolfgang heaved the tomb back against it, using all his muscle to push it along the rollers and back into place. *Has one of the others come, even though we told them not to? Bastian? Franco?* The goosebumps told him it wasn't a friend. It was the Stasi.

Wolfgang grabbed the rollers and tossed them outside. *How much time do I have?* He closed the tomb as quietly as possible, but stone grinding against stone didn't leave room for stealth. He locked the padlock and then grabbed the metal poles.

Two shadows rounded a corner. He recognized Eckhart and had no doubt who the other was. But then more shadows rounded the corner. The figures advanced toward Wolfgang. He ignored them and dropped all but one of the metal poles and used it to break apart the undisturbed earth. They'd barely started the grave, but at least they had something, so it didn't look as though he just started digging for the sake of it.

"*Herr* Kirschke," the familiar voice of Schwarzfuchs greeted.

Wolfgang turned, resting his hand on top of the metal pole. He wanted to look at Eckhart for answers but knew that Schwarzfuchs and the other Stasi agents wouldn't miss that discreet look.

"Good evening," Wolfgang said.

"Good evening indeed." Schwarzfuchs smiled.

Does he know? Is he about to arrest me? But how could he know about the tunnel? Unless someone else close to us has betrayed us? Wolfgang shoved the thoughts away—Schwarzfuchs would sense doubt instantly. But in this setting, the other Stasi agents were even more dangerous. While Wolfgang talked to Schwarzfuchs, the others scrutinized his every move, mannerism, and expression.

"What brings you here?" Wolfgang asked.

"I came to add to your collection," Schwarzfuchs said, holding up a small burlap pouch. "What remains of your friend," he added for clarity.

Wolfgang cheated his glance at Eckhart, unable to stop himself All that remained of a once great friend was ash inside a small bag. Schwarzfuchs wielded it like a weapon. The Stasi had always preferred psychological torment to physical. Seeing someone you deeply cared for reduced to nothing but ash was among the most lethal.

"What about his mother and father?" Wolfgang asked.

"They did not want to claim them. He was a traitor—an enemy of the state who betrayed his family name."

Wolfgang's knuckles whitened around the pole.

"Of course, we could just throw it in the trash? Down the toilet? That would be appropriate," Schwarzfuchs said.

"No," Wolfgang said. "I'll dig him a grave."

"I'll help," Eckhart said, marching forward to retrieve his own shovel.

"Of course, graves come at a cost," Schwarzfuchs said. Wolfgang and Eckhart paused. "Burial costs, grave costs, maintenance fees, transportation fees, cremation fees," Schwarzfuchs rambled off. "Normally, these expenses are covered by social insurance. But since your friend wanted to be a *Bonner*, the state should bear no financial burden for his demise."

"How much?" Wolfgang asked, cutting straight to the chase.

Schwarzfuchs wanted this to be a game, but he wouldn't play.

"200."

Wolfgang made 450 *Ostmarks* a month, Eckhart about the same. On paper, 200 didn't sound disastrous. But their salaries barely stretched to cover rent, rationed food, and the constant petty expenses of survival. Eckhart tensed. Either ready to swear or drop his shovel.

"Fine," Wolfgang said.

"Up front," Schwarzfuchs said.

"We don't carry that much on us," Eckhart said. "Let us pay you after."

"I'm afraid the word of two traitors does nothing for me. Pay now or I flush your friend into the sewers of Berlin."

Wolfgang pulled out his wallet and glanced at Eckhart for help. He'd understand if he didn't want to. Neither of them had forgiven Dietrich for what he'd done. He'd tried to atone, but not in the way they needed.

Eckhart reluctantly removed his wallet and added what he had. The total was over 200, but Wolfgang expected no change and received none.

"I shall supervise," Schwarzfuchs said.

"And them?" Wolfgang nodded to the other agents.

"They will make sure these grounds are up to standard."

Wolfgang avoided looking at Eckhart, praying his friend did the same. He wanted to pass off an expression that said *go ahead*, but he wasn't an actor. He couldn't fake emotion on command.

"Should I expect Mrs. Kleppelstein to deliver a late-night meal?" Schwarzfuchs asked.

"No," Wolfgang replied, feeling his arctic glare.

"I didn't think so."

Leading the way to the east boundary of the grounds, Wolfgang tried to keep his breathing even while Eckhart and Schwarzfuchs trailed silently behind him. Shade obscured most of this section, but there was a small patch that received daylight. It seemed the best place. Dietrich had loved summer. Loved the sun. When everyone else complained about how hot and unbearable it was, Dietrich had always had a smile.

Wolfgang dug the shovel into the ground, unearthing a small, shallow space. He paused, waiting for the ashes.

Schwarzfuchs stared at the hole. "Surely, you don't think a few inches of dirt is a fitting end—even for a traitor."

"It's just a small bag," Eckhart said.

Wolfgang cringed. No good would come from challenging Schwarzfuchs.

"No, he's right," Wolfgang said. "We should dig a proper grave."

At first, Schwarzfuchs looked displeased that the game had ended, but then nodded for them to commence. They'd dug enough graves to eyeball the size and get to work. All the while trying to be cognizant of what the other Stasi agents were doing.

But to do anything more than glance in their direction was too risky. Schwarzfuchs stood by and watched. Watching Eckhart and Wolfgang as if it were the most exciting thing he could be doing.

"You know, I'm not sure this is the best spot," Schwarzfuchs said, before cracking into laugher. "Relax. I am joking."

Dietrich's bagged remains lay on the ground, looking as though the ashes would spill out. Sometimes, it was just a bag of ash. Other times, Wolfgang remembered they were human remains— Dietrich's. And when that realization hit, it hit hard. But he couldn't show emotion in front of Schwarzfuchs. He'd use it as a weapon. Nor did he want to show it in front of Eckhart. He'd showed so much grief when Dietrich had been killed, and he knew how conflicted Eckhart must have felt. The pain Dietrich had caused his family.

Once the grave was six feet deep, something Wolfgang had developed an eye for, he and Eckhart climbed out. Wolfgang reached for the ashes, but Schwarzfuchs got there first. He opened the bag and showcased the ashes inside.

"Take a good look, gentlemen. If you do not tread with caution, this is the future that awaits you."

He handed the bag to Wolfgang. He stared at it, afraid to open it. To gaze inside. He'd never spread ashes before. It felt odd to keep them inside the bag, like it would keep Dietrich's soul prisoner. But he knew from his lessons with Father Langer that Dietrich's soul had moved on. *Where has it moved on to? Heaven or hell?*

Memories of Dietrich flashed in his mind. He reached inside the bag and grabbed a handful of ashes. His bottom lip trembled from the emotional weight of the moment. Eckhart tapped him on the shoulder. Wolfgang turned. Eckhart had tears in his eyes, too, and wanted to help spread Dietrich's ashes. Wolfgang offered the bag.

It's an incredibly bizarre thing to hold the ashes of someone you once held dear. Realizing this was once a person brought a wave of repulsion. But then it became something more.

Wolfgang silently repeated the prayer from the Book of Revelation. Then he opened his hands, letting the ashes of his friend trickle through his fingers into the grave. Eckhart followed by emptying the last of the ashes.

Wolfgang cleared the emotion in his throat, then started tossing dirt back into the grave. Taking all the anger Dietrich had caused and using it to fill the hole. *Why did he have to spy on us? Betray us? And why did he feel he needed to end his life?* Halfway through filling the grave, that anger faded. Anger never lasts. Grief replaces it, and grief is everlasting. Dietrich was gone from the face of the earth. His parents had labeled him a traitor and wouldn't even accept his remains. And now, two of the people he had betrayed laid him to rest.

Eckhart tossed the last bit of dirt onto the grave and smoothed it out with his shovel.

"I'll get a marker," Wolfgang said.

"No," Schwarzfuchs said. "A traitor to the state deserves neither remembrance nor reverence."

"He worked for you," Wolfgang said.

Eckhart sighed at the comment. Admittedly, it was a stupid thing to say. He'd fallen prey to emotion.

"I assure you I wouldn't resort to such vileness," Schwarzfuchs said.

Wolfgang didn't interject further. Dietrich had admitted the truth. Schwarzfuchs could deny it all he wanted. Wolfgang didn't press for a marker. He knew where Dietrich was buried. During the day, it would be where the shadows ended and the sun caressed. Schwarzfuchs and the Stasi could try to erase people from existence, but they never would succeed in erasing the memory of them.

The Stasi agents marched toward them, an excited, aggressive lurch in their step.

Schwarzfuchs turned toward them. "What is it?"

"Sir. You need to see this."

Obstacle or Omen

L ieselotte had spent days worrying about how far Wolfgang had gotten with the tunnel. Then, by some unexplainable grace, she realized it didn't matter how much ground he had—or hadn't—covered. 2,728 feet was the target. Knowing how far he'd gotten or how far he advanced each day wouldn't affect how hard she and her team worked, or how many hours they put in. They had the advantage—better tools, fewer eyes watching, and more people.

But she couldn't shake the feeling that something had happened in the East. Her mother's advice replayed: to listen to her heart, brain, and gut. Though her brain remained undecided, her heart and gut told her she was right. Something had happened. So, as soon as Tom walked into his office, she sprang on him.

"Have I told you you're relentless?" he said.

"No, but thank you."

"Not a compliment this time."

He nodded for her to take a seat. Lieselotte started to speak, but Tom cast a stern look at her and then raised his mug of coffee, took an exaggerated sip, and sighed dramatically.

"Better?" she asked.

"No. But it was worth a shot. Divulge." He gestured for her to go on. "What's got you pacing?"

"We're under the Wall. Past it, actually. We've dug 1,614 feet."

"And the tunnel needs to be what? 2,700?"

"2,728. I don't know how much they've been able to complete. But at the rate we're going, we will have it done by the end of the year. No question. I need to get word to Wolfgang."

Tom tilted his head, confused. "Won't he discover the tunnel is complete?"

"Not if he's had to stop digging."

She tried to sound calm. Anneliese blamed it on nerves. But Lieselotte couldn't explain the feeling. It felt undeniable. Not the creation of a worried mind. As if the connection between her and Wolfgang had been weakened. Not broken, but bent. It wasn't unrealistic to assume that something would happen that hindered his ability to dig.

"Why do you think that?" Tom asked.

Lieselotte shrugged, demurely. "I can't explain it. My mother always told me to listen to my heart, mind, and gut. To let the majority win."

Tom considered her words. "Do you know who Clare Hollingworth is?" Lieselotte shook her head. Tom frowned. "That's a shame. She was a reporter for *The Daily Telegraph*. On 28th August 1939, she had a feeling something was happening on the German-Polish border. So, she hopped in her car and drove. And what did she see? German troops, tanks, and armored cars poised for attack. She broke the news of World War II." Tom focused his gaze on Lieselotte. A mentor ready to deliver the moral of the story. "Trust those feelings."

"Even if they turn out to be wrong?"

"Yes, and pray they are wrong. Don't you think Hollingworth wished her hunch had been wrong?" The moment reminded her how grateful she was to work for Tom. "I can see if I can get access into East Berlin," he said.

"I want to go."

"We discussed this. It's dangerous."

"I have to go."

Tom waited for more. Lieselotte hesitated.

"If something happens … this will be the last time I'll ever see him. I need to see him."

Tom sighed. He'd told her he couldn't take part in digging the tunnel, and she'd already asked so much of him. Hell, he probably felt he might as well pick up a damn shovel at this point.

"I'll see what I can do," Tom said.

Lieselotte nodded, thanked him, and headed back to work. Her good mood lasted until she reached the basement of the grocery store. She'd expected the group to be hard at work, but everyone stood around, looking defeated.

"What's going on?" Lieselotte asked.

"We hit a snag," Rory said.

"Define snag," Anneliese said.

"I'll show you."

Lieselotte and Anneliese exchanged a glance, then followed Rory further and further into the tunnel. They passed the sign they'd hung directly beneath the Wall: *You are now crossing into East Berlin.* Deeper and deeper until they reached the end of their tunnel. But instead of the familiar sight of black dirt, a massive boulder sealed the tunnel.

"The *Titanic* just found its iceberg," Rory quipped.

Yes, it had. An iceberg of gray stone. Lieselotte put her hand against it, needing to feel that it was real, that it was actually stone. *How much does this behemoth weigh?* She couldn't even fathom a guess Her mind flickered with the faces of everyone counting on this tunnel—Wolfgang, Eckhart, Trude, Bastian, Emilia, and Franco. And for the first time in days, doubt crept in. *What if we've come all this way only to fail by a few feet?*

The three of them retreated and exited the tunnel. By this point, the people who knew about the boulder had shared the information with the new arrivals. A hum of chatter filled the basement. A chorus of questions and no answers.

"What are our choices?" Petyr asked.

"We could try to break it apart," Hansel said.

Lieselotte shook her head. "No, that would take too much time."

Chipping away at that massive boulder would take months. She tried to think like Wolfgang. Use his engineering knowledge. She'd been with him as he studied. He'd told her about so much in his letters and during those fleeting moments in person.

"If we remove that rock, we risk collapse. It's a natural load-bearing support," she added.

"So, we dig around it," Anneliese said.

"Dig around" was the last thing anyone wanted to hear. Everyone knew the shortest distance between two points was a straight line. So, it was rather disheartening to hear the phrase.

"We have to be incredibly cautious for cave-ins. Reinforce the wooden beams and cross-bracings," Lieselotte said.

"We can use shoring boards," Petyr said. "Press them against the walls to keep the soil in place."

"We don't have to divert the route too much," Anneliese said. "Just enough space for people to squeeze through."

Her comment was met with relieved expressions, even sighs.

"Johan. We'll base the size requirement off you," Lieselotte said.

He was the tallest and broadest person in the group, even larger than Eckhart and Wolfgang. It was the smartest choice when gauging how big the gap needed to be.

Lieselotte forced a smile—one to instill resolve. Then she excused herself and went upstairs so no one could witness that smile falter. She unlocked the front door and stepped outside. She needed to feel the fresh air, even if Mrs. Winterstein yelled at her for leaving the door unlocked.

Moments later, the door opened. Lieselotte turned, ready to apologize, but it wasn't Mrs. Winterstein. Instead, Anneliese stood there with a look of understanding.

"You okay?" she asked.

"One thing after another. And now, a literal boulder."

Anneliese contemplated it, looking like she wanted to speak but couldn't settle on what to say.

"Never known you to bite your tongue," Lieselotte teased.

"Maybe it's not an obstacle," Anneliese said.

"What?"

"I mean, it's obviously an obstacle. But what if it's a benefit?" Lieselotte stared at her best friend. Wanting to ask her what the hell she was talking about. "Maybe God put that rock there. Ironically, our biggest obstacle might be our biggest blessing."

"You need to explain yourself before I rush you to a hospital."

"You talk about support and load bearing. That rock is the biggest one. Like a natural anchor. Stronger than anything we could have fashioned."

Lieselotte grinned. It was exactly what she had needed to hear. To see the positive in the negative. She hugged Anneliese. "Ugh, I love you."

"Okay, easy. Now, who needs that hospital visit?"

They giggled and went back inside. Lieselotte wouldn't have to fake her resolve; it had been restored. This boulder wasn't a blunder or a hinderance, it was a gift. Changing that mindset was powerful. This route had led them to this boulder. She chose to believe it wasn't without reason. For all she knew, Wolfgang's tunnel was on the other side of it.

The Hollow Hour

Wolfgang thought he'd forgotten what nervousness felt like. He lived in a state of constant paranoia—awake or asleep. That had become his norm. Until the guard said they'd found something. Then panic surged through every cell. This wasn't fear. This was terror.

What have they found?

Looking at Eckhart might signal guilt. But not looking at him might do the same. Wolfgang settled on a middle ground—he turned in Eckhart's direction but stopped short of making eye contact.

"Shall we see what they found?" Schwarzfuchs asked.

Wolfgang didn't reply and let the guard lead. No reason to give him a hint of where to look. Schwarzfuchs and his men walked through the grave sites. Some cared more than others about trampling on graves. Schwarzfuchs ordered his men to be mindful of where they walked.

The middle-aged guard with a balding comb-over pointed to a locked mausoleum entrance. It wasn't the Von Haven Stein mausoleum. *Thank God. What has the guard seen to make them question this one?* But the answer came when he pointed to the padlock fence.

"It's locked," the guard said.

"Yes, it's private," Wolfgang said, trying to hide his relief.

"Open it," Schwarzfuchs commanded.

Eckhart fumbled with his keys, inserting the wrong one again and again.

"Do not waste my time," Schwarzfuchs said.

Eckhart held up the ring—over two dozen keys for gates, buildings, sheds, crypts. A silent protest. Finally, the key clicked. The stone door scraped open. The air reeked of musk and dust. A chipped stone angel stood in the corner, arms outstretched. The familial name of Goldschmidt was chiseled in stone. Ten graves all together from the late 1800s to the early 1920s.

"What did you want to see?" Eckhart asked.

Schwarzfuchs strolled the narrow space, eyes darting around like a hawk.

"It's filthy in here," Schwarzfuchs said.

"Yes," Wolfgang replied. "Some families do not want the crypts disturbed."

He wasn't sure what Eckhart would have answered. But if the Stasi were going to have them open every locked crypt and mausoleum, the Von Haven Stein mausoleum—with its signs of use—would draw scrutiny.

The Stasi agents traced the walls like they were hunting for secret doors. When they had concluded there was nothing to find, they stepped out and advanced to the next crypt. The next one was equally undisturbed—musty air, dust-covered floor. Each inspection brought them closer to the Von Haven Stein crypt. Eckhart knew its key by heart—but if he used it too quickly, it'd raise suspicion. And there was no way to warn him.

They advanced toward the Von Haven Stein mausoleum. Wolfgang's stomach was pure boiling battery acid. Bile rose in his throat. He waited for Eckhart to mindlessly insert the correct key on the first try.

But he didn't. Eckhart struggled to find the correct one, just like he had with the others. Finding it on the third try. He heaved the door open. This crypt was different—and the smell gave it away. The door had clearly been opened more often than the others. That musty smell had faded. It smelled like a strange combination of earth and incense from the candles placed in the votive holders.

Schwarzfuchs and two other agents stepped inside. Hunting for clues and signs of foul play.

"This is remarkably cleaner than the others," Schwarzfuchs said.

"Family pays us to keep the candles lit and sweep the floors," Wolfgang said.

It was a lie Schwarzfuchs could easily dispel. He could ask the day crew, the accountant of the cemetery, for financial proof; he could track down the descendants of this familial crypt. Wolfgang had no choice but to offer a harmless explanation—hoping it sounded too mundane to question.

There were a few clumps of dirt strewn about. Schwarzfuchs bent down and picked one up. *Is he studying it? Deciding if this came from topsoil or something deeper?*

"You should have greater respect than this," he said, rolling the dirt in his hands.

"We haven't cleaned it yet this week."

He hadn't rushed the Stasi during any other crypt examination and couldn't do so now. Even though he was sick to his stomach with worry, he needed to put on a front. That this was just another crypt. Nothing to see.

Schwarzfuchs crouched by the tomb, running his hands along it. It was far too heavy for him to push himself. Even with all the agents, they'd struggle. But if they used physics to their advantage, like Wolfgang had, they certainly could. *And if they did, what will I do? Pretend I know nothing about the tunnel? Act surprised?* Even if the Stasi believed they had nothing to do with it, it would get pinned on someone who worked here. Someone with access to the keys. Seeing someone innocent face the repercussions for something he had done would be horribly wrong. Something no different from what Dietrich had done.

If he couldn't deny it, he'd have to run. But warning Eckhart? Nearly impossible. If he kept by his vow to avoid arrest and not abandon Eckhart, he'd have to fight for his life. Try to get a hold of Schwarzfuchs's pistol.

"Very well," Schwarzfuchs said. "The remnant smells of these candles are nauseating. Onto the next."

Wolfgang and Eckhart stepped out of the way. Once Schwarzfuchs and the two agents stepped out, Eckhart closed the door and reapplied the padlock. Even though it was a chilly November night, Eckhart's hands were sweating. Wolfgang glanced at them, signaling for him to wipe them. Sweaty hands were a physical cue they couldn't reveal.

Wolfgang and Eckhart followed the Stasi agents. Schwarzfuchs lingered behind them—an incredibly unnerving thing. They examined every padlocked mausoleum. For some, they did nothing but give a courteous glance; others, they spent more time surveying.

"Well, it's getting late," Schwarzfuchs said, as if he had stopped over for a beer and lost track of time. "We shall check in on you from time to time."

Wolfgang escorted them to the cemetery office and then closed the gate behind them.

"Don't forget, *Herr* Kirschke—you owe me. And I always collect," Schwarzfuchs said, then strode away.

Eckhart had resumed digging the grave Wolfgang had started when he'd heard Schwarzfuchs. Wolfgang grabbed his shovel, not daring to speak. Even if they couldn't see the Stasi, they were around. Walking outside the grounds, lingering behind. While Wolfgang and Eckhart dug Dietrich's grave, the Stasi agents had been everywhere. Who knew where they had placed hidden microphones. They could be listening right now, waiting for Eckhart and Wolfgang to speak about the unexpected visit.

When Eckhart opened his mouth, Wolfgang snapped his hand up to silence him. He shook his head. Thankfully, Eckhart picked up the cue without interjection. Instead of asking his initial question, he pivoted seamlessly.

"We'll finish this grave, then put in the Joachim tombstone," he said.

Once their shift was over, they skipped taking the bus to have a few minutes of privacy on the sidewalks. The places they could speak openly and freely were becoming fewer and fewer.

"You think they planted something?" Eckhart asked.

Wolfgang shrugged, not speaking until they had crossed the street and a middle-aged couple had passed them.

"We can't risk it," he said.

"I don't get it," Eckhart said. "It's like they knew we were up to something."

It had been such an incredibly horrid feeling. So similar to the first arrest, yet different. With the first arrest, they had been waiting for them. Knew the exact time and place. All thanks to Dietrich. But this time, they didn't seem to know any details. They didn't know which crypt, but seemed to have targeted them. But was that even true? While he and Eckhart dug the grave for Dietrich's remains, they had traversed all over the cemetery. Inspected every meter of the place. The crypts and mausoleums were just the areas they needed access to see.

"You made the right call having the others stop coming," Eckhart said.

Wolfgang didn't answer. He was too busy disappearing into his mind, trying to answer unanswerable questions. Doing the calculations. *Has someone given them information? Someone in our small circle?* God, he didn't want to believe that. But how else would they have known? He asked Eckhart. There would have been a time when Eckhart would have snapped at Wolfgang for asking such a question. He had initially denied it was Dietrich. Defended him.

But that bitter truth had changed him. When the unthinkable happens, nothing ever again is unthinkable.

"Bastian would never betray me," Eckhart said.

Wolfgang said nothing. He wanted Eckhart to consider the next possibility. *What if the Stasi promised Trude her son back? Who could blame her for taking that deal?*

"I know what Trude could gain," Eckhart said. "But no. She wouldn't do that. And I know being best friends isn't much of a measuring stick anymore, but I don't see Emilia or Franco betraying us."

"If it was one in our group, they'd have known which mausoleum," Wolfgang said.

Eckhart agreed, feeling both relieved and guilty for questioning their group's loyalty.

"Someone is watching us," Wolfgang said.

The moment he said that, it seemed there were eyes everywhere. In every window. In every alley. On every roof.

Eckhart stated he would reiterate to Bastian and Trude the absolute need for secrecy and to pass that along to Franco and Emilia. All-important information was to be written on a single sheet of paper, burned after reading, and flushed.

Once they returned home, Eckhart and Wolfgang waited in line for the shower. Waiting for over an hour for their turn. *Is it someone in this line who is watching us? Detailing our activities to the Stasi?* After showering, with water well beyond lukewarm and approaching frigid, Wolfgang wanted to sleep, but his mind was too restless. Going over too many calculations and numbers and brutal truths. Even at the pace they would have been able to dig with just the two of them, it would take way too long to make any difference in the tunnel. And now, with Schwarzfuchs and the Stasi having stopped by once, they had to assume they would visit again. It was foolish and dangerous to do any work on the tunnel.

It was all on Lieselotte and her allies in the West. One miscalculation and their tunnels wouldn't align, meaning they would have to dig the full distance. *And even if they did, how would they ever notify me that the tunnel was ready?*

The Stasi had stopped all letters from her long ago, and now, he was living under the guise they had ended things, found closure, and moved on. To write a letter now would draw even more attention. Even if his letter got to her, they wouldn't let her letter get to him.

For the first time in months, that permanent nervous feeling in his stomach dissipated. Dread replaced it. An ache in his chest that felt so much like the twang of heartbreak.

The tunnel had failed. The escape attempt they had toiled over for months had been fruitless. The elation of breaking through the concrete and that first shovel into the dirt felt like a lifetime ago. He'd let everyone down. And on top of it, Lieselotte, Anneliese, and countless others had given up so much time to help.

Wolfgang waited for the tears. The moment warranted them. But he didn't cry. And that scared him. Instead of desolation, he just felt hollow. Like he could no longer feel desperation or grief. Wolfgang would never leave East Berlin. He had to accept that or reject that. It was a microcosm of live or die. Driving through the Wall had failed. Going under the Wall had failed. It was time he tried going over the Wall. Toss the dice and see where they lay. He'd have to tell Eckhart the news later, but for now he'd let him sleep. His friend could choose what he wanted to do. Accept life in East Berlin, or go out the same way as Wolfgang. Hands gripping the ledge of the Wall, feet scraping along the stone. And the crack of gunfire.

The Woman in the Mirror

Lieselotte pestered Tom for any updates on whether she—or he—might get a chance to enter the East. None came. There were plenty of worthy stories, but American news focused on the escalating war in Vietnam and the cultural clash between generations back home.

Lieselotte concentrated her attention on her job and the tunnel. They used extreme caution when shoveling around the boulder. Johan had successfully shimmied through the narrow opening with enough space for their pulley system to transport buckets full of dirt out of the tunnel.

When Lieselotte looked haggard, Mrs. Winterstein ordered her to nap. Though she appeared tough, Lieselotte suspected the icy woman was beginning to thaw—and might even enjoy the company. But she still hadn't looked at the tunnel. How was that possible? Was she not curious?

Though Lieselotte had wanted to continue working, they had made more progress than they had planned. The clay-like soil on the other side of the Wall was much easier to dig through. Her volunteers had given so much, and Lieselotte told them to take the night off. Lieselotte and Anneliese offered to buy a few rounds of beer. But first she wanted to speak with Mrs. Winterstein. Anneliese stayed behind with her, while her brother, Petyr, led the ravenous group to the nearest pub with enough money from Lieselotte and Anneliese for at least a few rounds.

After locking the door, Lieselotte and Anneliese lumbered up the stairs to Mrs. Winterstein's living quarters, their legs and backs sore from digging. They waited for permission, then entered.

"I sent the others home early," Lieselotte said.

"A respectable decision. They've worked hard," Mrs. Winterstein said.

"Would you like to see it?" Lieselotte asked. "The tunnel," she added. Lieselotte had learned from Mrs. Winterstein to say exactly what you wanted. To not hide behind vagueness. To not give people a way out with mock confusion.

"Would you like me to see it?"

"Yes, very much."

"Then I would like to see it."

It was like a verbal hug—the closest to intimacy Mrs. Winterstein displayed. She followed Lieselotte and Anneliese down the stairs, through the store, and down into the basement.

"Here," Anneliese offered, holding out a coat to help keep Mrs. Winterstein's bathrobe clean.

Lieselotte pointed out a pair of rubber boots for her to wear instead of her slippers. Anneliese powered the generator, and the lights of the tunnel flickered on, section by section, illuminating the dark, dank space in golden light.

Lieselotte led, with Mrs. Winterstein behind her, and Anneliese at the rear. They walked deeper into the tunnel until they reached the border crossing sign.

Mrs. Winterstein gasped when she read the sign. "The Wall is right above us?"

"Yes, directly," Lieselotte replied.

They advanced past the sign and crossed into East Berlin.

"I haven't been in the East since July of '61. I spent so much of my time there. It was my home. Back when it was just Berlin," Mrs. Winterstein said.

Even though they were underground with nothing to see, nothing to hear, and nothing to smell from the world above, Mrs.

Winterstein's emotions were palpable. Lieselotte, knowing her well, understood how much this moment meant.

They moved past the boulder to the end of their progress. By her calculation, they were at 1,782 feet. They retraced their steps out of the tunnel. Anneliese helped Mrs. Winterstein out of her coat.

"You have done incredible work. All of you," Mrs. Winterstein said.

"We couldn't have done this without you," Lieselotte said.

"Oh, please. I offered no help except the location."

"Which is more than anyone else did," Anneliese said.

Lieselotte and Anneliese said good night, then joined Petyr and the others at the pub. He had already spent the drinking money, and their team of diligent workers was sloshed. They roared and cheered when Anneliese and Lieselotte entered.

Lieselotte had a couple of beers, left enough money for more rounds, and said her goodbyes—fending off pleas to stay. Anneliese stayed out, which pleased Lieselotte. She needed to charge her social batteries frequently.

Lieselotte went to the store early, knowing most of her help would be nursing some major hangovers. She returned to work Monday, eagerly awaiting an answer from Tom. If he couldn't find a viable reason to go into the East, she would have to find a different way to get information to Wolfgang.

Tom arrived at work earlier than normal, but two of his assistants were already deep in conversation with him, offering Lieselotte no opportunity to ask him. His door stayed shut most of the day. It wasn't until she packed up at the end of her shift that he opened his door and asked her to come inside.

"I've got nothing for you. I'm sorry," he said.

She had expected this conclusion, but even though it hadn't blindsided her, it didn't mean it wasn't demoralizing.

"They're really cracking down on crossings," Tom added. Lieselotte forced a nod of understanding. "Don't do anything foolish."

"I won't," she assured him.

She thanked him and left the office. But doing something foolish was the only option she had left. Lieselotte Reisinger wasn't allowed access into the East, and even if she were, it was in her best interest not to go. Tom had warned her they could arrest her and accuse her of being a spy, which, depending on your definition of spy, wasn't far from the truth. After all, she was trying to help East Berliners escape.

So, if Lieselotte couldn't go into the East, she needed to be someone who could. She traveled to Anneliese's house, catching her before she left for Mrs. Winterstein's store.

"I need your help, no questions. Just help me pull it off, okay?" Lieselotte asked.

Anneliese paused. "I definitely don't like the sound of that."

"Please."

"What is it?"

"I need help creating a disguise so that I can get into East Berlin."

Anneliese's jaw dropped. "What?!"

"We need to give Wolfgang and the others an update. The date the tunnel will be complete. There's no other way."

Anneliese listed off the alternatives. Letters. Radio broadcasting secret messages. But Lieselotte countered. They'd have no guarantee Wolfgang and the others would hear the radio transmissions or understand them. Besides, it was dangerous.

Listening to Western radio was illegal. Anneliese took the loss in stride, trying to come up with more reasons before Lieselotte interjected.

"I appreciate your concern. But I've thought this through. It needs to be done."

"Then let me do it."

Lieselotte smiled. "I think by being my friend you've been brandished an enemy of the state. I won't risk that."

"And I'm supposed to let you risk it?"

Lieselotte didn't rebuke or comment further. Using silence as a powerful tool the way Mrs. Winterstein had shown her. Feeling awkward had defeated the resolve of millions.

"What do you have in mind?" Anneliese finally said.

"I'll need to change my hair color. The style. Maybe glasses. Different makeup. I am deferring to your expertise."

Anneliese sighed, annoyed and worried. "What about your passport?"

"I'll work on that."

Anneliese studied Lieselotte, and Lieselotte sensed when the moment shifted from Anneliese trying to talk her out of it to studying Lieselotte as if she were a canvas and she the artist deciding where to place her paintbrush.

"I have some ideas. But we need to go shopping," Anneliese said.

"Of course we do."

Anneliese's preferred solution to many of life's problems. They headed to the Ku'damm, to a beauty supply store called Golden Lily.

"We'll need to dye your hair," Anneliese said.

Though Lieselotte agreed, she loved her raven hair and hated the thought of losing it, even temporarily.

"Some of these aren't permanent. They'll come out in a few washes," Anneliese said. She studied the shelves, full of Clairol, L'Oréal, and Wella hair dyes ranging in color from platinum blonde to raven black, to kits to help conceal gray hair.

"Preference on color?" Anneliese asked.

"No. Surprise me," Lieselotte replied.

She turned away before Anneliese plucked a box from the shelf, then strolled over to the makeup aisle, where she grabbed a hodgepodge of concealers, eye shadows, and lipsticks.

"What's the cover story?" Anneliese asked.

Lieselotte had considered it. When crossing into East Berlin, guards would ask why she wanted to enter.

"A baptism," Lieselotte said.

"Okay …" Anneliese said, holding the word.

The more she heard, the more anxious she looked. Lieselotte understood that conflicting state—of wanting to know more, but knowing the more you knew, the more you had to worry about.

After Anneliese checked out, refusing to let Lieselotte pay for the supplies, they stepped out into the brisk autumnal air. Anneliese didn't head in the direction of either of their apartments.

"Where are you going?" Lieselotte asked.

"You're running this past Mrs. Winterstein."

"No, I'm not."

"Yes, you are. She's rational. I'm not asking you to change your mind, just to make sure you're aware of everything that could go … well, everything."

She didn't finish the last part—everything that could go wrong. Lieselotte didn't protest. She needed Anneliese's help, and these were her terms. So, they headed to Mrs. Winterstein's grocery store. It was after hours. Lieselotte used her key to unlock the door. They stopped to check in with the tunnel, asking for any unexpected hiccups. There hadn't been. Hansel said it had been smooth sailing. Odd phrasing for tunnel work, but better than stormy skies, Lieselotte supposed.

Then they headed back up the steps, through the store, and up the stairs to Mrs. Winterstein's living quarters. Anneliese knocked, then entered.

"What's all that?" Mrs. Winterstein asked, regarding the bag Anneliese held.

Anneliese turned to Lieselotte, making Lieselotte feel like a defendant thrown to the mercy of cross-examination. Lieselotte explained the plan and why she had to do it.

"You're not stupid," Mrs. Winterstein said. "So, why would you think this plan would work? The Stasi are not fools."

"I know."

Mrs. Winterstein regarded Lieselotte, trying to gauge if she truly understood how dangerous this idea was. Mrs. Winterstein had been in the circle of men like that. Cunning, sharp, and wicked.

"Well, use my sink to dye your hair. Lord help you if you stain it, though."

While Anneliese applied the temporary hair dye, Mrs. Winterstein unloaded her questions, not sounding much different in tone and intensity than a Stasi officer would.

"What is your reasoning for wanting to go into East Berlin?" she asked.

"A baptism."

"A baptism? A baptism for whom?"

"My cousin."

Mrs. Winterstein shook her head. "Oh, no, dear. They will eat you alive. These answers must not come to you; they must be in you."

Mrs. Winterstein restarted the questioning. "What is your reasoning for wanting to go into East Berlin?"

"A baptism for my cousin Eunice's child."

"Eunice who?"

"Kennedy."

Mrs. Winterstein's face shifted with discouragement. "Kennedy? As in the late American president's sister?"

Anneliese shot a look at Lieselotte that said the lie would have worked for her. Mrs. Winterstein hounded Lieselotte the whole while the hair dye burned her scalp and destroyed her beautiful dark hair. Mrs. Winterstein pressed for specifics. Telling Lieselotte that the Nazis had been excellent interrogators, but the Stasi had perfected the art. She critiqued the way Lieselotte answered the questions. Where her eyes went. When she swallowed, when she breathed. When her fingers clenched.

"The lies are in your eyes, dear," Mrs. Winterstein said.

"Sorry."

"Don't apologize to me. You'll be the one in a prison and responsible for Wolfgang and the others being forsaken."

Mrs. Winterstein had no deft touch—more sledgehammer than scalpel. But sometimes coaxing doesn't help. Sometimes a person needs to be pushed, to be challenged. The questioning continued. Lieselotte fought to maintain eye contact with Mrs. Winterstein, but when that faltered, Mrs. Winterstein told her to study her own mannerisms in the mirror—learning to mask any tells that could give her away.

"We should rinse the dye out," Anneliese said.

Lieselotte went over to the kitchen sink and leaned her head under the faucet. Anneliese turned the water on, testing the temperature before telling Lieselotte to lean forward. Anneliese worked the dye through, mindful not to splatter and risk Mrs. Winterstein's wrath.

"Here, dear," Mrs. Winterstein said, handing a towel to Anneliese to dry Lieselotte's hair.

She squeezed the ends and then scrubbed Lieselotte's hair until it was only damp.

"Well, take a look," Anneliese said, handing over a hand mirror.

Lieselotte raised the mirror. Her dark hair was gone. Replaced with a fiery red. Not a natural red by any means, but not polarizing enough to stand out.

"With it being cold out, I thought we could style the hair up. Hide the length," Anneliese said. "What do you think, Mrs. Winterstein?"

"Excellent suggestion. Church appropriate, too," she replied. "When are you planning on going?"

"The first day of Advent is the 28th."

"Of November?" Anneliese asked.

"Oh, heavens, dear. That's this Sunday," Mrs. Winterstein said.

Lieselotte elected not to disclose to Mrs. Winterstein that she still hadn't even started on her fake passport. She'd go full atomic if she knew that. Instead, Mrs. Winterstein continued her interrogation, making Lieselotte look into the mirror as she answered.

Every time Lieselotte anticipated the next question, Mrs. Winterstein asked an entirely new one. Questions that seemed pointless but required details most people would trip over.

Questions like: *Where did your cousin go to school? How did she meet the child's father?*

By the end of the torrent of questions, Lieselotte was exhausted. Mentally drained. Something that didn't go unnoticed by Mrs. Winterstein, who demanded Lieselotte take a nap. She wanted to fight it but knew to save her strength for another battle. When she woke, Anneliese and Mrs. Winterstein were playing cribbage at her small circular table. They'd moved the table out to fit a second chair in front of the wall.

After assuring Mrs. Winterstein that she was well rested, she and Anneliese left to dig the tunnel. Working well into the morning, so that by the time they left, Lieselotte would have only enough time for three hours of rest, and that was if she fell right to sleep.

She arrived at work early, knowing the graphic designer of the paper worked through the night laying out the aesthetics of the front page. Lieselotte knew little about Joachim Johansberg personally, but was aware of his reputation. His services predated the Second World War, when he forged passports for German agents. He was a stern-looking man. Tall but with small fingers that made them perfect for the surgical precision of creating counterfeits. Lieselotte introduced herself, stating her role within the Associated Press.

"Who?" he asked.

Lieselotte repeated herself.

"I'm hoping you can help me," she said.

"With?" Joachim asked.

"I need a passport to get into East Berlin."

"Why?"

Is he only capable of one-word questions? Lieselotte explained why— leaving out the tunnel but mentioning her criticism of the East

German government and her father's status, which barred her entry.

"I heard you're the best," Lieselotte added.

"I am. They won't be able to tell mine is fake. But it is up to you to sell it."

"I can."

Joachim stared at her, studying her. Lieselotte met his gaze, not backing down. Holding strong the same way Mrs. Winterstein had shown her.

"Are you going to do anything illegal?" he asked.

"Of course not."

"Apart from using a false identity?"

"Right. Apart from that."

But, yes, she may do something illegal. Tell a joke about the government. Perhaps her outfit would be seen as promoting Western decadence. She may be out too late without a purpose. She may photograph the wrong thing—perhaps a government building loomed in the background. All those actions could lead to her arrest. *Over there, freedom isn't tangible, it's abstract.*

"I'll need a photo," Joachim said.

Lieselotte had one. She'd had Anneliese take a photo of her at Mrs. Winterstein's standing in front of a white wall, and had developed it when she got in. Lieselotte handed the photo to him, as well as her own passport to copy the height and weight. Then she held out a wad of cash, unsure how much he required.

He looked at her with pity—as if ten years ago, he might've taken it all. But now he only grabbed what he considered fair. An amount that was less than what she had offered, but more than she had hoped. Joachim stated he'd have it done in a few days.

"I need it by Saturday evening," she said.

Trying to focus on work the next few days was terribly difficult. Fortunately, Tom was too busy to ask about her hair, only giving a confused look on his way to his office. She followed the stories coming out of Vietnam and her heart wrenched for every casualty report. But it was hard to be invested in the tribulations in a distant place. Then she chastised herself—she had once condemned the world for its indifference to Berlin.

When she arrived at the tunnel, she checked the clipboard for the daily progress. She needed to scrutinize the progress to keep Wolfgang accurately informed. Mrs. Winterstein was great with numbers, so she and Anneliese ran the clipboard up to her. While Mrs. Winterstein went over the numbers, she asked Lieselotte to brew a pot of coffee for the three of them. Lieselotte poured Mrs. Winterstein a cup, cheating a glance at the notes she had put together. Her handwriting had gotten shaky in her old age, but the lines were precise.

"You're averaging two feet per day since you started the tunnel," Mrs. Winterstein said. "However, since you implemented around-the-clock digging, you're averaging 3.86 feet."

"It would have been more if we could have kept using the power tools, but it's too risky on the other side of the Wall," Lieselotte said.

How much further would we be if we'd been able to use them?

"What if the other side hasn't started their section?" Anneliese asked. "How long before we hit 2,728?"

Mrs. Winterstein consulted the numbers she had put together. "Seventy-two more days."

How long can I ask Petyr and the others to dig? Seventy-two days? That would be with no time off and assuming she kept her entire volunteer force, which she wouldn't hold fault with anyone who decided to stop digging. Especially as the holidays approached. They were digging so that others could have the same freedom they had. To live life to the fullest. But were they even living life to the fullest? Digging a tunnel for months on end?

"That's incredibly demoralizing," Anneliese said.

"Mathematics isn't obligated to care about your feelings, dear," Mrs. Winterstein said.

Lieselotte glanced at the numbers, not doubting their correctness. Mrs. Winterstein's records were always meticulous. She studied them to understand them and what they needed to do to stay on track.

"We have to hope they've dug some amount of tunnel," Lieselotte said. She picked up the sheet of paper. "If I show this to Wolfgang, he'll be able to add his distances to this and calculate?"

"Yes, he can," Mrs. Winterstein said.

"I'm going to go tell the others the plan," Anneliese said.

Lieselotte thanked her. Not wanting to see how they reacted to the news. See their will and resolve break.

"What are you planning on wearing when you cross over to the East?" Mrs. Winterstein asked.

Lieselotte shrugged. "I don't know. I don't have a lot of outfits for a fake baptism."

"I have something for you," Mrs. Winterstein said.

Lieselotte hesitated, struck by Mrs. Winterstein's unexpected generosity—the way it had grown over the months, from subtle to overwhelming. But she also hesitated because they were of different shapes. Mrs. Winterstein was taller and stockier, and even if she had clothes from her youth, they were sure to be out of style.

"I wasn't always old," Mrs. Winterstein said, as if reading her mind.

She disappeared down her hallway and after ten minutes of searching, returned with a dark gray suit dress. Though the epitome of '40s fashion, it was timeless. And, most importantly, not Western.

"This will be perfect for a service. Style and church are not normally synonymous. It'll need to be hemmed, washed, and ironed, of course."

"It's beautiful," Lieselotte said. It was a striking suit.

"I want to be honest with you about this dress," Mrs. Winterstein said. "I wore it to many Nazi fundraisers. That pinhole in the lapel?" she pointed to it. "A swastika was pinned right there. I'll understand if that taints this dress, and you do not wish to wear it."

Did it? Yes—in some ways, in many ways—it did. Mrs. Winterstein had worn this dress around men like Hitler, Göring, and Goebbels. The stench of cigarettes and whiskey from parties long past still clung to the fabric. But this was also the dress of a woman Lieselotte had grown to admire and care for.

"There's one other thing you should wear," Mrs. Winterstein said, heading off to her bedside nightstand. It was a necklace—a simple silver band with a cross. "I was once a devout Catholic. Considered becoming a nun, if you can believe that. But once I married Manfred, and we joined the party, our allegiance was to them and no one else. After the war, after everything that came out, I didn't feel I had the right to wear this. Here."

She held out the cross for Lieselotte to take.

"I'd be honored to wear it." Lieselotte placed it over her head and around her neck. "But you always have the right to wear it."

Mrs. Winterstein bit her bottom lip and nodded. She was a woman at war with her past. Her mistakes. The mistakes of her husband. Forced to face the brunt of retribution for the heinous crimes her party committed. While cowards like Hitler and Goebbels killed themselves or fled to Argentina, Mrs. Winterstein had stayed to face the wrath. To be judged. To be juried. And, if so chosen, to be executed.

That Friday, by the time Lieselotte arrived at the Associated Press, her forged passport was on her desk, jutting out from under her typewriter. She grabbed it and brought it into the bathroom to examine. It was brilliant. The name displayed on it was Gertrude Mueller. The nationality was *Deutsch*, with "German" and "Allemand" listed beside it. A unique alphanumeric identifier, her date of birth, occupation of Housewife, and place of birth were all documented on it, confirming her citizenship in the Federal Republic of Germany.

When she arrived at Mrs. Winterstein's store, she had no hesitation showing the passport to her and Anneliese. Of all the things that could go wrong, she had the most faith in this passport. It was immaculate. Anneliese and Mrs. Winterstein could find no errors, nothing proving it was counterfeit. So, since the passport was not of concern, Mrs. Winterstein had Anneliese play the role of a VoPo while she hemmed the gray suit dress.

The lies came quickly and easily because she had created the full backstory of her cousin and her baby. Coming up with memories of their time in Kissing, Bavaria. How life had pulled them apart, but they had rekindled their relationship.

Lieselotte would cross at six the following night. Telling the border guard she'd be staying with her cousin overnight for the baptism mass Sunday morning and scheduled to leave Sunday around noon.

She hadn't planned to fall asleep on the couch while Anneliese and Mrs. Winterstein played cribbage, but she had. Truthfully, it was more comforting being here than alone in her apartment. She had expected Anneliese to wake her, but she hadn't. Lieselotte's constant thoughts finally quieted, giving her a much-needed night's sleep. By the time she woke, Mrs. Winterstein had left a plate of eggs and toast in front of her and was already working. Saturday was always the busiest day for the store.

She ate the eggs. They'd turned cold, which told her she really had overslept. The clock behind her desk showed 7:30, which may not seem late to some, but she'd fallen asleep around eight. Lieselotte headed down the steps, trying to spot Mrs. Winterstein. She was in the thick of the crowd, so she left, knowing she would stop here before she crossed over into East Berlin—or attempted to.

Forged Papers and Sacred Vows

Lieselotte took a long bath, refilling the tub with hot water when it went cold. She savored the quiet, her mind racing through every possible scenario. Her body needed the soak. She had demanded too much of it—too little sleep, too little food, too little care.

Things could go wrong. Being denied entry would thwart her plan to meet Wolfgang, but it was among the best-case failures. They could allow her into the East and then arrest her. She used a fake passport, a false identity. The Stasi had all the reason they would need to hold her as a spy. She could make things worse for Wolfgang. She needed a discreet way to reach him. Any unknown visitors would only cause the Stasi to keep an even closer eye on him. And yet, that nagging feeling twisted in her gut, a silent warning she couldn't explain.

Anneliese stopped over later to do Lieselotte's hair and makeup. She had a gift for knowing when a look turned from striking to clownish. Most importantly, she could alter a face with makeup. Using shadows, concealer, and blush to accentuate or hide certain features. The result made Lieselotte's face appear longer, leaner—almost unfamiliar. Anneliese styled Lieselotte's hair in a high bun—a style she never wore. It was a fashion that belonged more to the Second World War era, but it looked great. Elegant and classy. Making her look ten years older. *Will Wolfgang even recognize me?*

After Anneliese finished, she cleaned up while Lieselotte went into her room to change into her gray suit dress. Mrs. Winterstein had hemmed it perfectly.

"Let me come with you," Anneliese said.

"There's no need for us both to take the risk."

Anneliese wanted to argue, but it would do no good. She did not have a forged passport with a false identity, and Lieselotte was most likely correct in saying that Anneliese would be denied entrance based on her relationship with her. And without a disguise of her own, Anneliese's presence would also blow a hole in Lieselotte's cover, too.

They left Lieselotte's apartment and walked to Mrs. Winterstein's store. The weather had turned. Winter had arrived. The wind nipped at Lieselotte's nylon-covered legs. *How will this cold weather affect digging the tunnel?* Likely it would not, since they were beneath the frost line. But it was yet another thing to worry about.

Each time she reached the store, she braced for news of a tunnel collapse. The clay-like dirt was more prone to cave-ins, and that fragile soil filled the area around the Wall. The worry haunted her even in sleep.

The store was busy, people buying for the week ahead or picking up special ingredients for a recipe. Mrs. Winterstein retired at five, leaving the store to be run by a trusted employee. Lieselotte and Anneliese climbed the stairs to her living quarters. Mrs. Winterstein opened the door—something she never did. There was a manic nervousness to her that was normally absent.

"Anneliese, you've done wonders," Mrs. Winterstein said, her eyes scanning Lieselotte with a sharp, approving look. "I hardly recognize her."

The two women stepped inside, closing the door behind them. Mrs. Winterstein poured coffee. Lieselotte was jittery enough already but the coffee was poured, so she cradled the cup, grateful for the heat.

"You're all set on your answers?" Mrs. Winterstein asked.

Lieselotte nodded, but Mrs. Winterstein looked doubtful. Thankfully, she didn't start interrogating her. Either Lieselotte knew her cover story or she did not. No last-minute cramming session would save her.

No one drank their coffee. It was nothing but a prop, something to do with their hands. They watched the clock tick down until it was time for Lieselotte to leave.

When Lieselotte rose from the couch, Mrs. Winterstein put her hands on her shoulders. As close to a hug as the stern woman would give. But it meant as much as a hug. Anneliese took a different approach—throwing her arms around Lieselotte in an aggressive hug.

"Be safe. Be smart. Don't take unnecessary risks," she said.

Lieselotte nodded, her stomach churning as if she might be sick. Mrs. Winterstein went to her desk and grabbed a handful of peppermint starlights.

"Here. Suck on these. It'll help with the nerves."

Lieselotte popped one into her mouth, savoring the peppermint.

When her father had crossed into the East, he believed he'd return. Lieselotte didn't share that illusion. It'd been stolen from her at a young age when he was killed. She knew she may not make it back into the West. She couldn't go without Mrs. Winterstein knowing how much she appreciated everything she'd done. Knowing such sentimentality would make her uncomfortable, Lieselotte had written it in a letter and slid it onto her desk when Mrs. Winterstein's attention was on Anneliese.

"I'll see you tomorrow," she said.

It seemed like a jinx to say that, but it also felt unlucky not to. Like putting that statement out into the universe would bode good fortune. Like it was a favorable omen.

With wobbly legs, Lieselotte exited and climbed down the stairs and outside. Feeling the cold winter gusts attack her, pushing her away. As if warning her to stay out of the East. The gusts grew stronger the closer she came to Checkpoint Charlie and the Wall. Mother Nature's final warning. Lieselotte squeezed the fake passport, the weight of her decision settling in her chest. *Will it be enough to fool the Stasi—known for their meticulous attention to detail?* She had no choice but to trust it.

She advanced through, extending her passport. Sucking on that piece of candy, hoping it had calming medicinal properties. The guard snatched the passport from her hand. A wave of nausea washed over her. They had no reason to suspect her—but they suspected everyone. *What will happen if I'm branded a spy?*

"What is your business in the East?" he asked, studying her photograph.

"A family baptism."

They had decided to keep answers vague until pressed for more information.

The guard looked from the passport to her, then back again. "Whose baptism?"

"My cousin's child."

"Your cousin's child … does it not have a name?"

"Clara." The name rolled off her tongue.

A German Shepherd sniffed her leg, the ridge of hair on its back standing. The guard holding its lead tightened his grip. The guard lowered the passport and stared at Lieselotte. Sure, he was studying her, but he was also looking at her. Eyeing her breasts. Her curves. Her face.

"How long do you plan to be in East Berlin?"

"Until around noon tomorrow. After the baptism."

"Your purse. Hand it over."

Lieselotte did so. The guard handed the purse off to another VoPo, who looked inside it. He drew out a pair of white baby shoes.

"For Clara," Lieselotte said.

He found nothing incriminating and handed the purse back to her. Though he was finished with his inquiry, his superior was not. Having watched from a short distance away, he now strutted over.

"Good evening, *Fraulein*," he said.

He was a few inches taller than Lieselotte and a combination of brawn and bulk.

"Good evening," Lieselotte said, trying to keep her voice level.

"Your hair. It's dyed," he said.

"Yes, it is."

"Recently."

The guard stared at her, his gaze lingering on her dyed hair. Lieselotte kept her breathing steady, but her pulse quickened. *Can they see through my disguise?* The more he stared, the more unnerved his canine companions became. One snap of his fingers and those dogs would tear her apart.

"If I were to inquire, would I find other visits from you?" he asked.

Lieselotte shook her head. "I had no reason to come."

"Not even to see your precious cousin?"

"We were estranged until the birth."

"Cara," the man said.

"Clara," she corrected.

The strength in her legs vanished. Instinct urged her to look back toward the West, but to do so would be an admission of guilt. There was no turning back. *Will one of the American soldiers on the other side of the Wall help me if I need it?* No, they wouldn't. Their orders were to not interfere. They wouldn't risk nuclear war for her. She'd die the same way Peter Fechter had.

Alone.

"You do not look excited," the guard said. "You look nervous."

Lieselotte swallowed. "I am. I don't know how I'll be received."

The superior took the passport and gazed at it, rubbing it with his fingers. Looking for any signs of forgery. Lieselotte bit the inside of her cheek.

"Welcome to East Berlin," he said, as if sealing her fate.

He handed the passport back to his subordinate to stamp. Lieselotte retrieved the passport, thanked them, then stepped into East Berlin.

To her, it felt as though she had finagled her way through security into a tiger exhibit. Sure, getting through security was part of the process, but it was far from meaning the danger had passed. The Stasi's reach extended throughout the city. She would be watched wherever she went.

Now that she was in East Berlin, she hadn't thought of what her next step would be. There had always been a part of her, one she kept as silent as she could, that didn't think she'd be granted access into East Berlin. *Now that I'm here, what should I do?*

Stopping at Wolfgang's apartment would be foolish. His neighbors could be spies, reporting her appearance to the Stasi. *Should I go to the cemetery? Go to the pub he and Eckhart frequented and hope to spot him? But what if Dietrich was there? Would he recognize me through this disguise?*

But there was somewhere else she decided to go—not for the mission, but for peace of mind. St. Hedwig's Church, a grand Catholic landmark built after the Reformation in the 1700s by order of Frederick the Great. It featured a distinctive domed structure inspired by the Pantheon in Rome. Heavily damaged in the Second World War, it had undergone extensive reconstruction.

Lieselotte stepped inside, dipping her hand in the holy water and motioning the sign of the cross. The pews were arranged concentrically around the elevated altar. No mass was in session, but other troubled souls sat throughout the church. Some waited for the confessional to open.

Why have I come here? No doubt, partly because this had been her parish before her family had moved. She had memories of this church. Christmas Eve masses, Easter Sundays, getting a fit of giggles, and her father squeezing her hand at the end of the Lord's Prayer.

Lieselotte knew better than to trust a priest—he could be a Stasi informant. But just because she couldn't be honest with the priest didn't mean she couldn't unload her mind and receive spiritual guidance. She waited in the pew, praying silently. Once her turn came, she stepped into the confessional.

The priest, dressed in black slacks and shirt with a clerical collar, was a rotund man, making the intimidating space feel even smaller.

"Good evening," he said. "May I ask your name?"

She hated to question why he wanted the name. Did the priest simply want to know the name of the child of God he was talking to, or did he want to know so that he could file her away as more fodder for the Stasi? She gave her fake name, hoping God understood she wasn't lying in His house without good reason.

"What's troubling you?" he asked.

"I worry and want a positive outcome," she settled on.

"What do you worry about?"

"I cannot say."

The priest shifted uncomfortably. To be fair, he wasn't being given much to work with.

"But God knows," Lieselotte responded.

"Indeed, He does. Let us pray that through His grace and wisdom, His will be done."

She noted the phrasing—it was never her will, but God's. We can only hope His will aligns with our wishes. Together, she and the priest prayed. As she rose to leave, a clarity revealed itself. Not an idea but a name—one Wolfgang had spoken of.

"Do you know a Father Langer?" she asked.

"I do."

"Is he still practicing here in East Berlin?"

"No. He was at the Church of the Sacred Heart of Jesus, but he was replaced."

"Do you know where he is?"

"What's this about?"

Lieselotte didn't like the shift in his demeanor. No longer inquisitive but interrogative. She couldn't allow him to ask questions. Mrs. Winterstein had shown her how to command and control a room.

"Where does he live now?"

"Prenzlauer Berg. Right by the church. What is your business with Father Langer?"

"He was my priest when I was a child."

"Where did you say you attend church now?"

She hadn't and she wouldn't. "I hope he's well. Thank you for listening."

"Of course. Will you be visiting Father Langer?"

"Oh, no. Just a name from my childhood that I remembered."

Lieselotte stepped outside and left in a rush. Not wanting to wait and see if the priest would step out and motion for someone to follow her. She had no proof he was a Stasi informant, but she didn't like the feeling in her stomach. Her head also told her he was an informant. Even though her heart hoped that wasn't true, priests were men. Men are corruptible. She had to get to Father Langer's before the priest could get the word out. Father Langer had spent time in prison and helped orchestrate prisoner releases. The Stasi surely kept a close eye on him. Even casual curiosity could trigger surveillance.

The church was nearly two miles away—a long walk, but better than being trapped on a bus. She envisioned a Stasi officer stepping aboard and trapping her with nowhere to go. Solitude seemed her best friend. It wouldn't get her to the church fast, but if the priest called stating she would be visiting Father Langer, maybe it would be best if she waited if she couldn't arrive right away. So, she took her time walking over there. Turning the forty-minute walk into three hours, stopping in shops so it didn't look as though she aimlessly wandered. She strolled the street, scanning for any sign of Father Langer's residence. A late mass had just ended, and despite the chill, parishioners lingered—giving her the perfect excuse to observe.

A dreaded realization came with the cold wind—she had no idea what Father Langer looked like. Wolfgang had never even seen his face. Had only heard his voice. Sure, he had described it: deep and soothing. But how hard would it be to find someone by their voice when you yourself had never heard it? It'd require divine intervention.

There was a high probability that Father Langer was among these mingling guests. She scouted, listened. Wolfgang had thought he was older. Not elderly, but not young. So, she searched the crowd for men ages forty through seventy. She could eliminate men accompanied by women or who had children clinging to their legs. She spotted a tall man with a salt and pepper beard and a barrel chest. Not only did he fit those requirements, but he was also popular with the parishioners.

Her heart, head, and gut still weren't aligned. As the man crossed the street, she quickened her pace. She had to decide now.

"Father Langer?" she asked.

The man turned and looked at her. He didn't say yes or no but waited for her to say more. Her head told her not to say anything more, but her gut and heart told her to.

"I believe we have a mutual friend."

Father Langer was stoic in his silence.

"Wolfgang Kirschke."

The man's skeptical blue eyes shifted, lighting up with recognition and surprise. "Who are you?"

"Lieselotte."

Joy flashed across his aged face. "What are you doing here? Where is Wolfgang?"

"He's here in the East."

"What? I organized his release."

"You did. But they granted him his freedom only."

Father Langer bit his lip, wanting to say words that weren't very priestly.

"I need to get a message to Wolfgang," Lieselotte said.

Father Langer looked around, insuring there were no staring eyes. "I can do that. I need his address."

She gave him the address of Eternal Peace Cemetery. "I would like to meet him tonight if possible. At this church."

"That will be tough. I can try. Though if your information is confidential, you must be careful. The Stasi have planted their evil all over that church."

He asked her if she had a place to wait. She shook her head, having no idea.

"Stay at my place," he said. "It's bugged, so don't speak."

He escorted Lieselotte across the street and into a modest apartment. Reminding her more of the clinical bareness of a hospital than a home. But she knew this wasn't unique to Father Langer's place but for most of East Berlin. He left Lieselotte without a word, but the smile on his face said to make herself at home. Lieselotte didn't speak—doing nothing to alert whoever may be listening to her presence.

A flicker of doubt crept in. *What if he's not Father Langer? What if he alerts the Stasi?* Right or wrong, she searched the living room for signs of authenticity. She strolled into his bedroom. On the nightstand beside his bed was a battered copy of the Bible. The pages were frayed. The spine cracked and held in place with a rubber band. She picked it up, removed the rubber band, and gingerly opened the Bible. There were notes sprawled in the margins. Circled words, highlighted lines. Questions pertaining to certain passages. This wasn't a Bible for reading—it belonged to a man wrestling with faith, searching for understanding and answers.

She banded the Bible, set it on the nightstand, and then sat on the couch. He had a collection of other books—those approved by the state. There was such a bareness to the place. *Did the Stasi take his possessions when he was in prison? Making him restart with nothing?*

The sound of a key entering the lock drew her attention to the door. Her heartbeat quickened at the thought of seeing Wolfgang. But when the door opened, it was only Father Langer—though a far cry better than a Stasi agent.

Father Langer nodded that all had gone well. Lieselotte knew not to question any further, as he had warned her that his apartment was bugged. Father Langer removed his coat and hung it in the small closet by the door. He filled a glass of water and handed it to her. She thanked him with a smile. Then he scribbled a note and held it for her to read.

Asked to meet at the church at 9:15.

Lieselotte nodded. The clock showed it was an hour away. They spent that hour in silence. Jotting questions and scribbling answers took too long. She wanted to ask about Hohenschönhausen Prison. Ask how Father Langer had organized Wolfgang's freedom. Why had he? How did he know Wolfgang wasn't a Stasi spy? One planted in the prison, hoping the West would buy their freedom? Instead, Father Langer prayed out loud. It wasn't for Lieselotte, but for his own need and want. She recognized the power and soothing voice he possessed. How much it must have meant to Wolfgang at Hohenschönhausen.

When that hour was up, Lieselotte rose and moved to the door and waited, a silent question—*Is he coming with me?* Father Langer followed her outside but stopped in the entryway.

"Be careful with your words," Father Langer warned. "The Stasi have infiltrated the church. Trust no one."

Father Langer staying behind increased her odds. He knew how closely he was watched. Lieselotte thanked him and then rushed across the street and into the church. She was surprised to see half the church filled with people, but then noticed the sign stating there was a 9:30 mass.

Lieselotte motioned the sign of the cross and scanned the crowd for Wolfgang. A few men had dark, wavy hair, but she only saw them from behind. She couldn't check each face. *How can I be sure one of them is him?*

What she needed to do was get to the front of the church and then choose her seat. That way, she could scan the crowd for faces. *Would that be so odd? Scanning for family or friends so I can sit by them?*

Lieselotte walked along the left side of the pews and approached the front, surveying the crowd. None of the men she thought could be Wolfgang were him.

As she searched, another figure stepped into the church. Her eyes studied him. He was wearing gray slacks, work boots, and a thick jacket. His glasses fogged up from the cold. Lieselotte met his eyes.

Wolfgang.

He searched the crowd for Lieselotte. His eyes found her, but only because she was staring at him. Her disguise was nearly perfect—but once he met her eyes, he knew.

She took a seat in the back row, so that there was no one behind them to listen in on their whispered conversation or to try to read what she would show him. Wolfgang strolled down the pew. Every fiber of her being longed to leap into his arms, to rest her head against his chest and feel his strong arms wrap around her. She slid the sheet of paper with all of Mrs. Winterstein's calculations into the hymnbook.

Before Wolfgang could speak, the mighty church organ sprang to life, and the mass of people sprung to their feet as the priest and his two altar boys marched down the center aisle.

Lieselotte slid the book toward him. They kept a distance between them to show they were not together, but that distance felt like a magnet. There was so much uncertainty. To finally be near him and to keep this distance … wouldn't it be worth the risk? To just hold his hand and kiss him?

Wolfgang opened the hymnbook and saw the note. He and Lieselotte joined in singing the processional hymn, "O Come, O Come, Emmanuel." A fitting song for the first day of Advent.

Once the song ended and the parishioners took their seats, Wolfgang read the note. His eyes lit up when he saw how far they'd gotten. He looked over at Lieselotte. She risked a glance back. Then, from her pocket, she removed a small pencil almost sharpened to the nub. She rolled the pencil across the wooden pew. Before she had slipped the note into the hymnbook, she had written a question.

How far have you gotten?

Wolfgang scribbled a curt reply. He closed the hymnbook and subtly passed it back. Lieselotte reached for it but didn't open it. She'd wait until the next song. When it came, she opened the book.

478 feet. The Stasi are watching. Can no longer dig.

That terrible worry in her gut had been well-founded. There had been an issue that had caused Wolfgang to stop digging. Lieselotte took the nubbed pencil and wrote the most pressing question.

When will we finish?

She closed the hymnbook, set it between them, and waited for the next song. Listening to the priest's sermon. They needed to get the note out of the book before the Eucharist. She wouldn't trust this information here. A person could choose the wrong row and claim their spot. Or, if they were being watched, have an opportunity to steal the note.

As the priest discussed the first day of Advent, Wolfgang opened the hymnbook. Shielding it with his arms, he read the note. His eyes narrowed in concentration, biting the inside of his lip as he calculated. His eyes going back and forth on the numbers and averages Mrs. Winterstein had calculated. Then a soft smile spread across his lips.

He scribbled his reply and slid the book over. She flipped it open. This couldn't wait.

Christmas Eve.

She smiled. *Less than a month. What a Christmas!*

The priest consecrated the bread and wine, transforming them into the Body and Blood of Christ. Then the moment of mass Lieselotte and Wolfgang had longed for arrived: the Lord's Prayer. When the parishioners extend their hands to those around them, offering a valid reason to hold each other's hand.

She sighed as his fingers curled around hers, his thumb brushing the space between her fingers. After the prayer finished, people turned to each other to exchange the sign of peace. Lieselotte and Wolfgang faced each other for the first time. He looked beyond the disguise to the woman he knew so well. The woman he loved. The woman he knew in a way no one else did. Neither could break the intimate handshake. While those in the pews turned left and right, ahead and backward to share peace with as many people as possible, Wolfgang and Lieselotte kept their hands clasped.

But they had to break apart. Their fingers slipped away from each other. That final caress of fingertip against fingertip electric. Reluctantly, they distanced themselves and brought their gaze back to the priest. Lieselotte slid the note from the hymnbook and into her pocket.

The Communion began and row by row, people lined up to receive it. Wolfgang took the Body and Blood before Lieselotte. As she brought the chalice to her lips, she couldn't help but think his lips had been here.

Hands folded, she followed Wolfgang toward their seats, but before he turned into the pew, she reached for his hand, gently nudging him to continue forward and out of the church.

"Where are we going?" he whispered.

Together, they rushed toward the stairs. She had no idea where they led except away from prying eyes and listening ears. Up and up and up the steps, past the entrance where the organist played, to the very top where the church bell hung. A sign on the door read *Church Staff Only*. Lieselotte opened the door and dragged him inside.

She pressed her lips to his. It was reckless, foolish, even dangerous, but she didn't care. This wasn't desire, it was need. She needed to be near him, to feel his touch.

Wolfgang returned her kiss—sighing and gasping. It was the first breath of air after being underwater. But the kissing didn't stop—it escalated. Hands struggling to remove clothing, to feel and to hold and caress. Was it sacrilegious to do such a thing in a church? In a rational headspace, they both would have agreed it was. But they were drunk on each other. God had given them this moment.

As the organ's majestic, atmospheric tones carried through the church, Wolfgang lay sprawled atop Lieselotte. Their pile of clothes was strewn around them, a makeshift blanket.

"I want you inside me," she whispered.

He hesitated, looking into her eyes. She had always wanted to wait until they were married. It had mattered to her deeply, and he would never pressure her to abandon that principle.

"You're sure?" he asked.

"Never been more certain. I am going to marry you, Wolfgang. I won't deny us this moment."

Inside that small space, with the giant church bell above them, Lieselotte and Wolfgang embraced each other, savoring that blissful union. For those precious minutes, all was right in the world. But that postcoital clarity vanished cruelly fast.

After, they rushed to dress. Wolfgang told her to leave first and he would exit a few minutes later, so that they weren't seen together.

"Christmas Eve," she said. "11 p.m."

"Christmas Eve," Wolfgang said. "I can't believe you dug a tunnel for me."

"This is going to work. The rest of our lives is almost here."

There was so much more they wanted to say. To sit and talk all night. He wanted to tell her about Dietrich, about what digging that tunnel had required them to do. But there would be another time for that.

He drew her toward him, holding her against him. Their bodies swaying in dance to a silent song. Then he arched her chin toward him, lowered his head, and kissed her.

"Goodbye," he said.

"For now," she clarified.

He nodded. "For now."

Lieselotte opened the door and disappeared. For Wolfgang, the goodbye carried a painful finality. He didn't want to think about it—what he felt in his heart, in his soul—the feeling that he would never see her again. Yet if this was the last time, he couldn't have imagined a more perfect goodbye.

Snowfall and Silence

Wolfgang hurried back to the cemetery, thinking about the turn his night had taken. It felt surreal—like waking from a dream, unsure if it had really happened.

"What's going on?" Eckhart asked.

Wolfgang grabbed a twig and wrote in the dirt. *Lieselotte.*

Eckhart's eyes widened. Wolfgang erased the word and wrote: *Tunnel is far.*

Eckhart responded. *When?*

Wolfgang smiled and wrote: *24-12.*

Eckhart processed what Wolfgang had said—the wide spectrum of emotion he had to work through. Mere days ago, the tunnel had been a complete failure. He had to choose if he wanted to risk escape another way. Wolfgang had faced the same spectrum; he'd just had longer to process it.

Eckhart was silent. But even in the faint lighting, the emotion on his face was unmistakable. Lieselotte, Anneliese, and an unknown number of others had spent countless hours digging this tunnel.

There was no reason for Wolfgang and Eckhart to help dig— but they still wondered if doing so might shave off precious days. It was hard to be patient. To sit idly by. Not only because they wanted to escape as soon as possible, but because it felt wrong— lazy even—to sit and do nothing, while Lieselotte, Anneliese, and their team dug the tunnel.

On Sunday, Eckhart went to tell his brother and sister-in-law the great news. Wolfgang stayed behind. Safety and caution were their best play at this point. Eckhart returned before supper, recapping how elated they'd been at the news. Trude was nearing the end of her pregnancy, and the announcement only added to their excitement. Trude planned to meet with Emilia for coffee later and share the amazing development then.

Wolfgang didn't routinely visit his mother and father, but he visited them that following Sunday. Trying to hide the emotion in his voice. He knew this would be the last time he saw them. The thought made him question everything. *Could I ask them to leave? Could I risk tearing them from everything they know? And if there is a chance, shouldn't I broach that subject?*

His parents had lived through much. For them, surviving the constant bombing during the end of the Second World War and the horrors that followed, communism wasn't the end of the world the way it was for Wolfgang. They were older. Their dreams had either faded away or come to fruition. They were content. And that was fine. Across the world, many considered communism evil. It wasn't. For many, it worked. They enjoyed equal rights, the state-run programs for health care and transit. The lie was believing men like Stalin, Ulbricht, and Brezhnev lived with the same modest means. The *nomenklatura*—the ruling elite—lived lavish lifestyles. For the dreamers, like Wolfgang, it was a prison. His parents would never understand. They'd urge him to fall in line, to stop looking beyond the Wall for happiness.

"I am proud of you, son," his father said. "You're working hard. Atoning for your mistakes."

If he only knew.

"I love you," Wolfgang said, as he stood by the door to leave.

His parents didn't recognize the finality in his words, and he was thankful for that. His father had no idea how on that Christmas Eve all those years ago, he'd given Wolfgang and Lieselotte the most amazing gift. A skill that had allowed their relationship to flourish when it otherwise would have floundered.

He stepped out of the home he'd grown up in, knowing he'd never return. The finality devastated him. He tried to steady his heaving chest, stop the tears from falling. But he couldn't.

A wave of depression hit him all that week. He spent the rest of that Sunday sleeping. But once that depression lifted, the anxiety about the tunnel prevented him from sleeping and eating.

They had to plan that fateful Christmas Eve night. The cemetery would be unstaffed. *How best to get everyone there? At what time?*

Trude was due at any moment, and a wave of paranoia had struck her. She became overly emotional, fearing that if she gave birth in East Berlin, the Stasi would take her baby. She'd pleaded with Bastian that they needed to cross now. The rational explanation that the tunnel wasn't complete didn't register with her. No one blamed her fear. It was a mother's instinct, not madness.

Bastian met Eckhart and Wolfgang for beers at the Copper Cellar. Dietrich's ghost hung over the table, overwhelming them with memories. *How many beers had we shared here? More importantly, how many conversations?*

"Emilia and Franco will be at our place for Christmas Eve," Bastian said.

"I've been thinking about the others ... from before," Wolfgang said.

They'd never heard what had happened to the Schneiders or their children. Or Fresa.

"I have, too," Eckhart said.

For him, there was a sense of needed atonement. During their twenty-three months in the Submarine, he'd been convinced it had been one of the outsiders who had betrayed them.

"I've been thinking," Bastian said, his voice lower. "With this ... we're not limited by space."

In truth, the tunnel could accommodate countless people. *Is it wrong to limit it to the six of us? Or should more people be given the option to leave?*

"It's too dangerous," Eckhart whispered. "The risk isn't worth the reward."

Risk and reward were the basis of all of Wolfgang's decisions. Weighing the invisible scale to see the weight of a choice. *How many people in this crowded bar would risk the chance of escape for the reward of freedom? How many would betray us?*

Bastian finished his beer. "I'm leaving. Care to walk me out?"

Wolfgang and Eckhart polished their beers off, deciding to also leave. The frigid sting of winter assaulted them. Bastian exhaled. His cloud of breath mushroomed into the sky.

"If you do decide to tell anyone," Bastian said, "we don't say anything until the day of. The moment of."

"No chance for them to alert the Stasi," Wolfgang said.

Bastian nodded.

"It's still not without risk," Eckhart said.

"Nothing is, brother."

They walked further away from the pub. The dozens of conversations occurring inside faded away. Falling snow has a way of silencing the world. Normally, that silence is beautiful. But now it was only nerve-wracking. As if the Stasi could hear them all the better. Each snowflake, a potential spy.

"We'll see you on Christmas Eve," Bastian said.

Bastian hugged them both and went his separate way. Twelve days until Christmas Eve. *How will I survive the next twelve days? How will I eat? How will I sleep?*

"Do you have anyone in mind to ask?" Eckhart enquired.

Wolfgang shook his head. Eckhart nodded, looking relieved.

"Do you feel guilty about that?" Wolfgang asked.

Eckhart didn't answer. He didn't need to. There'd always be some level of guilt about that. Perhaps after they escaped, they could send word to someone in the East about the tunnel's existence. But how? A letter? The Stasi would find the tunnel if they escaped. And once they did, it would be destroyed.

Wolfgang and Eckhart tried to retain their normal routine. They avoided going within two blocks of the Wall. The Stasi hadn't returned since Schwarzfuchs had delivered Dietrich's remains. They were due for a visit, and that terrified him.

As the holidays approached, panic consumed Wolfgang. Plenty of times he struggled to breathe. He'd dunk his face in cold water or step outside to breathe in the invigorating frigid air. *What if Lieselotte can't meet the deadline?* He'd given some leeway, but the uncertainty gnawed at him. *What if they come across a problem? A massive boulder? A cave-in? What if we unlock that crypt, move to the tomb, and head into the tunnel to find a wall of dirt blocking us at 478 feet? What then? What if the Stasi are on our tail?*

Wolfgang couldn't keep living like this—anxious, restless, barely able to breathe. He stood at the window each night, staring at the dark, knowing sleep was impossible. This would end. And that was much more comforting than he could have imagined. Not even saying this would end with him on West Berlin soil. There was a chance it would end with his death. But that didn't faze him. Death was preferred to incarceration. This constant worry, this dread ... it would finally end.

The Right Side of History

Lieselotte returned to the West, presenting her passport to a guard unfamiliar with her planned baptism. Getting into East Berlin had been nearly impossible; getting out could be equally so. The guard examined the flawless West German passport, hunting for a defect. His eyes lingered on the photo, then her face, then back to the photo again. He called another guard over, nodding at Lieselotte. The second guard stared at the photo, then focused his gaze on Lieselotte. Her pulse hammered. She didn't look away.

Finally, the man handed back the passport and nodded for her to cross Checkpoint Charlie into West Berlin. She hurried across, bracing for a voice—or a gunshot. None came.

Lieselotte rushed to Mrs. Winterstein's store. She unlocked the main entrance and then dashed up the steps to Mrs. Winterstein's living quarters. She knocked. Mrs. Winterstein replied before the first rap of knuckles had ended. Anneliese sat up on the couch, waking from a nap. Mrs. Winterstein clutched her nightgown closed at the neck. Relief washed over her face.

"Tell us everything," Anneliese said.

Lieselotte did, everything but her private embrace with Wolfgang in the church tower.

"They've dug 478 feet?" Anneliese asked.

"But had to stop. Wolfgang did the calculations. We settled on a day and time," Lieselotte said.

"When?"

"Christmas Eve. 11 p.m."

Anneliese hugged Lieselotte, beaming. Mrs. Winterstein's joy was more reserved.

"Those were averages. He's left himself enough room for error?" Mrs. Winterstein asked.

Lieselotte nodded, even though Wolfgang had done all the calculations silently. Tonight was too joyous a night to contemplate cave-ins, obstacles, or anything else.

"We have to tell the team," Anneliese said.

Mrs. Winterstein stayed behind while Lieselotte and Anneliese went down into the basement. Music played out of a transistor radio. Empty bottles of Coca-Cola were strewn about (Mrs. Winterstein had provided them). Petyr and Johan shoveled dirt into the wheelbarrow.

"I have news!" Lieselotte said.

Petyr flicked the tunnel lights—off, then on—to signal those inside to come out. They waited a few minutes before the ten people inside came out. Faces streaked with dirt and sweat.

Lieselotte revealed the tunnel should be completed by Christmas Eve. She didn't disclose when Wolfgang and the others would escape—keeping that secret was critical. Apart from Petyr and his friends, no one knew the tunnel led to the Von Haven Stein mausoleum in Eternal Peace Cemetery.

The group looked around, no one matching Lieselotte's joy. They'd still be here on Christmas Eve, digging. The notion that they would have to spend the holidays here was a blow. But they didn't *have* to spend them here. *What if they say they will resume digging in the new year?* In all of Wolfgang and Mrs. Winterstein's calculations, they hadn't accounted for that.

"I know you've all sacrificed so much. Time and effort. I can't repay you, and I can't give you back your time, but I need your help to finish this."

"I can't think of anything more in the Christmas spirit than this," Anneliese said.

"I don't care much for digging on Christmas Eve," Petyr said. Lieselotte felt her spirit deflate. If they lost Petyr, they'd lose everybody. "So, why don't we finish a day early?"

Deadlines carry power. The finish line was within sight. In running, that second burst of energy is called the kick. It's when every last speck of will and effort drains from your body to finish the race. Lieselotte's news had invigorated the team. No one wanted to dig on Christmas Eve. They wanted to be at home with their families or here in the basement drinking champagne, waiting for the East Berliners to crawl out of the tunnel.

At the Associated Press the following morning, Tom approached Lieselotte while she typed an article. Normally, she would rush to get his attention. But this time, he wanted her attention.

He pointed at her. "My office. Now."

Bristling from his tone, she rose from her desk and followed him into his office, feeling the weight of the staff staring. She wanted to keep the door open, but he would insist she shut it. After the inevitable berating, she'd be grateful for the barrier.

"Care to tell me what you did this weekend?" Tom asked.

She could lie. Say she'd spent the weekend digging at the grocery store. She wouldn't, though. She could claim it was the moral high ground, but truthfully, she was too exhausted to lie. She'd rather get scolded and go on with her day.

"I went into the East," she said.

Tom sighed and rubbed the bridge of his nose. "That explains the hair. I'm glad it's back to normal. You realize how foolish that was?"

"I met with Wolfgang. I know the date of the escape."

Tom seemed at war. On the one hand, he wasn't done preaching to her about safety, which in its way was flattering that he cared enough about her to trump the story. His reporters weren't expendable. But the other part of him craved the dramatic details. The one that millions of readers would want to invest their time reading about.

"When?" he asked.

"Christmas Eve."

The headline wrote itself: *Christmas Miracle, Silent Night, Daring Flight*—endless possibilities.

"I just need to know you did this for him, not because I pushed you for the story."

"You didn't push me," Lieselotte replied.

He sighed with relief. The tension in his shoulders slacked. "Do you know how many are making the escape?"

Lieselotte shook her head. She'd be just as surprised as anybody by the number of people who came out of the tunnel. Wolfgang and the others would think about extending the escape. She hadn't pushed Wolfgang, though secretly, selfishly she hoped he didn't risk it. But she knew Anneliese, Petyr, and the others hadn't risked everything just for Wolfgang. If there was a possibility that others could escape, how could she hope they wouldn't embrace that chance?

"You got lucky," Tom said. "I don't need to ask where you got the fake ID. Joachim confessed yesterday."

"You didn't punish him, did you?"

"No. I wanted to kick his ass, though. No more risks."

"Of course." Lieselotte nodded, though it was a lie. She'd do whatever it took to get Wolfgang through the tunnel. There were risks at every turn. She couldn't avoid them. Couldn't shy away from them.

"We'll print on Christmas Day night," Tom said. "Are there any in your group who do not want their names mentioned in the paper?"

Lieselotte was unsure and told Tom she would ask the group. If they had any family in the East, being associated with helping East Berliners escape would cause repercussions for them. Firings. Evictions. Time in labor camps. Prison sentences.

She had a deadline, and this was the biggest story of her life. The opportunity to be on the front page. Her photographs. Her words. But she hadn't written a word of it yet. It seemed like a jinx to write it. What if everything went to hell? Every word she wrote would be hard-grained into her mind.

She finished developing photos from other reporters, enjoying the tranquil time in the red-tinted room. After work, she headed straight to the grocery store. They had a daily quota to meet, and she would do everything she could to meet it.

Even though they met that quota that day and the following day and week, Lieselotte asked for time off from the paper to ensure the digging went smoothly. She expected it to be unpaid, but Tom insisted she was reporting a story—and would be paid. It was incredibly generous and needed because she was almost out of funds.

Mrs. Winterstein had supplied drinks and snacks for the diggers, but Lieselotte couldn't let her do that without chipping in herself. She changed into the overcoat and followed Anneliese and Petyr into the tunnel. It never failed to give her a sense of wonder at what they had accomplished. Wooden support beams. Lights. Fans pumping in fresh air. They crossed through the border, touching the makeshift sign for good luck. Around the massive boulder, on and on, further and further into the tunnel.

All the way to 2,226 feet.

"With their 478 feet, that means we're down to the last twenty-four," Petyr said.

It was 20 December. They had four days to dig twenty-four feet. Even with a bad day, they would achieve completion by Christmas Eve.

That first strike through the cement wall felt so long ago. How daunting it had been to realize that first shovelful was just the beginning of thousands more. Now, they had dug over 2,000 feet of tunnel.

"I need to talk to the group," Lieselotte said.

She had stated earlier that she needed an all-hands-on-deck meeting. Even Mrs. Winterstein joined, standing on the basement steps. It was a collection of people, men and women, sisters and brothers, friends and coworkers.

Some she knew well, like Petyr and Anneliese. Some she knew, like Petyr's friends. Others she'd only welcomed and said thanks to. Strangers who had taken up the call to arms. Germans. Americans. French. Belgians. Italians.

"There may be information about this tunnel that makes the press," Lieselotte said. "I need to know who is okay with their name being listed, those who want to use an alias, and those who wish to be kept out entirely." She paused. People filled the basement and stairwell. "Think hard. If you have family in the East, they might suffer for what we've done."

No one spoke. But that wasn't uncommon in large groups. People uncomfortable to stand up or ask questions. Instead, coyly looking at the person beside themselves.

"I will leave a sign-in sheet. Tear a piece of paper and write your name if you are willing to have your name and photograph shared. Place it in the box."

Lieselotte set up her camera and tripod. "I would like to take a group photo. For those of you who do not sign, you will be blurred out."

Lieselotte lined them up near the tunnel entrance, moving people to achieve the best look—tallest in the back, shortest in the front. There were too many people to fit in the frame, so she, Petyr, and Anneliese crouched in front of the tunnel, leaving enough space at the top of the tunnel for the camera to capture the tunnel's depth.

But there was one notable person absent, trying to retreat up the stairs.

"Mrs. Winterstein. Front and center, please," Lieselotte said.

"I'm fine, dear."

"You have to join us," Anneliese chimed in.

Then Petyr and his friends echoed the sentiment. Once enough people did it, the rest joined in. Most of them had never interacted with Mrs. Winterstein. But none of them would be here and not a single inch of tunnel would have been dug if not for her.

Reluctantly, Mrs. Winterstein strode forward. Lieselotte positioned her beside herself and Anneliese and helped her into a kneeling position. She went to the camera, set the timer, and darted back.

"You're on the right side of history," Lieselotte whispered to Mrs. Winterstein.

The group stared into the camera as the giant flash lit the room. After, those who were not on duty left. Lieselotte and Anneliese crouched through the tunnel toward those last remaining feet. Digging spades and hand shovels into the dirt wall. Tearing it apart.

When Lieselotte finished for the day, sixteen feet, two inches of tunnel remained. She didn't go home. Neither did Anneliese. Instead, they sprawled out on Mrs. Winterstein's couch. Feet to head. Too exhausted to care how cramped they were. Mrs. Winterstein cooked them breakfast before they got back to work on the tunnel. The overnight crew had turned those sixteen feet, two inches into five feet, three inches. Less distance than a standard grave remained.

Lieselotte dug frantically, panic surging through her.

"Relax, you'll hurt yourself," Anneliese said.

"We're running out of time," Lieselotte said, ignoring Anneliese's warning.

"Look at the numbers. The averages. We're fine."

Still, Lieselotte couldn't trust the numbers. She wanted to feel her shovel break through to open air. Until it did, there would be panic. Panic that they wouldn't complete the tunnel in time and the even more panic-inducing problem that their tunnel would not align with Wolfgang's.

Anneliese tried to get Lieselotte to stop for the night, threatening to get Mrs. Winterstein to drag her out if she didn't listen. Most of their volunteers had left. Only Petyr, Hansel, Rory, Johan, and George remained.

Petyr promised he and his friends would continue digging, arguing they would accomplish more since they were fresh, and Lieselotte was at the tail end of a grueling shift.

"We'll wake you when we get close," he said. "I promise."

Lieselotte surrendered, dropping her shovel. Her hands stayed coiled as if they were still wrapped around the shovel, throbbing. Her back ached. She crouched through the tunnel, around the boulder, past the border crossing sign, and out. Feeling the relief of standing erect for the first time in hours. She barely had the energy to peel off her coat and rubber boots.

"Come on, just a bit further," Anneliese encouraged, but she sounded just as weak and tired as Lieselotte. It sent a wave of guilt through Lieselotte. Anneliese wouldn't stop while she continued to dig.

They were so exhausted they had forgotten to knock on Mrs. Winterstein's door. Mrs. Winterstein was at her desk, wrapped in her bathrobe, working on a crossword.

"Oh, you two look like death on vacation," she said. "For the love of God, lay down and rest."

Lieselotte collapsed on the couch, barely getting her shoes off before she fell asleep. She awoke to the sound of arguing. A one-sided argument. Mrs. Winterstein scolded Petyr, who stood at the doorway, looking like a commoner forced to tell a king he slept with his queen. His eyes darted to Lieselotte, flooding with relief that she was awake.

"What's wrong?" she asked.

"I just wanted to tell you we're close," Petyr said, ducking his head as if Mrs. Winterstein would throw something at him.

"You need to rest," Mrs. Winterstein said.

"I'm fine. I need to see this," Lieselotte assured her.

I can rest later. After this is over. In … how many days? The clock on the wall showed it was 6:15 in the morning. Meaning today was the 23rd.

Lieselotte tried to hide how hard it was just to put her shoes on and get to her feet. Anneliese put a supporting hand on her back. Lieselotte whispered her thanks.

"This is for both of us. I may topple over without using you to brace myself," Anneliese said.

"Thank God you woke up when you did. She's a shark," Petyr said.

Lieselotte smirked, but the smile faded as she descended the steps, each one like a blow to her feet. At the tunnel entrance, the men drank water, their clothes sodden with sweat.

"Finish it," George said with a smile.

Lieselotte entered, Anneliese behind her. The excitement of completing this tunnel trumped all her aches and pains as she passed the border sign, touching it for luck. When she passed the boulder, the excitement exploded.

The men gathered behind Lieselotte and Anneliese, arching their necks to see. They stayed silent—out of necessity to prevent sound from traveling and because the hum of anticipation traveled through the tunnel like an electrical current. Petyr raised Lieselotte's father's camera, ready to capture the moment.

Lieselotte lifted a shovel and stabbed it into the wall. Again and again. Until the wall collapsed, leaving a mountain of dirt around her knees. The camera flashed. There was just the smallest opening for her to gaze through.

"It's there," she whispered, trying to keep her voice soft.

She and Anneliese used their shovels to scrape the dirt toward them. They could carry it out later. Right now, they just needed enough room to get through. As they freed space, the first thing they noticed was that Wolfgang's tunnel was much narrower than theirs. Roughly a quarter narrower, equally on both sides.

With enough space created, she crawled through, followed by the others. There were no lights on this side of the tunnel and the lights from their side succumbed to darkness.

"Here, I have a flashlight," Hansel whispered.

They passed the flashlight from one to the next until Lieselotte had it. She scanned the walls. The tunnel was so much more primitive than theirs. The support beams weren't made from solid wood like theirs were. These had been pieced together.

"Are those … caskets?" Anneliese asked, shuddering.

Mikael examined one of the crossbeams. "They were desperate," he said, voice hushed.

George stepped closer. "But clever."

Johan crouched beside them, his large hands brushing along the wood. "Look how they've pieced this together …"

"It's like a different world," Rory said.

"It is," Mikael said.

It felt like discovering the relics of a long-ago civilization. This tunnel represented the divide between East and West. They had better tools and supplies, while Wolfgang's team had to use whatever they could, relying on ingenuity and determination. A testament to their resolve to escape and to breathe free air on free soil. They traveled the length of Wolfgang's tunnel, toward the ramp and the tunnel entrance.

"There's some pretty shoddy spots here," Petyr whispered.

"Some of these are rotted," Hansel added. "Is it even safe to be in here?"

Lieselotte trusted Wolfgang's engineering. It was his supplies she didn't. He said they'd had to stop digging because of Stasi observation. In that amount of time, the wooden beams had eroded. Were they groaning? Even with their own side of the tunnel, they were constantly checking the support beams.

"His cross braces are pretty ingenious," George said.

Lieselotte paused at the ramp. She kept her light low, not daring to draw attention. But the lack of light coming through signified the entrance was blocked. Just above her was the Von Haven Stein mausoleum.

"We should head back," Anneliese whispered, reaching for Lieselotte's hand.

Lieselotte turned, the last of them to exit the tunnel—snapping photographs as she retreated toward the store. The ramp, the casket-built support beams, the freshly cleared passage. If all went well, tomorrow night Wolfgang would crawl through the tunnel. To the West. To her.

Names on the List

Wolfgang weighed the choices: risk telling others about the tunnel or stay silent. He trusted Lieselotte to complete it by Christmas Eve, but things could still go wrong. *What if I invite others only to discover the tunnel had caved in?* Anyone they asked risked imprisonment.

The weeks leading up to Christmas were busy for Eternal Peace. People grieving recent losses visited the cemetery often. Most visits were during the day, but several people came during the early part of Wolfgang and Eckhart's shift. Most visitors knew where to go; some needed help after dark. Eckhart and Wolfgang laid wreathes and flowers on graves, dusted the snow off tombstones so that the epitaphs could be read.

The snow covered the ground, hiding Dietrich's grave. Unless Schwarzfuchs remembered, only Eckhart and Wolfgang knew where it rested. When they left for the West, no one would know. No one would visit his grave.

"Someone's coming," Eckhart said, standing up after placing a wreath on a tombstone.

Wolfgang turned to look, then checked his watch. 11:47. Near the back entrance, the silhouettes of a half dozen men and a dog waited. Wolfgang and Eckhart headed toward them.

"*Herr* Kirschke, *Herr* Kleppelstein, Merry Christmas," Schwarzfuchs said.

Though they hadn't opened the crypt in weeks, Schwarzfuchs and his faceless henchmen still haunted the grounds.

"What can I do for you?" Wolfgang asked.

"Are we not able to exchange niceties as friends?" Schwarzfuchs asked, with mock offense.

"I apologize, but we're rather busy," Wolfgang said.

"With them?" Schwarzfuchs darted his head toward the tombs. "They're dead. They have forever to wait."

Wolfgang bit the inside of his lip and waited for Schwarzfuchs to speak. The cold had gnawed through his coat and pants. Schwarzfuchs, probably having just recently come out of a heated building, wasn't affected by it yet.

"You had a new eternal guest buried here. Gerhard Adenbauer. Age forty-seven."

"Yes," Wolfgang said.

"You know where he is buried?"

Wolfgang stated he did. When he went into the specific location, Schwarzfuchs shushed him. He extended his hand toward one of his henchmen. The young agent handed over a sealed glass jar. Inside was a piece of fabric—looking like a torn piece of cotton shirt. He unsealed it and held it in front of the dog. The dog's ears perked up.

"Find him," he said with calmness.

The dog sprinted; ears pressed back. Schwarzfuchs followed at a leisurely pace. Wolfgang and Eckhart exchanged scared, apprehensive looks. The dog ran back and forth, searching. Sniffing the ground. Then the air. Picking up the scent, it beelined to a freshly dug grave. No tombstone marked the grave yet, but it was the grave of Gerhard Adenbauer. Schwarzfuchs bent down and praised the dog, scratching its muscular neck. A sick heat surged in Wolfgang's gut. Bile rose in his throat.

"This is the grave," Schwarzfuchs stated.

"It is," Eckhart replied.

"You can never escape us. Not even in death," Schwarzfuchs said. His eyes glowed in the darkness, unblinking and piercing. "As you know by experience, there are many who would risk leaving our great country," Schwarzfuchs said. "To keep our city and our country safe, these people must be monitored."

Eckhart's stare burned into Wolfgang.

"I know nothing about anyone wanting to escape," Wolfgang said.

"And what about you?" Schwarzfuchs asked, turning his head to study Eckhart.

"I am content here," Wolfgang said.

"Content?"

"Content."

"But not happy?"

Wolfgang shook his head. He wouldn't lie. Telling Schwarzfuchs he was happy would be suspicious.

"I don't love my job, and I don't have a woman who loves me. But would I risk an escape just to end up in prison again? Never."

And that was true. He wouldn't end up in prison again. He would escape—or die.

"You've paid your dues, *Herr* Kirschke. As have you, *Herr* Kleppelstein. Tell me, are you happy?"

"No," Eckhart answered.

"For the same reasons?"

"Mostly."

"What if I told you I could give you more? Better jobs? Better pay? Better living quarters? Women?"

"I would ask why you would do that?" Wolfgang said.

If Schwarzfuchs wanted to play games, he could play them with Wolfgang. Not Eckhart.

391

"Become my informants."

Wolfgang's first desire was to cackle at him like a madman. Become his informants? His second reaction was unfiltered anger. Did he think so lowly of Wolfgang and Eckhart that they would sell their soul to betray people?

"I do not believe you have accepted that your fate is here in East Berlin," Schwarzfuchs said, stamping the ground for emphasis. "This will be your future: digging graves until you're in one. Perhaps you think that if I die, your lives will be easier. No, gentlemen. They will not. I am one of Hydra's many heads. Do you think yourselves Hercules? Can you slay us all?" Wolfgang and Eckhart stayed silent. "Inform for me. I will see that you are an engineer at the company of your choice. And you, *Herr* Kleppelstein, you shall reclaim your role at the auto plant. A state-provided home for each of you. No more sharing a bathroom with an entire building. Women to warm your bed. And you, *Herr* Kleppelstein, spy for me and I will return your nephew."

Wolfgang braced himself, ready to restrain Eckhart. To stop his rage from blinding him and causing him to lash out like a feral animal. But Eckhart didn't react. He was wise to the games of the Stasi, too.

For Wolfgang, it was ironic how Schwarzfuchs had tried to entice him with promises of better—better jobs, better homes, a better lifestyle. All things they condemned the West for. Everyone was equal in communism, or so they said.

Schwarzfuchs removed a list from his pocket and held it out for Wolfgang to take. Assuming he had no choice, Wolfgang took it. Schwarzfuchs fumbled for his cigarette case and offered one to Eckhart and Wolfgang. Both refused. He gave a small lift of his brow—a silent *suit yourself*—and lit his own.

"What is this?" Wolfgang asked.

He held it out for Eckhart, but with only starlight, it was hard to read.

"Are these names?" Eckhart asked.

Schwarzfuchs nodded, exhaling smoke. "These are people we believe are planning an escape."

Schwarzfuchs flicked his lighter and used his hand to shield the flame from the wind, offering Eckhart and Wolfgang enough light to read. Wolfgang scanned the names.

"My brother is on this list ..." Eckhart said.

"So he is. His wife, too," Schwarzfuchs said.

"Why do you think he's planning on escaping?"

"We have our sources."

"He would have said something to me."

"Well, it was your misplaced trust in your friend that cost him and his wife last time. Cost them their child. I would think it would be only intelligent to do everything possible to prevent that from happening again. She is due any day now."

Wolfgang read through the names. Emilia and Franco were on the list. But it was the two names at the end that made his stomach drop.

"Why are we on here?" Wolfgang asked.

Schwarzfuchs smirked, but only momentarily before a stern glare replaced it. "Please. I consider that a great insult. I am exceptional at my job. I know you are planning an escape."

Eckhart scoffed, a valiant attempt. But Wolfgang only stared at Schwarzfuchs.

"How do you know that?" Wolfgang asked, delivered in a way that didn't admit to anything.

He didn't divert his eyes. He stared at Schwarzfuchs. Sure, he'd felt confident in his trust with the others during their first escape attempt and that had proven foolish. But he trusted Eckhart,

Bastian, Trude, Emilia, and Franco. Absolutely. He wouldn't betray them, and they wouldn't betray him. So, that meant Schwarzfuchs had nothing but rumors and mumblings, and an unsubstantiated, unprovable hunch in his gut.

"I think I was onto something when I came here with the traitor's ashes," Schwarzfuchs said. "The other four coming here for nightly visits. You were planning an escape. Our extended surveillance and my arrival thwarted your plans. Whether postponed or canceled, it matters not. You will plan another escape, *Herr* Kirschke. And I will be here to catch you. Holding a jar filled with your scent." He stepped in close, daring Wolfgang to flinch. "And when the beast drags you down, tearing your flesh with bared teeth … I will be standing over you. I promise you that what will happen to you will make your time in Hohenschönhausen feel like a summer camp." He let the words sink into Wolfgang's bones. "Here is what you will do for me. You will resume your escape plans, recruiting those on that list. Then you tell me the location, date, and time, and I shall do the rest. If you don't, this will be the last Christmas you spend on the outside. I assure you that you will never see light again. You will wilt away in a dark cell like vermin. Your friends on that list will face the same fate as you. Cold. Dark. And alone."

Wolfgang stared at the names, the letters blurring into meaningless lines and curves. He turned to Eckhart. Meeting his eyes. His friend looked to him for guidance.

"We don't have a choice …" Wolfgang said.

"Wonderful!" Schwarzfuchs reached into his pocket yet again and drew out two chocolate bars. He tossed one to each of them and strutted away. "A Christmas gift! We shall speak soon! Merry Christmas!"

Wolfgang and Eckhart watched their shadows disappear.

"Wolfgang …" Eckhart said.

"Relax. I am not working for them," Wolfgang whispered.

Did Schwarzfuchs really think I would betray my character for a chocolate bar? Not even twenty pieces of silver.

"They're onto us, Wolfgang! They know!"

Wolfgang shook his head, placing his hands on Eckhart's shoulders. "Quiet." He couldn't be sure that the Stasi hadn't planted listening devices. "If they knew, they would've sealed it," Wolfgang whispered.

"What about those names?" Eckhart asked.

Wolfgang couldn't stop the smirk from curling on his lips.

"Why are you smirking?" Eckhart asked, looking at Wolfgang as if he had gone mad.

"He just gave us a list of people who want to escape. He handed us what we were searching for."

Eckhart considered it. "What if it's a trap? What if those people are informants?"

No doubt some were. Schwarzfuchs wouldn't trust so blindly.

"He told us to recruit as if we're escaping. We tell these people tomorrow. At the last minute."

"How do we find them?"

"I know someone who can help with that."

The Last Night

Wolfgang's confidence faltered. Schwarzfuchs was always a step ahead. The list of names felt too easy—too good to be true. For it to be a trap, Schwarzfuchs would need to know the exact time and location of the escape. If he suspected the cemetery, he could only know the specifics if someone in the group had leaked the details. And they hadn't.

But what about Lieselotte's group? Had one of them let the date slip? The Stasi had spies in West Berlin. Had one of them infiltrated her group? Providing feedback to Schwarzfuchs as they went along? Was there a chance that Schwarzfuchs had far more information on the tunnel than Wolfgang thought?

It'd been so long since Father Langer had recited the Bible to him. So many of those passages had faded into the far reaches of his memory. Father Langer would know of the perfect passage to ease his mind.

On 22 December, Wolfgang slid a note under Father Langer's door, knocked, and then dashed across the street into the Church of the Sacred Heart of Jesus for the 9:30 mass. He was nervous Father Langer wasn't home—or hadn't received the note. There was also the issue of what Father Langer even looked like. Lieselotte had described him as best she could that night in the church—trying to offer more than generic callouts like height and hair color, which Father Langer himself had once described to Wolfgang in Hohenschönhausen. Though he didn't know exactly what he looked like, he'd recognize his voice anywhere. The voice that had gotten him through Hohenschönhausen. The surrogate voice of God.

Wolfgang scanned the rows ahead. The priests and altar boys strode down the center row toward the front of the church. *What if Father Langer doesn't show? What is the backup plan?* The hymn began, followed by readings and the priest's sermon. When Communion commenced, Wolfgang watched as the rows of people emptied.

A tall man with blue-white hair rounded the pews, locking eyes with Wolfgang. He continued on. Wolfgang lost track of him as he advanced in line, deciding that turning around to look would draw attention. He accepted the Body and Blood of Christ, then turned to scan the congregation for the man with blue-white hair. But he was gone. *Hadn't the man locked eyes with me? As if he had wanted to be seen?*

Discouraged, Wolfgang reclaimed his lone seat in the pew. But his eyes caught the hymnbook lying on the pew. *Had that been there before?* No. He had put it back in the hymnal rack.

Wolfgang grabbed the hymnbook and flipped through the pages. About three-quarters in, he found a folded note. He kept it flat, pretending to search for the closing song as he opened the note.

St. Mary's School. Koppenstraße. 11:30. Roof.

Wolfgang slid the note out of the book, scrunched it up, and left the mass as discreetly as he could. Wolfgang wasn't familiar with the school and hadn't expected to have to jog to meet that 11:30 deadline. The dilapidated school had been abandoned decades ago. Swings creaked in the wind. Wolfgang struggled with the door; leaves and dirt were scattered across the floor. In the shadows, animals had made their home. Wolfgang advanced up the stairs, keeping a sure hand on the railing, not trusting their integrity.

The entrance to the roof still had a sign hanging on the door that stated *No Students.* Wolfgang put his hand on the door handle and paused.

What if this is the trap?

The safest choice was to walk away. His escape was less than a day away. *Why risk that? For strangers?* He trusted Father Langer, but what if it wasn't him that delivered this note? What if the Stasi had taken the note he left? How did he know this wasn't an intricate plot concocted by Schwarzfuchs?

The weight of the names in his pocket pressed on him. All those people who yearned for freedom. If he had the power to help them, did that mean he had the responsibility to?

Wolfgang was new to faith, still trying to grasp it. So often people pray to God. He had whispered those same prayers inside the Submarine. But it wasn't until after his lessons with Father Langer that Wolfgang felt he understood God. God rarely used divine intervention. He didn't require that. Instead, He sent others in His place. In prison, He had given Wolfgang Father Langer. All these people on that list had prayed for God's help. What if God's answer was to send Wolfgang?

Ask him after he was arrested, and he'd wished he'd thought this through with a more practical mind. Eckhart would say he was crazy. Most would. But right now, it felt right. That this was the answer. So, he opened the door and walked up the steps—half expecting Schwarzfuchs and Stasi agents to arrest him. But there was only one person on the roof. The man with the blue-white hair, barrel chest, and graying beard.

He smiled the most genial, authentic smile Wolfgang had ever seen. There was no way that it could have been faked or forced.

"We finally meet face-to-face," the man said.

Wolfgang recognized the voice—one he remembered fondly. A remarkable feat, given the harshness of the prison. Wolfgang extended his hand. Father Langer shook it.

"I never got the chance to thank you," Wolfgang said.

"Please. I'm sorry they didn't release you into the West. It was the arrangement we made with them."

Wolfgang didn't question who "we" was or who "them" were. That was the past. He needed to focus on tomorrow.

"You have something for me?" Father Langer asked.

Instinctively, Wolfgang looked around as if he could spot a recording device.

"This school closed after the war. Like so many buildings here, it was neglected and left to rot," Father Langer said.

Meaning there'd be no reason for listening devices. Wolfgang removed his left shoe and then his sock, digging his hand into it to retrieve the list of names. He unfolded it and extended it out for Father Langer to take.

"I have a way out," Wolfgang said.

Father Langer glanced up from the list when Wolfgang had said that. "How did you get these names?"

"A Stasi agent."

Father Langer gave Wolfgang a deserved look that said *are you serious?* It sounded reckless, so he explained Schwarzfuchs wanted Wolfgang to become an informant and orchestrate a bogus escape attempt so that he could arrest every person on that list.

"Your worry is that this is a trap," Father Langer said, lifting the paper for emphasis.

"There are six names on that list I trust. I happen to be one of them. The other five are involved."

He didn't elaborate on the word involved. It was obvious what that meant, but if there were any listening devices, it was something he could try to claim as being vague. Probably a fool's hope, but one he had to try.

"Do you recognize any of those names?" Wolfgang asked.

Father Langer's eyes scanned across the page, left to right, top to bottom.

"Apart from the same six names? No, I do not."

"What if it's a trap? That one of those people is an informant?" Wolfgang asked.

"That is certainly a possibility."

Not the assurance he'd hoped for—nor the confirmation he feared.

"Do you know why you were chosen to be freed?" Father Langer asked. Wolfgang shook his head. It was a question he wrestled with every day. "Because I knew your character. You didn't betray your friends or offer to become an informant. You could have given them everything you knew and made up what you didn't know, but you didn't. You stayed true to yourself."

Wolfgang hesitated. "So, you think I should help them?"

Father Langer shook his head. "No, I'm saying I trust your judgement." He reviewed the list once more. "Your potential ask is that I find these people and invite them to your 'way out'?"

Wolfgang nodded. "Is that something you could do?"

"Oh, yes. I cannot vouch for the character of the people on this list, though. What you fear, I cannot vanquish."

"I wish I could pretend I didn't have this list—or that they're all spies."

"That would make it easier," Father Langer agreed.

"You're not going to talk me into it?" Wolfgang asked.

Father Langer chuckled. "No, dear Wolfgang. I would not do that. You've waited a long time for this way out. You were betrayed once before. It's only natural for you to be suspicious. You'd be a fool if you weren't."

From up here, with most of the city's buildings in the distance, it offered a better view of the stars that the city and smog otherwise blocked. But the wind bit hard.

"Being a name on this list, I'd hope that if someone had a way out, they'd take a chance on me," Wolfgang said.

Father Langer only listened. Wolfgang felt more at ease keeping his gaze ahead. He'd never spoken with Father Langer face-to-face before. Hearing and not seeing was more natural.

"Is it foolish—or even sacrilegious—to think God is using me?" Wolfgang asked.

"God doesn't use us. He empowers us. Every one of us. Every day."

"You told me once about Peter doubting."

"Matthew 14:28-31," Father Langer recited. *"Peter said, 'Lord, if it's you, call me.' Jesus replied, 'Come.' Peter stepped onto the water but, frightened, began to sink. 'Lord, save me!' he cried. Jesus caught him and said, 'You of little faith, why did you doubt?'"*

"It's about courage. Faith. Trust. About taking that step even in the face of fear and uncertainty," Wolfgang said.

"It is."

"It's not fair for me to risk this for Eckhart and the others." Wolfgang turned toward him. "I'll need them to meet somewhere else. From there, I'll lead them where they need to go." He paused, thinking it through. "I'll stagger and lead them in smaller groups. No one knows where it is until I walk them there. That way, no one can betray the position, because they won't know."

"I must inform you that there is still the risk that while you lead a group, those who remain could betray you," Father Langer said.

Maybe Eckhart or Bastian could escort the group while I stayed behind.

"May I suggest meeting here?" Father Langer said.

"It's quite the walk. Over five miles."

"Do you have an automobile?"

Wolfgang scoffed. "I don't have a bicycle."

Father Langer fished into his pockets and tossed a set of keys. "It screams like a demon when it starts, but it's dependable. It can seat five."

Wolfgang calculated how long each trip could take, factoring in enough additional time for any hiccups.

"10 p.m. Here. Tomorrow. No parking at the school," Wolfgang said.

He'd promised Lieselotte eleven, but he wouldn't make it. Waiting until later at night seemed the smartest play.

"I will send word. Can I keep this?" Father Langer gestured to the note.

"You can. I have another copy in my right sock."

Father Langer smiled.

"Will you come with us?" Wolfgang asked.

"God has work for me to do here."

"You're sure?"

"*Lord, if it's you, tell me to come to you on the water.* He has not led me astray yet."

They shared a look—one of grace and gratitude, wordless but complete.

"I can't tell you how much … you kept me sane in there," Wolfgang said. "I can never repay you for any of it."

"Walk in the Lord's light. That's all He asks of any of us."

Wolfgang had Father Langer's keys but elected to walk home instead. It was a good three miles and damn cold. Shivering and exercising made his mind focus on survival. Even if his life wasn't in danger. It wiped all thoughts clean in a way nothing else did apart from a dreamless sleep.

Once he returned to his apartment, he wanted nothing but to crash on his bed and sleep. But he had to tell Eckhart. He was on the couch drinking a Vista Cola—East Germany's darker, citrusy, less-sweet answer to Coca-Cola—a favorite among many Germans.

"Care for a walk?" Wolfgang asked.

He didn't want to walk—and judging by Eckhart clutching his blanket, neither did he. The heat was unreliable in this hunk of junk apartment. They slept in their coats. But Eckhart wanted to know how Wolfgang's meeting went, and it wasn't safe to talk about it in the apartment. Wolfgang set their course to Bastian's, filling Eckhart in with everything he and Father Langer had discussed, and ultimately, Wolfgang's decision to have faith and provide a way out for those on the list.

"You don't have to have any part in it. You and the others … you go," Wolfgang said.

"Shit, Wolfgang," Eckhart said, letting out a frustrated sigh.

"I had to tell you. It wasn't right for me to decide without telling you and the others about it."

"I hate how selfless you're being," Eckhart said.

Wolfgang gave a short laugh. "Me, too."

They shared a brief smirk.

Eckhart cursed then sighed. "I'll do it," he said, already regretting it.

"You don't have to."

"We made a promise. We all escape or none of us."

Three people had made that promise. One had broken it, and now, two reforged it.

"You drive," Wolfgang said. "I'll stay with the group."

Eckhart unlocked Bastian's door, flicked on the light, and called out. A bedroom light flickered on, and Bastian stepped out.

"Eckhart? What the hell are you doing here?" he whispered.

"We need to talk, but first make some *Muckefuck*. I'm freezing," Eckhart said.

Wolfgang asked Bastian to wake Trude, stating she needed to come as well. With her due date days away and the stress of impending escape, she'd barely slept. But Eckhart was adamant she needed to hear this.

Trude shuffled out, wearing flannel pajamas and thick socks. Her bathrobe couldn't close around the girth of her stomach. She eased her way into the living room. The hard wooden kitchen chairs wreaked havoc on her back, so this conversation would take place in the living room.

They did a quick sweep for bugs—under the couch, between chair cushions, inside lamps, even unscrewing bulbs. Ten minutes later, Bastian returned with *Muckefuck*. Wolfgang clutched his cup, savoring the warmth against his face.

"Tomorrow …" Trude asked, holding the word. Its tone questioning if it was still on.

Wolfgang nodded as he removed the copy of the list from his right sock. Bastian turned on their Stern-Radio Berlin. State-approved Christmas music sprang out. Most of it had emphasis on winter rather than religion. With the radio covering their conversation, Wolfgang explained the change in plan and the visit from the Stasi.

"You're dumb," Bastian said in a voice higher than a whisper. Trude cast a stern look at him to lower his voice. "Both of you. Idiots. You," a nod at Eckhart, "I expected this from. But you," a follow-up nod at Wolfgang, "I thought you were smart."

"This doesn't have to change your plans," Wolfgang said.

"You and Trude go," Eckhart added.

Bastian sighed. "The hell I can. You're my brother. I'm not leaving you."

"Well, I can't leave you," Trude said. The thought horrified her, almost bringing her to tears.

Bastian squeezed her hand, his voice soft but urgent. "We'll be fine. Go through with Emilia and Franco. There will be people on the other side." He shot a glance at Wolfgang for confirmation. He reiterated that Lieselotte and Anneliese would be there.

"Gives you a chance to meet my future wife," Eckhart joked.

Wolfgang and Eckhart filled the silence that followed by drinking their *Muckefuck*. Letting that hot brew burn a trail down their chests.

"There's something else I need to tell you," Eckhart said. "Tomorrow, we start anew. I want to leave all this behind."

Bastian looked from Eckhart to Wolfgang. By Eckhart's expression, he was going to tell Bastian the secret they'd been carrying since they were released from prison.

"It was Dietrich. He betrayed us."

Bastian paused, staring at his brother in disbelief—too stunned for any other reaction. But it would come.

"I'm so sorry," Eckhart said.

"Why didn't you tell me?"

"Because you would have killed him and spent the rest of your life in prison."

Bastian didn't refute that he would have killed him. That wasn't up for debate.

"You all knew?" Bastian asked, looking around the room.

"I had to protect you," Trude said.

"I'm sorry, Bastian," Wolfgang said.

"It's why you two stopped seeing so much of him. I thought that was odd, but you said he was content staying here. That he'd changed." He paused. "He deserved the death he got."

Wolfgang understood the pain Bastian felt. It was warranted. But Dietrich had been more than a rat. More than the Judas of their group. Before that, he was their friend. Any explanation for why Dietrich had betrayed them would only come across as a defense of him, so Wolfgang didn't speak.

"It's too cold for you two to walk back," Bastian said. "Sleep here. There're extra blankets in the closet down the hall."

He disappeared into his room. Eckhart helped Trude up from the couch. Before she joined her husband, she reached out to Wolfgang and Eckhart, drawing them close.

"I do not blame either of you," Trude said. "Do you hear me?" They both nodded, though not convincingly. "No. Do you hear me? His actions were his own. It's time to let it go."

Wolfgang hadn't realized the guilt he'd held onto for so long. Her blessing, her cleansing of his self-inflicted sins, was everything. Eckhart tried to hold back his tears. Trude stroked his face. She didn't rush him, didn't stop stroking his face while she held Wolfgang's hand with the other. Once Eckhart calmed, he escorted her to her bedroom. Eckhart returned with a couple of extra blankets, tossing one to Wolfgang.

Neither took the couch, both electing to take an armchair instead. Wolfgang was exhausted. Sleep should come to him easily, but his restless mind wouldn't let him sleep. The past, the present, and the future all melded into a volatile compound. An explosive charge of nerves, excitement, dread, worry, and fear.

"Huh," Eckhart said.

"What?"

"We'll never sleep in our apartment again."

Wolfgang had known there'd be a last time. But he hadn't known that the previous night would be the last time he'd lay in that small twin bed, constantly switching positions to avoid the nasty poking springs. He hated that place. The ice box it was in winter and the oven it was in summer. Yet, it was hard not to be emotional about losing a home.

"This is our last night sleeping in East Berlin," Wolfgang whispered.

No Way Back

Sleep was a generous term. Wolfgang dozed off in fits, his nerves giving him cotton mouth. He'd drink a glass of water, then need to use the bathroom—an endless cycle. When he managed to sleep, Eckhart's snoring woke him. But to be fair, Wolfgang's pacing and frequent trips to the sink had woken Eckhart, too.

They had planned to slip away before Bastian and Trude woke, but Trude, also restless, insisted they stay for breakfast. Neither man liked the idea of a pregnant woman cooking for them, but Trude wouldn't hear of it.

"Is Bastian still asleep?" Eckhart asked.

"Oh, yes," Trude said, cracking an egg over the frying pan. "I think last night was freeing for him. That wonder ... not knowing ... I should have told him after Dietrich's death."

Wolfgang and Eckhart didn't comment. Couldn't pretend to know what was best. Not knowing was a pain and knowing was a pain.

Wolfgang and Eckhart scarfed down their eggs and toast and then washed their plates. At the door, putting their coats and boots on, Bastian stepped out of the bedroom.

"Be here for dinner at 5:30," Bastian said. He looked at Wolfgang. "You, too."

"No, you don't have to feed me," Wolfgang politely refused.

"Nonsense," Trude said. "You're family. You're having Christmas Eve dinner with us."

Wolfgang nodded his appreciation. On the walk back, the Ghost of Christmas Past filled his mind—his father teaching him and Lieselotte codes, the holidays with his parents, the sewer where he met Lieselotte last Christmas, and now, God willing, the tunnel that would bring freedom. In another life, he and Lieselotte would be heading to his parents' house for their annual Christmas Eve party, laughter spilling from the windows, music drifting into the snowy street, and *Glühwein* warming their chests.

Everything made him emotional. Not just the profound—like realizing he might never see his parents again. That thought devastated him, sending him to his room in tears. But it was also the mundane, the seemingly inconsequential things—things he hadn't truly cared about before. Like the kitchen table. How many card games have they played at that table?

Nostalgia and loss hit in waves. They'd leave everything behind, except for a few precious items that fit in their pockets—anything more invited interrogation. Wolfgang pocketed his pictures of Lieselotte and his parents. Then he and Eckhart left their apartment for the final time.

Though they wanted that final time to be because they were escaping into the West, that wasn't a predetermined fate. There was a possibility, a high one at that, that this could not just be their last day in East Berlin, but their last day on Earth. This escape could cost them their lives.

Wolfgang and Eckhart strolled through the cold winter air to Bastian and Trude's. The sidewalks were less crowded with pedestrians, but the streets were alive with holiday traffic. How many people can't spend time with those they love because of that monstrous Wall?

When they stepped inside Bastian and Trude's apartment, the smell of baking filled the air. Roasted meats, steaming vegetables, cinnamon, clove, garlic, melting butter. He couldn't process what Trude was cooking, but his stomach growled from the intoxicating smells, even though he was far from hungry.

Bastian pleaded with Trude to rest as she moved about the kitchen, preparing the meal.

"I am fine, Bastian," she snapped.

Bastian wisely retreated. Eckhart drew attention to his and Wolfgang's arrival.

"I hope you're hungry. I'm cooking everything we have," Trude said.

While Bastian and Trude cooked, Eckhart and Wolfgang played cards in the living room. Offering to help every so often only for Trude to state they were fine. Bastian's look said otherwise.

Franco and Emilia set? Eckhart wrote on a sheet of paper.

Bastian scribbled, *We stopped over there this morning after you left.*

Wolfgang grabbed the sheet of paper and pen. *You told them about the plan?*

Bastian shook his head, writing a quick reply. *They'll be with Trude. First to go through the tunnel. No need to worry them.*

Wolfgang agreed. No reason to add more worry.

"I need to shovel the sidewalk," Bastian said with a look at Eckhart and Wolfgang that implied they should join him outside.

Wolfgang picked up on the hint sooner than Eckhart. While Wolfgang slipped his coat and shoes on, Eckhart made a dramatic show of it, not eager to go back out in the cold. Coming from inside, it felt even colder than it had on the walk over. Eckhart shivered, his arms crossed, and his hands buried into his armpits.

"I need to ask something of you both," Bastian said. "If something happens to me tonight … I ask that you look after Trude and my child."

Eckhart turned away, frustrated. "Don't talk like that. You're getting in that tunnel with Trude."

"I can't let you stay behind. Promise me."

"Trude needs you. Wolfgang and I can handle it. I can't let you risk it."

"You can't let me risk it?" Bastian asked with a smile. "I'm the big brother here."

"Older," Eckhart corrected.

"And bigger."

"Debatable."

Bastian's smile faded. "I have to know that you'll look after her if something happens." He turned to Wolfgang. "Please."

"Of course," Wolfgang said.

Eckhart hated to even consider it, like making this promise put a bad omen out into the world. "I promise," he finally relented.

"Let me take over," Wolfgang said, reaching for the shovel Bastian held. Bastian refused, but Wolfgang insisted. "It'll help me stay calm. I'm getting restless."

Bastian relinquished the shovel, and he and Eckhart went inside. Wolfgang shoveled, the scrape of metal on concrete steadying his nerves. But the calm didn't last. Inside, the anxiety returned. After a few more rounds of cards, listening to Christmas music on the radio, dinner was ready. The countertops overflowed with food—barely enough room for plates. A true hodgepodge of a feast.

Trude had spent hours preparing it and Wolfgang tried his best to eat, but he had never felt less hungry in his life. And after a few quick bites, the food lay untouched, each of them lost in their own thoughts, united in the same quiet terror.

After dinner, Wolfgang put on his hat and gloves and buttoned his wool overcoat. He would attend the Christmas Eve mass before retrieving Father Langer's car. Then he'd pick Eckhart up at a mechanic shop halfway between Bastian and Trude's apartment and Eternal Peace. Bastian, Trude, Emilia, and Franco would arrive at the cemetery in Franco's truck. Before Wolfgang and Eckhart drove to the abandoned school, they had to make sure the tunnel was ready. He tried to believe that if Lieselotte hadn't finished the tunnel, she would've found a way to warn him.

But what if she couldn't?

That question nagged, buzzing around his ear like a threatened bee ready to sting.

Wolfgang walked the couple of miles to the Sacred Heart church and sat in the last pew. Praying to God, hearing the priest's sermon but not listening. He recalled Father Langer's words about Joseph and Mary's strength and faith and tried to channel the same for himself. He left after Communion so that no one from the church would see him drive away in Father Langer's car.

True to his word, Father Langer's Wanderer W24, a prewar relic, sounded like a demon when it started and had a distinct rattling sound when idling. Wolfgang drove to the mechanic shop. The beast jerked to a stop. Eckhart jogged out from the alley and hopped inside, refraining from mentioning how much of a hunk of junk the car was, but it was written all over his face.

Wolfgang circled the fence line of Eternal Peace a handful of times, scanning for any unfamiliar cars or loitering people. After more than a year working at the cemetery, they knew the vehicles owned by the nearby residents. But tonight, several unrecognized cars lined the street. *Do they belong to visitors spending Christmas Eve with family—or Stasi agents ready to pounce?*

When all looked clear, Wolfgang parked, avoiding the streetlights. He and Eckhart jogged to the cemetery entrance. Eckhart fished the keys out of his pocket. Their eyes scanned—a feeling of being watched crawling along their skin. Trees, grass, and tombstones all cast shadows—each one temporarily looking like the outline of Schwarzfuchs. *Good evening,* Herr *Kirschke.*

Eckhart unlocked the Von Haven Stein mausoleum. The paranoia was debilitating.

"Shit!" Eckhart said.

"What?" Wolfgang asked, snapping his attention to Eckhart.

"The rollers are gone."

They'd gotten rid of them during Schwarzfuchs's surprise visit. It'd been over a month since they'd been inside the mausoleum. How had they forgotten that? Panic threatened to paralyze him but that would do no good. Wolfgang needed to keep his head.

"Can we try pushing it?" Eckhart asked.

It was worth an attempt, though they both doubted it would work. It had been a beast to move when it was the six of them. Still, they tried and quickly realized it wouldn't budge.

"The truck!" Eckhart said. "Let's use that again."

They jogged to where the truck should have been—but it was gone.

"What the hell?" Eckhart asked.

They looked around, as if tall grass or shadow could somehow hide a truck.

"Maybe it's getting fixed," Wolfgang said.

Eckhart cursed. "I can't believe this."

Wolfgang checked his watch—9:15. Bastian, Trude, Emilia, and Franco weren't due for another forty-five minutes. If the tunnel wasn't ready by then, the entire schedule unraveled. *What would all those people gathering at the school think? That they had been betrayed? Duped?* The longer this went on, the more likely it was that they would be discovered.

"Okay, we can do this," Wolfgang said. "Just have to think it through."

Eckhart continued to curse, so it was on Wolfgang to figure it out. The ticking clock in his mind grew louder. He breathed in slowly and exhaled. *Time to get to work.*

"Okay. I need you to get some sandbags from the shed," Wolfgang said. Eckhart bombarded him with questions. Wolfgang grabbed his shoulders. "Calm down, okay? We can do this. I need the bags. Shovels, too. And rope. Okay?" Eckhart nodded, but the sweat on his forehead showed his mind was elsewhere. Racing. Panicking. "Bags. Shovels. Rope," Wolfgang repeated calmly.

Eckhart exhaled. "I'm on it."

He took off toward the shed by the main building. Wolfgang freed the rusted chain from around the crypt. What he had in mind was a block-and-tackle system. He wrapped it around the side of the tomb, verifying there were no kinks and the chain was evenly placed.

Eckhart ran back, the rope wrapped around his shoulders, trying to keep the two shovels in his hands from smacking his knees. He dropped the supplies in front of Wolfgang.

Wolfgang tossed the chain over the tree. "The tree acts as the pivot point."

"I'm not going to understand this, so just do it," Eckhart said with a nervous smile.

"Okay. Fill those sacks with dirt and stones. The heavier the better," Wolfgang instructed.

Eckhart grabbed a bag and hand-shoveled dirt into the sacks. Then he looked for stones. Wolfgang rushed to help, filling their six bags with as many stones as they could. Then they secured those sacks to the chain. The combined weight pressed down like a grip. Together, Wolfgang and Eckhart lifted the sacks off the ground. The counterweight pulled taut. The tomb inside shifted with a grating groan. Wolfgang and Eckhart sandwiched the shovels in between the created gap.

"Can you fit?" Wolfgang asked.

It was tight, but Eckhart squeezed through.

"I can make it down. Trude will be able to, too," he said.

"Make sure the tunnel is complete," Wolfgang said. Though he knew if it wasn't, Lieselotte would have gotten word to him. Somehow. Some way.

Eckhart disappeared into the depths of the tunnel. 478 feet of desperation and hope lay behind them. Every second that passed was good news. A few minutes later, he returned. Wolfgang helped him out of the tunnel. Eckhart broke out in the biggest smile of his life.

"They did it! They really did it!" he said.

Wolfgang smiled, too. A smile loaded with emotion. What Lieselotte, Anneliese, and an unknown number of people had done was truly beyond comprehension. Beyond words.

"Not going to lie. I kind of wanted to keep going," Eckhart said.

"I don't blame you. It's why I sent you. I'd be in West Berlin by now," Wolfgang joked.

There was no time to rest on their laurels. They had to get the chain off the gnarled branch. They could toss the sacks of rocks and dirt somewhere—there was nothing overly suspicious about that. Their goal wasn't long-term deception anymore.

They'd shifted the tomb just enough for people to slip through and still close the mausoleum door. Eckhart slid it shut. Bastian and Franco would have no trouble getting it open.

A prickle crawled up Wolfgang's spine as if someone was watching. So much of his body, his heart, his mind pleaded for him to leave now. Whispering to him that he may not get another chance. Would he regret this decision for the rest of his life? But he wouldn't have to live with that regret long. His promise to escape or die held true.

Wolfgang and Eckhart ran as fast as they could to Father Langer's Wanderer, trying to leave the scene as fast as possible, not only due to watching eyes but because they wanted to remove the temptation of escape. They had longed for this day since 13 August 1961—Barbed Wire Sunday. It was finally here.

"We're doing the right thing, aren't we?" Wolfgang asked.

Eckhart hesitated. "The right thing? I don't know. The honorable thing? Yeah."

Eckhart drove off toward the school, keeping his speed within the limit. Wolfgang had already checked the taillights and headlights worked. Nothing about the car or their driving would give the police a reason to pull them over. When they pulled into the barren school parking lot, their stomachs dropped. An unease crawled over them—like stepping into a haunted house after dark. Father Langer had gotten the word out, leaving as little time as possible for those names on the list to betray them. But there was a chance the Stasi were here, waiting for them.

Wolfgang had to get out of the car, but every cell in his body screamed to stay put and cling to the safety the car provided.

"I'll go in. Keep the car running," Wolfgang said. "If I don't come out in a minute or two, you drive off."

Eckhart shook his head. "We said we're in this together."

"This was my choice. There's no reason for both of us …"

He trailed off. The answer wasn't "to be arrested." It was "to die." Wolfgang wouldn't surrender. Those Stasi agents would have to use their weapons.

Wolfgang opened the door and cautiously dipped one leg out. Waiting for flashlights to shine on him, dogs to bark, agents to shout. But they wouldn't do it with him still in the car. They'd wait until he had no way out. He trembled, stepping out of the car, holding onto the door's frame to keep himself upright. He took slow steps toward the school entrance. The inside was pitch black. He didn't dare call out or announce his presence.

No one was inside. Did he have the wrong address? No. This was the same school he'd met Father Langer in last night. Had the people on the list gone to the wrong school? Had there been a mix-up in information? Or had none of them decided to come, thinking it was a setup?

Wolfgang turned to head back to the car when faint voices carried through the cold air. A man's voice. Then a woman's and a child's. He followed those voices to the school's old gymnasium. Dust covered the cracked wooden floor. The gym overflowed— shoulder to shoulder, far more people than the list accounted for.

The questions rang out at Wolfgang. *Who are you? Why are we here?* Wolfgang struggled to process the sheer number of people.

"I have a way out," Wolfgang said. "I know what you are risking being here. I also know that some of you in this gym are Stasi informants." A nervous murmur took hold, people looking at each other apprehensively. "You do this because they have something on you. You feel you have no way out—that you must do what they ask. I'm telling you, I have a way out. I couldn't offer my friend that way out—but I can offer it to you." He paused. Letting those words permeate whatever brainwashing or threat the Stasi had on these people. "Now, we'll need to travel in groups of five."

Getting people to fall into line was always a difficult process. They'd all been waiting for him and now they were told to form into a line. Those closest to him had an advantage. Arguments and accusations broke out. The vocal trying to suppress the silent. The strong trying to intimidate the weak.

We don't have time for this.

"Please. We can all make it out if we don't waste time!" Wolfgang yelled. *To hell with waiting.* He grabbed a woman by the elbow; her husband followed, and their children clung to him, their fear palpable. He led them through the school and outside.

Wolfgang gave a thumbs-up to Eckhart and told the family who Eckhart was. As the family got into the Wanderer, Wolfgang leaned into the car through Eckhart's open window.

"There's more than we thought," Wolfgang said. "The list must've been adults only."

"How many more?" Eckhart asked.

Wolfgang shrugged. "Twice as many. If not more."

Eckhart's eyes said it all. They hadn't planned for this amount of people. This amount of time. Every single trip they took, they were subject to a long list of variables and none of them good.

"Wish Father Langer drove a bus," Eckhart remarked.

Wolfgang stepped back and tapped the top of the car. Eckhart drove away. Wolfgang rushed back inside, expecting silence, but instead he faced a barrage of questions. *Where are you taking us? Where did they go? How are you getting us out of here?*

"For the safety of everyone, I will not divulge that. No one is allowed to leave," Wolfgang said.

"The hell we're not allowed to leave!" a man shouted from the back.

"We can't let anyone leave and risk them alerting the Stasi. You all made the choice to come here. You must see this through."

No one liked being called a potential informant—but it had to be said. Right now, their questions came from fear. But fear could twist into anger—irrational, dangerous anger. This crowd could become a mob, and if it did, Wolfgang would be powerless to stop them.

To the End of the Line

Franco parked outside Eternal Peace Cemetery. Emilia checked her watch: 9:58.

"Looks clear," Emilia said, scouting the street with her side mirror.

The two couples stepped out of the truck, closing the doors as quietly as they could. Hopefully, people were preoccupied—gathered around the table, playing games, singing carols, or asleep. Anything to keep their eyes off the street.

Bastian held Trude's hand while Franco supported her other arm as they entered Eternal Peace. They moved as quickly as Trude's body would allow. Breaking into a cemetery was eerie enough. Doing it while trying to escape made it worse. Fear crept over their skin as they approached the Von Haven Stein mausoleum.

"They have it open for us," Trude said.

"I need your truck," Bastian said to Franco.

Franco looked confused, as if he hadn't translated it correctly. Bastian explained that there were others wanting to escape, and Wolfgang and Eckhart were bringing them here.

"Then I help, too. We do this together," Franco said.

There wasn't time to argue, at least not for Bastian. Emilia grabbed her husband's hands and kissed him hard.

"You make it back here," she said.

Franco nodded, then helped Emilia into the tunnel.

"I'll be there," Bastian said.

"Don't … leave me. You make it," Trude said.

"I will. I promise."

He helped Trude to the opening, her pregnant belly barely fitting through.

"Is it complete?" Bastian called down.

In the tunnel, Emilia ran the length of the tunnel to the spot they had marked at 478, then beyond it. A smile spread and she whispered-shouted to Trude.

"She says it's complete!" Trude said.

"Go! Tell Lieselotte there'll be more coming," Bastian said. "Lots more. I love you."

Trude echoed the sentiment before Bastian and Franco darted across the cemetery and back to Franco's truck.

Wolfgang urged the crowd to quiet—and finally, they did. There were a few whispers, but nothing resembling the mob-like mentality they'd had before.

If they hadn't quieted, he would have missed the sound of a car door shutting. *Eckhart can't be back this soon?* It'd only been minutes. A second car door closed. Nothing more than a faint thud.

Oh, God. Is it the Stasi?

The gym had only one exit. If the crowd panicked, they'd bull-rush him—trampling him and anyone in their way to reach it. Others had heard the car doors, too. If Wolfgang looked panicked, they would reciprocate that fear. All these people could be arrested. Children torn from their families. The thought made him ill. How could he keep that from showing on his face?

Wolfgang turned and faced the door. Curling his hand into a fist. Ready to die.

"Wolfgang?" a familiar voice whispered.

"Bastian?" Wolfgang replied.

Bastian and Franco emerged into the gym. All the built-up tension in Wolfgang's body loosened with a hearty sigh. Like a taut rubber band finally released.

"Franco wanted to help," Bastian said. "We have his truck."

Wolfgang sprang at Franco and hugged him. Franco chuckled. Without a second vehicle, this would have taken all night and into the morning. God had answered his prayers. He'd sent Franco.

"Okay, the second group of five, come forward," Wolfgang said.

The next group—men around his age—didn't move forward. They stepped aside.

"Let the families go first," one of them said.

A mother with her two sons and daughter stepped forward.

"Room for one more," Wolfgang said.

A woman in her forties claimed the spot.

"Franco will drive you," Wolfgang told them.

Bastian stayed behind with Wolfgang.

"Trude and Emilia are in the tunnel. They did it, Wolfgang. They did it!" he said.

They shared a victorious smile, even if they were here in the East. No matter what happened tonight, Trude and Emilia had made it.

"So, what can we do while we wait?" Bastian asked.

"We need to take a head count," Wolfgang replied.

They needed exact counts of how many people and groups were here. Wolfgang and Bastian walked on either side of the lines, counting. At the end, they compared their numbers.

"Forty-seven," Wolfgang said.

"Forty-three, but you counted the babies."

"I did."

"Their mothers will hold them, so they won't take up a seat."

Forty-seven people, forty-three seats. Some children could sit on laps. That would help.

"Figuring out how many trips it'll take?" Bastian asked.

Wolfgang nodded, going over the numbers in his head. Four infants, sixteen children—half under five. Two vehicles with five available spots.

"Attention!" Wolfgang shouted. Bastian put his fingers in his mouth and whistled. Wolfgang thanked him then continued. "I want one line with families. If your children are small enough to sit on your lap, do not count them. But we want five per group. Those traveling without children are the second group. We have two vehicles that will take you to the site. Please be patient."

"How long do we think it'll take Eckhart?" Bastian asked.

Wolfgang hesitated. Unsure of the answer or how to even guess. Eckhart would have to drive slowly. Change the routes he took to Eternal Peace and the routes back here to St. Mary's School. Then shepherd the group through the cemetery and to the Von Haven Stein mausoleum. Each trip could take anywhere from fifteen to thirty minutes, depending on a myriad of conditions.

"Does anybody have a car?" Wolfgang asked the large group.

A collection of answers rang out. Mostly noes. The few yeses came from people who'd left them at home. Even on Christmas Eve, when travel was common, neighbors might notice them driving off and report them to the Stasi. It was what Wolfgang expected, but a question that needed to be asked.

"You know what I just thought of?" Bastian asked.

"No. Do I want to?" Wolfgang asked.

"No. But I'm bringing it up, anyway. What's stopping the people he dropped off from sneaking off and warning the Stasi?"

It was the last thing he wanted to add to his already worried mind. But it was a valid point. Something he should have considered.

"You go with the next group," Wolfgang said. "Monitor the tunnel. Make sure everyone that goes in stays in."

"Why me?"

"Because if shit goes wrong, you can make it into the tunnel. To Trude. To your child."

Before Bastian countered, the faint shutting of a car door garnered their attention. Moments later, Eckhart rushed in.

"Everything went well," he said. "Bastian, what the hell are you doing?"

"Can't let you be the only hero," Bastian said with a smile.

Wolfgang explained Bastian would be going with him and guarding the tunnel.

"Good idea," Eckhart said. "I should have thought of that."

Wolfgang turned to the crowd. "I need a group of four."

"Four?! You just put us into groups of five!" someone bellowed.

"Yes, I know. But I need a seat for Bastian. He's going to stay at the site for added safety."

Wolfgang didn't wait for a group of four to come forward or acknowledge complaints. He went to the non-family line and gave a forceful nudge to four people to follow Eckhart.

"You're sure you don't want to go?" Bastian asked.

"And miss all this complaining? I'm good. Go," Wolfgang said.

Bastian half sighed with reluctance but nodded and followed Eckhart.

"Be back soon," Eckhart called out.

About seven minutes later, by Wolfgang's watch, Franco returned. Though he'd worry no matter what, he needed a better estimate of how long this would take. He was a man of numbers. He asked the crowd if anyone had a scrap piece of paper. An older woman, a grandmother judging by her wispy gray hair and two young girls clinging to her legs, had a pen, while a young mother tore a sheet from a coloring book.

Franco left at 10:17 and returned at 10:39—twenty-two minutes. Thirty-eight people in total remained. Five per trip, meant eight runs. With two cars, four trips each. At twenty-two minutes per trip, that was nearly two hours. The world can change in a second. Plenty of time for the Stasi to stop a fairy tale ending.

While waiting, there wasn't much to do. Children nudged their parents, asking questions, unaware of the danger around them. The adults swayed nervously, biting nails and grinding teeth. They'd risked everything to be here.

Twenty-two minutes came and went. At twenty-six minutes, Eckhart returned. Wolfgang jotted the time, adjusting the estimates he'd put together.

"Any issues?" Wolfgang asked.

Eckhart shook his head. "No. I'm taking different routes, though."

"Bastian good?"

"Yes. He's guarding the site."

The crowd had finally stopped asking where the escape would happen and how it would be done. It was a leap of faith now—a moment to step out of the boat, like Peter.

Eckhart guided the next group of five to Father Langer's Wanderer. Wolfgang stood and waited, unease knotting his stomach. They were like gazelles grazing, surrounded by a pride of lions they couldn't see. Trapped in this gym.

Franco returned at thirty-one minutes. Wolfgang tried not to let the growing average get to him, but it was hard not to. They had to be finished before dawn. Even on Christmas, the streets wouldn't be empty. People would be heading to the homes of friends or relatives, or to church.

Eckhart returned in nineteen minutes. Wolfgang wanted to hug him. That time helped the average.

"Have you seen anything suspicious?" Wolfgang asked Eckhart before he headed back out.

"I mean, there's plenty of cars parked on the roads," Eckhart said. "I have no idea if anyone is in them, though."

Wolfgang nodded, then at Eckhart to get going. Franco returned at twenty-one minutes. Wolfgang had enough data to gauge their finish time. Around 1:30 a.m.

With each trip, the crowd thinned. The rest stood in tight-lipped patience. Each moment that passed was beyond brutal. The constant state of fight-or-flight Wolfgang experienced exhausted him. His body teetered on collapse, but he couldn't show it—not to these people. They had put blind trust in him. If he looked worried or panicked, they would, too. A few more hours. Then, one way or another, this would be over.

Franco returned. Only two trips remained. The packed gym had emptied to a handful of people.

"*Buona fortuna*," Franco said to Wolfgang.

They hugged, and then Franco left with the penultimate group—the young men who had selflessly given their spots earlier. They had deferred again, but the last family decided to wait for Father Langer's car, which would be far easier for the two pregnant women to climb into than the tall truck. The women were twins, both gorgeous with curly, fiery ginger hair. Their parents stood behind them. Their third daughter looked to be younger than twenty and had the same curls as her sisters, but in a subdued brown hue.

Time crawled. Nineteen minutes since Eckhart left—longer than Wolfgang hoped. Then twenty-four minutes. The exact average time the trips had taken. But then twenty-eight minutes passed. Then thirty-two minutes—the longest trip yet. At forty minutes, Wolfgang was incapable of hiding his panic.

"They're not coming back for us," the youngest daughter said.

Her father didn't even try to dispel that. No other trip had taken this length of time. Something had gone wrong. *Had Eckhart been stopped? Arrested? Killed?* A dizzying sensation sloshed through Wolfgang, leaving him silently begging that this was nothing more than a nightmare.

Wolfgang had promised Eckhart that he would share his fate. How could he fulfill that promise if he didn't know what that fate had been?

"Let me check," Wolfgang said.

He walked out of the gym and through the barren, dark halls to the entrance door. He glanced out, half expecting two dozen vehicles to swarm into the parking lot. But it was empty.

Should he go? What if Eckhart returned and found him gone? Or what if the Stasi had forced his hand and Eckhart used the chaos to escape?

But then a shadow sprinted across the parking lot and to the entrance. Wolfgang recognized Eckhart's run. He pushed open the door for him.

"What happened? Where's the car?" Wolfgang asked.

"I got stopped on the way back!" Eckhart said.

Wolfgang's eyes darted to the street. "What?!"

"Police." Eckhart hunched over, trying to catch his breath. "They parked me in. Forced me out of the car. I ran for it."

"Do you think they know about the tunnel?" Wolfgang asked.

Eckhart shook his head. "I think they noticed me driving around."

Wolfgang glanced back in the gym's direction, where the last family waited.

"We'll have to walk," Wolfgang said.

They headed inside the gymnasium. Any thoughts that Franco would return were slim. For all he knew, Eckhart was on his way back to the school to pick up the last group of people. When he escorted his group into the tunnel, he'd join them. Perhaps Bastian would wait, but Wolfgang didn't mention that. If Bastian went looking for them, they'd never find him. They couldn't sit around and wait. Hopefully, Bastian would come to that conclusion and go into the tunnel himself, or at the bare minimum, wait at the entrance.

"What's wrong?" the mother asked.

"We have to walk," Wolfgang said.

The moment he said it, he realized this was the worst group to make the walk. The father had a severe limp, grimacing as he shifted his weight. It didn't help that he was overweight. Then there were the two pregnant women. Not as far along as Trude, but late into the second trimester. The youngest daughter and mother were in heels. And none of them were dressed to walk miles in the cold.

"Walk? How far?" the mother asked.

"It's not too far," Wolfgang said, deciding to lie.

But what choice did they have? Would they really return home? Not even try for freedom?

Wolfgang turned back to Eckhart. "Thanks for coming back to tell us."

"You would have done it for me. We share the same fate."

"We share the same fate."

The two led the family toward the door. Before pushing it open, Wolfgang eyed up their outfits one final time. Dress suits for the women and a suit coat and fedora for the man. *Did they come right from church?*

Even if there might be something in this abandoned school they could wear or use for added layers, there was no time to waste searching.

"Stay close. Stay quiet," Wolfgang said.

He pushed open the door. The wintry winds howled, like opportunistic scavengers recognizing easy prey. Wolfgang and Eckhart led, standing on either side of the group, eyes scanning for prying eyes.

It was a five-mile walk—far shorter than the winding fifteen- to thirty-minute drives they'd taken to avoid suspicion. *How long would a wobble, limp, or shuffle take?*

"How much further?" the father asked a few minutes later.

Wolfgang hoped they didn't turn around. If they did, they'd still see the school's outline.

"It's a ways further," Wolfgang said.

The father stuck his hand out, seizing Wolfgang at the wrist. "Please tell us the truth. We're risking everything for this."

What would it hurt to tell them now? Who would they rat him out to? Especially given how slowly they moved. Wolfgang and Eckhart could outrun them before they could tell anyone.

"It's about four miles from here."

"Four miles?" the mother croaked.

The two pregnant women cried out in a gasp.

"It's a tunnel," Wolfgang said.

"A tunnel?" the father asked.

"Yes. A tunnel into the West. I promise you it's there. Trust me."

The father studied Wolfgang's eyes. Faced with the powerful, awesome responsibility of making a choice for his entire family. Studying Wolfgang's character, his belief in this plan. Then he nodded.

"Come on. Let's go," he told his family.

With their resolve refreshed, they covered the next mile faster than the first half—but the wind, the cold, and their failing bodies crippled that pace. No matter how many "Come on, just a bit furthers" and "Keep movings" were said, their pace slowed and slowed.

"How much further?" Wolfgang whispered to Eckhart at an intersection. The family was far enough behind that they couldn't hear.

"About two and a half miles," Eckhart replied. "There's a shorter route, but there are streetlights and homes."

"And police searching for you?"

"Yes, and that."

They waited for the family, and once they'd caught up, they crossed the road. Wolfgang couldn't help but gawk at the shoes the two pregnant sisters had on. Flat shoes. Walking through slush and snow. No padding for their feet. Nothing to keep them warm.

Two miles to the tunnel. Then 2,728 feet to freedom. He stood in between the two pregnant women, locking his arms between theirs to help support them while their father and younger sister did the same on the outside.

His body wanted to run. His legs were dying to spring forward. But he couldn't leave the family behind. And besides, running down the street drew attention. Being slow meant staying invisible. But instincts, animal and ancient, screamed that slow meant dead.

One and a half miles.

One mile.

Wolfgang now practically held up both pregnant women. His arms burned and cramped. They had vice-like grips on him. If he was this sore, the fact their father and younger sister still hung on was a testament to their familial bond.

Eckhart stopped dead in his tracks, then waved them back. In one giant mass, they stumbled into an alleyway. The fence line of Eternal Peace was just down this street. But bridging that divide was a row of cars and people in military uniforms patrolling on foot.

"It's the Stasi," the mother uttered, her voice quivering with fear.

Had we made it this far only to fall short? Wolfgang glanced at the family. The father and mother tried to console their adult children. Hugging and sobbing together. Their choice to escape would cost them everything. They'd be separated. Imprisoned. Perhaps their children would be taken away like Bastian and Trude's had. All because they had put their faith in Wolfgang.

How had the Stasi known? Had the police officer recognized Eckhart? Was this an innocent search? But why would they bring so many officers to look for someone who had simply driven around the block one too many times?

"They know about the tunnel," Eckhart said.

"I don't think so," Wolfgang said. "As far as I can see, they're on the street. Not in the cemetery grounds."

"We'll never make it. They're swarming the place."

"No, *we'll* never make it."

Eckhart locked eyes with his best friend. "What are you saying?"

"You need to lead them to the tunnel. I'll cause a distraction. Try to get them to follow me."

"No." Eckhart shook his head. "To hell with that. We share the same fate."

Wolfgang put his hand on Eckhart's shoulder. "I started this. Let me finish it." He turned to the family. "You're going to make it. Eckhart will lead you the rest of the way."

The family reached for Wolfgang's hand, showing their gratitude for what he'd done and for what he was about to do.

Wolfgang fished in his coat pocket for a letter. He'd written it once he had found the courage and clarity to help others escape. Knowing by doing so he had infinitely worsened his own chances of escape.

"Give this to Lieselotte, okay?" Wolfgang said, thrusting it into Eckhart's open palm and then pulling his friend's hand closed. "Make sure she gets that."

It was the last letter he'd ever write to her. He had poured his heart into that letter. Not worried about who would read it or what they redacted. It was unfiltered. The draining of his soul onto the written page. It was an ode, a declaration of love. The last line written in cipher. It had to be.

Everything had come full circle. He had met Lieselotte on Christmas all those years ago. It was only fitting that it ended on Christmas now. There was a beauty to that. A poetry.

"Don't look back," Wolfgang said.

He stepped out of the alley and marched down the street toward the agents. Just far enough to be seen.

In the shadows of the streetlights, Wolfgang surveyed the elongated silhouettes. He recognized one of them—Schwarzfuchs. The Stasi agent turned and stared in Wolfgang's direction. The alternating light and shadow turned the street between Wolfgang and Schwarzfuchs into a giant chessboard. *How fitting.*

The transition from calm to pandemonium was instantaneous. Whistles shrieked. Dogs barked. A dozen flashlight beams sliced through the night to illuminate Wolfgang.

Wolfgang turned and sprinted east down the street, parallel with the cemetery, as the Stasi and dogs gave chase. This would be the closest to the tunnel he would get. The closest to freedom he would ever reach.

The Last Letter

Lieselotte stood at the tunnel entrance in West Berlin. She began her vigilant watch at 8:30—well before Wolfgang's scheduled journey. Anneliese had tried to get her to step away, to do something to ease her mind, or at least sit. Most of the volunteer diggers weren't here—they were with family and friends. It was Christmas Eve, after all. Only Mrs. Winterstein, Anneliese, and Petyr joined her. His core group of friends who had helped from the beginning would arrive shortly. Mrs. Winterstein had packed brown lunch bags with a Coke, an apple, and a peanut butter sandwich for those who came over from the East.

Lieselotte had stocked shelves and faced every aisle at the store earlier, just to keep busy. Not the Christmas activities she had wanted to do. But she'd have the rest of her Christmases to create new traditions.

Mrs. Winterstein and Anneliese had tried to get Lieselotte to play cards, and though they succeeded, she quickly excused herself from the game. Cards couldn't distract her.

At 9:30, she'd been pacing the basement for an hour. She would have forgotten about documenting the moment if Anneliese hadn't reminded her. They set up the colored camera on a tripod, placing it in front of the tunnel but flush against the back wall. Her father's camera was draped around her neck. She rubbed it subconsciously, feeling the ghost of his long-ago touch.

When ten o'clock arrived, her nerves went nuclear. Her legs wobbled. Her mouth went dry. Bile crept up her throat. Wolfgang should be arriving at the cemetery. It wouldn't be an instant thing. But that dread and worry that something had gone horribly wrong consumed her.

Mikael, Rory, Johan, George, and Hansel arrived, carrying cases of Schultheiss beer for the celebration. No one dared crack one open until it was over. For now, the cases sat in the corner, growing warm.

"There's a faint light," Petyr called out.

Lieselotte was too nervous to take photographs. It felt wrong—disrespectful—to do it, but she had given her word she would document the escape in exchange for funding. So, while Petyr manned the camera on the tripod, she raised her father's camera and began to shoot.

A woman Lieselotte recognized as Eckhart's sister-in-law emerged through the entrance, a protective hand on her pregnant belly. Another woman, whom she recognized as Emilia, was right behind Trude, supporting her. Anneliese offered her hand to help Trude out of the tunnel as Lieselotte snapped a photograph.

Trude looked around in overwhelming disbelief. She turned to Emilia and hugged her, tears of joy streaming down their faces. Lieselotte and Petyr captured every moment.

"Welcome to West Berlin," Lieselotte said.

"Thank you, thank you so much!" Trude said.

Trude embraced Lieselotte—a hug for her, and for Wolfgang. They had never met, yet through him, their lives had been intertwined for years. When they parted, Emilia pulled Lieselotte into the same embrace, her smile just as warm.

Mrs. Winterstein guided Trude and Emilia to the two foldable lounge chairs in the corner for them to comfortably wait for the others. She gave them each a packed bag of snacks, telling them to drink up and rest. Lieselotte kept her eyes on the tunnel, willing for Wolfgang, Eckhart, Franco, and Bastian to appear. But they didn't.

"Where are the others?" Lieselotte asked Trude and Emilia.

"Wolfgang had a list of people who wanted to escape. He, Bastian, Eckhart, and Franco are escorting them to the tunnel in groups," Trude said.

Lieselotte pressed for more information. *How many people? Who are they?* Introducing a variable this late into the escape was incredibly risky. She knew he had pondered the idea—knew why he'd risk it—and she loved him all the more for it.

Roughly fifteen minutes later, faint voices and footsteps drifted out of the tunnel. Lieselotte and Anneliese exchanged glances. *Who are these people?* A man and his family tentatively stepped out, wide-eyed—unsure if they were ecstatic or terrified.

"Is this West Berlin?" he asked.

"This is West Berlin," Lieselotte answered.

The parents' demeanor transformed from cautious fear to overwhelming joy. The husband and wife clutched each other, their children sandwiched between them, crying tears of gratitude. They reached out to thank her, Anneliese, and everyone they could reach.

Mrs. Winterstein handed each of them a paper bag of snacks and surmised they weren't going to have enough at the rate they came. Nor would they have enough room down in the basement.

"Follow me upstairs," she said. "You can wait up there."

Mrs. Winterstein led the family upstairs and then started preparing more snack bags. The mother and her children helped her. Every fifteen to twenty minutes, more groups arrived. Families and individuals emerged, exhausted and overwhelmed. The basement swelled with voices and tears.

With each new group, Lieselotte, Anneliese, Petyr, and his friends grew more shocked. They had spent months digging this tunnel, expecting to save six people. Yet three times that number had already escaped through it.

Lieselotte's father had died documenting the cries and pleas of thousands of Berliners. Now, she documented their escape to freedom. He had never set his camera down—not even when the shots were fired. She channeled his courage, snapping photographs that captured the grime, the grit, and the relief.

Still, they kept coming—group after group. She captured the looks of exhaustion and disbelief. Each similar, yet different. All profound and moving.

Even as joy came with each arrival, her thoughts stayed fixed on the four still in the East. The next group stepped out of the tunnel, staring in wide-eyed wonder. Faces covered in swaths of dirt, drops of sweat, and tracks of tears.

"Franco!" Emilia yelled.

She dashed toward him and flung her arms around him. Lieselotte captured their heartwarming reunion. Franco's dazzling smile, his crooked newsboy cap. The look of love and relief displayed in her eyes.

Franco turned to Trude. "Bastian, he is at the tunnel entrance—making sure everyone who goes in does not come back out."

A smart choice to ensure no one left to alert the Stasi.

"No one went back in," Petyr confirmed. "They're all upstairs. My friends are making sure no one leaves until the last have come through the tunnel."

A final safety precaution to ensure no one alerted the Stasi, though the risk of that was minimal. If there were Stasi informants, they had escaped their invisible leash and were no longer beholden to them.

"Bastian, he's waiting for the last group," Franco said.

"Eckhart and Wolfgang?" Lieselotte asked.

Franco confirmed with a nod. While Lieselotte's team conversed with Wolfgang's team, Mrs. Winterstein shepherded everyone else upstairs. Euphoria grew in each of them as the reality set in. They were in West Berlin. But Lieselotte couldn't share in that limitless joy. Wolfgang was still in the East.

She had expected to wait twenty to twenty-five minutes—that seemed the average time between groups. But that time duration came and went. Then half an hour.

Petyr and Anneliese exchanged worried glances. Franco removed his newsboy cap and squeezed it. Trude, no longer able to sit, struggled to her feet to wait. Emilia clutched her arm, supporting her in more ways than one.

Forty minutes.

Fifty minutes.

An hour.

Lieselotte kept her eyes on the tunnel, her breathing hitched. The voices around her distorted—Petyr and Franco's low murmuring, Mrs. Winterstein whispering reassurances to Trude and Emilia. They felt a world away. Her world was somewhere on the other side of that tunnel. She would not cry. Not yet.

But her body betrayed her. A single sob escaped—shallow and shaky. This was a carbon copy of that fateful January night in '63. Waiting on the other side of the Wall. Her heart told her. Her brain told her. Her gut told her. It was unanimous.

Something had gone wrong.

A hand rested lightly on her back—Anneliese. Just long enough to say *I'm here.* Then it was gone. No words. None were needed.

But finally, voices approached. She wanted to sprint into the tunnel but held back—she'd only clog the path. She waited, eyes wide, camera ready, heart racing.

A man in his fifties, dressed in a suit and wearing a fedora, limped out, then turned to help his wife out. Then two pregnant women and a younger woman—two with curly red hair and the youngest, dark—stepped out.

Lieselotte turned to Franco, hoping he had the answers. He had said one last group. This was a group. But this couldn't be the last.

437

Trude's expression collapsed. Mrs. Winterstein grabbed her other arm for support. Nothing came out of the tunnel but silence. No one dared to move out of fear if they did, they would miss something.

Then the sound of feet shuffling along the tunnel floor carried into the basement. Bastian stepped out. With surprising grace and explosiveness, Trude broke free from the supportive hold Emilia and Mrs. Winterstein had on her and leaped at Bastian. Eckhart stepped out of the tunnel, head down.

Neither wore the expression of joy or euphoria the dozens and dozens of others had worn. Eckhart's face was solemn. Anneliese hugged him, stroking his face. She wanted to kiss him but read the somber tone the basement had taken on. Eckhart squeezed her hand as he brought his gaze to Lieselotte.

"I'm so sorry," he said, holding out the letter Wolfgang had given him.

She didn't need to see the faint handwriting visible through the folded page to know who it was from. Petyr snapped a photograph. Anneliese glared at him. He'd been told to photograph throughout. There was nothing malicious intended.

"The Stasi had the entrance to the cemetery covered. About a mile from the tunnel, Wolfgang told us to run. To let him draw the Stasi away. The last glimpse I had—he was still running, buying us time," Eckhart said.

Lieselotte stared at the letter in her trembling hands. Pain and hurt etched into her face. Her eyes brimmed. One final message—a proof of love, and sacrifice sealed in ink. The last letter from Wolfgang Kirschke she would ever receive.

The Roof and the Hounds

Wolfgang wasn't being chased—he was being hunted. He powered his legs and arms, trying to ignore the stabbing pain in his side and the fire in his lungs. He darted across intersections, shimmied through alleyways—running too fast to think, let alone remember Father Langer's car Eckhart had left behind. Maybe the keys were in it. His thoughts reduced to a single instinct—*run*. Nothing more. Nothing less.

The dogs' barks echoed around the neighborhood—terrifying on their own, but more so in how they warped and reverberated through the narrow streets. Wolfgang ducked behind a dumpster, gulping air. His mind screamed danger, but his body refused to cooperate.

"*Herr* Kirschke!" Schwarzfuchs's voice carried through the night.

It was tough to gauge where it had come from. It bent, careened, and echoed around buildings. But it was close. Wolfgang had two ways out of this alley. If he chose wrong, he'd run right into Schwarzfuchs. Or maybe it didn't matter—there could be Stasi and police waiting at both exits. He waited for Schwarzfuchs to speak again, needing to home in on his location.

"Let us speak as men!" Schwarzfuchs shouted.

It'd come from the way Wolfgang had entered the alley. The dogs' growls and barks neared. He sprinted away from them. His feet throbbed, sweat dripping off his forehead even in the cold. He reached a rusted fire escape. Could he jump high enough? Maybe on a good day. Tonight, he needed adrenaline to make up the difference. He crouched and leaped. His left hand caught the rung—iron so cold it burned. He grabbed ahold with his right, but the escape didn't lower. A combination of neglect and cold had yielded it inoperable. Wolfgang used his momentum to swing up.

Then, as quickly and quietly as he could, he climbed the stairs to the roof.

He sprawled out, heat rising from his skin. Not even the stars could break through the thick, suffocating East Berlin smog. Chest heaving, he lay there until his body calmed enough to allow him to think beyond *run*.

His vow to never return to prison held firm. He preferred escape, but he'd be running as long as he remained in East Berlin. Soon, the Stasi and police would surround him. He needed to control how it unfolded, couldn't allow himself to be taken alive. And being torn apart by dogs was not the way he wanted to go.

Shot. That was how he wanted to die. Trick Schwarzfuchs into thinking he had a weapon—force them to fire before the dogs reached him. *What do I have?* He looked around the roof. He patted his pockets. His hands hitting the hard, cylindrical flashlight. He pulled it from his pocket and held it like a gun. In the dark, it might look convincing enough. So, that was his play. Wait for them to come for him and then draw the flashlight. Pray that they shot him before the fearless dogs charged at him and dragged him down— his useless flashlight spinning across the concrete.

"*Herr* Kirschke!" Schwarzfuchs yelled, his voice amplified by a bullhorn. "You have been bested! Do you really think I trusted you to turn? Those names were plants! I knew you would betray me!"

A flicker of satisfaction crossed Wolfgang's grim face. *Your plants didn't stay loyal. They chose freedom.*

Fifty-seven people breathed free air because of him. Schwarzfuchs had overplayed his hand. If he'd known about the tunnel, they would have stopped the escapes. Instead, he got lucky when the police pulled Eckhart over for what they considered "driving aimlessly." Once Eckhart ran, they notified the Stasi, and Schwarzfuchs sprang into action.

What did his face look like when he received that call? Was he eating Christmas dinner? Enjoying a nightcap by the tree?

"Surrender," Schwarzfuchs called. "Spend your days at a labor camp—be of use to your country and your countrymen!" He paused, the echo hanging in the cold air. "Or I could have the dogs tear you apart! Which fate do you prefer?" He stopped, listening for any reply. "I must confess, *Herr* Kirschke, your selflessness surprises me. If not for your friend's encounter with the police, your plan might have worked." His voice hardened. "What was it? Over the Wall? Through it? Under it?" Another pause. "This is your last chance! Come out now, or I open your scent jar and let the dogs decide your fate!"

His voice drew closer. Wolfgang crouched, advancing toward the far edge of the roof. He glanced down, then across, gauging the distance. He exhaled. This leap might kill him. If he missed, he'd hit the next building face-first, then plummet to the street below.

He turned and looked toward Eternal Peace, then the Wall. He'd had a chance to escape—been inside the Von Haven Stein mausoleum. Now escape was farther away than ever. He'd never be that close again—to freedom or to Lieselotte.

But as he stared at the dark cemetery, searching for the Von Haven Stein mausoleum, his eyes caught movement.

A silhouette emerged from the crypt.

Flash and Fire

The letter was a pin-pulled grenade. Words are the most powerful entity—they can heal or destroy, lift or bury. But no matter how lovingly Wolfgang had written them, these words would destroy her. Another before-and-after moment. Her life would never be the same after reading them.

Anneliese kept her hand on Lieselotte's shoulder. Mrs. Winterstein looked on, knowing there was nothing she could do. Eckhart, Bastian, Emilia, Franco, and Trude stood in a tight circle, stealing glances at Lieselotte. A joyous moment turned on its head—the epitome of bittersweet.

Lieselotte unfolded the letter and drew a sharp, pained breath. The handwriting was instantly familiar—once a source of butterflies, a constant in her life since she was eleven. Now each line, every curve was a blade that cut deep.

When I was young, I wanted a friend. When I became a man, I longed for someone to share my life with. When I felt stuck and hopeless in East Berlin, I needed someone who shared my troubles. When I was in prison, I prayed someone would save me.

In prison, Father Langer told me about God. About how He sends people to do His bidding. I found the positives in my predicament. It gave me time to think. To ponder and reflect. When I was young and wanted a friend, you came to my house that Christmas Eve. When I became a man and longed for someone to share my life with, we saw the same movie at the same showtime in the same theater. When I felt stuck and hopeless, I had Eckhart. And in prison, when I prayed for God to save me, He sent me Father Langer. I realized God sent me everything I had asked for. He sent the people I needed. He sent Father Langer. Eckhart. And He sent me you.

When Schwarzfuchs gave me the list of names of people under watch for an escape attempt, I knew there was a chance it was a ruse. A game. But I also knew that at least some, if not most, of those people on that list wanted to escape. Had prayed to God for a way out. And I believe God answered those prayers by sending me.

If you're reading this, it means God's will differed from my will and your will. For that, I'm sorry.

I wake in light, longing—always lovingly watching, always yearning. Splendid love outshines vows. Eternally yours. Only us.

Forever yours,

Wolfgang.

She closed her eyes and squeezed the paper. She deciphered the ending, her lip trembling with every letter revealed. *I will always love you.* Half of her wanted to destroy it—to never see it or hold it again. It would always destroy her. But the other half couldn't let it go. It held a piece of his soul. She'd keep it forever, until the corners frayed and the white paper aged to sepia.

"Let's give her a few moments," Anneliese said.

Eckhart wanted to stay behind, but Anneliese waved him toward the stairs along with everyone else. Lieselotte leaned against the edge of the tunnel entrance, head bowed. Wolfgang's words echoed in her mind—about how God sends people in His stead. Well, if God sent people in His stead, then He could send her. She wouldn't sit at this tunnel entrance as she had once stood before the looming Wall on that cold January night in 1963—powerless, only able to stare up at its menacing height, with no way into the East. Now she had a way. 2,728 feet worth of tunnel.

Her legs wavered. *What am I doing?* The tunnel was a one-way path back into a world that imprisoned its citizens. She had no weapon, no plan—but she would try. It was what Wolfgang would have done—for her.

Seizing her moment of isolation, Lieselotte lunged forward into the tunnel. Before Anneliese or anyone else could return and stop her—before her gut, mind, and heart could cast their vote—she followed the string of lights deeper into the passage. As fast as she could. Passing under the sign marking entrance into East Berlin, touching it for luck, past the boulder and into the section Wolfgang and the others had dug. Up the ramp and into the mausoleum.

She squeezed past the marble tomb, her body begging her to turn back. The cold attacked her; her heart thudded like a war drum. But she couldn't turn back. She wouldn't.

The waxing crescent moon offered little light to trickle inside. She stepped out, turning toward the sound of dogs barking and a distorted voice booming through a bullhorn. The buildings stood in silhouette, a patchwork of dark and golden-lit windows. But her eyes found the shape of a person as black as onyx crouching on a roof. Only one person would have a rational reason to be on the roof in the cold, wintery early hours of Christmas.

Wolfgang.

She didn't bother dusting off. The dirt helped her blend with the shadows as she searched for an exit. The cold assaulted her, and she had no defenses for it. Nothing except for her adrenaline. She'd left without a coat.

A faded white truck was parked outside the rear entrance— Franco's. He had no reason to keep the keys, so he'd left them in the truck. She opened the door and checked the back seat. Emilia had left a sweater on the floor. *Praise God.* She put it on, rubbing the thick wool into her cold skin. Then she brought the truck to life and crept down the street. Its engine overpowered everything but the barking dogs. As she drove away from Eternal Peace, waves of flashlights swept the streets.

She darted her eyes across the intersection, gauging where she should turn—trying to spot the building where she'd seen Wolfgang. It had looked so obvious from far away, so easy to find. Now it was a labyrinth. As she got closer, the buildings took shape.

Different colors of brick from tan to red to terracotta, with the tops of the buildings stretching far above what she could see. Lieselotte parked the truck, shut off the headlights, and killed the engine. She scanned the windshield and mirrors.

Nothing.

No approaching shadows or elongated silhouettes. No flashlight beams. She opened the truck door and stepped out. Her heartbeat drummed in her chest, even in her wrists. Fear ignited her nerves. *Think rationally.* The Stasi didn't know they should be looking for her. They were looking for Wolfgang. She had an advantage. Her outfit—black tights, a charcoal dress—felt too Western, but Emilia's sweater helped her blend in. Even if they came across her, if she walked slowly and kept her composure, she would be invisible. Unless Schwarzfuchs was here. He knew what she looked like.

Her father's camera swung from her neck, like a cherished heirloom. Lieselotte glanced up at the buildings. Choosing one, she slipped into a narrow alleyway toward a fire escape. She pulled the stairs down and dragged the sweater over her hands before gripping the ice-cold bar. The iron groaned beneath her weight.

Lieselotte climbed onto the roof. Crouching, she scanned her surroundings, trying to gauge where the Stasi were and where Wolfgang might be. She moved to the far edge. With gaps less than three feet wide, she confidently leaped to the next rooftop. A sea of flashlights swept beneath her.

Lieselotte clung to the center of the roof, away from eyes below, and hurried to the building's edge. She paused. A shadow stretched across the roof. Someone hid behind the access door.

Please be him.

It had to be him. She couldn't think of any way to gain his attention that wouldn't also gain the attention of the Stasi. It would be a farther jump to that roof than the others had been—roughly six feet instead of three.

She took a few steps away from the ledge, steadying her breathing. Then Lieselotte sprinted forward and leaped. As her foot left the ledge, one thought screamed inside her: *Please let it be him. Please.*

Her landing wasn't as graceful as she had hoped. She jammed her knee and slid awkwardly into the splits. The shadow stepped out, holding a gun.

They were nothing but shadows and silhouettes. But she knew that outline. And he knew hers. In a moment that required absolute trust, they acted on faith.

Lieselotte's face shifted, lighting with relief and joy that only Wolfgang could gift. But his showed horror. By instinct—by overwhelming need—they collided in a rush of relief and disbelief. Lips met. Hands reached. Hair tangled between fingers.

"What are you doing here?" he asked, voice strained with anger and worry.

"You said God sent you to help those people," Lieselotte said. Wolfgang's confusion didn't wane; he just stared, as if trying to make sense of her words. "God sent me to save you."

His anger melted into awe. How could it not? Her loyalty—the lengths she'd gone to. No man was ever more fortunate. She had crossed a wall, a city, a world for him.

He pulled her into his chest, kissing the top of her head. "I don't know who He's going to send to save us."

"We're together. That's all that matters."

Even if it was temporary. Wolfgang hadn't planned—or wanted—to be taken alive, but he didn't expect or want Lieselotte to share that fate. Nor did he want her to face prison. The Submarine. The constant interrogations, long stretches of darkness followed by even longer stretches of blinding light that made it impossible to keep track of time. He didn't want her to succumb to that feeling of being less than human.

"Listen," he said, taking her hands in his and guiding them to their knees to reduce the risk of being seen. "I won't be taken alive."

Lieselotte wasn't horrified by what he'd said—she was devastated by the finality in his voice. No wavering. No uncertainty. No emotion. He hadn't just come to his decision. There was peace in his voice—the kind that comes only after months of painful contemplation. That he had borne it alone destroyed her.

"I'm with you to the end," she said.

Wolfgang stared into her blue eyes—the resolve in them, the quiet fire that had carried her across the Wall to find him. His own resolve faltered. This wasn't something he'd ever prepared for— not this kind of ending. The only grace he'd clung to was knowing she was alive and free in the West. Now, seeing her here, hiding in the dark, tore through every conviction he'd made peace with. Her love for him would cost her her life.

"Do you have a gun?" she asked.

Wolfgang let out a quiet, broken laugh, then removed the flashlight from his pocket. "I'm hoping they think this is one."

Lieselotte looked at the flashlight, then to Wolfgang. He had no plan—he'd given up hope. "Don't give up on me just yet. I have a plan."

Wolfgang wrapped his jacket around her. He could do nothing to keep her safe, but he could keep her warm.

"Franco's truck is parked nearby," she said. "If we can get to it, we drive like hell to the cemetery. To the tunnel."

He didn't mention the Stasi or the dogs. Surely, she'd noticed. But it was better than sitting around and waiting.

"They're looking for a single male," Lieselotte said, reading his objections.

Wolfgang nodded, forcing a reassuring smile. He crouched and tried the access door handle—it was unlocked. If there was one supposed blessing to life in East Berlin, it was the illusion that crime didn't exist. The state simply buried or rewrote the numbers. Whether this shop owner believed the lie or never imagined a robbery from the roof, Wolfgang couldn't say.

They headed down the stairs into a department store. Rows of clothing stretched across the store, with a glass counter full of fragrances near the back.

"Change your clothes," she said.

While Wolfgang stripped out of his shirt and pants, Lieselotte dashed to the counter of fragrances. She grabbed a bottle of cologne, not caring what the scent was. Wolfgang slid into a pair of dress pants and a long peacoat. Lieselotte doused him in cologne, the sharp scent assaulting both their senses.

"Hopefully, that throws the dogs off," she said.

She threw on a peacoat, trying to make them look like a young couple on their way home from midnight mass.

"Your glasses," she said. "Take them off."

"I won't be able to see."

"I'll guide you."

Wolfgang took them off, his eyes narrowing into slits. Lieselotte hooked her arm in his and led him to the back entrance of the store. She unlocked it, opened it, and glanced both ways. She paused.

"What's wrong?" Wolfgang asked.

"Do we try to avoid being seen or walk like we belong here?" she asked.

Cling to the shadows or walk in the light?

"If we appear to be hiding, it's more suspicious. How far is the truck?" Wolfgang asked.

Lieselotte thought on it, trying to shake the disorienting feeling of being back on the ground. Everything looked close on the roof.

"Three blocks that way," she said, pointing.

Wolfgang only saw a blur of hand motion. "You decide."

It was a race against time. Her goal: reach the truck—quickly, but not running unless absolutely necessary.

Arm in arm, with a rushed gait, Lieselotte led them to an intersection. A faint stream of light twirled around the corner. She stopped, clutching Wolfgang's arm to halt him, too. The light grew in strength and coverage. Boots clacked.

Someone approached.

There was no time to run. Wolfgang didn't have his glasses on. To ask him to run blindly would result in disaster.

In a flash of insanity—or ingenuity—she shoved Wolfgang against the brick and kissed him, guiding his hands to her waist, fingers tangling his hair. A harsh light flared, blinding them. They both shielded their eyes.

"Hands up!" the police officer said.

Lieselotte stepped away, shocked. Both she and Wolfgang threw their hands up, squinting and hiding from the harsh light.

"What are you doing?" the officer asked, aiming the flashlight at them. But he found his answer in the lipstick covering Wolfgang's lips and cheeks.

"Sorry. Just coming home from midnight mass," Wolfgang said.

"Papers. Give them to me."

"We don't have our papers," Lieselotte said. "They're at home."

The officer looked annoyed, deciding whether to stay to interrogate them or continue searching. Then the dogs erupted—sharp, urgent barks that signaled discovery.

"Found something! Come here!" someone shouted.

No doubt the dogs had found Wolfgang's clothes in the shop. If they stayed here any longer, it wouldn't take long for someone to shout that he had changed clothes. And with the aid of the scent jar, those dogs wouldn't be fooled by the cologne.

The officer hesitated, flashlight still trained on Wolfgang's lipstick-smeared face. Then he looked over his shoulder toward the shouting—something more pressing than lovers breaking curfew.

"Get home," the officer warned, then ran toward the sound of the barking dogs.

They rounded the corner and decided now was the time to run. Wolfgang dug out his glasses and slipped them on. Hand in hand, they sprinted, adrenaline and fear surging through them.

"Just up ahead," Lieselotte said.

They were closing in on Franco's truck—just across the street now.

So close.

"Stop!"

A shot ripped through the night, sending a pulse of fear through their bodies.

"Turn around."

Wolfgang and Lieselotte slowly turned, arms raised. Schwarzfuchs aimed his Makarov PM sidearm at them. His eyes lighting with recognition when he saw Lieselotte. A leering smirk spread across his cold, calculating face.

"Oh, how tragic is this? A Shakespearean end for you two lovers. But this story doesn't end with your deaths—no, no, no."

He waved a finger and tsked repeatedly. "No, it ends with you in separate prisons—spending the rest of your lives wondering what became of the other. Or perhaps I'll put her in the cell right beside you—so close, yet so far away. One in perpetual light, the other in endless darkness. Questioning your reality. The only proof time has passed will be the wrinkling of your hands. Nothing but time. Time to accept—even if it takes decades—that your great love was nothing but whispers through the Wall. Nothing more."

He had never understood—never appreciated—the power of those whispers. Those whispers were embers, and they'd sparked an unstoppable flame.

Deep down, void of hope, this was the ending Wolfgang had always expected. But Lieselotte was here. If Schwarzfuchs shot him first, she'd be taken alive—condemned to rot in some godforsaken prison. He couldn't let that happen. He'd have to use her as a shield, free her from the worst fate. Could he override the instinct to protect her? Would she understand? He hoped Schwarzfuchs would shoot him next. If not, he'd spend the rest of his life in that cell. But better him than Lieselotte.

Schwarzfuchs briefly turned his attention to the alleyway behind him to see where his reinforcements were. Lieselotte lifted her camera. As he spun back toward them, she pressed the shutter button. The flash hit him like a bolt of lightning—sharp, sudden, and disorienting.

Schwarzfuchs flinched, shielding his eyes with his hand. Seizing the moment, Wolfgang exploded forward, grabbing the Stasi agent's gun hand and driving him backward with enough force to knock them both to the ground.

Lieselotte dove for the gun. Wolfgang and Schwarzfuchs wrestled for dominance, exchanging blows. Lieselotte had never fired a gun before. Her aim would be poor. But it didn't matter. When you hear the crack of a gunshot, fear paralyzes you.

She fired the shot wide, unwilling to risk hitting Wolfgang. They both paused. Lieselotte's hands trembled from the recoil.

"Go!" Lieselotte shouted.

Wolfgang shoved Schwarzfuchs off and bolted with Lieselotte toward Franco's truck. They dove inside. Lieselotte in the driver's seat; he in the passenger seat.

"They're getting away!" Schwarzfuchs yelled, crawling to his feet.

Down the alley, beams of flashlights danced, boots clattered, and dogs barked as they charged at the truck.

"Shoot them!" Schwarzfuchs ordered.

If the truck wouldn't start, it was over—but it roared to life. Lieselotte yanked the shifter into drive. Bullets tore into the truck's side as Schwarzfuchs hollered, sprinting after with his men.

"Go, go, go!" Wolfgang yelled.

His eyes stayed on the rearview mirror. The terrifying dogs chased after them, leaving their human masters far behind—but only for a moment. The Stasi and police piled into Wartburg 311 sedans. "They're coming!" Wolfgang shouted. Lieselotte slammed her foot on the pedal, pushing it to the floor.

"Hold on!" she yelled, approaching a stop sign she had no intention of obeying. She blew through it, grimacing in anticipation of being sideswiped. There was no time to circle around to the entrance gate. The truck picked up speed, groaning louder and louder as it missiled toward the tall black iron fence.

Wolfgang braced his hands against the dashboard. The truck barreled into the unforgiving wrought-iron fence. Any hopes of driving through it were dashed. The iron gate bent but didn't break. The impact whiplashed their bodies, knocking the air from their lungs. For a few precious seconds, they were stunned by the sheer force—unable to move.

The dogs clawed at the doors, jolting them awake. Headlights bore down behind them. Opening a door meant getting torn apart.

One word defined their fate: *trapped*.

"Windshield!" Wolfgang said.

He drew his flashlight and used it as a baton to break the spider-webbed glass. He crawled through, then offered his hand to Lieselotte. The dogs snapped and clawed at the truck, desperate to climb aboard. Wolfgang and Lieselotte scrambled onto the roof.

"You go first," Wolfgang said, guiding Lieselotte onto the fence.

She gripped the cold iron, fighting her way upward toward the top of the fence. Wolfgang was right behind her. The headlights of the approaching vehicles grew from distant pinpoints into blinding orbs—the wrath of their harsh light fixed on Wolfgang and Lieselotte.

Lieselotte's foot slipped. Her body jerked downward. Wolfgang thrust his arm beneath her, catching her before she fell. She secured her footing and heaved herself over the fence. Pain exploded through her body. She rolled out of the way, groaning. Wolfgang crashed beside her. She struggled to her feet and tried to heave Wolfgang to his.

"Come on—"

A crack rang out. Then another. A tombstone beside them exploded in stone shrapnel.

"Run!" Wolfgang yelled.

His whole body pulsated with pain. He tried to ignore it. Tried to tell his nerve endings to rest just for a bit until he was safe. After that, they could throb and light up all they wanted.

Lieselotte reached for his hand, entwining her fingers with his. They both knew they should separate—make themselves smaller targets—but neither could let go. Not now. Not after so long apart. Not even with death closing in.

The Stasi and East German police took crack shots, not caring about accuracy. Every bullet fired had a chance. And they would take them until they were out of ammo.

The Von Haven Stein mausoleum loomed ahead, identical to the others—except for Wolfgang. He knew every inch of it. It was their haven, their sanctuary, their way out.

Dozens of police and Stasi sprinted around the fence line, searching for the entrances. Those far from an entrance stopped and fired through the fence. Gunfire came from the north, from the south, from the east, and from the west. The Stasi and East German police turned the cemetery into a war zone.

Schwarzfuchs, the dogs, and a handful of agents had driven to the entrance. They had the advantage of fresh legs, hadn't fallen to the unforgiving ground, and they had weapons. Even wounded and fatigued, Wolfgang and Lieselotte would beat Schwarzfuchs and his minions to the mausoleum. The dogs were another question.

The mausoleum was less than ten feet away for Wolfgang and Lieselotte. Thirty for the dogs—but they were faster, tireless. They'd been told Wolfgang and Lieselotte were threats and they would eliminate them. Failure wasn't an option.

Wolfgang pushed Lieselotte into the mausoleum. He turned—a German Shepherd pounced. He dodged the first, but a second sank its teeth into his forearm and dragged him to the ground.

"Go!" he yelled to Lieselotte.

She wouldn't leave him. She lifted the dog's back legs. With its balance lost, its grip on Wolfgang lessened enough for him to roll free. He pushed Lieselotte, forcing her into the tunnel.

"Stop!" Schwarzfuchs yelled.

Wolfgang lunged over the sarcophagus, face-first toward the entrance as Schwarzfuchs fired. Dogs charged. Wolfgang rolled down the ramp like an avalanche. His body spit out onto the tunnel floor.

"Wolfgang!" Lieselotte shouted.

"I'm okay! Go! Keep moving!"

Schwarzfuchs fired blindly into the tunnel. Even with death a whisper away, Wolfgang wished he could see Schwarzfuchs's face when he saw the tunnel—the shock of realizing how long this had taken, and how utterly he'd failed.

"Checkmate!" Wolfgang shouted.

He couldn't help himself. After everything Schwarzfuchs had put him through—all his snide comments, his arrogance, his threats, real and idle—he had earned this moment.

"Yes, *Herr* Kirschke," Schwarzfuchs said. "Checkmate indeed."

But his tone held no defeat. Just venom.

A sharp metallic click echoed into the tunnel. Then came the unmistakable clatter of a Soviet grenade, small and deadly, bouncing down the ramp toward Wolfgang. Lieselotte saw it, too. Her soul clenched. *I can't lose him again. Not like this.*

"Run!" Wolfgang screamed.

Wolfgang surged forward with every ounce of strength he had left—desperate to create life-saving distance. The grenade exploded in a blinding flash and a deafening roar. The concussive force rattled his bones and nearly burst his eardrums. The tunnel groaned. Searing shrapnel sliced through his back, but he kept running. Nearing the 478-foot mark he and the others had dug. Support beam by support beam collapsed, filling the tunnel with cascading earth.

Crossing Over

The explosion had ripped through the tunnel, destroying everything Wolfgang and the others had built. He didn't know how far he'd gone before the shockwave slammed him down. When he came to, he was face down, dirt clinging to his mouth and face. He rolled onto his side, hacking up dirt and rubbing it from his eyes.

He looked back, fearing Schwarzfuchs or the dogs had followed. But it was pitch black in the tunnel. He couldn't even see his own hands. He fished for his flashlight and flicked it on. The tunnel had caved in some twenty feet behind him. He swiveled the flashlight in the direction of West Berlin. Another barrier of earth blocked the tunnel.

He was trapped. Boxed into a suffocating, coffin-sized space—just fourteen feet long and barely four feet wide. The tunnel groaned. The repurposed coffin wood creaked—one collapse away from burying him alive. If they held, he'd run out of air. How much air he had depended on how much he breathed. He needed to sip, not gulp. But it didn't matter. It was only a matter of time. Eventually, he'd suffocate.

Is Lieselotte okay? Was she able to make it out? God, he prayed she had. The support beams above him were from the grave Franco had accidentally selected. The wood from that coffin was hard, not rotten like most of the others. That mistake had saved Wolfgang's life. Temporarily, at least. He was about 460-some feet into the tunnel. Nowhere near the border. He didn't even have the grim satisfaction of dying in West Berlin.

The explosion had set off a terrifying chain of events. Not just the initial explosion from the grenade itself, but the sound of the support beams failing. Cracking. Wood splintering. The sound of the earth groaning and reclaiming itself. It was the most terrifying moment of Lieselotte's life.

She hadn't reached the border sign, but she'd made it past the massive boulder. The boulder had diverted the shockwave, protecting the integrity of the support beams behind it. The thing that had been such an obstacle, a source of demoralization, had been a blessing. The lights had flickered but stayed on. *Thank God.*

Lieselotte cried out to Wolfgang again and again. But there was no reply. She clawed at the dirt, but it was packed tight as concrete. Her fingers bled, her hands useless against it. She needed tools.

"I'll be back! I promise!" she shouted, praying he could hear.

The moment she moved, her body throbbed in pain. But she couldn't let it stop her. Grimacing, she limped through the tunnel, past the border crossing, until a faint glow appeared in the darkness. People gawked at her from the entrance, their faces pale and wide-eyed.

"What the hell were you thinking?!" Mrs. Winterstein cursed.

"Wolfgang's trapped in the tunnel! I need supplies to help free him!" she said.

Eckhart, Bastian, and Franco snapped into action, grabbing the shovels Petyr and his friends had stood against the back wall. Lieselotte led, with Bastian, Franco, and Eckhart following closely behind. Eckhart asked for information, and she gave them everything she could, as succinctly as possible.

"Did you hear from him after the collapse?" Eckhart asked.

"No."

She didn't need to look back to know the look they shared. Her heart threatened to crack. Every second that passed meant there was less air, less time, and less hope.

They crossed into East Berlin, then to the massive boulder. The narrow distance the men had shimmied through was now impassable.

"This boulder stopped the shockwave," Bastian said.

He didn't finish his train of thought. He didn't have to. Lieselotte knew. Until that boulder, the shockwave had traveled freely, collapsing and burying everything in dirt. Including Wolfgang.

Lieselotte used her hand shovel and stabbed it into the dirt, but it made little impact.

"Stand back," Eckhart said. "Let me try to free it with this."

He raised the shovel, and once Lieselotte shimmied behind him, he speared the end of it into the dirt. Over and over, trying to break it apart. The force of the explosion had packed the dirt into near rock-like strength. But he kept stabbing away. Loosening dirt grain by grain. But it wasn't enough.

The flashlight died, plunging Wolfgang into space-like darkness. As the air ran out, it first felt like a shortness of breath, as if he had exerted himself too much. But then it became more shallow and rapid. Each breath less satisfying than the last. Like breathing through a wet cloth. His limbs sagged like lead. His hearing warped—muffled and distant. But then a voice. Not imagined. This time real.

"Wolfgang!"

A beam of light broke through the darkness. Wolfgang stared at it but was too weak to crawl toward it. The sound faded. Maybe it had been imagined. His breath slowed, each one shallower than the last.

The rescuers exchanged glances, then worked in a frenzy. Working together, they struck, stabbed, and shoveled the dirt free. Then finally, Bastian's well-placed strike caused the mountain of dirt to collapse and cascade on both sides of the boulder. Lieselotte climbed over. The tunnel was nearly filled with dirt and earth. Only two feet of space remained between earth and the ceiling, forcing Lieselotte and the others to crawl through and ignore the innate claustrophobic feeling of being buried alive. She turned her head to keep the dirt out of her mouth and nose. Her lungs desperately trying to suck in air, but there was little to be had.

Then she came to another mound of dirt that sealed off the tunnel. She placed her hand on it, as if it were a tomb. But the clay-like soil crumbled. Leaving an opening. Lieselotte pressed her face into the hole.

"Wolfgang!" she called.

He sat against the tunnel wall, head lolled to the side. "Lieselotte?" he gasped.

"It's me! We're working to get you out! Are you—"

She didn't know how to finish that sentence. *Buried alive? Okay? Dying?*

"I'm … I'm …"

His words drifted. Bastian and Franco shimmied ahead, stabbing their hand shovels into the soil. It gave like a wave of dirt, sending Lieselotte sliding down. She crawled to Wolfgang and stroked his cheek. The oppressive heat swarmed her as if she had crawled into an oven.

"You're alive!"

Bastian and Eckhart muscled through. Wolfgang took quick, deep breaths. Each one rejuvenated him. The two brothers slung their arms over each other's shoulders, smiling and laughing.

"*Madonna mia*, what is happening?!" Franco asked.

"He's okay!" Bastian shouted back.

The two brothers hoisted Wolfgang to his feet and up onto raised earth, where Franco dragged him through.

Once they reached the boulder and crossed, Lieselotte draped Wolfgang's arm over her shoulder. Franco led the way. Eckhart followed last, prepared to help if needed.

"… Thirsty," Wolfgang said.

"The tunnel's in a grocery store, so plenty of choices for a beverage," Eckhart quipped.

Up ahead, the border sign shone like a beacon.

"Hold on," Wolfgang said.

You are now crossing into West Berlin.

He reached the spot he'd dreamed of for years—and nearly died to reach. His breath hitched. Tears washed the dirt from his face, leaving trails of clean skin. One more step and Wolfgang would be in West Berlin. Something that had seemed impossible. Even now, it felt as though something would stop him. But the only thing that did was his reflection on the magnitude of this moment and everything that had led to it. He reached for the sign and took it down, putting it around his neck like a necklace. Together with Lieselotte, he stepped into West Berlin—then kept going, deeper into the tunnel.

The tunnel Lieselotte and her team had fashioned was far superior to what Wolfgang and his team had created. String lights ran the length of the tunnel. Fresh air pumped in from a generator, and the support beams were from hearty oak. Every inch of tunnel was testament to Lieselotte and the others who had devoted the last year to making this possible. The tunnel would have been his tomb if Lieselotte hadn't come back for him.

As they neared the tunnel entrance, Anneliese snapped a photograph from the tripod: Wolfgang wearing the Berlin crossing sign. Lieselotte's father's camera dangled from her neck like a charm, each swing a memory. Applause broke out from those on the basement floor. From Trude and Emilia, Petyr, Mikael, Hansel, Rory, Johan, and George. Mrs. Winterstein had a bottle of water for Wolfgang, exchanging it for the sign. He gulped it down.

Lieselotte snapped photographs without hesitation. The world needed to see what freedom cost—and what it was worth. With Eckhart's support, Wolfgang climbed the steps. Lieselotte stayed close behind. Once they stepped out into the grocery store, the fifty-seven people he had helped escape, along with the countless teams of diggers who had rushed to see the culmination of their hard work, applauded and cheered. Reaching out to shake his hand, pat his back. Whistling and cheering.

Lieselotte captured the moments before letting the camera dangle from her neck. She took Wolfgang's hands in hers. Their embrace was part hug, part dance, part resurrection. They were caked in dirt, sodden with sweat, and tinged with blood. But they were finally free. Finally, together.

"Merry Christmas, Wolfgang."

Wolfgang smirked. "Merry Christmas, Lieselotte."

At last, their lives had truly begun.

The Long Chord of History

During the Wall's existence, countless East Germans risked everything to escape—over the Wall, through it, or beneath it. Each attempt more daring than the last, culminating in the 1979 escape of two families who sewed a homemade hot-air balloon and floated into West Berlin.

Lieselotte and Wolfgang followed those attempts closely, celebrating each ingenious success and mourning every valiant failure. Lieselotte's article and photographs for the Associated Press captured the world's attention, sparking headlines, conversations, and debates. The image of Wolfgang and Lieselotte embracing in a grocery store, surrounded by applause, became iconic—evoking the emotional resonance of *Raising the Flag on Iwo Jima*, *V-J Day in Times Square*, and *The Execution of Nguyen Van Lem*.

How had Schwarzfuchs reacted when he saw those photographs? Read the article? Discovered how long that tunnel had been in the works? Had he been reprimanded for his failure?

Wolfgang and Lieselotte adjusted to a relationship that was rooted in physical intimacy and face-to-face conversation. They were married in 1967 on Christmas Eve—surrounded by a small circle of friends and family, including Mrs. Winterstein. Christmas had been such an integral part of their relationship—it seemed there could be no other day for them to be wed. It was Mrs. Winterstein's last Christmas. She passed shortly into the new year of 1968. At her funeral, nearly everyone who had crawled through that tunnel came to pay their respects. Each one of them carrying the weight of knowing that without the stern woman's generosity, none of them would have lived the life they now enjoyed. Mrs. Winterstein, no doubt, would have hated the fuss made.

Anneliese and Eckhart dated, broke up bitterly, reconciled, and eventually spent years as friends before realizing they belonged together. They married in June 1971.

Living in West Berlin—a raft of democracy in a sea of communism—left Wolfgang gripped with an unshakeable paranoia that infiltrated his soul. He flinched at knocks on the door, scanned streets before stepping outside. Even innocent conversations felt like traps. The worry that the Stasi would try to kidnap him led to many sleepless nights. Freedom, he'd learned, was not always the same as safety.

Finally, Lieselotte couldn't let him live that way any longer. Lieselotte, thanks to her world-famous article and photographs and a great recommendation from Tom Jackson, secured a job at the *Milwaukee Journal*. Together with her mother, they moved to Milwaukee in the spring of 1969.

Wolfgang got a job at Schlitz, a brewing company, becoming an industrial engineer before taking a promotion with Milwaukee County to help with the urban renewal. He joined Lieselotte wherever her job took her, and they traveled often—Rome, London, and finally Paris, where Lieselotte took Wolfgang to the Givre Strudel, to reunite with Anneliese and Eckhart over apple strudel. Those days in Paris, reconnecting with their best friends, were some of the best days of their lives.

Their home overflowed with photographs—more than most would consider reasonable, but for them, each image was proof: *We endured. We lived. We are free.* They adorned the living room walls, the fireplace mantel, the hallway, dressers, and refrigerators. Photos were tucked into purses and wallets, stashed in drawers, cabinets, and shoeboxes—testaments of memory and survival at every turn.

They had six children—the first likely conceived the day of Wolfgang's escape. In 1981, the call to return home was too great to ignore, and they moved back to Germany. Though they returned to Milwaukee often, especially in the summers. America had become a home. They reunited with Bastian and Trude and their family, their daughter, Renate, having been born a week after their escape on New Year's Eve. Anneliese and Eckhart and their family, and Franco and Emilia, provided so much joy. Yet the pain and tribulations they'd gone through together couldn't be ignored.

When the news broke on 9 November 1989, that the Soviet Union was allowing free travel from the East into the West, Wolfgang and Lieselotte had to see it for themselves.

Thousands gathered on both sides of the Wall. The cold November air bit at cheeks and stiffened fingers, but no one left. Youths climbed atop the Wall. Concrete dust and cigarette smoke hung in the air. Powerful chants of the collective voices of those thousands and thousands of people rang into the autumnal night.

"We are the people!"

"The Wall must go!"

And the most shiver-inducing of them all: "Freedom!"

Wolfgang squeezed Lieselotte's hand. Tears filled his eyes—not just for what was happening, but for what they had survived. The same sort of mass gathering that had cost her father his life. But now there were no soldiers. No tanks. Nothing to stand in the way of change.

People chiseled away at the Wall. Sledgehammers struck the concrete. When a panel crashed to the pavement, the crowd erupted in a deafening cheer. Wolfgang and Lieselotte, hands clasped, stepped through the breach with their six children. Their youngest daughter, Elfriede, tugged on Wolfgang's sleeve.

"Papa … is this safe?"

He crouched beside her and nodded. "It wasn't for a long time. But it is now."

Crossing the border had been impossible. Wolfgang couldn't believe he'd been able to simply walk across it now—and sharing that moment with Lieselotte and their children felt essential.

The fall of East Germany didn't bring the instant unity many had hoped for. Reunification wasn't clean. For many East Germans, freedom came at a bitter cost. Files revealed betrayals by neighbors, friends—even family. Trust, already frayed by decades of surveillance and fear, collapsed under the weight of truth.

Wolfgang and Lieselotte stood in line outside the former Stasi headquarters, their six children beside them. Around them, others clutched faded ID cards and old photographs, desperate to know who had watched them, who had whispered their names behind closed doors.

Inside, torn papers spilled from bins. Scent jars lined the shelves like grotesque trophies. Shelves bowed under the weight of crumbling folders. The Stasi had accumulated enough files to stretch nearly sixty-nine miles—over 39 million index cards, thousands of hours of audio recordings, surveillance reports, photographs, and scent samples. In a country of roughly 16 million, the Stasi had over 91,000 full-time officers and 189,000 unofficial informants. One in every sixty East Germans participated in the machine of repression.

The Stasi had tried to destroy much of the evidence— shredding, burning, tearing files into pieces—but citizens storming the headquarters had arrived just in time to save what remained. It was overwhelming, sobering, and heartbreaking.

The Wall stood for twenty-eight years—destroying lives, isolating families, and crushing dreams. For Wolfgang and Lieselotte, it would never cease to amaze them each time they drove through the Brandenburg Gate. How easy it was now and how impossible it had been before. Seeing his parents in East Berlin in the same home he'd grown up in was an incredibly emotional experience. Wolfgang never expected to be in that house again or to see his parents. Never thought his children would be able to meet them in person.

Wolfgang and Lieselotte and their family, along with Eckhart and Anneliese and their two sons, Bastian and Trude and their three children, and Franco and Emilia returned to Eternal Peace. Overcome with emotion. Wolfgang and Lieselotte had paid for a proper tombstone to be placed where Dietrich's remains resided.

Bastian and Trude had tried to get information on their firstborn son, but if there were records on the family who had taken him in, they had been destroyed. It was the final closure for them: they'd never know.

Franco pointed out the grave he had wrongly dug up. The fence Lieselotte had driven Franco's truck into was still warped and bent. It had rusted in place—frozen in time, like a scar that never faded. The memory of their escape returned in vivid detail—sound, image, and emotion. Schwarzfuchs still loomed in Wolfgang's memory—that final exchange replaying often. He never found out what happened to him. Had he died sometime between Wolfgang's escape and the Wall's collapse? Retreated to Russia, where his brand of cruelty might still be of use? Or had he, like so many before him, taken his own life to avoid the justice he was owed? Or had he slipped away in anonymity, living among the masses here in Berlin?

As Wolfgang and the others looked on at the Von Haven Stein mausoleum, it showed no signs a tunnel had been there. It was locked, but there was no doubt the tunnel entrance had been sealed with concrete.

As the adults told the story of their escape to their children, Wolfgang couldn't help but think that history was played on one long chord. How the assassination of Archduke Franz Ferdinand had sparked the Great War, which led to a brutal treaty that put immense reparations on Germany that eventually led to the rise of Hitler and the Nazi Party and a quest for world domination. When that failed, Germany had been ripped in half, and ultimately, a wall was built to keep them separate. The echoes of that wall still reverberated—through their family, through Germany, through the world.

What notes were being struck now? How long would they echo—and would the world ever learn the melody they carried?

About the Author

Inspired by the power of storytelling after watching *Titanic* in 1997, Bret Kissinger embarked on a journey to entwine fact and fiction, to bring history to life, and to create stories that linger long after the final page. His books have been read in more than a dozen countries and are known for their compelling characters, immersive settings, and emotional depth.

He lives in Wisconsin. Follow him on Facebook and Instagram and visit www.bretkissinger.com to learn more about his captivating tales of love, loss, and adventure.